THE WORKS OF

H. RIDER HAGGARD

ERIC BRIGHTEYES

WILDSIDE PRESS
Berkeley Heights, NJ 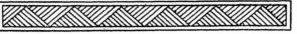 1999

BIBLIOGRAPHICAL NOTE.

First printed April 1891. *Reprinted September* 1891.

Reissued in 'THE SILVER LIBRARY,' *June* 1893. *Reprinted August* 1895, *July* 1898, *October* 1902, *June* 1905, *August* 1908, *October* 1912, *and May* 1916.

Colonial Edition, June 1893. *Reprinted August* 1895, *July* 1898, *June* 1905, *August* 1908, *October* 1912, *and May* 1916.

WILDSIDE PRESS
P.O. Box 45
Gillette, NJ 07933-0045

Dedication

MADAM,

You have graciously conveyed to me the intelligence that during the weary weeks spent far from his home—in alternate hope and fear, in suffering and mortal trial—a Prince whose memory all men must reverence, the Emperor Frederick, found pleasure in the reading of my stories : that ' they interested and fascinated him.'

While the world was watching daily at the bedside of your Majesty's Imperial husband, while many were endeavouring to learn courage in our supremest need from the spectacle of that heroic patience, a distant writer little knew that it had been his fortune to bring to such a sufferer an hour's forgetfulness of sorrow and pain.

This knowledge, to an author, is far dearer than any praise, and it is in gratitude that, with your Majesty's permission, I venture to dedicate to you the tale of Eric Brighteyes.

The late Emperor, at heart a lover of peace, though by duty a soldier of soldiers, might perhaps have cared to interest himself in a warrior of long ago, a hero of our Northern stock, whose days were spent in strife, and whose latest desire was Rest. But it may not be ; like the Golden Eric of this Saga, and after a nobler fashion, he has passed through the Hundred Gates into the Valhalla of Renown.

To you then, Madam, I dedicate this book, a token, however slight and unworthy, of profound respect and sympathy.

I am, Madam,
Your Majesty's most obedient servant,

H. RIDER HAGGARD.

November 27, 1889.

To H.I.M. VICTORIA, Empress Frederick of Germany.

INTRODUCTION

'ERIC BRIGHTEYES' is a romance founded on, or, to be more accurate, fashioned from the model of, the Icelandic Sagas. 'What is a saga?' 'Is it a fable or a true story?' The answer is not altogether simple. For such sagas as those of Burnt Njal and Grettir the Strong partake both of truth and fiction: historians dispute as to the proportions. This was the manner of the saga's growth: In the early days of the Iceland community—that republic of aristocrats—say, between the dates 900 and 1100 of our era, a quarrel would arise between two great families. As in the case of the Njal Saga, its cause, probably, was the ill doings of some noble woman. This quarrel would lead to manslaughter. Then blood called for blood, and a vendetta was set on foot that ended only with the death by violence of a majority of the actors in the drama and of large numbers of their adherents. In the course of the feud, men of heroic strength and mould would come to the front and perform deeds worthy of the iron age which bore them. Women also would help to fashion the tale, for good or ill, according to their natural gifts and characters. At last the tragedy was covered up by death and time, leaving only a few dinted shields and haunted cairns to tell of those who had played its leading parts.

But its fame lived on in the minds of men. From generation to generation skalds wandered through the winter snows, much as Homer may have wandered in his day across the Grecian vales and mountains, to find a welcome at every stead, because of the old-time story they had to tell. Here, night after night, they would sit in the ingle and while away the weariness of the dayless dark with histories of the times when men carried their lives in their hands, and thought them well lost if there might be a song in the ears of folk to come. To alter the tale was one of the greatest of crimes : the skald must repeat it as it came to him ; but by degrees undoubtedly the sagas did suffer alteration. The facts remained the same indeed, but around them gathered a mist of miraculous occurrences and legends. To take a single instance : the account of the burning of Bergthorsknoll in the Njal Saga is not only a piece of descriptive writing that for vivid, simple force and insight is scarcely to be matched out of Homer and the Bible, it is also obviously true. We feel as we read, that no man could have invented that story, though some great skald threw it into shape. That the tale is true, the writer of 'Eric' can testify, for, saga in hand, he has followed every act of the drama on its very site. There he who digs beneath the surface of the lonely mound that looks across plain and sea to Westman Isles may still find traces of the burning, and see what appears to be the black sand with which the hands of Bergthora and her women strewed the earthen floor some nine hundred years ago, and even the greasy and clotted remains of the whey that they threw upon the flame to quench it. He may discover the places where Flosi drew up his men, where Skarphedinn died, singing while his legs were burnt from off him, where Kari leapt from the flaming ruin, and the dell in which he laid down to rest—at every step, in short, the truth of the narrative becomes more obvious. And yet the tale has been added to, for, unless we may believe that some human beings are gifted with second sight, we cannot accept as true the prophetic vision that came to Runolf, Thorstein's son ; or that of Njal who, on the evening of the onslaught, like Theoclymenus in the Odyssey, saw the whole board and the meats upon it 'one gore of blood.'

Thus, in the Norse romance now offered to the reader, the tale of Eric and his deeds would be true ; but the dream of Asmund, the witchcraft of Swanhild, the incident of the speaking head, and the visions of Eric and Skallagrim, would owe their origin to the imagination of successive generations of skalds ; and, finally, in the fifteenth or sixteenth century, the story would have been written down with all its supernatural additions.

The tendency of the human mind—and more especially of the Norse mind—is to supply uncommon and extraordinary reasons for actions and facts that are to be amply accounted for by the working of natural forces. Swanhild would have needed no 'familiar' to instruct her in her evil schemes ; Eric would have wanted no love-draught to bring about his overthrow. Our common experience of mankind as it is, in opposition to mankind as we fable it to be, is sufficient to teach us that the passion of the one and the human weakness of the other would suffice to these ends. The natural magic, the beauty and inherent power of such a woman as Swanhild, are things more forceful than any spell that magicians have invented, or any demon they are supposed to have summoned to their aid. But no saga would be complete without the intervention of such extraneous forces : the need of them was always felt, in order to throw up the acts of heroes and heroines, and to invest their persons with an added importance. Even Homer experienced this need, and did not scruple to introduce not only second sight, but gods and goddesses, and to bring their supernatural agency to bear directly on the personages of his chant, and that far more freely than any Norse sagaman. A word may be added in explanation of the appearances of 'familiars' in the shapes of animals, an instance of which will be found in this story. It was believed in Iceland, as now by the Finns and Eskimo, that the passions and desires of sorcerers took visible form in such creatures as wolves or rats. These were called 'sendings,' and there are many allusions to them in the Sagas.

Another peculiarity that may be briefly alluded to as eminently characteristic of the Sagas is their fatefulness. As we read we seem to hear the voice of Doom speaking continually. '*Things will happen as they are fated :*' that is the keynote of them all. The Norse mind had little belief in free will, less even than we have to-day. Men and women were born with certain characters and tendencies, given to them in order that their lives should run in appointed channels, and their acts bring about an appointed end. They do not these things of their own desire, though their desires prompt them to the deeds: they do them because they must. The Norns, as they name Fate, have mapped out their path long and long ago; their feet are set therein, and they must tread it to the end. Such was the conclusion of our Scandinavian ancestors—a belief forced upon them by their intense realisation of the futility of human hopes and schemings, of the terror and the tragedy of life, the vanity of its desires, and the untravelled gloom or sleep, dreamless or dreamful, which lies beyond its end.

Though the Sagas are entrancing, both as examples of literature of which there is but little in the world and because of their living interest, they are scarcely known to the English-speaking public. This is easy to account for: it is hard to persuade the nineteenth century world to interest itself in people who lived and events that happened a thousand years ago. Moreover, the Sagas are undoubtedly difficult reading. The archaic nature of the work, even in a translation; the multitude of its actors; the Norse sagaman's habit of inter-weaving endless side-plots, and the persistence with which he introduces the genealogy and adventures of the ancestors of every unimportant character, are none of them to the taste of the modern reader.

'Eric Brighteyes' therefore, is clipped of these peculiarities, and, to some extent, is cast in the form of the romance of our own day, archaisms being avoided as much as possible. The author will be gratified should he succeed in exciting interest in the troubled lives of our Norse forefathers, and still more so if his difficult experiment brings readers to the Sagas—to the prose epics of our own race. Too ample, too prolix, too crowded with detail, they cannot indeed vie in art with the epics of Greece; but in their pictures of life, simple and heroic, they fall beneath no literature in the world, save the Iliad and the Odyssey alone.

CONTENTS

ERIC BRIGHTEYES

CHAPTER I

HOW ASMUND THE PRIEST FOUND GROA THE WITCH

HERE lived a man in the south, before Thangbrand, Wilibald's son, preached the White Christ in Iceland. He was named Eric Brighteyes, Thorgrimur's son, and in those days there was no man like him for strength, beauty and daring, for in all these things he was the first. But he was not the first in good-luck.

Two women lived in the south, not far from where the Westman Islands stand above the sea. Gudruda the Fair was the name of the one, and Swanhild, called the Fatherless, Groa's daughter, was the other. They were half-sisters, and there were none like them in those days, for they were the fairest of all women, though they had nothing in common except their blood and hate.

Now of Eric Brighteyes, of Gudruda the Fair, and of Swanhild the Fatherless, there is a tale to tell.

These two fair women saw the light in the self-same hour. But Eric Brighteyes was their elder by five years. The father of Eric was Thorgrimur Iron-Toe. He had been a mighty man; but in fighting with a Baresark,[1] who fell upon

[1] The Baresarks were men on whom a passing fury of battle came; they were usually outlawed.

him as he came up from sowing his wheat, his foot was hewn
from him, so that afterwards he went upon a wooden leg
shod with iron. Still, he slew the Baresark, standing on one
leg and leaning against a rock, and for that deed people
honoured him much. Thorgrimur was a wealthy yeoman,
slow to wrath, just, and rich in friends. Somewhat late in life
he took to wife Saevuna, Thorod's daughter. She was the best
of women, strong in mind and second-sighted, and she could
cover herself in her hair. But these two never loved each
other overmuch, and they had but one child, Eric, who was born
when Saevuna was well on in years.

The father of Gudruda was Asmund Asmundson, the
Priest of Middalhof. He was the wisest and the wealthiest
of all men who lived in the south of Iceland in those days,
owning many farms and, also, two ships of merchandise and
one long ship of war, and having much money out at interest.
He had won his wealth by viking's work, robbing the English
coasts, and black tales were told of his doings in his youth on
the sea, for he was a 'red-hand' viking. Asmund was a hand-
some man, with blue eyes and a large beard, and, moreover, he
was very skilled in matters of law. He loved money much,
and was feared of all. Still, he had many friends, for as he
aged he grew more kindly. He took in marriage Gudruda,
the daughter of Björn, who was very sweet and kindly of
nature, so that they called her Gudruda the Gentle. Of this
marriage there were two children, Björn and Gudruda the
Fair ; but Björn grew up like his father in his youth, strong
and hard, and greedy of gain, while, except for her wonderful
beauty, Gudruda was her mother's child alone.

The mother of Swanhild the Fatherless was Groa the
Witch. She was a Finn, and it is told of her that the ship
on which she sailed, trying to run under the lee of the Westman Isles in a great gale from the north-east, was dashed to
pieces on a rock, and all those on board of her were caught in
the net of Ran [1] and drowned, except Groa herself, who was saved   .
by her magic art. This at the least is true, that, as Asmund
the Priest rode down by the sea-shore on the morning after

---

[1] The Norse goddess of the sea.

the gale, seeking for some strayed horses, he found a beautiful woman, who wore a purple cloak and a great girdle of gold, seated on a rock, combing her black hair and singing the while; and, at her feet, washing to and fro in a pool, was a dead man. He asked whence she came, and she answered:

'Out of the Swan's Bath.'

Next he asked her where were her kin. But, pointing to the dead man, she said that this alone was left of them.

'Who was the man, then?' said Asmund the Priest.

She laughed again and sang this song:—

> Groa sails up from the Swan's Bath,
> Death Gods grip the Dead Man's hand.
> Look where lies her luckless husband,
> Bolder sea-king ne'er swung sword!
> Asmund, keep the kirtle-wearer,
> For last night the Norns were crying,
> And Groa thought they told of thee:
> Yea, told of thee and babes unborn.

'How knowest thou my name?' asked Asmund.

'The sea-mews cried it as the ship sank, thine and others —and they shall be heard in story.'

'Then that is the best of luck,' quoth Asmund; 'but I think that thou art fey.'[1]

'Ay,' she answered, 'fey and fair.'

'True enough thou art fair. What shall we do with this dead man?'

'Leave him in the arms of Ran. So may all husbands lie.'

They spoke no more with her at that time, seeing that she was a witchwoman. But Asmund took her up to Middalhof, and gave her a farm, and she lived there alone, and he profited much by her wisdom.

Now it chanced that Gudruda the Gentle was with child, and when her time came she gave a daughter birth—a very fair girl, with dark eyes. On the same day, Groa the witchwoman brought forth a girl-child, and men wondered who

---

[1] *I.e.* subject to supernatural presentiments, generally connected with approaching doom.

was its father, for Groa was no man's wife. It was women's talk that Asmund the Priest was the father of this child also; but when he heard it he was angry, and said that no witchwoman should bear a bairn of his, howsoever fair she was. Nevertheless, it was still said that the child was his, and it is certain that he loved it as a man loves his own; but of all things, this is the hardest to know. When Groa was questioned she laughed darkly, as was her fashion, and said that she knew nothing of it, never having seen the face of the child's father, who rose out of the sea at night. And for this cause some thought him to have been a wizard or the wraith of her dead husband; but others said that Groa lied, as many women have done on such matters. But of all this talk the child alone remained and she was named Swanhild.

Now, but an hour before the child of Gudruda the Gentle was born, Asmund went up from his house to the Temple, to tend the holy fire that burned night and day upon the altar. When he had tended the fire he sat down upon the cross-benches before the shrine, and, gazing on the image of the Goddess Freya, he fell asleep and dreamed a very evil dream.

He dreamed that Gudruda the Gentle bore a dove most beautiful to see, for all its feathers were of silver; but that Groa the Witch bore a golden snake. And the snake and the dove dwelt together, and ever the snake sought to slay the dove. At length there came a great white swan flying over Coldback Fell, and its tongue was a sharp sword. Now the swan saw the dove and loved it, and the dove loved the swan; but the snake reared itself, and hissed, and sought to kill the dove. But the swan covered her with his wings, and beat the snake away. Then he, Asmund, came out and drove away the swan, as the swan had driven the snake, and it wheeled high into the air and flew south, and the snake swam away also through the sea. But the dove drooped and now it was blind. Then an eagle came from the north, and would have taken the dove, but it fled round and round, crying, and always the eagle drew nearer to it. At length, from the south the swan came back, flying heavily, and about its neck was twined the golden snake, and with it came a raven. And it saw the eagle and loud it trumpeted, and shook the snake from it so that it fell like a gleam of gold into the sea. Then the eagle and the swan met in battle, and the swan drove the eagle down and broke it with his wings, and, flying to the dove, comforted it. But those in the house ran out and shot at the swan with bows and drove it away, but now he, Asmund, was not with them. And once more the dove drooped. Again the swan came back, and with it the raven, and a great host were gathered against them, and, among them, all Asmund's kith and kin, and the men of his quarter and some of his priesthood, and many whom he did not know by face. And the swan flew at Björn his son, and shot out the sword of its tongue and slew him, and many a man it slew thus. And the raven, with a beak and claws of steel, slew also many a man, so that Asmund's kindred fled and the swan slept by the dove. But as it slept the golden snake crawled out of the sea, and hissed in the ears of men, and they rose up to follow it. It came to the swan and twined itself about its neck. It struck at the dove and slew it. Then the swan awoke and the raven awoke, and they did battle till all who remained of Asmund's kindred and people were dead. But still the snake clung about the swan's neck, and presently snake and swan fell into the sea, and far out on the sea there burned a flame of fire. And Asmund awoke trembling and left the Temple.

Now as he went, a woman came running, and weeping as she ran.

'Haste, haste!' she cried; 'a daughter is born to thee, and Gudruda thy wife is dying!'

'Is it so?' said Asmund; 'after ill dreams ill tidings.'

Now in the bed-closet off the great hall of Middalhof lay Gudruda the Gentle and she was dying.

'Art thou there, husband?' she said.

'Even so, wife.'

'Thou comest in an evil hour, for it is my last. Now hearken. Take thou the new-born babe within thine arms and kiss it, and pour water over it, and name it with my name.'

This Asmund did.

'Hearken, my husband. I have been a good wife to thee, though thou hast not been all good to me. But thus shalt thou atone : thou shalt swear that, though she is a girl, thou wilt not cast this bairn forth to perish, but wilt cherish and nurture her.'

'I swear it,' he said.

'And thou shalt swear that thou wilt not take the witch-woman Groa to wife, nor have anything to do with her, and this for thine own sake : for, if thou dost, she will be thy death. Dost thou swear ? '

'I swear it,' he said.

'It is well ; but, husband, if thou dost break thine oath, either in the words or in the spirit of the words, evil shall overtake thee and all thy house. Now bid me farewell, for I die.'

He bent over her and kissed her, and it is said that Asmund wept in that hour, for after his fashion he loved his wife.

'Give me the babe,' she said, ' that it may lie once upon my breast.'

They gave her the babe and she looked upon its dark eyes and said :

'Fairest of women shalt thou be, Gudruda—fair as no woman in Iceland ever was before thee ; and thou shalt love with a mighty love—and thou shalt lose—and, losing, thou shalt find again.'

Now, it is said that, as she spoke these words, her face grew bright as a spirit's, and, having spoken them, she fell back dead. So they laid her in earth, and Asmund mourned her much.

But, when all was over and done, the dream that he had dreamed lay heavy on him. Now of all diviners of dreams Groa was the most skilled, and when Gudruda had been in earth seven full days, Asmund went to Groa, though doubtfully, because of his oath.

He came to the house and entered. On a couch in the chamber lay Groa, and her babe was on her breast and she was very fair to see.

'Greeting, lord ! ' she said. ' What wouldest thou here ? '

'I have dreamed a dream, and thou alone canst read it.'

'That is as it may be,' she answered. 'It is true that I have some skill in dreams. At the least I will hear it.'

Then he unfolded it to her every word.

'What wilt thou give me if I read thy dream?' she said.

'What dost thou ask? Methinks I have given thee much.'

'Yea, lord,' and she looked at the babe upon her breast. 'I ask but a little thing: that thou shalt take this bairn in thy arms, pour water over it and name it.'

'Men will talk if I do this, for it is the father's part.'

'It is a little thing what men say: talk goes by as the wind. Moreover, thou shalt give them the lie in the child's name, for it shall be Swanhild the Fatherless. Nevertheless that is my price. Pay it if thou wilt.'

'Read me the dream and I will name the child.'

'Nay, first name thou the babe: for then no harm shall come to her at thy hands.'

So Asmund took the child, poured water over her, and named her.

Then Groa spoke: 'This, lord, is the reading of thy dream, else my wisdom is at fault: The silver dove is thy daughter Gudruda, the golden snake is my daughter Swanhild, and these two shall hate one the other and strive against each other. But the swan is a mighty man whom both shall love, and, if he love not both, yet he shall belong to both. And thou shalt send him away; but he shall return and bring bad luck to thee and thy house, and thy daughter shall be blind with love of him. And in the end he shall slay the eagle, a great lord from the north who shall seek to wed thy daughter, and many another shall he slay, by the help of that raven with the bill of steel who shall be with him. But Swanhild shall triumph over thy daughter Gudruda, and this man, and the two of them, shall die at her hands, and, for the rest, who can say? But this is true—that the mighty man shall bring all thy race to an end. See now, I have read thy rede.'

Then Asmund was very wroth. 'Thou wast wise to be-guile me to name thy bastard brat,' he said; 'else had I been its death within this hour.'

'This thou canst not do, lord, seeing that thou hast held it in thy arms,' Groa answered, laughing. 'Go rather and lay out Gudruda the Fair on Coldback Hill; so shalt thou make an end of the evil, for Gudruda shall be its very root. Learn this, moreover: that thy dream does not tell all, seeing that thou thyself must play a part in the fate. Go, send forth the babe Gudruda, and be at rest.'

'That cannot be, for I have sworn to cherish it, and with an oath that may not be broken.'

'It is well,' laughed Groa. 'Things will befall as they are fated; let them befall in their season. There is space for cairns on Coldback and the sea can shroud its dead!'

And Asmund went from the house, angered and fearful at heart.

CHAPTER II

HOW ERIC TOLD HIS LOVE TO GUDRUDA IN THE SNOW ON COLDBACK

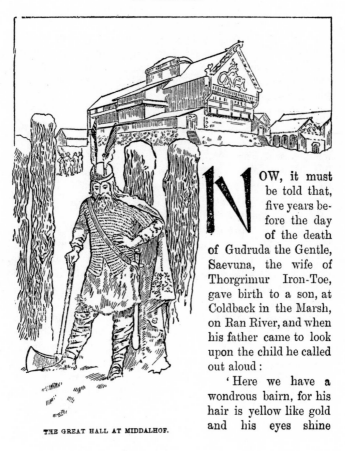

THE GREAT HALL AT MIDDALHOF.

NOW, it must be told that, five years before the day of the death of Gudruda the Gentle, Saevuna, the wife of Thorgrimur Iron-Toe, gave birth to a son, at Coldback in the Marsh, on Ran River, and when his father came to look upon the child he called out aloud:

'Here we have a wondrous bairn, for his hair is yellow like gold and his eyes shine

bright as stars.' And Thorgrimur named him Eric Brighteyes.

Now, Coldback is but an hour's ride from Middalhof, and
it chanced, in after years, that Thorgrimur went up to Middalhof, to keep the Yule feast and worship in the Temple, for he
was in the priesthood of Asmund Asmundson, bringing the
boy Eric with him. There also was Groa with Swanhild, for
now Asmund had forgotten his oath and she dwelt at Middalhof; so it came about that the three fair children were set
together in the hall to play, and men thought it great sport
to see them. Now, Gudruda had a horse of wood and wished
to ride it while Eric pushed the horse along. But Swanhild
smote her from the horse and called to Eric to make it move;
but he comforted Gudruda and would not, and at that Swanhild was angry and lisped out :

' Push thou must, if I will it, Eric.'

Then he pushed sideways and with such good will that
Swanhild fell almost into the fire of the hearth, and, leaping
up, she snatched a brand and threw it at Gudruda, firing
her clothes. Men laughed at this; but Groa, standing apart,
frowned and muttered witch-words.

' Why lookest thou so darkly, housekeeper ? ' said Asmund ;
' the boy is bonny and high of heart.'

' Ah, he is bonny as no child is, and he shall be bonny all
his life-days. Nevertheless, he shall not stand against his ill
luck. This I prophesy of him : that women shall bring him
to his end, and he shall die a hero's death, but not at the
hand of his foes.'

And now the years went by peacefully. Groa dwelt with
her daughter Swanhild up at Middalhof and was the love
of Asmund Asmundson. But, though he forgot his oath thus
far, yet he would never take her to wife. The witchwife was
angered at this, and she schemed and plotted much to bring
it about that Asmund should wed her. But still he would not,
though in all things else she led him as it were by a halter.

Twenty full years had gone by since Gudruda the Gentle

was laid in earth ; and now Gudruda the Fair and Swanhild the
Fatherless were women grown.   Eric, too, was a man of five-
and-twenty years, and no such man had lived in Iceland.   For
he was strong and great of stature, his hair was yellow as
gold, and his grey eyes shone with the light of swords.   He
was gentle and loving as a woman, and even as a lad his
strength was the strength of two men ; and there were none
in all the quarter who could leap or swim or wrestle against
Eric Brighteyes.   Men held him in honour and spoke well of
him, though as yet he had done no deeds, but lived at home
on Coldback, managing the farm, for now Thorgrimur Iron-
Toe, his father, was dead.   But women loved him much, and that
was his bane—for of all women he loved but one, Gudruda the
Fair, Asmund's daughter.   He loved her from a child, and
her alone till his day of death, and she, too, loved him and
him only.   For now Gudruda was a maid of maids, most
beautiful to see and sweet to hear.   Her hair, like the hair
of Eric, was golden, and she was white as the snow on
Hecla ; but her eyes were large and dark, and black lashes
drooped above them.   For the rest she was tall and strong
and comely, merry of face, yet tender, and the most witty of
women.

Swanhild also was very fair; she was slender, small of
limb, and dark of hue, having eyes blue as the deep sea, and
brown curling hair, enough to veil her to the knees, and a
mind of which none knew the end, for, though she was open
in her talk, her thoughts were dark and secret.   This was her
joy : to draw the hearts of men to her and then to mock them.
She beguiled many in this fashion, for she was the cunningest
girl in matters of love, and she knew well the arts of women,
with which they bring men to nothing.   Nevertheless she
was cold at heart, and desired power and wealth greatly, and
she studied magic much, of which her mother Groa also had
a store.   But Swanhild, too, loved a man, and that was the joint
in her harness by which the shaft of Fate entered her heart, for
that man was Eric Brighteyes, who loved her not.   But she
desired him so sorely that, without him, all the world was dark
to her, and her soul but as a ship driven rudderless upon a

winter night. Therefore she put out all her strength to win
him, and bent her witcheries upon him, and they were not few
nor small. Nevertheless they went by him like the wind, for
he dreamed ever of Gudruda alone, and he saw no eyes but
hers, though as yet they spoke no word of love one to the
other.

But Swanhild in her wrath took counsel with her mother
Groa, though there was little liking between them ; and, when
she had heard the maiden's tale, Groa laughed aloud :

'Dost think me blind, girl ?' she said ; 'all of this I have
seen, yea and foreseen, and I tell thee thou art mad. Let
this yeoman Eric go and I will find thee finer fowl to fly at.'

'Nay, that I will not,' quoth Swanhild : 'for I love this man
alone, and I would win him ; and Gudruda I hate, and I would
overthrow her. Give me of thy counsel.'

Groa laughed again. 'Things must be as they are fated.
This now is my rede : Asmund would turn Gudruda's beauty
to account, and that man must be rich in friends and money
who gets her to wife, and in this matter the mind of Björn is
as the mind of his father. Now we will watch, and, when a
good time chances, we will bear tales of Gudruda to Asmund
and to her brother Björn, and swear that she oversteps her
modesty with Eric. Then shall Asmund be wroth and drive
Eric from Gudruda's side. Meanwhile, I will do this : In the
north there dwells a man mighty in all things and blown up
with pride. He is named Ospakar Blacktooth. His wife is
but lately dead, and he has given out that he will wed the fairest
maid in Iceland. Now, it is in my mind to send Koll the Half-
witted, my thrall, whom Asmund gave to me, to Ospakar as
though by chance. He is a great talker and very clever, for
in his half-wits is more cunning than in the brains of most ;
and he shall so bepraise Gudruda's beauty that Ospakar will
come hither to ask her in marriage ; and in this fashion, if
things go well, thou shalt be rid of thy rival, and I of one who
looks scornfully upon me. But, if this fail, then there are two
roads left on which strong feet may travel to their end ; and
of these, one is that thou shouldest win Eric away with thine
own beauty, and that is not little. All men are frail, and I

have a draught that will make the heart as wax ; but yet the other path is surer.'

' And what is that path, my mother ? '

'It runs through blood to blackness. By thy side is a knife and in Gudruda's bosom beats a heart. Dead women are unmeet for love ! '

Swanhild tossed her head and looked upon the dark face of Groa her mother.

'Methinks, with such an end to win, I should not fear to tread that path, if there be need, my mother.'

' Now I see thou art indeed my daughter. Happiness is to the bold. To each it comes in uncertain shape. Some love power, some wealth, and some—a man. Take that which thou lovest—I say, cut thy path to it and take it ; else shall thy life be but a weariness : for what does it serve to win the wealth and power when thou lovest a man alone, or the man when thou dost desire gold and the pride of place ? This is wisdom : to satisfy the longing of thy youth ; for age creeps on apace and beyond is darkness. Therefore, if thou seekest this man, and Gudruda blocks thy path, slay her, girl—by witchcraft or by steel—and take him, and in his arms forget that thine own are red. But first let us try the easier plan. Daughter, I too hate this proud girl, who scorns me as her father's light-of-love. I too long to see that bright head of hers dull with the dust of death, or, at the least, those proud eyes weeping tears of shame as the man she hates leads her hence a bride. Were it not for her I should be Asmund's wife, and, when she is gone, with thy help—for he loves thee much and has cause to love thee— this I may be yet. So in this matter, if in no other, let us go hand in hand and match our wit against her innocence.'

' So be it,' said Swanhild ; ' fail me not and fear not that I shall fail thee.'

Now, Koll the Half-witted went upon his errand, and the time passed till it lacked but a month to Yule, and men sat indoors, for the season was dark and much snow fell. At length came frost, and with it a clear sky, and Gudruda, ceas- ing from her spinning in the hall, went to the women's porch, and, looking out, saw that the snow was hard, and a great longing came upon her to breathe the fresh air, for there was still an hour of daylight. So she threw a cloak about her and walked forth, taking the road towards Coldback in the Marsh that is by Ran River. But Swanhild watched her till she was over the hill. Then she also took a cloak and followed on that path, for she always watched Gudruda.

Gudruda walked on for the half of an hour or so, when she became aware that clouds gathered in the sky, and that the air was heavy with snow to come. Seeing this she turned homewards, and Swanhild hid herself to let her pass. Now flakes floated down as big and soft as fifa flowers. Quicker and more quick they came till all the plain was one white maze of mist, but through it Gudruda walked on, and after her crept Swanhild, like a shadow. And now the darkness gathered and the snow fell thick and fast, covering up the track of her footsteps and she wandered from the path, and after her wandered Swanhild, being loath to show herself. For an hour or more Gudruda wandered and then she called aloud and her voice fell heavily against the cloak of snow. At the last she grew weary and frightened, and sat down upon a shelving rock whence the snow had slipped away. Now, a little way behind was another rock and there Swanhild sat, for she wished to be unseen of Gudruda. So some time passed, and Swanhild grew heavy as though with sleep, when of a sudden a moving thing loomed upon the snowy darkness. Then Gudruda leapt to her feet and called. A man's voice answered:

'Who passes there?'

'I, Gudruda, Asmund's daughter.'

The form came nearer; now Swanhild could hear the snorting of a horse, and now a man leapt from it, and that man was Eric Brighteyes.

'Is it thou indeed, Gudruda!' he said with a laugh, and his great shape showed darkly on the snow mist.

'Oh, is it thou, Eric?' she answered. 'I was never more joyed to see thee; for of a truth thou dost come in a good hour. A little while and I had seen thee no more, for my eyes grow heavy with the death-sleep.'

'Nay, say not so. Art lost, then? Why, so am I. I came out to seek three horses that are strayed, and was overtaken by the snow. May they dwell in Odin's stables, for they have led me to thee. Art thou cold, Gudruda?'

'But a little, Eric. Yea, there is place for thee here on the rock.'

So he sat down by her on the stone, and Swanhild crept nearer; for now all weariness had left her. But still the snow fell thick.

'It comes into my mind that we two shall die here,' said Gudruda presently,

'Thinkest thou so?' he answered. 'Well, I will say this, that I ask no better end.'

'It is a bad end for thee, Eric: to be choked in snow, and with all thy deeds to do.'

'It is a good end, Gudruda, to die at thy side, for so I shall die happy; but I grieve for thee.'

'Grieve not for me, Brighteyes, worse things might befall.'

He drew nearer to her, and now he put his arm about her and clasped her to his bosom; nor did she say him nay. Swanhild saw and lifted herself up behind them, though for a while she heard nothing but the beating of her heart.'

'Listen, Gudruda,' Eric said at last. 'Death draws near to us, and before it comes I would speak to thee, if speak I may.'

'Speak on,' she whispers from his breast.

'I would say this, then: that I love thee, and that I ask no better fate than to die in thy arms.'

'First shalt thou see me die in thine, Eric.'

'Be sure, if that is so, I shall not tarry for long. Oh! Gudruda, since I was a child I have loved thee with a great love, and now thou art all to me. Better to die thus than to live without thee. Speak, then, while there is time.'

'I will not hide from thee, Eric, that thy words are sweet in my ears.'

And now Gudruda sobs and the tears fall fast from her dark eyes.

'Nay, weep not. Dost thou, then, love me?'

'Ay, sure enough, Eric.'

'Then kiss me before we pass. A man should not die thus, and yet men have died worse.'

And so these two kissed, for the first time, out in the snow on Coldback, and though their lips were cold that first kiss was long and sweet.

Swanhild heard and her blood seethed within her as water seethes in a boiling spring when the fires wake beneath. She put her hand to her kirtle and gripped the knife at her side. She half drew it, then drove it back.

'Cold kills as sure as steel,' she said in her heart. 'If I slay her I cannot save myself or him. Let us die in peace, and let the snow cover up our troubling.' And once more she listened.

'Ah, sweet,' said Eric, 'even in the midst of death there is hope of life. Swear to me, then, that if by chance we live thou wilt love me always as thou lovest me now.'

'Ay, Eric, I swear that and readily.'

'And swear, come what may, that thou wilt wed no man but me.'

'I swear, if thou dost remain true to me, that I will wed none but thee, Eric.'

'Then I am sure of thee.'

'Boast not overmuch, Eric : if thou dost live thy days are all before thee, and with times come trials.'

Now the snow whirled down faster and more thick, till these two, clasped heart to heart, were but a heap of white, and all white was the horse, and Swanhild was nearly buried.

'Where go we when we die, Eric ?' said Gudruda; 'in Odin's house there is no place for maids, and how shall my feet fare without thee ?'

'Nay, sweet, my May, Valhalla shuts its gates to me, a deedless man ; up Bifrost's rainbow bridge I may not travel, for I do not die with byrnie on breast and sword aloft. To Hela shall we go, and hand in hand.'

'Art thou sure, Eric, that men find these abodes ? To say sooth, at times I misdoubt me of them.'

'I am not so sure but that I also doubt. Still, I know this : that where thou goest there I shall be, Gudruda.'

'Then things are well, and well work the Norns.[1] Still,

[1] The Northern Fates.

Eric, of a sudden I grow fey : for it comes upon me that I shall not die to-night, but that, nevertheless, I shall die with thy arms about me, and at thy side. There, I see it on the snow ! I lie by thee, sleeping, and one comes with hands outstretched, and sleep falls from them like a mist—by Freya, it is Swanhild's self ! Oh ! it is gone.'

'It was nothing, Gudruda, but a vision of the snow—an untimely dream that comes before the sleep. I grow cold and my eyes are heavy ; kiss me once again.'

'It was no dream, Eric, and ever I doubt me of Swanhild, for I think that she loves thee also, and she is fair and my enemy,' says Gudruda, laying her snow-cold lips on his lips. 'Oh, Eric, awake ! awake ! See, the snow is done.'

He stumbled to his feet and looked forth. Lo ! out across the sky flared the wild Northern fires, throwing light upon the darkness.

'Now it seems that I know the land,' said Eric. 'Look : yonder are Golden Falls, though we did not hear them because of the snow ; and there, out at sea, loom the Westmans ; and that dark thing is the Temple Hof, and behind it stands the stead. We are saved, Gudruda, and thus far indeed thou wast fey. Now rise, ere thy limbs stiffen, and I will set thee on the horse, if he still can run, and lead thee down to Middalhof before the witchlights fail us.'

'So it shall be, Eric.'

Now he led Gudruda to the horse—that, seeing its master, snorted and shook the snow from its coat, for it was not frozen—and set her on the saddle, and put his arm about her waist, and they passed slowly through the deep snow. And Swanhild, too, crept from her place, for her burning rage had kept the life in her, and followed after them. Many times she fell, and once she was nearly swallowed in a drift of snow and cried out in her fear.

'Who called aloud ?' said Eric, turning ; 'I thought that I heard a voice.'

'Nay,' answers Gudruda, 'it was but a night-hawk screaming.'

Now Swanhild lay quiet in the drift, but she said in her heart:

c 2

'Ay, a night-hawk that shall tear out those dark eyes of thine, my enemy!'

The two go on and at length they come to the banked roadway that runs past the Temple to Asmund's hall. Here Swanhild leaves them, and, climbing over the turf-wall into the home meadow, passes round the hall by the outbuildings and so comes to the west end of the house, and enters by the men's door unnoticed of any. For all the people, seeing a horse coming and a woman seated on it, were gathered in front of the hall. But Swanhild ran to that shut bed where she slept, and, closing the curtain, threw off her garments, shook the snow from her hair, and put on a linen kirtle. Then she rested a while, for she was weary, and, going to the kitchen, warmed herself at the fire.

Meanwhile Eric and Gudruda came to the house and there Asmund greeted them well, for he was troubled in his heart about his daughter, and very glad to know her living, seeing that men had but just begun to search for her, because of the snow and the darkness.

Now Gudruda told her tale, but not all of it, and Asmund bade Eric to the house. Then one asked about Swanhild, and Eric said that he had seen nothing of her, and Asmund was sad at this, for he loved Swanhild. But as he told all men to go and search, an old wife came and said that Swanhild was in the kitchen, and while the carline spoke she came into the hall, dressed in white, very pale and with shining eyes and fair to see.

'Where hast thou been, Swanhild?' said Asmund. 'I thought certainly thou wast perishing with Gudruda in the snow, and now men go to seek thee while the witchlights burn.'

'Nay, foster-father, I have been to the Temple,' she answered, lying. 'So Gudruda has but narrowly escaped the snow, thanks be to Brighteyes yonder! Surely I am glad of it, for we could ill spare our sweet sister,' and, going up to her, she kissed her. But Gudruda saw that her eyes burned like fire and felt that her lips were cold as ice, and shrank back wondering.

CHAPTER III

HOW ASMUND BADE ERIC TO HIS YULE-FEAST

OSPAKAR.

OW it was supper-time and men sat at meat while the women waited upon them. But as she went to and fro, Gudruda always looked at Eric, and Swanhild watched them both. Supper being over, people gathered round the hearth, and, having finished her service, Gudruda came and sat by Eric, so that her sleeve might touch his arm. They spoke no word, but there they sat and were happy. Swanhild saw and bit her lip. Now, she was seated by Asmund and Björn his son.

'Look, foster-father,' she said ; 'yonder sit a pretty pair! '

'That cannot be denied,' answered Asmund. 'One may ride many days to see such another man as Eric Brighteyes, and no such maid as Gudruda flowers between Middalhof and London town, unless it be thou, Swanhild. Well, so her mother said that it should be, and without doubt she was foresighted at her death.'

'Nay, name me not with Gudruda, foster-father; I am but a grey goose by thy white swan. But these shall be well wed and that will be a good match for Eric.'

'Let not thy tongue run on so fast,' said Asmund sharply.
'Who told thee that Eric should have Gudruda?'

'None told me, but in truth, having eyes and ears, I grew
certain of it,' said Swanhild. 'Look at them now: surely
lovers wear such faces.'

Now it chanced that Gudruda had rested her chin on her
hand, and was gazing into Eric's eyes beneath the shadow of
her hair.

'Methinks my sister will look higher than to wed a simple
yeoman, though he is large as two other men,' said Björn
with a sneer. Now Björn was jealous of Eric's strength and
beauty, and did not love him.

'Trust nothing that thou seest and little that thou hearest,
girl,' said Asmund, raising himself from thought: 'so shall
thy guesses be good. Eric, come here and tell us how thou
didst chance on Gudruda in the snow.'

'I was not so ill seated but that I could bear to stay,'
grumbled Eric beneath his breath; but Gudruda said 'Go.'

So he went and told his tale; but not all of it, for he intended to ask Gudruda in marriage on the morrow, though
his heart prophesied no luck in the matter, and therefore he
was not overswift with it.

'In this thing thou hast done me and mine good service,'
said Asmund coldly, searching Eric's face with his blue eyes.
'It had been sad if my fair daughter had perished in the snow,
for, know this: I would set her high in marriage, for her honour
and the honour of my house, and so some rich and noble man
had lost great joy. But take thou this gift in memory
of the deed, and Gudruda's husband shall give thee another
such upon the day that he makes her wife,' and he drew a
gold ring off his arm.

Now Eric's knees trembled as he heard, and his heart
grew faint as though with fear. But he answered clear and
straight:

'Thy gift had been better without thy words, ring-giver;
but I pray thee to take it back, for I have done nothing to win
it, though perhaps the time will come when I shall ask thee
for a richer.'

'My gifts have never been put away before,' said Asmund, growing angry.

' This wealthy farmer holds the good gold of little worth. It is foolish to take fish to the sea, my father,' sneered Björn.

' Nay, Björn, not so,' Eric answered : ' but, as thou sayest, I am but a farmer, and since my father, Thorgrimur Iron-Toe, died things have not gone too well on Ran River. But at the least I am a free man, and I will take no gifts that I cannot repay worth for worth. Therefore I will not have the ring.'

' As thou wilt,' said Asmund. ' Pride is a good horse if thou ridest wisely,' and he thrust the ring back upon his arm.

Then people go to rest; but Swanhild seeks her mother, and tells her all that has befallen her, nor does Groa fail to listen.

' Now I will make a plan,' she says, ' for these things have chanced well and Asmund is in a ripe humour. Eric shall come no more to Middalhof till Gudruda is gone hence, led by Ospakar Blacktooth.'

' And if Eric does not come here, how shall I see his face ? for, mother, I long for the sight of it.'

' That is thy matter, thou lovesick fool. Know this : that if Eric comes hither and gets speech with Gudruda, there is an end of thy hopes ; for, fair as thou art, she is too fair for thee, and, strong as thou art, in a way she is too strong. Thou hast heard how these two love, and such loves mock at the will of fathers. Eric will win his desire or die beneath the swords of Asmund and Björn, if such men can prevail against his might. Nay, the wolf Eric must be fenced from the lamb till he grows hungry. Then let him search the fold and make spoil of thee, for, when the best is gone, he will desire the good.'

' So be it, mother. As I sat crouched behind Gudruda in the snow at Coldback I had half a mind to end her love-words with this knife, for so I should have been free of her.'

'Yes, and fast in the doom-ring, thou wildcat. The gods
help this Eric, if thou winnest him. Nay, choose thy time and,
if thou must strike, strike secretly and home. Remember also
that cunning is mightier than strength, that lies pierce further
than swords, and that witchcraft wins where honesty must
fail. Now I will go to Asmund, and he shall be an angry man
before to-morrow comes.'

Then Groa went to the shut bed where Asmund the
Priest slept He was sitting on the bed and asked her why
she came.

'For love of thee, Asmund, and thy house, though thou
dost treat me ill, who hast profited so much by me and my
foresight. Say now: wilt thou that this daughter of thine,
Gudruda the Fair, should be the light May of yonder long-
legged yeoman?'

'That is not in my mind,' said Asmund, stroking his
beard.

'Knowest thou, then, that this very day your white
Gudruda sat on Eric's lap in the snow, while he fondled her
to his heart's content?'

'Most likely it was for warmth. Men do not dream on love
in the hour of death. Who saw this?'

'Swanhild, who was behind, and hid herself for shame,
and therefore she held that these two must soon be wed!
Ah, thou art foolish now, Asmund. Young blood makes
light of cold or death. Art thou blind, or dost thou not see
that these two turn to each other like birds at nesting-time?'

'They might do worse,' said Asmund, 'for they are a
proper pair, and it seems to me that each was born for
each.'

'Then all goes well. Still, it is a pity to see so fair a maid
cast like rotten bait upon the waters to hook this troutlet
of a yeoman. Thou hast enemies, Asmund; thou art too
prosperous, and there are many who hate thee for thy state
and wealth. Were it not wise to use this girl of thine to build
a wall about thee against the evil day?'

'I have been more wont, housekeeper, to trust to my
own arm than to bought friends. But tell me, for at the least

thou art far-seeing, how may this be done? As things are, though I spoke roughly to him this night, I am inclined to let Eric Brighteyes take Gudruda. I have always loved the lad, and he will go far.'

'Listen, Asmund! Surely thou hast heard of Ospakar Blacktooth—the priest who dwells in the north?'

'Ay, I have heard of him, and I know him; there is no man like him for ugliness, or strength, or wealth and power. We sailed together on a viking cruise many years ago, and he did things at which my blood turned, and in those days I had no chicken heart.'

'With time men change their temper. Unless I am mistaken, this Ospakar wishes above all to have Gudruda in marriage, for, now that everything is his, this alone is left for him to ask—the fairest woman in Iceland as a housewife. Think then, with Ospakar for a son-in-law, who is there that can stand against thee?'

'I am not so sure of this matter, nor do I altogether trust thee, Groa. Of a truth it seems to me that thou hast some stake upon the race. This Ospakar is evil and hideous. It were a shame to give Gudruda over to him when she looks elsewhere. Knowest thou that I swore to love and cherish her, and how runs this with my oath? If Eric is not too rich, yet he is of good birth and kin, and, moreover, a man of men. If he take her good will come of it.'

'It is like thee, Asmund, always to mistrust those who spend their days in plotting for thy weal. Do as thou wilt: let Eric take this treasure of thine—for whom earls would give their state—and live to rue it. But I say this: if he have thy leave to roam here with his dove the matter will soon grow, for these two sicken each to each, and young blood is hot and ill at waiting, and it is not always snow-time. So betroth her or let him go. And now I have said.'

'Thy tongue runs too fast. The man is quite unproved and I will try him. To-morrow I will warn him from my door; then things shall go as they are fated. And now peace, for I weary of thy talk, and, moreover, it is false; for thou lackest one thing—a little honesty to season all thy craft. What fee has Ospakar paid thee, I wonder. Thou at least hadst never refused the gold ring to-night, for thou wouldst do much for gold.'

'And more for love, and most of all for hate,' Groa said, and laughed aloud; nor did they speak more on this matter that night.

Now, early in the morning Asmund rose, and, going to the hall, awoke Eric, who slept by the centre hearth, saying that he would talk with him without. Then Eric followed him to the back of the hall.

'Say now, Eric,' he said, when they stood in the grey light outside the house, 'who was it taught thee that kisses keep out the cold on snowy days?'

Now Eric reddened to his yellow hair, but he answered: 'Who was it told thee, lord, that I tried this medicine?'

'The snow hides much, but there are eyes that can pierce the snow. Nay, more, thou wast seen, and there's an end. Now know this—I like thee well, but Gudruda is not for thee; she is far above thee, who art but a deedless yeoman.'

'Then I love to no end,' said Eric; 'I long for one thing only, and that is Gudruda. It was in my mind to ask her in marriage of thee to-day.'

'Then, lad, thou hast thy answer before thou askest. Be sure of one thing: if but once again I find thee alone with Gudruda, it is my axe that shall kiss thee and not her lips.'

'This may yet be put to the proof, lord,' said Eric, and turned to seek his horse, when suddenly Gudruda came and stood between them, and his heart leapt at the sight of her.

'Listen, Gudruda,' Eric said. 'This is thy father's word: that we two speak together no more.'

'Then it is an ill saying for us,' said Gudruda, laying her hand upon her breast.

'Saying good or ill, so it surely is, girl,' answered Asmund. 'No more shalt thou go a-kissing, in the snow or in the flowers.'

'Now I seem to hear Swanhild's voice,' she said. 'Well, such things have happened to better folk, and a father's wish is to a maid what the wind is to the grass. Still, the sun is behind the cloud and it will shine again some day. Till then, Eric, fare thee well ! '

'It is not thy will, lord,' said Eric, 'that I should come to thy Yule-feast as thou hast asked me these ten years gone ? '

Now Asmund grew wroth, and pointed with his hand towards the great Golden Falls that thunder down the mountain named Stonefell that is behind Middalhof, and there are no greater water-falls in Iceland.

'A man may take two roads, Eric, from Coldback to Middalhof, one by the bridle-path over Coldback and the other down Golden Falls ; but I never knew traveller to choose this way. Now, I bid thee to my feast by the path over Golden Falls ; and, if thou comest that way, I promise thee this : if thou livest I will greet thee well, and if I find thee dead in the great pool I will bind on thy Hell-shoes and lay thee to earth neighbourly fashion. But if thou comest by any other path, then my thralls shall cut thee down at my door.' And he stroked his beard and laughed.

Now Asmund spoke thus mockingly because he did not think it possible that any man should try the path of the Golden Falls.

Eric smiled and said, 'I hold thee to thy word, lord ; perhaps I shall be thy guest at Yule.'

But Gudruda heard the thunder of the mighty Falls as the wind turned, and cried 'Nay, nay—it were thy death ! '

Then Eric finds his horse and rides away across the snow.

Now it must be told of Koll the Half-witted that at length he came to Swinefell in the north, having journeyed hard across the snow. Here Ospakar Blacktooth had his great hall, in which day by day a hundred men sat down to meat. Now Koll entered the hall when Ospakar was at supper, and looked at him with big eyes, for he had never seen so wonderful a man. He was huge in stature—his hair was black, and black his beard, and on his lower lip there lay a great black fang. His eyes were small and narrow, but his cheekbones were set wide apart and high, like those of a horse. Koll thought him an ill man to deal with and half a troll,[1] and grew afraid of his errand, since in Koll's half-wittedness there lay hid much cunning—for it was a cloak in which he wrapped himself. But as Ospakar sat in the high seat, clothed in a purple robe, with his sword Whitefire on his knee, he saw Koll, and called out in a great voice:

'Who is this red fox that creeps into my earth?'

For, to look at, Koll was very like a fox.

'My name is Koll the Half-witted, Groa's thrall, lord. Am I welcome here?' he answered.

'That is as it may be. Why do they call thee half-witted?'

'Because I love not work overmuch, lord.'

'Then all my thralls are wholly mad and fellow to thee. Say, what brings thee here!'

'This, lord. It was told among men down in the south that thou wouldst give a good gift to him who should discover to thee the fairest maid in Iceland. So I asked leave of my mistress to come on a journey and tell thee of her.'

'Then a lie was told thee. Still, I love to hear of fair maids, and seek one for a wife if she be but fair enough. So speak on, Koll the Fox, and lie not to me, I warn thee, else I will knock what wits are left there from that red head of thine.'

So Koll took up the tale and greatly bepraised Gudruda's beauty; nor in truth, for all his talk, could he praise it too much. He told of her dark eyes and the whiteness of her skin, of the nobleness of her shape and the gold of her hair, of her wit and gentleness, till at length Ospakar grew afire to see this flower of maids.

'By Thor, thou Koll,' he said, 'if the girl be but half of what thou sayest, her luck is good, for she shall be wife to Ospakar. But if thou hast lied to me about her, beware! for soon there shall be a knave the less in Iceland.'

Now a man rose in the hall and said that Koll spoke truth, for

[1] An able-bodied Goblin.

he had seen Gudruda the Fair, Asmund's daughter, and there was no maid like her in Iceland.

' I will do this now,' said Blacktooth. ' To-morrow I will send a messenger to Middalhof, saying to Asmund the Priest that I purpose to visit him at the time of the Yule-feast ; then I shall see if the girl pleases me. Meanwhile, Koll, take thou a seat among the thralls, and here is something for thy pains,' and he took off the purple cloak and threw it to him.

' Thanks to thee, Gold-scatterer,' said Koll. ' It is wise to go soon to Middalhof, for such a bloom as this maid does not lack a bee. There is a youngling in the south, named Eric Brighteyes, who loves Gudruda, and she, I think, loves him, though he is but a yeoman of small wealth and is only twenty-five years old.'

' Ho ! ho ! ' laughed great Ospakar, ' and I am forty-five. But let not this suckling cross my desire, lest men call him Eric Holloweyes ! '

Now the messenger of Ospakar came to Middalhof, and his words pleased Asmund and he made ready a great feast. And Swanhild smiled, but Gudruda was afraid

CHAPTER IV

HOW ERIC CAME DOWN GOLDEN FALLS

NOW Ospakar rode up to Middalhof on the day before the Yule-feast. He was splendidly apparelled, and with him came his two sons, Gizur the Lawman and Mord, young men of promise, and many armed thralls and servants. Gudruda, watching at the women's door, saw his face in the moonlight and loathed him.

'What thinkest thou of him who comes to seek thee in marriage, foster-sister?' asked Swanhild, watching at her side.

'I think he is like a troll, and that, seek as he will, he shall not find me. I had rather lie in the pool beneath Golden Falls than in Ospakar's hall.'

'That shall be proved,' said Swanhild. 'At the least he is rich and noble, and the greatest of men in size. It would go hard with Eric were those arms about him.'

'I am not so sure of that,' said Gudruda; 'but it is not likely to be known.'

'Comes Eric to the feast by the road of Golden Falls, Gudruda?'

'Nay, no man may try that path and live.'

'Then he will die, for Eric will risk it.'

Now Gudruda thought, and a great fire burned in her heart and shone through her eyes. 'If Eric dies,' she said, 'on thee be his blood, Swanhild—on thee and that dark mother of thine, for ye have plotted to bring this evil on us. How have I harmed thee that thou shouldst deal thus with me?'

Swanhild turned white and wicked-looking, for passion mastered her, and she gazed into Gudruda's face and answered: 'How hast thou harmed me? Surely I will tell thee. Thy beauty has robbed me of Eric's love.'

'It would be better to prate of Eric's love when he had told it thee, Swanhild.'

'Thou hast robbed me and therefore I hate thee, and therefore I will deliver thee to Ospakar, whom thou dost loath — ay and yet win Brighteyes to myself. Am I not also fair, and can I not also love, and shall I watch thee snatch my joy? By the Gods, never! I will see thee dead, and Eric with thee, ere it shall be so! but first I will see thee shamed!'

'Thy words are ill-suited to a maiden's lips, Swanhild! But of this be sure: I fear thee not, and shall

GOLDEN FALLS.

never fear thee. And one thing I know well, that, whether thou
or I prevail, in the end thou shalt harvest the greatest shame,
and in times to come men shall speak of thee with hatred and
name thee by ill names. Moreover, Eric shall never love
thee ; from year to year he shall hate thee with a deeper hate,
though it may well be that thou wilt bring ruin on him. And
now I thank thee that thou hast told me all thy mind, show-
ing me what indeed thou art ! ' And Gudruda turned scornfully
upon her heel and walked away.

Now Asmund the Priest went out into the courtyard, and
meeting Ospakar Blacktooth, greeted him heartily, though he
did not like his looks, and took him by the hand and led him
to the hall, that was bravely decked with tapestries, and seated
him by his side on the high seat. And Ospakar's thralls
brought good gifts for Asmund, who thanked the giver well.

Now it was supper time, and Gudruda came in, and after
her walked Swanhild. Ospakar gazed hard at Gudruda and a
great desire entered into him to make her his wife. But she
passed coldly by, nor looked on him at all.

' This, then, is that maid of thine of whom I have heard
tell, Asmund ? I will say this : fairer was never born of
woman.'

Then men ate and Ospakar drank much ale, but all the
while he stared at Gudruda and listened for her voice. But
as yet he said nothing of what he came to seek, though all
knew his errand. And his two sons, Gizur and Mord, stared
also at Gudruda, for they thought her most wonderfully fair.
But Gizur found Swanhild also fair.

And so the night wore on till it was time to sleep.

On this same day Eric rode up from his farm on Ran
River and took his road along the brow of Coldback till he
came to Stonefell. Now all along Coldback and Stonefell
is a steep cliff facing to the south, that grows ever higher till
it comes to that point where Golden River falls over it and,
parting its waters below, runs east and west—the branch to
the east being called Ran River and that to the west Laxà—
for these two streams girdle round the rich plain of Middalhof,

till at length they reach the sea. But in the midst of Golden River, on the edge of the cliff, a mass of rock juts up called Sheep-saddle, dividing the waters of the fall, and over this the spray flies, and in winter the ice gathers, but the river does not cover it. The great fall is thirty fathoms deep, and shaped like a horseshoe, of which the points lie towards Middalhof. Yet if he could but gain the Sheep-saddle rock that divides the midst of the waters, a strong and hardy man might climb down some fifteen fathoms of this depth and scarcely wet his feet.

Now here at the foot of Sheep-saddle rock the double arches of waters meet, and fall in one torrent into the bottomless pool below. But, some three fathoms from this point of the meeting waters, and beneath it, just where the curve is deepest, a single crag, as large as a drinking-table and no larger, juts through the foam, and, if a man could reach it, he might leap from it some twelve fathoms, sheer into the spray-hidden pit beneath, there to sink or swim as it might befall. This crag is called Wolf's Fang.

Now Eric stood for a long while on the edge of the fall and looked, measuring every thing with his eye. Then he went up above, where the river swirls down to the precipice, and looked again, for it is from this bank that the dividing island-rock Sheep-saddle must be reached.

'A man may hardly do this thing; yet I will try it,' he said to himself at last. 'My honour shall be great for the feat, if I chance to live, and if I die—well, there is an end of troubling after maids and all other things.'

So he went home and sat silent that evening. Now, since Thorgrimur Iron-Toe's death, his housewife, Saevuna, Eric's mother, had grown dim of sight, and, though she peered and peered again from her seat in the ingle nook, she could not see the face of her son.

'What ails thee, Eric, that thou sittest so silent? Was not the meat, then, to thy mind at supper?'

'Yes, mother, the meat was well enough, though a little undersmoked.'

'Now I see that thou art not thyself, son, for thou hadst no meat, but only stock-fish—and I never knew a man forget

D

his supper on the night of its eating, except he was distraught
or deep in love.'

'Was it so?' said Brighteyes.

'What troubles thee, Eric?—that sweet lass yonder?'

'Ay, somewhat, mother.'

'What more, then?'

'This, that I go down Golden Falls to-morrow, and I do not
know how I may come from Sheep-saddle rock to Wolf's Fang
crag and keep my life whole in me; and now, I pray thee,
weary me not with words, for my brain is slow, and I must
use it.'

When she heard this Saevuna screamed aloud, and threw
herself before Eric, praying him to forego his mad venture.
But he would not listen to her, for he was slow to make up
his mind, but, that being made up, nothing could change it.
Then, when she learned that it was to get sight of Gudruda
that he purposed thus to throw his life away, she was very
angry and cursed her and all her kith and kin.

'It is likely enough that thou wilt have cause to use such
words before all this tale is told,' said Eric; 'nevertheless,
mother, forbear to curse Gudruda, who is in no way to blame
for these matters.'

'Thou art a faithless son,' Saevuna said, 'who wilt slay
thyself striving to win speech with thy May, and leave thy
mother childless.'

Eric said that it seemed so indeed, but he was plighted to
it and the feat must be tried. Then he kissed her, and she
sought her bed, weeping.

Now it was the day of the Yule-feast, and there was no sun
till one hour before noon. But Eric, having kissed his mother
and bidden her farewell, called a thrall, Jon by name, and
giving him a sealskin bag full of his best apparel, bade him
ride to Middalhof and tell Asmund the Priest that Eric
Brighteyes would come down Golden Falls an hour after midday, to join his feast; and thence go to the foot of the Golden
Falls, to await him there. And the man went, wondering, for
he thought his master mad.

Then Eric took a good rope and a staff tipped with iron, and, so soon as the light served, mounted his horse, forded Ran River, and rode along Coldback till he came to the lip of Golden Falls. Here he stayed a while till at length he saw many people streaming up the snow from Middalhof far beneath, and, among them, two women who by their stature should be Gudruda and Swanhild, and, near to them, a great man whom he did not know. Then he showed himself for a space on the brink of the gulf and turned his horse up stream. The sun shone bright upon the edge of the sky, but the frost bit like a sword. Still, he must strip off his garments, so that nothing remained on him except his sheepskin shoes, shirt, and hose, and take the water. Now here the river runs mightily, and he must cross full thirty fathoms of the swirling water before he can reach Sheep-saddle, and woe to him if his foot should slip on the boulders, for then certainly he must be swept over the brink.

Eric rested the staff against the stony bottom and, leaning his weight on it, took the stream, and he was so strong that it could not prevail against him till at length he was rather more than half-way across and the water swept above his shoulders. Now he was lifted from his feet and, letting the staff float, he swam for his life, and with such mighty strokes that he felt little of that icy cold. Down he was swept—now the lip of the fall was but three fathoms away on his left, and already the green water boiled beneath him. A fathom from him was the corner of Sheep-saddle. If he may grasp it, all is well ; if not, he dies.

Three great strokes and he held it. His feet were swept out over the brink of the fall, but he clung on grimly, and by the strength of his arms drew himself on to the rock and rested a while. Presently he stood up, for the cold began to nip him, and the people below became aware that he had swum the river above the fall and raised a shout, for the deed was great. Now Eric must begin to clamber down Sheep-saddle, and this was no easy task, for the rock is almost sheer, and slippery with ice, and on either side the waters rushed and thundered, throwing their blinding spray about him as they leapt to the depths beneath. He looked, studying the rock ;

then, feeling that he grew afraid, made an end of doubt and, grasping a point with both hands, swung himself down his own length and more. Now for many minutes he climbed down Sheep-saddle, and the task was hard, for he was bewildered with the booming of the waters that bent out on either side of him like the arc of a bow, and the rock was very steep and slippery. Still, he came down all those fifteen fathoms and fell not, though twice he was near to falling, and the watchers below marvelled greatly at his hardihood.

'He will be dashed to pieces where the waters meet,' said Ospakar, 'he can never gain Wolf's Fang crag beneath; and, if so it be that he come there and leaps to the pool, the weight of water will drive him down and drown him.'

'It is certainly so,' quoth Asmund, 'and it grieves me much; for it was my jest that drove him to this perilous adventure, and we cannot spare such a man as Eric Brighteyes.'

Now Swanhild turned white as death; but Gudruda said: 'If great heart and strength and skill may avail at all, then Eric shall come safely down the waters.'

'Thou fool!' whispered Swanhild in her ear, 'how can these help him? No troll could live in yonder cauldron. Dead is Eric, and thou art the bait that lured him to his death!'

'Spare thy words,' she answered; 'as the Norns have ordered so it shall be.'

Now Eric stood at the foot of Sheep-saddle, and within an arm's length the mighty waters met, tossing their yellow waves and seething furiously as they leapt to the mist-hid gulf beneath. He bent over and looked through the spray. Three fathoms under him the rock Wolf's Fang split the waters, and thence, if he can come thither, he may leap sheer into the pool below. Now he unwound the rope that was about his middle, and made one end fast to a knob of rock— and this was difficult, for his hands were stiff with cold—and the other end he passed through his leathern girdle. Then Eric looked again, and his heart sank within him. How might he give himself to this boiling flood and not be shattered? But as he looked, lo! a rainbow grew upon the face of the water,

ERIC ON SHEEP-SADDLE ROCK.

and one end of it lit upon him, and the other, like a glory from the Gods, fell full upon Gudruda as she stood a little way apart, watching at the foot of Golden Falls.

'Seest thou that,' said Asmund to Groa, who was at his

side, ' the Gods build their Bifrost bridge between these two.
Who now shall keep them asunder ? '

' Read the portent thus,' she answered : ' they shall be
united, but not here. Yon is a Spirit bridge, and, see: the
waters of Death foam and fall between them ! '

Eric, too, saw the omen and it seemed good to him,
and all fear left his heart. Round about him the waters
thundered, but amidst their roar he dreamed that he heard a
voice calling :

' Be of good cheer, Eric Brighteyes ; for thou shalt live to
do mightier deeds than this, and in guerdon thou shalt win
Gudruda.'

So he paused no longer, but, shortening up the rope, pulled
on it with all his strength, and then leapt out upon the arch
of waters. They struck him and he was dashed out like a
stone from a sling ; again he fell against them and again was
dashed away, so that his girdle burst. Eric felt it go and clung
wildly to the rope and lo ! with the inward swing, he fell on
Wolf's Fang, where never a man has stood before and never a
man shall stand again. Eric lay a little while on the rock till
his breath came back to him, and he listened to the roar of
the waters. Then, rising on his hands and knees, he crept to
its point, for he could scarcely stand because of the trembling
of the stone beneath the shock of the fall ; and when the
people below saw that he was not dead, they raised a great
shout, and the sound of their voices came to him through the
noise of the waters.

Now, twelve fathoms beneath him was the surface of the
pool ; but he could not see it because of the wreaths of spray.
Nevertheless, he must leap and that swiftly, for he grew cold.
So of a sudden Eric stood up to his full height, and, with a loud
cry and a mighty spring, he bounded out from the point of
Wolf's Fang far into the air, beyond the reach of the falling
flood, and rushed headlong towards the gulf beneath. Now
all men watching held their breath as his body travelled, and
so great is the place and so high the leap that through the
mist Eric seemed but as a big white stone hurled down the
face of the arching waters.

He was gone, and the watchers rushed down to the foot of
the pool, for there, if he rose at all, he must pass to the
shallows. Swanhild could look no more, but sank upon the
ground. The face of Gudruda was set like a stone with doubt
and anguish. Ospakar saw and read the meaning, and he
said to himself: 'Now Odin grant that this youngling rise
not again! for the maid loves him dearly, and he is too much
a man to be lightly swept aside.'

Eric struck the pool. Down he sank, and down and down
—for the water falling from so far must almost reach the
bottom of the pool before it can rise again—and he with it.
Now he touched the bottom, but very gently, and slowly began
to rise, and, as he rose, was carried along by the stream. But
it was long before he could breathe, and it seemed to him that
his lungs would burst. Still, he struggled up, striking great
strokes with his legs.

'Farewell to Eric,' said Asmund, 'he will rise no more
now.'

But just as he spoke Gudruda pointed to something that
gleamed, white and golden, beneath the surface of the current,
and lo! the bright hair of Eric rose from the water, and he
drew a great breath, shaking his head like a seal, and, though
but feebly, struck out for the shallows that are at the foot of
the pool. Now he found footing, but was swept over by the
fierce current, and cut his forehead, and he carried that scar
till his death. Again he rose, and with a rush gained the
bank unaided and fell upon the snow.

Now people gathered about him in silence and wondering,
for none had known so great a deed. And presently Eric
opened his eyes and looked up, and found the eyes of Gudruda
fixed on his, and there was that in them which made him
glad he had dared the path of Golden Falls.

CHAPTER V

HOW ERIC WON THE SWORD WHITEFIRE

NOW Asmund the priest bent down, and Eric saw him and spoke:

'Thou badest me to thy Yule-feast, lord, by yonder slippery road and I have come. Dost thou welcome me well?'

'No man better,' quoth Asmund. 'Thou art a gallant man, though foolhardy; and thou hast done a deed that shall be told of while skalds sing and men live in Iceland.'

'Make place, my father,' said Gudruda, 'for Eric bleeds.' And she loosed the kerchief from her neck and bound it about his wounded brow, and, taking the rich cloak from her body, threw it on his shoulders, and no man said her nay.

THE WRESTLING SHOES.

Then they led him to the hall, where Eric clothed himself and rested, and he sent back the thrall Jon to Coldback, bidding him tell Saevuna, Eric's mother, that he was safe. But he was somewhat weak all that day, and the sound of waters roared in his ears.

Now Ospakar and Groa were ill pleased at the turn things had taken; but all the others rejoiced much, for Eric was well loved of men and they would have grieved if the waters had prevailed against his might. But Swanhild brooded bitterly, for Eric never turned to look on her.

The hour of the feast drew on, and, according to custom, it was held in the Temple, and thither went all men. When they were seated in the nave of the Hof, the fat ox that had been made ready for sacrifice was led in and dragged before the altar on which the holy fire burned. Now Asmund the Priest slew it, amid silence, before the figures of the Gods, and, catching its blood in the blood-bowl, he sprinkled the altar and all the worshippers with the blood-twigs. Then the ox was cut up, and the figures of the almighty Gods were anointed with its molten fat and wiped with fair linen. Next the flesh was boiled in the cauldrons that were hung over fires lighted all down the nave, and the feast began.

Now men ate, and drank much ale and mead, and all were merry. But Ospakar Blacktooth did not grow glad, though he drank much, for he saw that the eyes of Gudruda watched Eric's face and that they smiled on each other. He was wroth at this, for he knew that the bait must be good and the line strong that should win this fair fish to his angle, and as he sat, unknowingly his fingers loosed the peace-strings of his sword Whitefire, and he half drew it, so that its brightness flamed in the firelight.

'Thou hast a wondrous blade there, Ospakar!' said Asmund, 'though this is no place to draw it. Whence came it? Methinks no such swords are fashioned now.'

'Ay, Asmund, a wondrous blade indeed. There is no other such in the world, for the dwarfs forged it of old, and he shall be unconquered who holds it aloft. This was King Odin's sword, and it is named Whitefire. Ralph the Red took it from King Eric's cairn in Norway, and he strove long with the Barrow-Dweller[1] before he wrenched it from his grasp. But my father won it and slew Ralph, though he had never done this had Whitefire been aloft against him. But Ralph the Red, being in drink when the ships met in battle, fought with an axe, and was slain by my father, and since then Whitefire has

---

[1] The ghost in the cairn.

been the last light that many a chief's eyes have seen. Look at it, Asmund.'

Now he drew the great sword, and men were astonished as it flashed aloft. Its hilt was of gold, and blue stones were set therein. It measured two ells and a half from crossbar to point, and so bright was the broad blade that no one could look on it for long, and all down its length ran runes.

'A wondrous weapon, truly!' said Asmund. 'How read the runes?'

'I know not, nor any man—they are ancient.'

'Let me look at them,' said Groa, 'I am skilled in runes.' Now she took the sword, and heaved it up, and looked at the runes and said, 'A strange writing truly.'

'How runs it, housekeeper?' said Asmund.

'Thus, lord, if my skill is not at fault:—

Whitefire is my name—Dwarf-folk forged me—
Odin's sword was I—Eric's sword was I—Eric's sword shall I be—
And where I fall there he must follow me.'

Now Gudruda glanced at Eric Brighteyes wonderingly, and Ospakar saw it and became very angry.

'Look not so, maiden,' he said, 'for it shall be another Eric than yon flapper-duck who holds Whitefire aloft, though it may well chance that he shall feel its edge.'

Now Gudruda bit her lip, and Eric burned red to the brow and spoke:

'It is ill, lord, to throw taunts like an angry woman. Thou art great and strong, yet I may dare a deed with thee.'

'Peace, boy! Thou canst climb a waterfall well, I gainsay it not; but beware ere thou settest up thyself against my strength. Say now, what game wilt thou play with Ospakar?'

'I will go on holmgang with thee, byrnie-clad or baresark,[1] and fight thee with axe or sword, or I will wrestle with thee, and Whitefire yonder shall be the winner's prize.'

'Nay, I will have no bloodshed here at Middalhof,' said

[1] To a duel, usually fought, in mail or without it, on an island—'holm'—within a circle of hazel-twigs.

Asmund sternly. 'Make play with fists, or wrestle if ye will, for that were great sport to see ; but weapons shall not be drawn.'

Now Ospakar grew mad with anger and drink—and he grinned like a dog, till men saw the red gums beneath his lips.

'Thou wilt wrestle with me, youngling—with *me* whom no man has ever so much as lifted from my feet ? Good ! I will lay thee on thy face and whip thee, and Whitefire shall be the stake—I swear it on the holy altar-ring ; but what hast thou to set against the precious sword ? Thy poor hovel and its lot of land shall be all too little.'

'I set my life on it ; if I lose Whitefire let Whitefire slay me,' said Eric.

'Nay, that I will not have, and I am master here in this Temple,' said Asmund. 'Bethink thee of some other stake, Ospakar, or let the game be off.'

Now Ospakar gnawed his lip with his black fang and thought. Then he laughed aloud and spoke :

'Bright is Whitefire and thou art named Brighteyes. See now : I set the great sword against thy right eye, and, if I win the match, it shall be mine to tear it out. Wilt thou play this game with me ? If thy heart fails thee, let it go ; but I will set no other stake against my good sword.'

'Eyes and limbs are a poor man's wealth,' said Eric : 'so be it. I stake my right eye against the sword Whitefire, and we will try the match to-morrow.'

'And to-morrow night thou shalt be called Eric One-eye,' said Ospakar—at which some few of his thralls laughed.

But most of the men did not laugh, for they thought this an ill game and a worse jest.

Now the feast went on, and Asmund rose from his high seat in the centre of the nave, on the left hand looking down from the altar, and gave out the holy toasts. First men drank a full horn to Odin, praying for triumph on their foes. Then they drank to Frey, asking for plenty ; to Thor, for strength in battle ; to Freya, Goddess of Love (and to her Eric drank heartily) ; to the memory of the dead ; and, last of all, to Bragi,

God of all delight. When this cup was drunk, Asmund rose again, according to custom, and asked if none had an oath to swear as to some deed that should be done.

For a while there was no answer, but presently Eric Bright-eyes stood up.

' Lord,' he said, ' I would swear an oath.'

' Set forth the matter, then,' said Asmund.

' It is this,' quoth Eric. ' On Mosfell mountain, over by Hecla, dwells a Baresark of whom all men have ill knowledge, for there are few whom he has not harmed. His name is Skallagrim ; he is a mighty man and he has wrought much mischief in the south country, and brought many to their deaths and robbed more of their goods : for none can prevail against him. Still, I swear this, that, when the days lengthen, I will go up alone against him and challenge him to battle, and conquer him or fall.'

' Then, thou yellow-headed puppy-dog, thou shalt go with one eye against a Baresark with two,' growled Ospakar.

Men took no heed of his words, but shouted aloud, for Skallagrim had plagued them long, and there were none who dared to fight with him any more. Only Gudruda looked askance, for it seemed to her that Eric swore too fast. Nevertheless he went up to the altar, and, taking hold of the holy ring, he set his foot on the holy stone and swore his oath, while the feasters applauded, striking their cups upon the board.

And after that the feast went merrily, till all men were drunk, except Asmund and Eric.

Now Eric went to rest, but first he rubbed his limbs with the fat of seals, for he was still sore from the beating of the waters, and they must needs be supple on the morrow if he would keep his eye. Then he slept sound, and rose strong and well, and going to the stream behind the stead he bathed, and anointed his limbs afresh. But Ospakar did not sleep well, because of the ale that he had drunk. Now as Eric came back from bathing, in the dark of the morning, he met Gudruda, who watched for his coming, and, there being none to see, he kissed her often ; but she chided him because of the match that he had made with Ospakar and the oath that he had sworn.

' Surely,' she said, ' thou wilt lose thine eye, for this
Ospakar is a giant, and strong as a troll ; also he is merciless.
Still, thou art a mighty man, and I shall love thee as well with
one eye as with two. Oh ! Eric, methought I should have
died yesterday when thou didst leap from Wolf's Fang ! My
heart seemed to stop within me.'

' Yet I came safely to shore, sweetheart, and well does this
kiss pay for all I did. And as for Ospakar, if but once I get
these arms about him, I fear him little, or any man, and I
covet that sword of his greatly. But we can talk more
certainly of these things to-morrow.'

Now Gudruda clung to him and told him all that had befallen, and of the doings and words of Swanhild.

' She honours me beyond my worth,' he said, ' who am in
no way set on her, but on thee only, Gudruda.'

' Art thou so sure of that, Eric ? Swanhild is fair and wise.'

' Ay and evil. When I love Swanhild, then thou mayst
love Ospakar.'

'It is a bargain,' she said, laughing. ' Good luck go with
thee in the wrestling,' and with a kiss she left him, fearing lest
she should be seen.

Eric went back to the hall, and sat down by the centre
hearth, for all men slept, being still heavy with drink, and
presently Swanhild glided up to him, and greeted him.

' Thou art greedy of deeds, Eric,' she said. ' Yesterday
thou camest here by a path that no man has travelled, to-day
thou dost wrestle with a giant for thine eye, and presently
thou goest up against Skallagrim ! '

' It seems that this is true,' said Eric.

' Now all this thou doest for a woman who is the betrothed
of another man.'

' All this I do for fame's sake, Swanhild. Moreover,
Gudruda is betrothed to none.'

' Before another Yule-feast is spread, Gudruda shall be
the wife of Ospakar.'

' That is yet to be seen, Swanhild.'

Now Swanhild stood silent for a while and then spoke :
' Thou art a fool, Eric—yes, drunk with folly. Nothing but evil

shall come to thee from this madness of thine. Forget it and
pluck that which lies to thine hand,' and she looked sweetly
at him.

'They call thee Swanhild the Fatherless,' he answered,
'but I think that Loki, the God of Guile, was thy father, for
there is none to match thee in craft and evil-doing, and in
beauty one only. I know thy plots well and all the sorrow
that thou hast brought upon us. Still, each seeks honour
after his own manner, so seek thou as thou wilt; but thou
shalt find bitterness and empty days, and thy plots shall come
back on thine own head—yes, even though they bring Gudruda
and me to sorrow and death.'

Swanhild laughed. 'A day shall dawn, Eric, when thou
who dost hate me shalt hold me dear, this I promise thee.
Another thing I promise thee also : that Gudruda shall never
call thee husband.'

But Eric did not answer, fearing lest in his anger he should
say words that were better unspoken.

Now men rose and sat down to meat, and all talked of the
wrestling that should be. But in the morning Ospakar re-
pented of the match, for it is truly said that *ale is another
man*, and men do not like that in the morning which seemed
well enough on yester eve. He remembered that he held
Whitefire dear above all things, and that Eric's eye had no
worth to him, except that the loss of it would spoil his beauty,
so that perhaps Gudruda would turn from him. It would be
very ill if he should chance to lose the play—though of this
he had no fear, for he was held the strongest man in Iceland
and the most skilled in all feats of strength—and, at the
best, no fame is to be won from the overthrow of a deedless
man, and the plucking out of his eye. Thus it came to pass
that when he saw Eric he called to him in a big voice :

'Hearken, thou Eric.'

'I hear thee, thou Ospakar,' said Eric, mocking him,
and people laughed ; while Ospakar grinned angrily and
said, 'Thou must learn manners, puppy. Still, I shall find
no honour in teaching thee in this wise. Last night we made a
match in our cups, and I staked my great sword Whitefire and

thou thine eye. It would be bad that either of us should lose
sword or eye; therefore, what sayest thou, shall we let it pass?'

'Ay, Blacktooth, if thou fearest; but first pay thou forfeit
of the sword.'

Now Ospakar grew very mad and shouted, 'Thou wilt indeed stand against me in the ring! I will break thy back anon,
youngster, and afterwards tear out thine eye before thou diest.'

'It may so befall,' answered Eric, 'but big words do not
make big deeds.'

Presently the light came and thralls went out with spades
and cleared away the snow in a circle two rods across, and
brought dry sand and sprinkled it on the frozen turf, so that
the wrestlers should not slip. And they piled the snow in a
wall around the ring.

But Groa came up to Ospakar and spoke to him apart.

'Knowest thou, lord,' she said, 'that my heart bodes ill of
this match? Eric is a mighty man, and, great though thou
art, I think that thou shalt lout low before him.'

'It will be a bad business if I am overthrown by an untried
man,' said Ospakar, who was troubled in his mind, 'and it would
be evil moreover to lose the sword. For no price would I
have it so.'

'What wilt thou give me, lord, if I bring thee victory?'

'I will give thee two hundred in silver.'

'Ask no questions and it shall be so,' said Groa.

Now Eric was without, taking note of the ground in the
ring, and presently Groa called to her the thrall Koll the Half-
witted, whom she had sent to Swinefell.

'See,' she said, 'yonder by the wall stand the wrestling
shoes of Eric Brighteyes. Haste thee now and take grease, and
rub the soles with it, then hold them in the heat of the fire, so
that the fat sinks in. Do this swiftly and secretly, and I will
give thee twenty pennies.'

Koll grinned, and did as he was bid, setting back the shoes
just as they were before. Scarcely was the deed done when Eric
came in, and made himself ready for the game, binding the
greased shoes upon his feet, for he feared no trick.

Now everybody went out to the ring, and Ospakar and Eric

stripped for wrestling.   They were clad in tight woollen jerkins
and hose, and sheep-skin shoes were on their feet.

They named Asmund master of the game, and his word
must be law to both of them.   Eric claimed that Asmund
should hold the sword Whitefire that was at stake, but Ospakar
gainsaid him, saying that if he gave Whitefire into Asmund's
keeping, Eric must also give his eye—and about this they de-
bated hotly.   Now the matter was brought before Asmund as
umpire, and he gave judgment for Eric, ' for,' he said, 'if Eric
yields up his eye into my hand, I can return it to his head
no more if he should win ; but if Ospakar gives me the good
sword and conquers, it is easy for me to pass it back to
him unharmed.'

Men said that this was a good judgment.

Thus then was the arm-game set.   Ospakar and Eric
must wrestle thrice, and between each bout there would be a
space while men could count a thousand.   They might strike
no blow at one another with hand, or head, or elbow, foot
or knee ; and it should be counted no fall if the haunch and
the head of the fallen were not on the ground at the self-same
time.   He who suffered two falls would be adjudged conquered
and lose his stake.

Asmund called these rules aloud in the presence of wit-
nesses, and Ospakar and Eric said that they should bind them.

Ospakar drew a small knife and gave it to his son Gizur
to hold.

' Thou shalt soon know, youngling, how steel tastes in the
eyeball,' he said.

' We shall soon know many things,' Eric answered.

Now they threw off their cloaks and stood in the ring.
Ospakar was great beyond the bigness of men and his arms
were clothed with black hair like the limbs of a goat.   Beneath
the shoulder joint they were almost as thick as a girl's thigh.
His legs also were mighty, and the muscles stood out upon him
in knotty lumps.   He seemed a very giant, and fierce as a Baresark, but still somewhat round about the body and heavy in
movement.

From him men looked at Eric.

'Lo! Baldur and the Troll!' said Swanhild, and everybody laughed, since so it was indeed; for, if Ospakar was black and hideous as a troll, Eric was beautiful as Baldur, the loveliest of the Gods. He was taller than Ospakar by the half of a hand and as broad in the chest. Still, he was not yet come to his greatest strength, and, though his limbs were well knit, they seemed but as a child's against the limbs of Ospakar. But he was quick as a cat and lithe, his neck and arms were white as whey, and beneath his golden hair his bright eyes shone like spears.

Now they stood face to face, with arms outstretched, waiting the word of Asmund. He gave it and they circled round each other with arms held low. Presently Ospakar made a rush and, seizing Eric about the middle, tried to lift him, but with no avail. Thrice he strove and failed, then Eric moved his foot and lo! it slipped upon the sanded turf. Again Eric moved and again he slipped, a third time and he slipped a third time, and before he could recover himself he was full on his back and fairly thrown.

Gudruda saw and was sad at heart, and those around her said that it was easy to know how the game would end.

'What said I?' quoth Swanhild, 'that it would go badly with Eric were Ospakar's arms about him.'

'All is not done yet,' answered Gudruda. 'Eric's feet slipped most strangely, as though he stood on ice.'

But Eric was very sore at heart and could make nothing of this matter—for he was not overthrown by strength.

He sat on the snow and Ospakar and his sons mocked him. But Gudruda drew near and whispered to him to be of good cheer, for fortune might yet change.

'I think that I am bewitched,' said Eric, sadly: 'my feet have no hold of the ground.'

Gudruda covered her eyes with her hand and thought. Presently she looked up quickly. 'I seem to see guile here,' she said. 'Now look narrowly on thy shoes.'

He heard, and, loosening the string, drew a shoe from his foot and looked at the sole. The cold of the snow had hardened the fat, and there it was, all white upon the leather.

E

Now Eric rose in wrath. 'Methought,' he cried, 'that I dealt with men of honourable mind, not with cheating tricksters. See now! it is little wonder that I slipped, for grease has been rubbed upon my shoes—and, by Thor! I will cleave the man who did it to the chin,' and as he said it his eyes blazed so dreadfully that folk fell back from him. Asmund took the shoes and looked at them. Then he spoke:

'Brighteyes tells the truth, and we have a sorry knave among us. Ospakar, canst thou clear thyself of this ill deed?'

'I will swear on the holy ring that I know nothing of it, and if any man in my company has had a hand therein he shall die,' said Ospakar.

'That we will swear also,' cried his sons Gizur and Mord.

'This is more like a woman's work,' said Gudruda, and she looked at Swanhild.

'It is no work of mine,' quoth Swanhild.

'Then go and ask thy mother of it,' answered Gudruda.

Now all men cried aloud that this was the greatest shame, and that the match must be set afresh; only Ospakar bethought him of that two hundred in silver which he had promised to Groa, and looked around, but she was not there. Still, he gainsaid Eric in the matter of the match being set afresh.

Then Eric cried out in his anger that he would let the game stand as it was, since Ospakar swore himself free of the shameful deed. Men thought this a mad saying, but Asmund said it should be so. Still, he swore in his heart that, even if he were worsted, Eric should not lose his eye—no not if swords were held aloft to take it. For of all tricks this seemed to him the very worst.

Now Ospakar and Eric faced each other again in the ring, but this time the feet of Eric were bare.

Ospakar rushed to get the upper hold, but Eric was too swift for him and sprang aside. Again he rushed, but Eric dropped and gripped him round the middle. Now they were face to face, hugging each other like bears, but moving little. For a time things went thus, while Ospakar strove to lift Eric, but in nowise could he stir him. Then of a sudden Eric put out his strength, and they staggered round the ring, tearing at each other till their jerkins were rent from them, leaving them almost bare to the waist. Suddenly, Eric seemed to give, and Ospakar put out his foot to trip him. But Brighteyes was watching. He caught the foot in the crook of his left leg, and threw his weight forward on the chest of Blacktooth. Backward he went, falling with the thud of a tree on snow, and there he lay on the ground, and Eric over him.

Then men shouted ' A fall! a fair fall! ' and were very glad, for the fight seemed most uneven to them, and the wrestlers rolled asunder, breathing heavily.

Gudruda threw a cloak over Eric's naked shoulders.

' That was well done, Brighteyes,' she said.

' The game is still to play, sweet,' he gasped, ' and Ospakar is a mighty man. I threw him by skill, not by strength. Next time it must be by strength or not at all.'

Now breathing-time was done, and once more the two were face to face. Thrice Ospakar rushed, and thrice did Eric slip away, for he would waste Blacktooth's strength. Again Ospakar rushed, roaring like a bear, and fire seemed to come from his eyes, and the steam went up from him and hung upon the frosty air like the steam of a horse. This time Eric could not get away, but was swept up into that great grip, for Ospakar had the lower hold.

' Now there is an end of Eric,' said Swanhild.

' The arrow is yet on the bow,' answered Gudruda.

Blacktooth put out his might and reeled round and round the ring, dragging Eric with him. This way and that he twisted, and time on time Eric's leg was lifted from the ground, but so he might not be thrown. Now they stood almost still, while men shouted madly, for no such wrestling had been known in the southlands. Grimly they hugged and strove : forsooth it was a mighty sight to see. Grimly they hugged, and their muscles strained and cracked, but they could stir each other no inch.

Ospakar grew fearful, for he could make no play with this youngling. Black rage swelled in his heart. He ground his fangs, and thought on guile. By his foot gleamed the naked foot of Eric. Suddenly he stamped on it so fiercely that the skin burst.

'Ill done! ill done!' folk cried; but in his pain Eric moved his foot.

Lo! he was down, but not altogether down, for he did but sit upon his haunches, and still he clung to Blacktooth's thighs, and twined his legs about his ankles. Now with all his strength Ospakar strove to force the head of Brighteyes to the ground, but still he could not, for Eric clung to him like a creeper to a tree.

'A losing game for Eric,' said Asmund, and as he spoke Brighteyes was pressed back till his yellow hair almost swept the sand.

Then the folk of Ospakar shouted in triumph, but Gudruda cried aloud:

'Be not overthrown, Eric; loose thee and spring aside.'

Eric heard, and of a sudden loosed all his grip. He fell on his outspread hand, then, with a swing sideways and a bound, once more he stood upon his feet. Ospakar came at him like a bull made mad with goading, but he could no longer roar aloud. They closed and this time Eric had the better hold. For a while they struggled round and round till their feet tore the frozen turf, then once more they stood face to face. Now the two were almost spent; yet Blacktooth gathered up his strength and swung Eric from his feet, but he found them again. He grew mad with rage, and hugged him till Brighteyes was nearly pressed to death, and black bruises shewed upon the whiteness of his flesh. Ospakar grew mad, and madder yet, till at length in his fury he fixed his fangs in Eric's shoulder and bit till the blood spurted.

'Ill kissed, thou rat!' gasped Eric, and with the pain and rush of blood, his strength came back to him. He shifted his grip swiftly, now his right hand was beneath the fork of Blacktooth's thigh and his left on the hollow of Blacktooth's back. Twice he lifted—twice the bulk of Ospakar rose from the ground —a third mighty lift—so mighty that the wrapping on Eric's forehead burst, and the blood streamed down his face—and lo! great Blacktooth flew in air. Up he flew, and backward he fell into the bank of snow, and was buried there almost to the knees.

CHAPTER VI

HOW ASMUND THE PRIEST WAS BETROTHED TO UNNA

FOR a moment there was silence, for all that company was wonderstruck at the greatness of the deed. Then they cheered and cheered again, and to Eric it seemed that he slept, and the sound of shouting reached him but faintly, as though he heard through snow. Suddenly he woke and saw a man rush at him with axe aloft. It was Mord, Ospakar's son, mad at his father's overthrow. Eric sprang aside, or the blow had been his bane, and, as he sprang, smote with his fist, and it struck heavily on the head of Mord above the ear, so that the axe flew from his hand, and he fell senseless on his father in the snow.

Now swords flashed out, and men ringed round Eric to guard him, and it came near to the spilling of blood, for the people of Ospakar gnashed their teeth to see so great a hero overthrown by a youngling, while the southern folk of Middalhof and Ran River rejoiced loudly, for Eric was dear to their hearts.

'Down swords,' cried Asmund the priest, 'and haul yon carcass from the snow.'

This then they did, and Ospakar sat up, breathing in great gasps, the blood running from his mouth and ears, and he was an evil sight to see, for what with blood and snow and rage his face was like the face of the Swinefell Goblin.

But Swanhild spoke in the ear of Gudruda :

'Here,' she said, looking at Eric, 'we two have a man worth loving, foster-sister.'

'Ay,' answered Gudruda, 'worth and well worth!'

Now Asmund drew near and before all men kissed Eric
Brighteyes on the brow.

'In sooth,' he said, 'thou art a mighty man, Eric, and
the glory of the south. This I prophesy of thee : that thou
shalt do deeds such as have not been done in Iceland. Thou
hast been ill served, for a knave unknown greased thy
shoes. Yon swarthy Ospakar, the most mighty of all men in
Iceland, could not overthrow thee, though, like a wolf, he
fastened his fangs in thee, and, like a coward, stamped upon
thy naked foot. Take thou the great sword that thou hast won
and wear it worthily.'

Now Eric took snow and wiped the blood from his brow.
Then he grasped Whitefire and drew it from the scabbard,
and high aloft flashed the war-blade. Thrice he wheeled it
round his head, then sang aloud :

> Fast, yestermorn, down Golden Falls,
> Fared young Eric to thy feast,
> Asmund, father of Gudruda—
> Maid whom much he longs to clasp.
> But to-day on Giant Blacktooth
> Hath he done a needful deed :
> Hurling him in heaped-up snowdrift ;
> Winning Whitefire for his wage.

And again he sang :

> Lord, if in very truth thou thinkest
> Brighteyes is a man midst men,
> Swear to him, the stalwart suitor,
> Handsel of thy sweet maid's hand :
> Whom, long loved, to win, down Goldfoss
> Swift he sped through frost and foam ;
> Whom to win, to troll-like Ogre,
> He, 'gainst Whitefire, waged his eye.

Men thought this well sung, and turned to hear Asmund's
answer, nor must they wait long.

'Eric,' he said, 'I will promise thee this, that if thou goest
on as thou hast begun, I will give Gudruda in marriage to no
other man.'

'That is good tidings, lord,' said Eric.

' This I say further : in a year I will give thee full answer according as to how thou dost bear thyself between now and then, for this is no light gift thou askest ; also that, if ye will it, you twain may now plight troth, for the blame shall be yours if it is broken, and not mine, and I give thee my hand on it.'

Eric took his hand, and Gudruda heard her father's words and happiness shone in her dark eyes, and she grew faint for very joy. And now Eric turned to her, all torn and bloody from the fray, the great sword in his hand, and he spoke thus :

' Thou hast heard thy father's words, Gudruda ? Now it seems that there is no great need of troth-plighting between us two. Still, here before all men I ask thee, if thou dost love me and art willing to take me to husband ? '

Gudruda looked up into his face, and answered in a sweet, clear voice that could be heard by everyone :

' Eric, I say to thee now, what I have said before, that I love thee alone of men, and, if it be my father's wish, I will wed no other whilst thou dost remain true to me and hold me dear.'

' Those are good words,' said Eric. ' Now, in pledge of them, swear this troth of thine upon my sword that I have won.'

Gudruda smiled, and, taking great Whitefire in her hand, she said the words again, and, in pledge of them, kissed the bright blade.

Then Eric took back the war-sword and spoke thus : ' I swear that I will love thee, and thee only, Gudruda the Fair, Asmund's daughter, whom I have desired all my days ; and, if I fail of this my oath, then our troth is at an end, and thou mayst wed whom thou wilt,' and in turn he put his lips upon the sword, while Swanhild watched him.

Now Ospakar was recovered from the fight, and he sat there upon the snow, with bowed head, for he knew well that he had won the greatest shame, and had lost both wife and sword. Black rage filled his heart as he listened, and he sprang to his feet.

'I came hither, Asmund,' he said, 'to ask this maid of thine in marriage, and that had been a good match for her and thee. But I have been overthrown by witchcraft of this man in a wrestling-bout, and thereby lost my good word; and now I must seem to hear him betrothed to the maid before me.'

'Thou hast heard aright, Ospakar,' said Asmund, 'and thy wooing is soon sped. Get thee back whence thou camest and seek a wife in thine own quarter, for thou art unfit in age and aspect to have so sweet a maid. Moreover, here in the south we hold men of small account, however great and rich they be, who do not shame to seek to overcome a foe by foul means. With my own eyes I saw thee stamp on the naked foot of Eric, Thorgrimur's son; with my own eyes I saw thee, like a wolf, fasten that black fang of thine upon him—there is the mark of it; and, as for the matter of the greased shoes, thou knowest best what hand thou hadst in it.'

'I had no hand. If any did this thing, it was Groa the Witch, thy Finnish bedmate. For the rest, I was mad and know not what I did. But hearken, Asmund: ill shall befall thee and thy house, and I will ever be thy foe. Moreover, I will yet wed this maid of thine. And now, thou Eric, hearken also: I will have another game with thee. This one was but the sport of boys; when we meet again—and the time shall not be long—swords shall be aloft, and thou shalt learn the play of men. I tell thee that I will slay thee, and tear Gudruda, shrieking, from thy arms to be my wife! I tell thee that, with yonder good sword Whitefire, I will yet hew off thy head!'—and he choked and stopped.

'Thou art much foam and little water,' said Eric. 'These things are easily put to proof. If thou willest it, to-morrow I will come with thee to a holmgang, and there we may set the twigs and finish what we have begun to-day.'

'I cannot do that, for thou hast my sword; and, till I am suited with another weapon, I may fight no holmgang. Still, fear not: we shall soon meet with weapons aloft and byrnie on breast.'

'Never too soon can that hour come, Blacktooth,' said
Eric, and, turning on his heel, he limped to the hall to clothe
himself afresh. On the threshold of the men's door he met
Groa the Witch.

'Thou didst put grease upon my shoes, carline and witch-
hag that thou art,' he said.

'It is not true, Brighteyes.'

'There thou liest, and for all this I will repay thee. Thou
art not yet the wife of Asmund, nor shalt be, for a plan
comes into my head about it.'

Groa looked at him strangely. 'If thou speakest so, take
heed to thy meat and drink,' she said. 'I was not born among
the Finns for nothing; and know, I am still minded to wed
Asmund. For thy shoes, I would to the Gods that they were
Hell-shoon, and that I was now binding them on thy dead feet.'

'Oh! the cat begins to spit,' said Eric. 'But know this:
thou mayest grease my shoes—fit work for a carline!—
but thou mayest never bind them on. Thou art a witch, and
wilt come to the end of witches; and what thy daughter is,
that I will not say,' and he pushed past her and entered the
hall.

Presently Asmund came to seek Eric there, and prayed him
to be gone to his stead on Ran River. The horses of Ospakar
had strayed, and he must stop at Middalhof till they were
found; but, if these two should abide under the same roof,
bloodshed would come of it, and that Asmund knew.

Eric said yea to this, and, when he had rested a while, he
kissed Gudruda, and, taking a horse, rode away to Coldback,
bearing the sword Whitefire with him, and for a time he saw
no more of Ospakar.

When he came there, his mother Saevuna greeted him
as one risen from the dead, and hung about his neck. Then
he told her all that had come to pass, and she thought it a
marvellous story, and sorrowed that Thorgrimur, her husband,
was not alive to know it. But Eric mused a while, and spoke.

'Mother,' he said, 'now my uncle Thorod of Greenfell
is dead, and his daughter, my cousin Unna, has no home.
She is a fair woman and skilled in all things. It comes

into my mind that we should bid her here to dwell with
us.'

'Why, I thought thou wast betrothed to Gudruda the
Fair,' said Saevuna. 'Wherefore, then, wouldst thou bring
Unna hither?'

'For this cause,' said Eric: 'because it seems that Asmund
the Priest wearies of Groa the Witch, and would take another
wife, and I wish to draw the bands between us tighter, if it
may befall so.'

'Groa will take it ill,' said Saevuna.

'Things cannot be worse between us than they are now,
therefore I do not fear Groa,' he answered.

'It shall be as thou wilt, son; to-morrow we will send to
Unna and bid her here, if it pleases her to come.'

Now Ospakar stayed three more days at Middalhof, till his
horses were found, and he was fit to travel, for Eric had shaken
him much. But he had no words with Gudruda and few
with Asmund. Still, he saw Swanhild, and she bid him to
be of good cheer, for he should yet have Gudruda. For
now that the maid had passed from him the mind of
Ospakar was set on winning her. Björn also, Asmund's
son, spoke words of good comfort to him, for he envied Eric
his great fame, and he thought the match with Blacktooth
would be good. And so at length Ospakar rode away to
Swinefell with all his company; but Gizur, his son, left his
heart behind.

For Swanhild had not been idle this while. Her heart was
sore, but she must follow her ill-nature, and so she had put
out her woman's strength and beguiled Gizur into loving her.
But she did not love him at all, and the temper of Asmund the
Priest was so angry that Gizur dared not ask her in marriage.
So nothing was said of the matter.

Now Unna came to Coldback, to dwell with Saevuna, Eric's
mother, and she was a fair and buxom woman. She had been
once wedded, but within a month of her marriage her husband
was lost at sea, this two years gone. At first Gudruda was
somewhat jealous of this coming of Unna to Coldback; but

Eric showed her what was in his mind, and she fell into the plan, for she hated and feared Groa greatly, and desired to be rid of her.

Since this matter of the greasing of Eric's wrestling-shoes great loathing of Groa had come into Asmund's mind, and he bethought him often of those words that his wife Gudruda the Gentle spoke as she lay dying, and grieved that the oath which he swore then had in part been broken. He would have no more to do with Groa now, but he could not be quit of her ; and, notwithstanding her evil doings, he still loved Swanhild. But Groa grew thin with spite and rage, and wandered about the place glaring with her great black eyes, and people hated her more and more.

Now Asmund went to visit at Coldback, and there he saw Unna, and was pleased with her, for she was a blithe woman and a bonny. The end of it was that he asked her in marriage of Eric ; at which Brighteyes was glad, but said that he must know Unna's mind. Unna hearkened, and did not say no, for though Asmund was somewhat gone in years, still he was an upstanding man, wealthy in lands, goods, and moneys out at interest, and having many friends. So they plighted troth, and the wedding-feast was to be in the autumn after hay-harvest. Now Asmund rode back to Middalhof somewhat troubled at heart, for these tidings must be told to Groa, and he feared her and her witchcraft. In the hall he found her, standing alone.

'Where hast thou been, lord ? ' she asked.

'At Coldback,' he answered.

'To see Unna, Eric's cousin, perchance ? '

'That is so.'

'What is Unna to thee, then, lord ? '

'This much, that after hay-harvest she will be my wife, and that is ill news for thee, Groa.'

Now Groa turned and grasped fiercely at the air with her thin hands. Her eyes started out, foam was on her lips, and she shook in her fury like a birch-tree in the wind, looking so evil that Asmund drew back a little way, saying :

'Now a veil is lifted from thee and I see thee as thou art.

Thou hast cast a glamour over me these many years, Groa, and it is gone.'

'Mayhap, Asmund Asmundson—mayhap thou knowest me; but I tell thee that thou shalt see me in a worse guise before thou weddest Unna. What! have I borne the greatest shame, lying by thy side these many years, and shall I live to see a rival, young and fair, creep into my place with honour? That I will not while runes have power and spells can conjure the evil thing upon thee. I call down ruin on thee and thine —yea and on Brighteyes also, for he has brought this to pass. Death take ye all! May thy blood no longer run in mortal veins anywhere on the earth! Go down to Hela, Asmund, and be forgotten!' and she began to mutter runes swiftly.

Now Asmund turned white with wrath. 'Cease thy evil talk,' he said, 'or thou shalt be hurled as a witch into Goldfoss pool.'

'Into Goldfoss pool?—yea, there I may lie. I see it!—I seem to see this shape of mine rolling where the waters boil fiercest—but thine eyes shall never see it! *Thy* eyes are shut, and shut are the eyes of Unna, for ye have gone before!—I do but follow after,' and thrice Groa shrieked aloud, throwing up her arms, then she fell foaming on the sanded floor.

'An evil woman and a fey!' said Asmund as he called people to her. 'It had been better for me if I had never seen her dark face.'

Now it is to be told that Groa lay beside herself for ten full days, and Swanhild nursed her. Then she found her sense again, and craved to see Asmund, and spoke thus to him:

'It seems to me, lord, if indeed it be aught but a vision of my dreams, that before this sickness struck me I spoke mad and angry words against thee, because thou hast plighted troth to Unna, Thorod's daughter.'

'That is so, in truth,' said Asmund.

'I have to say this, then, lord: that most humbly I crave thy pardon for my ill words, and ask thee to put them away from thy mind. Sore heart makes sour speech, and thou knowest well that, howsoever great my faults, at least I have always loved thee and laboured for thee, and methinks that in some fashion thy fortunes are the debtor to my wisdom. Therefore when my ears heard that thou hadst of a truth put me away, and that another woman comes an honoured wife to rule in Middalhof, my tongue forgot its courtesy, and I spoke words that are of all words the farthest from my mind. For I know well that I grow old, and have put off that beauty with which I was adorned of yore, and that held thee to me. "*Carline*" Eric Brighteyes named me, and "carline" I am—an old hag, no more! Now, forgive me, and, in memory of all that has been between us, let me creep to my place in the ingle and still watch and serve thee and thine till my service is outworn. Out of Ran's net I came to thee, and, if thou drivest me hence, I tell thee that I will lie down and die upon thy threshold, and when thou sinkest into eld surely the memory of it shall grieve thee.'

Thus she spoke and wept much, till Asmund's heart softened in him, and, though with a doubting mind, he said it should be as she willed.

So Groa stayed on at Middalhof, and was lowly in her bearing and soft of speech.

CHAPTER VII

HOW ERIC WENT UP MOSFELL AGAINST SKALLAGRIM THE BARESARK

THE BARESARK PROPHESIES.

NOW Atli the Good, earl of the Orkneys, comes into the story.

It chanced that Atli sailed to Iceland in the autumn on a business about certain lands that had fallen to him in right of his mother Helga, who was an Icelander, and he had wintered west of Reyjanes. Spring being come, he wished to sail home, and, when his ship was bound, he put to sea full early in the year. But it chanced that bad weather came up from the south-east, with mist and rain, so he must needs beach his ship in a creek under shelter of the Westman Islands.

Now Atli asked what people dwelt in these parts, and, when he heard the name of Asmund Asmundson the Priest, he was glad, for in old days he and Asmund had gone many a viking cruise together.

'We will leave the ship here,' he said, 'till the weather clears, and go up to Middalhof to stay with Asmund.'

So they made the ship snug, and left men to watch her; but two of the company, with Earl Atli, rode up to Middalhof.

It must be told of Atli that he was the best of the earls who lived in those days, and he ruled the Orkneys so well that men gave him a by-name and called him Atli the Good. It was said of him that he had never turned a poor man away unsuccoured, nor bowed his head before a strong man, nor drawn his sword without cause, nor refused peace to him who prayed it. He was sixty years old, but age had left few marks on him, except that of his long white beard. He was keen-eyed, and well fashioned of form and face, a great warrior and the strongest of men. His wife was dead, leaving him no children, and this was a sorrow to him ; but as yet he had taken no other wife, for he would say : ' Love makes an old man blind,' and ' When age runs with youth, both shall fall,' and again, ' Mix grey locks and .golden and spoil two heads.' For this earl was a man of many wise sayings.

Now Atli came to Middalhof just as men sat down to meat and, hearing the clatter of arms, all sprang to their feet, think-ing that perhaps Ospakar was come again as he had promised. But when Asmund saw Atli he knew him at once, though they had not met for nearly thirty years, and he greeted him lovingly, and put him in the high seat, and gave place to his men upon the cross-benches. Atli told all his story, and Asmund bade him rest a while at Middalhof till the weather grew clearer.

Now the Earl saw Swanhild and thought the maid wondrous fair, and so indeed she was, as she moved scornfully to and fro in her kirtle of white. Soft was her curling hair and deep were her dark blue eyes, and bent were her red lips as is a bow above her dimpled chin, and her teeth shone like pearls.

' Is that fair maid thy daughter, Asmund ? ' asked Atli.

' She is named Swanhild the Fatherless,' he answered, turning his face away.

Well,' said Atli, looking sharply on him, ' were the maid sprung from me, she would not long be called the " Fatherless," for few have such a daughter.'

' She is fair enough,' said Asmund, ' in all save in temper, and that is bad to cross.'

' In every sword a flaw,' answers Atli ; ' but what has an old man to do with young maids and their beauty ? ' and he sighed.

' I have known younger men who would seem less brisk at bridals,' said Asmund, and at that time they talked no more of the matter.

Now, Swanhild heard something of this speech, and she guessed more; and it came into her mind that it would be the best of sport to make this old man love her, and then to mock him and say him nay. So she set herself to the task, as it ever was her wont, and she found it easy. For all day long, with downcast eyes and gentle looks, she waited upon the Earl, and now, at his bidding, she sang to him in a voice soft and low, and now she talked so wisely that Atli thought no such maid had trod the earth before. But he checked himself with many learned saws, and on a day when the weather had grown fair, and they sat alone, he told her that his ship was bound for Orkney Isles.

Then, as though by chance, Swanhild laid her white hand in his, and on a sudden looked deep into his eyes, and said with trembling lips, 'Ah, go not yet, lord!—I pray thee, go not yet!'—and, turning, she fled away.

But Atli was much moved, and he said to himself: 'Now a strange thing is come to pass: a fair maid loves an old man; and yet, methinks, he who looks into those eyes sees deep waters,' and he beat his brow and thought.

But Swanhild in her chamber laughed till the tears ran from those same eyes, for she saw that the great fish was hooked and now the time had come to play him.

For she did not know that it was otherwise fated.

Gudruda, too, saw all these things and knew not how to read them, for she was of an honest mind, and could not understand how a woman may love a man as Swanhild loved Eric and yet make such play with other men, and that of her free will. For she guessed little of Swanhild's guilefulness, nor of the coldness of her heart to all save Eric; nor of how this was the only joy left to her: to make a sport of men and put them to grief and shame. Atli said to himself that he would watch this maid well before he uttered a word to Asmund, and he deemed himself very cunning, for he was wondrous cautious after the fashion of those about to fall. So he set himself to watching, and Swanhild set herself to smiling, and he told her tales of warfare and of daring, and she clasped her hands and said:

'Was there ever such a man since Odin trod the earth?'

And so it went on, till the serving-women laughed at the old man in love and the wit of her that mocked him.

Now upon a day, Eric having made an end of sowing his corn, bethought him of his vow to go up alone against Skalla-grim the Baresark in his den on Mosfell over by Hecla. Now, this was a heavy task: for Skallagrim was held so mighty among men that none went up to fight him any more; and at times Eric thought of Gudruda, and sighed, for it was likely that she would be a widow before she was made a wife. Still, his oath must be fulfilled, and, moreover, of late Skallagrim, having heard that a youngling named Eric Brighteyes had vowed to slay him single-handed, had made a mock of him in this fashion. For Skallagrim rode down to Coldback on Ran River and at night-time took a lamb from the fold. Holding the lamb beneath his arm, he drew near to the house and smote thrice on the door with his battle-axe, and they were thundering knocks. Then he leapt on to his horse and rode off a space and waited. Presently Eric came out, but half clad, a shield in one hand and Whitefire in the other, and, looking, by the bright moonlight he saw a huge black-bearded man seated on a horse, having a great axe in one hand and the lamb beneath his arm.

'Who art thou?' roared Eric.

'I am called Skallagrim, youngling,' answered the man on the horse. 'Many men have seen me once, none have wished to see me twice, and some few have never seen aught again. Now, it has been echoed in my ears that thou hast vowed a vow to go up Mosfell against Skallagrim the Baresark, and I am come hither to say that I will make thee right welcome. See,' and with his axe he cut off the lamb's tail on the pommel of his saddle: 'of the flesh of this lamb of thine I will brew broth and of his skin I will make me a vest. Take thou this tail and when thou fittest it on to the skin again, Skallagrim will own a lord,' and he hurled the tail towards him.

'Bide thou there till I can come to thee,' shouted Eric; 'it will spare me a ride to Mosfell.'

'Nay, nay. It is good for lads to take the mountain air,' and Skallagrim turned his horse away, laughing.

Eric watched Skallagrim vanish over the knoll, and then, though he was very angry, laughed also and went in. But first he picked up the tail, and on the morrow he skinned it.

Now the time was come when the matter must be tried, and Eric bade farewell to Saevuna his mother, and Unna his cousin, and girt Whitefire round him and set upon his head a golden helm with wings on it. Then he found the byrnie which his father Thorgrimur had stripped, together with the helm, from that Baresark who cut off his leg—and this was a good piece, forged by the Welshmen—and he put it on his breast, and taking a stout shield of bull's hide studded with nails, he rode away with one thrall, the strong carle named Jon.

But the women misdoubted them much of this venture; nevertheless Eric might not be gainsayed.

Now, the road to Mosfell runs past Middalhof and thither he came. Atli, standing at the men's door, saw him and cried aloud : ' Ho! a mighty man comes here.'

Swanhild looked out and saw Eric, and he was a goodly sight in his war-gear. For now, week by week, he seemed to grow more fair and great, as the full strength of his manhood rose in him, like sap in the spring grass, and Gudruda was very proud of her lover. That night Eric stayed at Middalhof, and sat hand in hand with Gudruda and talked with Earl Atli. Now the heart of the old viking went out to Eric, and he took great delight in him and in his strength and deeds, and he longed much that the Gods had given him such a son.

' I prophesy of thee, Brighteyes,' he cried : ' that it shall go ill with this Baresark thou seekest—yes, and with all men who come within sweep of that great sword of thine. But remember this, lad: guard thy head with thy buckler, cut low beneath his shield, if he carries one, and mow the legs from him : for ever a Baresark rushes on, shield up.'

Eric thanked him for his good words and went to rest. But, before it was light, he rose, and Gudruda rose also and came into the hall, and buckled his harness on him with her own hands.

'This is a sad task for me, Eric!' she sighed, 'for how do I know that Baresark's hands shall not loose this helm of thine ?'

'That is as it may be, sweet,' he said ; 'but I fear not the Baresark or any man. How goes it with Swanhild now ? '

'I know not. She makes herself sweet to that old Earl and he is fain of her, and that is beyond my sight.'

'I have seen as much,' said Eric. 'It will be well for us if he should wed her.'

'Ay, and ill for him ; but it is to be doubted if that is in her mind.'

Now Eric kissed her soft and sweet, and went away, bidding her look for his return on the day after the morrow.

Gudruda bore up bravely against her fears till he was gone, but then she wept a little.

Now it is to be told that Eric and his thrall Jon rode hard up Stonefell and across the mountains and over the black sand, till, two hours before sunset, they came to the foot of Mosfell, having Hecla on their right. It is a grim mountain, grey with moss, standing alone in the desert plain ; but between it and Hecla there is good grassland.

'Here is the fox's earth. Now to start him,' said Eric.

He knew something of the path by which this fortress can be climbed from the south, and horses may be ridden up it for a space. So on they went. till at length they came to a flat place where water runs down the black rocks, and here Eric drank of the water, ate food, and washed his face and hands. This done, he bid Jon tend the horses—for hereabouts there is a little grass—and be watchful till he returned, since he must go up against Skallagrim alone. And there with a doubtful heart Jon stayed all that night. For of all that came to pass he saw but one thing, and that was the light of Whitefire as it flashed out high above him on the brow of the mountain when first Brighteyes smote at a foe.

Eric walked warily up the Baresark path, for he would keep his breath in him, and the light shone redly on his golden helm. High he went, till at length he came to a pass narrow and dark and hedged on either side with sheer cliffs, such as two armed men might hold against a score. He peered down this path, but he saw no Baresark, though it was worn by

Baresark feet. He crept along its length, moving like a sun-
beam through the darkness of the pass, for the light gathered
on his helm and sword, till suddenly the path turned and he
was on the brink of a gulf that seemed to have no bottom,
and, looking across and down, he could see Jon and the horses
more than a hundred fathoms beneath. Now Eric must stop,
for this path leads but into the black gulf. Also he was
perplexed to know where Skallagrim had his lair. He crept
to the brink and gazed. Then he saw that a point of rock
jutted from the sheer face of the cliff and that the point was
worn with the mark of feet.

'Where Baresark passes, there may yeoman follow,' said
Eric and, sheathing Whitefire, without more ado, though he
liked the task little, he grasped the overhanging rock and
stepped down on to the point below. Now he was perched like
an eagle over the dizzy gulf and his brain swam. Backward
he feared to go, and forward he could not, for there was nothing
but air. Beside him, growing from the face of the cliff, was a
birch-bush. He grasped it to steady himself. It bent beneath
his clutch, and then he saw, behind it, a hole in the rock
through which a man could creep, and down this hole ran foot-
marks.

'First through air like a bird; now through earth like a
fox,' said Eric and entered the hole. Doubling his body till his
helm almost touched his knee he took three paces and lo! he
stood on a great platform of rock, so large that a hall might
be built on it, which, curving inwards, cannot be seen from
the narrow pass. This platform, that is backed by the sheer
cliff, looks straight to the south, and from it he could search
the plain and the path that he had travelled, and there once
more he saw Jon and the horses far below him.

'A strong place, truly, and well chosen,' said Eric and
looked around. On the floor of the rock and some paces from
him a turf fire still smouldered. By it were sheep's bones,
and beyond, in the face of the overhanging precipice, was the
mouth of a cave.

'The wolf is at home, or has been but lately,' said Eric;
'now for his lair;' and with that he walked warily to the

mouth of the cave and peered in. He could see nothing yet a
while, but surely he heard a sound of snoring ?

Then he crept in, and, presently, by the red light of the
burning embers, he saw a great black-bearded man stretched
at length upon a rug of sheepskins, and at his side an axe.

'Now it would be easy to make an end of this cave-dweller,'
thought Eric ; 'but that is a deed I will not do—no, not even
to a Baresark—to slay him in his sleep,' and therewith he
stepped lightly to the side of Skallagrim, and was about to
prick him with the point of Whitefire, when ! as he did so,
another man sat up
behind Skallagrim.

'By Thor ! for two
I did not bargain,' said
Eric, and sprang from
the cave.

Then, with a grunt
of rage, that Baresark
who was behind Skal-
lagrim came out like
a she-bear robbed of
her whelps, and ran
straight at Eric, sword
aloft. Eric gives before
him right to the edge
of the cliff. Then the
Baresark smites at him

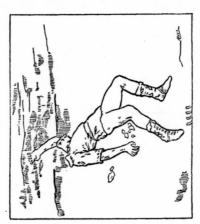

'FALLS A HUNDRED FATHOMS DOWN.'

and Brighteyes catches the blow on his shield, and smites in
turn so well and truly, that the head of the Baresark flies from
his shoulders and spins along the ground, but his body, with
outstretched arms yet gripping at the air, falls over the edge of
the gulf sheer into the water, a hundred fathoms down. It
was the flash that Whitefire made as it circled ere it smote
that Jon saw while he waited in the dell upon the mountain
side. But of the Baresark he saw nothing, for he passed down
into the great fire-riven cleft and was never seen more, save
once only, in a strange fashion that shall be told. This was
the first man whom Brighteyes slew.

Now the old tale tells that Eric cried aloud : ' Little chance had this one,' and that then a wonderful thing came to pass. For the head on the rock opened its eyes and answered :
' Little chance indeed against thee, Eric Brighteyes. Still, I tell thee this : that where my body fell there thou shalt fall, and where it lies there thou shalt lie also.'

Now Eric was afraid, for he thought it a strange thing that a severed head should speak to him.

' Here it seems I have to deal with trolls,' he said ; ' but at the least, though he speak, this one shall strike no more,' and he looked at the head, but it answered nothing.

Now Skallagrim slept through it all and the light grew so dim that Eric thought it time to make an end this way or that. Therefore, he took the head of the slain man, though he feared to touch it, and rolled it swiftly into the cave, saying, ' Now, being so glib of speech, go tell thy mate that Eric Brighteyes knocks at his door.'

Then came sounds as of a man rising, and presently Skallagrim rushed forth with axe aloft and his fellow's head in his left hand. He was clothed in nothing but a shirt and the skin of Eric's lamb was bound on his chest.

' Where now is my mate ? ' he said. Then he saw Eric leaning on Whitefire, his golden helm ablaze with the glory of the passing sun.

' It seems that thou holdest somewhat of him in thine hand, Skallagrim, and for the rest, go seek it in yonder rift.'

' Who art thou ? roared Skallagrim.

' Thou mayest know me by this token,' said Eric, and he threw towards him the skin of that lamb's tail which Skallagrim had lifted from Coldback.

Now Skallagrim knew him and the Baresark fit came on. His eyes rolled, foam flew from his lips, his mouth grinned, and he was awesome to see. He let fall the head, and, swinging the great axe aloft, rushed at Eric. But Brighteyes is too swift for him. It would not be well to let that stroke fall, and it must go hard with aught it struck. He springs forward, he louts low and sweeps upwards with Whitefire. Skallagrim sees the sword flare and drops almost to his knee, guarding his

head with the axe ; but Whitefire strikes on the iron haft
of the axe and shears it in two, so that the axe-head falls to
earth. Now the Baresark is weaponless but unharmed, and it
would be an easy task to slay him as he rushes by. But it came
into Eric's mind that it is an unworthy deed to slay a swordless
man, and this came into his mind also, that he desired to match
his naked might against a Baresark in his rage. So, in the
hardihood of his youth and strength, he cast Whitefire aside,
and crying ' Come, try a fall with me, Baresark,' rushed on
Skallagrim.

' Thou art mad,' yells the Baresark, and they are at it
hard. Now they grip and rend and tear. Ospakar was strong,
but the Baresark strength of Skallagrim is more than the
strength of Ospakar, and soon Brighteyes thinks longingly on
Whitefire that he has cast aside. Eric is mighty beyond the
might of men, but he can scarcely hold his own against this mad
man, and very soon he knows that only one chance is left to him,
and that is to cling to Skallagrim till the Baresark fit be passed
and he is once more like other men. But this is easier to tell
of than to do, and presently, strive as he will, Eric is upon
his back, and Skallagrim on him. But still he holds the
Baresark as with bands of iron, and Skallagrim cannot free
his arms, though he strive furiously. Now they roll over and
over on the rock, and the gloom gathers fast about them till
presently Eric sees that they draw near to the brink of that
mighty rift down which the severed head of the cave-dweller
has foretold his fall.

' Then we go together,' says Eric, but the Baresark does
not heed. Now they are on the very brink, and here as
it chances, or as the Norns decree, a little rock juts up and
this keeps them from falling. Eric is uppermost, and Skallagrim cannot turn him on his back again. Still, Brighteyes'
strength may not endure very long, for he grows faint, and his
legs slip slowly over the side of the rift till now he clings,
as it were, by his ribs and shoulder-blades alone, that rub
against the little rock. The light dies away, and Eric thinks
on sweet Gudruda and makes ready to die also, when suddenly
a last ray from the sun falls on the fierce face of Skalla-

grim, and lo ! Brighteyes sees it change, for the madness goes
out of it, and in a moment the Baresark becomes but as a
child in his mighty grip.

'Hold ! ' said Skallagrim, ' I crave peace ' and he loosed his
clasp.

' Not too soon, then,' gasped Eric as, drawing his legs from
over the brink of the rift, he gained his feet and, staggering to
his sword, grasped it very thankfully.

'I am fordone ! ' said Skallagrim ; ' come, drag me from
this place, for I fall ; or, if thou wilt, hew off my head.'

' I will not serve thee thus,' said Eric. ' Thou art a gallant
foe,' and he put out his hand and drew him into safety.

For a while Skallagrim lay panting, then he gained his
hands and knees and crawled to where Eric leaned against the
rock.

' Lord,' he said, ' give me thy hand.'

Eric stretched forth his left hand, wondering and Skallagrim took it. He did not stretch out his right, for, fearing guile,
he gripped Whitefire in it.

' Lord,' Skallagrim said again, ' of all men who ever were,
thou art the mightiest. Five other men could not have stood
before me in my rage, but, scorning thy weapon, thou didst
overcome me in the noblest fashion, and by thy naked strength
alone. Now hearken. Thou hast given me my life, and it is
thine from this hour to the end. Here I swear fealty to thee.
Slay me if thou wilt, or use me if thou wilt, but I think it
will be better for thee to do this rather than that, for there is
but one who has mastered me, and thou art he, and it is borne
in upon my mind that thou wilt have need of my strength,
and that shortly.'

' That may well be, Skallagrim,' said Eric, ' yet I put
little trust in outlaws and cave-dwellers. How do I know,
if I take thee to me, that thou wilt not murder me in my
sleep, as it would have been easy for me to do by thee but
now ? '

' What is it that runs from thy arm ? ' asked Skallagrim.

' Blood,' said Eric.

' Stretch out thine arm, lord.'

Eric did so, and the Baresark put his lips to the scratch and sucked the blood, then said :

' In this blood of thine I pledge thee, Eric Brighteyes ! May Valhalla refuse me and Hela take me ; may I be hunted like a fox from earth to earth ; may trolls torment me and wizards sport with me o' nights ; may my limbs shrivel and my heart turn to water ; may my foes overtake me, and my bones be crushed across the doom-stone—if I fail in one jot from this my oath that I have sworn ! I will guard thy back, I will smite thy enemies, thy hearthstone shall be my temple, thy honour my honour. Thrall am I of thine, and thrall I will be, and whiles thou wilt we will live one life, and, in the end, we will die one death.'

' It seems that in going to seek a foe I have found a friend,' said Eric, ' and it is likely enough that I shall need one. Skalla-grim, Baresark and outlaw as thou art, I take thee at thy word. Henceforth, we are master and man and we will do many a deed side by side, and in token of it I lengthen thy name and call thee Skallagrim Lambstail. Now, if thou hast it, give me food and drink, for I am faint from that hug of thine, old bear.'

CHAPTER VIII

HOW OSPAKAR BLACKTOOTH FOUND ERIC BRIGHTEYES AND SKALLAGRIM LAMBSTAIL ON HORSE-HEAD HEIGHTS

Now Skallagrim led Eric to his cave and fed the fire, and gave him flesh to eat and ale to drink. When he had eaten his fill Eric looked at the Baresark. He had black hair streaked with grey that hung down upon his shoulders. His nose was hooked like an eagle's beak, his beard was wild and his sunken eyes were keen as a hawk's. He was somewhat bent and not over tall, but of a mighty make, for his shoulders must pass many a door sideways.

'Thou art a great man,' said Eric, 'and it is something to have overcome thee. Now tell me what turned thee Baresark.'

'A shameful deed that was done against me, lord. Ten years ago I was a yeoman of small wealth in the north. I owned but one good thing, and that was the fairest housewife in those parts—Thorunna by name—and I loved her much, but we had no children. Now, not far from my stead is a place called Swinefell, and there dwells a mighty chief named Ospakar Blacktooth ; he is an evil man and a strong——'

Eric started at the name and then bade Skallagrim take up the tale.

'It chanced that Ospakar saw my wife Thorunna and de- sired to take her, but at first she did not listen. Then he pro- mised her wealth and all good things, and she was weary of our hard way of life and hearkened. Still, she would not go away openly, for that must have brought shame on her, but plotted with Ospakar that he should come and take her as though by force. So it came about, as I lay heavily asleep one night at Thorunna's side, having drunk somewhat too deeply of the autumn ale, that armed men seized me, bound me, and haled me from my bed. There were eight of them, and with them was Ospakar. Then Blacktooth bid Thorunna rise, clothe herself and come to be his May, and she made pretence to weep at this, but fell to it readily enough. Now she bound her girdle round her and to it a knife hung.

'"Kill thyself, sweet," I cried: "death is better than shame."

'"Not so, husband," she answered. "It is true that I love but thee ; yet a woman may find another love, but not another life," and I saw her laugh through her mock tears. Now Ospakar rode in hot haste away to Swinefell and with him went Thorunna, but his men stayed a while and drank my ale, and, as they drank, they mocked me who was bound before them, and little by little all the truth was told of the doings of Ospakar and Thorunna my housewife, and I learned that it was she who had planned this sport. Then my eyes grew dark and I drew near to death from very shame and bitterness. But of a sudden something leaped up in my heart, fire raged before my eyes and voices in my ears called on to war and vengeance. I was Baresark—and like hay bands I burst my cords. My axe hung on the wainscot. I snatched it thence, and of what befell I know this alone, that, when the madness passed, eight men lay stretched out before me, and all the place was but a gore of blood.

' Then I drew the dead together and piled drinking-tables over them, and benches, and turf, and anything else that would burn, and put cod's oil on the pile, and fired the stead above them, so that the tale went abroad that all these men were burned in their cups, and I with them.

' But I took the name of Skallagrim and swore an oath against all men, ay, and women too, and away I went to the wood-folk and worked much mischief, for I spared few, and so on to Mosfell. Here I have stayed these five years, awaiting the time when I shall find Ospakar and Thorunna the harlot, and I have fought many men, but, till thou camest up against me, none could stand before my might.'

'A strange tale, indeed,' said Eric; 'but now hearken thou to a stranger, for of a truth it seems that we have not come together by chance,' and he told him of Gudruda and the wrestling and of the overthrow of Blacktooth, and showed him Whitefire which he won out of the hand of Ospakar.

Skallagrim listened and laughed aloud. 'Surely,' he said, 'this is the work of the Norns. See, lord, thou and I will yet smite this Ospakar. He has taken my wife and he would take thy betrothed. Let it be! Let it be! Ah, would that I had been there to see the wrestling—Ospakar had never risen from his snow-bed. But there is time left to us, and I shall yet see his head roll along the dust. Thou hast his goodly sword and with it thou shalt sweep Blacktooth's head from his shoulders—or perchance that shall be my lot,' and with these words Skallagrim sprang up, gnashing his teeth and clutching at the air.

'Peace,' said Eric. 'Blacktooth is not here. Save thy rage until it can run along thy sword and strike him.'

'Nay, not here, nor yet so far off, lord. Hearken: I know this Ospakar. If he has set eyes of longing on Gudruda, Asmund's daughter, he will not rest one hour till he have her or is slain; and if he has set eyes of hate on thee—then take heed to thy going and spy down every path before thy feet tread it. Soon shall the matter come on for judgment and even now Odin's Valkyries[1] choose their own.'

'It is well, then,' said Eric.

'Yea, lord, it is well, for we two have little to fear from any six men, if so be that they fall on us in fair fight. But I do not altogether like thy tale. Too many women are mixed up in it, and women stab in the back. A man may deal with swords aloft, but not with tricks, and lies, and false women's witchery. It was a woman who greased thy wrestling soles; mayhap it will be a woman that binds on thy Hell-shoes when all is done—ay! and who makes them ready for thy feet.'

[1] The 'corse-choosing sisters' that were bidden by Odin to single out those warriors whose hour had come to die in battle and win Valhalla.

'Of women, as of men,' answered Eric, ' there is this to be said, that some are good and some evil.'

' Yes, lord, and this also, that the evil ones plot the ill of their evil, but the good do it of their blind foolishness. Forswear women and so shalt thou live happy and die in honour—cherish them and live in wretchedness and die an outcast.'

'Thy talk is foolish,' said Eric. ' Birds must to the air, the sea to the shore, and man must to woman. As things are so let them be, for they will soon seem as though they had never been. I had rather kiss my dear and die, if so it pleases me to do, than kiss her not and live, for at the last the end will be one end, and kisses are sweet ! '

' That is a good saying,' said Skallagrim, and they fell asleep side by side and Eric had no fear.

Now they awoke and the light was already full, for they were weary and their sleep had been heavy.

Hard by the mouth of the cave is a little well of water that gathers there from the rocks above and in this Eric washed himself. Then Skallagrim showed him the cave and the goodly store of arms that he had won from those whom he had slain and robbed.

' A wondrous place, truly,' said Eric, ' and well fitted to the uses of such a chapman [1] as thou art ; but, say, how didst thou find it ? '

'I followed him who was here before me and gave him choice—to go, or to fight for the stronghold. But he chose to fight and that was his bane, for I slew him.'

' Who was that, then,' said Eric, ' whose head lies yonder ? '

' A cave-dweller, lord, whom I took to me because of the lonesomeness of the winter tide. He was an evil man, for though it is good to be Baresark from time to time, yet to dwell with one who is always Baresark is not good, and thou didst a useful deed in smiting his head from him—and now let it go to find its trunk,' and he rolled it over the edge of the great rift.

[1] Merchant.

G

'Knowest thou, Skallagrim, that this head spoke to me after it had left the man's shoulders, saying that where its body fell there I should fall, and where it lay there I should lie also?'

'Then, lord, that is likely to be thy doom, for this man was foresighted, and, but the night before last, as we rode out to seek sheep, he felt his head, and said that, before the sun sank again, a hundred fathoms of air should link it to his shoulders.'

'It may be so,' answered Eric. 'I thought as I lay in thy grip yonder that the fate was near. And now arm thyself, and take such goods as thou needest, and let us hence, for that thrall of mine who waits me yonder will think thou hast been too mighty for me.'

Skallagrim went to the edge of the rift and searched the plain with his hawk eyes.

'No need to hasten, lord,' he said. 'See yonder rides thy thrall across the black sand, and with him goes thy horse. Surely he thought thou camest no more down the path by which thou wentest up, and it is not thrall's work to seek Skallagrim in his lair and ask for tidings.'

'Wolves take him for a fool!' said Eric in anger. 'He will ride to Middalhof and sing my death-song there, and that will sound sadly in some ears.'

'It is pleasant, lord,' said Skallagrim, 'when good tidings dog the heels of bad, and womenfolk can spare some tears and be little poorer. I have horses in a secret dell that I will show thee, and on them we will ride hence to Middalhof—and there thou must claim peace for me.'

'It is well,' said Eric ; 'now arm thyself, for if thou goest with me thou must make an end of thy Baresark ways, or keep them for the hour of battle.'

'I will do thy bidding, lord,' said Skallagrim. Then he entered the cave and set a plain black steel helm upon his black locks, and a black chain byrnie about his breast. He took the great axe-head also and fitted to it the haft of another axe that lay among the weapons. Then he drew out a purse of money and a store of golden rings, and set them in a bag of otter skin, and buckled it about him. But the other goods he wrapped up in skins and hid behind some stones which were at the bottom of the cave—purposing to come another time and fetch them.

Then they went forth by that same perilous path which Eric had trod, and Skallagrim showed him how he might pass the rock in safety.

'A rough road this,' said Eric as he gained the deep cleft.

'Yea, lord, and, till thou camest, one that none but wood-folk have trodden.'

'I wish to tread it no more,' said Eric again, 'and yet that fellow thief of thine said that I should die here,' and for a while his heart was heavy.

Now Skallagrim Lambstail led him by secret paths to a dell rich in grass, that is hid in the round of the mountain, and here three good horses were feeding. Then, going to a certain rock, he brought out bits and saddles, and they caught the horses, and mounting them, rode away from Mosfell.

Now Eric and his henchman Skallagrim the Baresark rode four hours and saw nobody, till at length they came to the brow of a hill that is named Horse-Head Heights, and, crossing it, found themselves almost in the midst of a score of armed men who were about to mount their horses.

'Now we have company,' said Skallagrim.

'Yes and bad company,' answered Eric, 'for yonder I spy Ospakar Blacktooth, and Gizur and Mord his sons, ay and others. Down, and back to back, for they will show us little gentleness.'

Then they sprang to earth and took their stand upon a mound of rising ground—and the men rode towards them.

'I shall soon know what thy fellowship is worth,' said Eric.

'Fear not, lord,' answered Skallagrim. 'Hold thou thy head and I will hold thy back. We are met in a good hour.'

'Good or ill, it is likely to be a short one. Hearken:

if thou must turn Baresark when swords begin to flash, at
the least stand and be Baresark where thou art, for if thou
rushest on the foe, my back will be naked and I must soon be
sped.'

'It shall be as thou sayest, lord.'

Now men rode round them, but at first they did not
know Eric, because of the golden helm that hid his face in
shadow.

'Who are ye?' called Ospakar.

'I think that thou shouldst know me, Blacktooth,'
Eric answered, 'for I set thee heels up in the snow but lately
—or, at the least, thou wilt know this,' and he drew great
Whitefire.

'Thou mayest know me also, Ospakar,' cried the Baresark.
'Skallagrim men called me, Lambstail, Eric Brighteyes calls
me, but once thou didst call me Ounound. Say, lord, what
tidings of Thorunna?'

Now Ospakar shook his sword, laughing. 'I came out
to seek one foe, and I have found two,' he cried. 'Hearken,
Eric: when thou art slain I go hence to burn and kill at
Middalhof. Shall I bear thy head as keepsake from thee to
Gudruda? For thee, Ounound, I thought thee dead; but,
being yet alive, Thorunna, my sweet love, sends thee this,' and
he hurled a spear at him with all his might.

But Skallagrim catches the spear as it flies and hurls it
back. It strikes right on the shield of Ospakar and pierces it,
ay and the byrnie, and the shoulder that is beneath the byrnie,
so that Blacktooth was made unmeet for fight, and howled
with pain and rage.

'Go, bid Thorunna draw that splinter forth,' says Skallagrim, 'and heal the hole with kisses.'

Now Ospakar, writhing with his hurt, shouts to his men to
slay the two of them, and then the fight begins.

One rushes at Eric and smites at him with an axe.
The blow falls on his shield, and shears off the side of it, then
strikes the byrnie beneath, but lightly. In answer Eric sweeps
low at him with Whitefire, and cuts his leg from under him
between knee and thigh, and he falls and dies.

Another rushes in. Down flashes Whitefire before he can smite, and the carle's shield is cloven through. Then he chooses to draw back and fights no more that day.

Skallagrim slays a man, and wounds another sore. A tall chief with a red scar on his face comes at Brighteyes. Twice he feints at the head while Eric watches, then lowers the sword beneath the cover of his shield, and sweeps suddenly at Eric's legs. Brighteyes leaps high into the air, smiting downward with Whitefire as he leaps, and presently that chief is dead, shorn through shoulder to breast.

Now Skallagrim slays another man and grows Baresark. He looks so fierce that men fall back from him.

Two rush on Eric, one from either side. The sword of him on the right falls on his shield and sinks in, but Brighteyes twists the shorn shield so strongly that the sword is wrenched from the smiter's hand. Now the other sword is aloft above him, and that had been Eric's bane, but Skallagrim glances round and sees it about to fall. He has no time to turn, but he dashes the hammer of his axe backward. It falls full on the swordsman's head, and the head is shattered.

'That was well done,' says Eric as the sword goes down.

'Not so ill but it might be worse,' growls Skallagrim.

Presently all men drew back from these two, for they have had enough of Whitefire and the Baresark's axe.

Ospakar sits on his horse, his shield pinned to his shoulder and curses aloud.

'Close in, you cowards!' he yells, 'close in and cut them down!' but no man stirs.

Then Eric mocks them. 'There are but two of us,' he says, 'will no man try a game with me? Let it not be sung that twenty were overcome by two.'

Now Ospakar's son Mord hears, and he grows mad with rage. He holds his shield aloft and rushes on. But Gizur the Lawman does not come, for Gizur was a coward.

Skallagrim turns to meet Mord, but Eric says:—

'This one for me, comrade,' and steps forward.

Mord strikes a mighty blow. Eric's shield is all shattered and cannot stay it. It crashes through and falls full on the golden helm, beating Brighteyes to his knee. Now he is up again and blows fall thick and fast. Mord is a strong man, unwearied, and skilled in war, and Eric's arms grow faint and his strength sinks low. Mord smites again and wounds him somewhat on the shoulder.

Eric throws aside his cloven shield and, shouting, plies Whitefire with both arms. Mord gives before him, then rushes and smites; Eric leaps aside. Again he rushes and lo! Brighteyes has dropped his point, and it stands a full span through the back of Mord, and instantly that was his bane.

Now men run to their horses, mount in hot haste and ride away, crying that these are trolls whom they have to do with here, not men. Skallagrim sees, and the Baresark fit takes him. With axe aloft he charges after them, screaming as he comes. There is one man, the same whom he had wounded. He cannot mount easily, and when the Baresark comes he still lies on the neck of his horse. The great axe wheels on high and falls, and it is told of this stroke that it was so mighty that man and horse sank dead beneath it, cloven through and through. Then the fit leaves Skallagrim and he walks back, and they are alone with the dead and dying.

Eric leans on Whitefire and speaks :

' Get thee gone, Skallagrim Lambstail ! ' he said ; ' get thee gone ! '

' It shall be as thou wilt, lord,' answered the Baresark ; ' but I have not befriended thee so ill that thou shouldst fear for blows to come.'

' I will keep no man with me who puts my word aside, Skallagrim. What did I bid thee ? Was it not that thou shouldst have done with the Baresark ways, and where thou stoodest there thou shouldst bide ? and see : thou didst forget my word swiftly ! Now get thee gone ! '

' It is true, lord,' he said. ' He who serves must serve wholly,' and Skallagrim turned to seek his horse.

' Stay,' said Eric ; ' thou art a gallant man and I forgive thee : but cross my will no more. We have slain seven men and

Ospakar goes hence wounded. We have got honour, and they loss and the greatest shame. Nevertheless, ill shall come of this to me, for Ospakar has many friends and will set a law-suit on foot against me at the Althing,[1] and thou didst draw the first blood.'

'Would that the spear had gone more home,' said Skalla-grim.

'Ospakar's time is not yet,' answered Eric ; 'still, he has something by which to bear us in mind.'

---

[1] The annual assembly of free men which, in Iceland, performed the functions of a Parliament and Supreme Court of law.

CHAPTER IX

HOW SWANHILD DEALT WITH GUDRUDA

OW Jon, Eric's thrall, watched all night on Mosfell, but saw nothing except the light of Whitefire as it smote the Baresark's head from his shoulders. He stayed there till daylight, much afraid; then, making sure that Eric was slain, Jon rode hard and fast for Middalhof, whither he came at evening.

Gudruda was watching by the women's door. She strained her eyes towards Mosfell to catch the light gleaming on Eric's golden helm, and presently it gleamed indeed, white not red.

'See,' said Swanhild at her side, 'Eric comes!'

'Not Eric, but his thrall,' answered Gudruda, 'to tell us that Eric is sped.'

They waited in silence while Jon galloped towards them.

'What news of Brighteyes?' cried Swanhild.

'Little need to ask,' said Gudruda, 'look at his face.'

Now Jon told his tale and Gudruda listened, clinging to the door-post. But Swanhild cursed him for a coward, so that he shrank before her eyes.

Gudruda turned and walked into the hall and her face was like the face of death. Men saw her, and Asmund asked why she wore so strange a mien. Then Gudruda sang this song :

Up to Mosfell, battle eager,
Rode helmed Brighteyen to the fray.
Back from Mosfell, battle shunning.
Slunk yon coward thrall I ween.
Now shall maid Gudruda never
Know a husband's dear embrace ;
Widowed is she—sunk in sorrow,
Eric treads Valhalla's halls !

And with this she walked from the stead, looking neither to the right nor to the left.

'Let the maid be,' said Atli the Earl. ' Grief fares best alone. But my heart is sore for Eric. It should go ill with that Baresark if I might get a grip of him.'

'That I will have before summer is gone,' said Asmund, for the death of Eric seemed to him the worst of sorrows.

Gudruda walked far, and, crossing Laxà by the stepping stones, climbed Stonefell till she came to the head of Golden Falls, for, like a stricken thing, she desired to be alone in her grief. But Swanhild saw her and followed, coming on her as she sat watching the water thunder down the mighty cleft. Presently Swanhild's shadow fell athwart her, and Gudruda looked up.

' What wouldst thou with me, Swanhild ? ' she asked. 'Art thou come to mock my grief ? '

' Nay, foster-sister, for then I must mock my own. I come to mix my tears with thine. See, we loved Eric, thou and I, and Eric is dead. Let our hate be buried in his grave, whence neither may draw him back.'

Gudruda looked upon her coldly, for nothing could stir her now.

' Get thee gone,' she said. ' Weep thine own tears and leave me to weep mine. Not with thee will I mourn Eric.'

Swanhild frowned and bit upon her lip. ' I will not come to thee with words of peace a second time, my rival,' she said. ' Eric

is dead, but my hate that was born of Eric's love for thee lives
on and grows, and its flower shall be thy death, Gudruda ! '

'Now that Brighteyes is dead, I would fain follow on his
path : so, if thou listest, throw the gates wide,' Gudruda
answered, and heeded her no more.

Swanhild went, but not far. On the further side of a knoll
of grass she flung herself to earth and grieved as her fierce
heart might. She shed no tears, but sat silently, looking with
empty eyes adown the past, and onward to the future, and
finding no good therein.

But Gudruda wept as the weight of her loss pressed
upon her—wept heavy silent tears and cried in her heart to
Eric who was gone—cried upon death to come to her and
bring her sleep or Eric.

So she sat and so she mourned till, quite outworn with sorrow, sleep stole upon her and she dreamed. Gudruda dreamed
that she was dead and that she sat nigh to the golden door
that is in Odin's house at Valhalla, by which the warriors pass
and repass for ever. There she sat from age to age, listening
to the thunder of ten thousand thousand tramping feet, and
watching the fierce faces of the chosen as they marched out
in armies to do battle in the meads. And as she sat, at length
a one-eyed man, clad in gleaming garments, drew near and
spoke to her. He was glorious to look on, and old, and she
knew him for Odin the Allfather.

'Whom seekest thou, maid Gudruda ?' he asked, and the
voice he spoke with was the voice of waters.

'I seek Eric Brighteyes,' she answered, 'who passed
hither a thousand years ago, and for love of whom I am
heart-broken.'

'Eric Brighteyes, Thorgrimur's son?' quoth Odin· 'I know
him well ; no brisker warrior enters at Valhalla's doors, and
none shall do more service at the coming of grey wolf Fenrir.[1]
Pass on and leave him to his glory and his God.'

Then, in her dream, she wept bitterly, and prayed of Odin
by the name of Freya that he would give Eric to her for a
little space.

[1] The foe destined to bring destruction on the Norse gods.

'What wilt thou pay, then, maid Gudruda?' said Odin.

'My life,' she answered.

'Good,' he said; 'for a night Eric shall be thine. Then die, and let thy death be his cause of death.' And Odin sang this song:

> Now, corse-choosing Daughters, hearken
> To the dread Allfather's word:
> When the gale of spears' breath gathers
> Count not Eric midst the slain,
> Till Brighteyen once hath slumbered,
> Wedded, at Gudruda's side—
> Then, Maidens, scream your battle call;
> Whelmed with foes, let Eric fall!

And Gudruda awoke, but in her ears the mighty waters still seemed to speak with Odin's voice, saying:

> Then, Maidens, scream your battle call;
> Whelmed with foes, let Eric fall!

She awoke from that fey sleep and looked upwards, and lo! before her, with shattered shield and all besmeared with war's red rain, stood gold-helmed Eric. There he stood, great and beautiful to see, and she looked on him trembling and amazed.

'Is it indeed thou, Eric, or is it yet my dream?' she said.

'I am no dream, surely,' said Eric; 'but why lookest thou thus on me, Gudruda?'

She rose slowly. 'Methought,' she said, 'methought that thou wast dead at the hand of Skallagrim.' And with a great cry she fell into his arms and lay there sobbing.

It was a sweet sight thus to see Gudruda the Fair, her head of gold pillowed on Eric's war-stained byrnie, her dark eyes afloat with tears of joy; but not so thought Swanhild, watching. She shook in jealous rage, then crept away, and hid herself where she could see no more, lest she should be smitten with madness.

'Whence camest thou? ah! whence camest thou?' said Gudruda. 'I thought thee dead, my love; but now I dreamed that I prayed Odin, and he spared thee to me for a little.'

'Well, and that he hath, though hardly,' and he told her all that had happened, and how, as he rode with Skallagrim, who yet sat yonder on his horse, he caught sight of a woman seated on the grass and knew the colour of the cloak.

Then Gudruda kissed him for very joy, and they were happy each with each—for of all things that are sweet on earth, there is nothing more sweet than this: to find him we love, and thought dead and cold, alive and at our side.

And so they talked, and were very glad with the gladness of youth and love, till Eric said he would go on to Middalhof before the light failed, for he could not come on horseback the way that Gudruda took, but must ride round the shoulder of the hill; and, moreover, he was spent with toil and hunger, and Skallagrim grew weary of waiting.

'Go!' said Gudruda; 'I will be there presently!'

So he kissed her and went, and Swanhild saw the kiss and saw him go.

'Well, lord,' said Skallagrim, 'hast thou had thy fill of kissing?'

'Not altogether,' answered Eric.

They rode a while in silence.

'I thought the maid seemed very fair!' said Skallagrim.

'There are women less favoured, Skallagrim.'

'Rich bait for mighty fish!' said Skallagrim. 'This I tell thee: that, strive as thou mayest against thy fate, that maid shall be thy bane and mine also.'

'Things foredoomed will happen,' said Eric; 'but if thou fearest a maid, the cure is easy: depart from my company.'

'Who was the other?' asked the Baresark—'she who crept and peered, listened, then crept back again, hid her face in her hands, and talked with a grey wolf that came to her like a dog?'

'That must have been Swanhild,' said Eric, 'but I did not see her. Ever does she hide like a rat in the thatch, and as for

the wolf, he must be her Familiar ; for, like Groa, her mother,
Swanhild plays much with witchcraft. Now I will away
back to Gudruda, for my heart misdoubts me of this matter.
Stay thou here till I come, Lambstail ! ' And Eric turns and
gallops back to the head of Goldfoss.

When Eric left her, Gudruda drew yet nearer to the edge
of the mighty falls, and seated herself on their very brink.
Her breast was full of joy, and there she sat and let the splen-
dour of the sight and the greatness of the rushing sounds
sink into her heart. Yonder shone the setting sun, poised, as
it were, on Westman's distant peaks, and here sped the waters,
and by that path Eric had come back to her. Yea, and there
on Sheep-saddle was the road that he had trod down Goldfoss ; and but now he had slain one Baresark and won another
to be his thrall, and they two alone had smitten the company
of Ospakar, and come thence with honour and but little harmed.
Surely no such man as Eric had ever lived—none so fair and
strong and tender ; and she was right happy in his love ! She
stretched out her arms towards him whom but an hour gone
she had thought dead, but who had lived to come back to her
with honour, and blessed his beloved name, and laughed aloud
in her joyousness of heart, calling :

'*Eric ! Eric !*'

But Swanhild, creeping behind her, did not laugh. She
heard Gudruda's voice and guessed Gudruda's gladness, and
jealousy arose within her and rent her. Should this fair rival
live to take her joy from her ?

'*Grey Wolf, Grey Wolf ! what sayest thou ?* '

See, now, if Gudruda were gone, if she rolled a corpse in
those boiling waters, Eric might yet be hers ; or, if he was not
hers, yet Gudruda's he could never be.

'*Grey Wolf, Grey Wolf ! what is thy counsel ?*'

Right on the brink of the great gulf sat Gudruda. One
stroke and all would be ended. Eric had gone ; there was
no eye to see—none save the Grey Wolf's ; there was no
tongue to tell the deed that might be done. Who could call
her to account ? The Gods ! Who were the Gods ? What

were the Gods? Were they not dreams? There were no
Gods save the Gods of Evil—the Gods she knew and com-
muned with.

'*Grey Wolf, Grey Wolf! what is thy rede?*'

There sat Gudruda, laughing in the triumph of her joy, with
the sunset-glow shining on her beauty, and there, behind her,
Swanhild crept—crept like a fox upon his sleeping prey.

Now she is there—

'*I hear thee, Grey Wolf! Back to my breast, Grey
Wolf!*'

SWANHILD WHISPERING TO HER GREY WOLF.

Surely Gudruda heard something? She half turned her
head, then again fell to calling aloud to the waters:

'Eric! beloved Eric!—ah! is there ever a light like the
light of thine eyes—is there ever a joy like the joy of thy kiss?'

Swanhild heard, and her springs of mercy froze. Hate
and fury entered into her. She rose upon her knees and
gathered up her strength:

'Seek, then, thy joy in Goldfoss,' she cried aloud, and with
all her force she thrust.

Gudruda fell a fathom or more, then, with a cry, she

clutched wildly at a little ledge of rock, and hung there, her feet resting on the shelving bank. Thirty fathoms down, swirled and poured and rolled the waters of the Golden Falls. A fathom above, red in the red light of evening, lowered the pitiless face of Swanhild. Gudruda looked beneath her and saw. Pale with agony she looked up and saw, but she said naught.

'Let go, my rival ; let go!' cried Swanhild : 'there is none to help thee, and none to tell thy tale. Let go, I say, and seek thy marriage-bed in Goldfoss!'

But Gudruda clung on and gazed upwards with white face and piteous eyes.

'What! art thou so fain of a moment's life ? ' said Swanhild. 'Then I will save thee from thyself, for it must be ill to suffer thus!' and she ran to seek a rock. Now she finds one and, staggering beneath its weight to the brink of the gulf, peers over. Still Gudruda hangs. Space yawns beneath her, the waters roar in her ears, the red sky glows above. She sees Swanhild come and shrieks aloud.

Eric is there, though Swanhild hears him not, for the sound of his horse's galloping feet is lost in the roar of waters. But that cry comes to his ears, he sees the poised rock, and all grows clear to him. He leaps from his horse, and even as she looses the stone, clutches Swanhild's kirtle and hurls her back. The rock bounds sideways and presently is lost in the waters.

Eric looks over. He sees Gudruda's white face gleaming in the gloom. Down he leaps upon the ledge, though this is no easy thing.

'Hold fast! I come ; hold fast!' he cries.

'I can no more,' gasps Gudruda, and one hand slips.

Eric grasps the rock and, stretching downward, grips her wrist ; just as her hold loosens he grips it, and Gudruda swings loose, her weight hanging on his arm.

Now he must needs lift her up and that with one hand, for the ledge is narrow and he dare not loose his hold of the rock above. She swings over the great gulf and she is senseless as one dead. He gathers all his mighty strength and lifts. His

H

feet slip a little, then catch, and once more Gudruda swings. The sweat bursts out upon his forehead and his blood drums through him. Now it must be, or not at all. Again he lifts and his muscles strain and crack, and she lies beside him on the narrow ledge !

All is not yet done. The brink of the cleft is the height of a man above him. There he must lay her, for he may not leave her to find aid, lest she should wake and roll into the chasm. Loosing his hold of the cliff, he turns, facing the rock, and, bending over Gudruda, twists his hands in her kirtle below the breast and above the knee. Then once more Eric puts out his might and draws her up to the level of his breast, and rests. Again with all his force he lifts her above the crest of his helm and throws her forward, so that now she lies upon the brink of the great cliff. He almost falls backward at the effort, but, clutching the rock, he saves himself, and with a struggle gains her side, and lies there, panting like a wearied hound of chase.

Of all trials of strength that ever were put upon his might, Eric was wont to say, this lifting of Gudruda was the greatest ; for she was no light woman, and there was little to stand on and almost nothing to cling to.

Presently Brighteyes rose and peered at Gudruda through the gloom. She still swooned. Now he gazed about him— but Swanhild, the witchgirl, was gone.

Then he took Gudruda in his arms, and, leading the horse, stumbled through the darkness, calling on Skallagrim. The Baresark answered, and presently his large form was seen looming in the gloom.

Eric told his tale in few words.

'The ways of womankind are evil,' said Skallagrim ; 'but of all the deeds that I have known done at their hands, this is the worst. It had been well to hurl the wolf-witch from the cliff.'

'Ay, well,' said Eric ; 'but that song must yet be sung.'

Now dimly lighted of the rising moon by turns they bore Gudruda down the mountain side, till at length, utterly fordone, they saw the fires of Middalhof.

CHAPTER X

HOW ASMUND SPOKE WITH SWANHILD

NOW as the days went, though Atli's ship was bound for sea, she did not sail, and it came about that the Earl sank ever deeper in the toils of Swanhild. He called to mind many wise saws, but these availed him little: for when Love rises like the sun, wisdom melts like the mists. So at length it came to this, that on the day of Eric's coming back, Atli went to Asmund the Priest, and asked him for the hand of Swanhild the Fatherless in marriage. Asmund heard and was glad, for he knew well that things went badly between Swanhild and Gudruda, and it seemed good to him that seas should be set between them. Nevertheless, he thought it honest to warn the Earl that Swanhild was apart from other women.

'Thou dost great honour, earl, to my foster-daughter and my house,' he said. ' Still, it behoves me to move gently in this matter. Swanhild is fair, and she shall not go hence a wife undowered. But I must tell thee this: that her ways are dark and secret, and strange and fiery are her moods, and I think that she will bring evil on the man who weds her. Now, I love thee, Atli, were it only for our youth's sake, and thou

н 2

art not altogether fit to mate with such a maid, for age
has met thee on thy way. For, as thou wouldst say, youth
draws to youth as the tide to the shore, and falls away from
eld as the wave from the rock. Think, then : is it well that
thou shouldst take her, Atli ? '

'I have thought much and overmuch,' answered the Earl,
stroking his grey beard ; ' but ships old and new drive before
a gale.'

'Ay, Atli, and the new ship rides, where the old one
founders.'

'A true rede, a heavy rede, Asmund ; yet I am minded to
sail this sea, and, if it sink me—well, I have known fair weather!
Great longing has got hold of me, and I think the maid
looks gently on me, and that matters may yet go well between
us. I have many things to offer such as women love. At the
least, if thou givest me thy good word, I will risk it, Asmund :
for the bold thrower sometimes wins the stake. Only I say
this, that, if Swanhild is unwilling, let there be an end of my
wooing, for I do not wish to take a bride who turns from my
grey hairs.'

Asmund said that it should be so, and they made an end
of talking just as the light failed.

Now Asmund went out seeking Swanhild, and presently
he met her near the stead. He could not see her face, and
that was well, for it was not good to look on, but her mien was
wondrous wild.

'Where hast thou been, Swanhild ? ' he asked.

'Mourning Eric Brighteyes,' she made answer.

'It is meeter for Gudruda to mourn over Eric than for
thee, for her loss is heavy,' Asmund said sternly. 'What hast
thou to do with Eric ? '

'Little, or much, or all—read it as thou wilt, foster-
father. Still, all wept for are not lost, nor all who are lost
wept for.'

'Little do I know of thy dark redes,' said Asmund.
'Where is Gudruda now ? '

'High is she or low, sleeping or perchance awakened :
naught reck I. She also mourned for Eric, and we went nigh

to mingling tears—near together were brown curls and golden,' and she laughed aloud.

'Thou art surely fey, thou evil girl!' said Asmund.

'Ay, foster-father, fey: yet is this but the first of my fey-dom. Here starts the road that I must travel, and my feet shall be red ere ever the journey's done.'

'Leave thy dark talk,' said Asmund, 'for to me it is as the wind's song, and listen: a good thing has befallen thee—ay, good beyond thy deserving.'

'Is it so? Well, I stand greatly in need of good. What is thy tidings, foster-father?'

'This: Atli the Earl asks thee in marriage, and he is a mighty man, well honoured in his own land, and set higher, moreover, than I had looked for thee.'

'Ay,' answered Swanhild, 'set like the snow above the fells, set in the years that long are dead. Nay, foster-father, this white-bearded dotard is no mate for me. What! shall I mix my fire with his frost, my breathing youth with the creeping palsy of his age? Never! If Swanhild weds she weds not so, for it is better to go maiden to the grave than thus to shrink and wither at the touch of eld. Now is Atli's wooing sped, and there's an end.'

Asmund heard and grew wroth, for the matter seemed strange to him; nor are maidens wont thus to put aside the word of those set over them.

'There is no end,' he said; 'I will not be answered thus by a girl who lives upon my bounty. It is my command that thou weddest Atli, or else thou goest hence. I have loved thee, and for that love's sake I have borne thy wickedness, thy dark secret ways, and evil words; but I will be crossed no more by thee, Swanhild.'

'Thou wouldst drive me hence with Groa my mother, though perchance thou hast yet more reason to hold me dear, foster-father. Fear not: I will go—perhaps further than thou thinkest,' and once more Swanhild laughed, and passed from him into the darkness.

But Asmund stood looking after her. 'Truly,' he said in his heart, 'ill-deeds are arrows that pierce him who shot them.

I have sowed evilly, and now I reap the harvest. What means
she with her talk of Gudruda and the rest?'

Now as he thought, he saw men and horses draw near, and
one man, whose helm gleamed in the moonlight, bore something in his arms.

'Who passes?' he called,

'Eric Brighteyes, Skallagrim Lambstail, and Gudruda,
Asmund's daughter,' answered a voice; 'who art thou?'

Then Asmund the Priest sprang forward, most glad at
heart, for he never thought to see Eric again.

'Welcome, and thrice welcome art thou, Eric,' he cried;
'for, know, we deemed thee dead.'

'I have lately gone near to death, lord,' said Eric, for he
knew the voice; 'but I am hale and almost whole, though
somewhat weary.'

'What has come to pass, then?' asked Asmund. 'and why
holdest thou Gudruda in thy arms? Is the maid dead?'

'Nay, she does but swoon. See, even now she stirs,' and
as he spake Gudruda awoke, shuddering, and with a little cry
threw her arms about the neck of Eric.

He set her down and comforted her, then once more turned
to Asmund:

'Three things have come about,' he said. 'First, I
have slain one Baresark, and won another to be my thrall, and
for him I crave thy peace, for he has served me well. Next,
we two were set on by Ospakar Blacktooth and his fellowship, and, fighting for our hands, have wounded Ospakar, slain
Mord his son, and six other men of his following.'

'That is good news and bad,' said Asmund, 'since Ospakar
will ask a great weregild [1] for these men, and thou wilt be
outlawed, Eric.'

'That may happen, lord. There is time enough to think
of it. Now there are other tidings to tell. Coming to the
head of Goldfoss I found Gudruda, my betrothed, mourning
my death and spoke with her. Afterwards I left her, and
presently returned again, to see her hanging over the gulf, and
Swanhild hurling rocks upon her to crush her.'

[1] The penalty for manslaying.

'These are tidings in truth,' said Asmund—'such tidings as my heart feared ! Is this true, Gudruda ? '

'It is true, my father,' answered Gudruda, trembling. 'As I sat on the brink of Goldfoss, Swanhild crept behind me and thrust me into the gulf. There I clung above the waters, and she brought a rock to hurl upon me, when suddenly I saw Eric's face, and after that my mind left me and I can tell no more.'

Now Asmund grew as one mad. He plucked at his beard and stamped on the ground. 'Maid though she be,' he cried, ' yet shall Swanhild's back be broken on the Stone of Doom for a witch and a murderess, and her body hurled into the pool of faithless women, and the earth will be well rid of her ! '

Now Gudruda looked up and smiled : ' It would be ill to wreak such a vengeance on her, father,' she said ; ' and the deed would also bring the greatest shame on thee, and all our house. I am saved, by the mercy of the Gods and the might of Eric's arm, and my counsel is that nothing be told of this tale, but that Swanhild be sent away where she can harm us no more.'

' She must be sent to the grave, then,' said Asmund, and fell to thinking. Presently he spoke again : ' Bid yon man fall back, I would speak with you twain,' and Skallagrim went grumbling.

' Hearken now, Eric and Gudruda : only an hour ago hath Atli the Good asked Swanhild of me in marriage. But now I met Swanhild here, and her mien was wild. Still, I spoke of the matter to her, and she would have none of it. Now, this is my counsel : that choice be given to Swanhild, either that she go hence Atli's wife, or take her trial in the Doom-ring.'

' That will be bad for the Earl then,' said Eric. ' He is too good a man to be played on thus.'

' Bairn first, then friend,' answered Asmund.

' Now I will tell thee something that, till this hour, I have hidden from all, for it is my shame. This Swanhild is my daughter, and therefore I have loved her and put away her evil deeds, and she is half-sister to thee, Gudruda. See, then, how sore is my strait, who must avenge daughter upon daughter.'

'Knows thy son Björn of this?' asked Eric.

'None knew it till this hour, except Groa and I.'

'Yet I have feared it long, father,' said Gudruda, 'and therefore I have also borne with Swanhild, though she hates me much and has striven hard to draw my betrothed from me. Now thou canst only take one counsel, and it is: to give choice to Swanhild of these two things, though it is unworthy that Atli should be deceived, and at the best little good can come of it.'

'Yet it must be done, for honour is often slain of heavy need,' said Asmund. 'But we must first swear this Baresark thrall of thine, though little faith lives in Baresark's breast.'

Now Eric called to Skallagrim and charged him strictly that he should tell nothing of Swanhild, and of the wolf that he saw by her, and of how Gudruda was found hanging over the gulf.

'Fear not,' growled the Baresark, 'my tongue is now my master's. What is it to me if women do their wickedness one on another? Let them work magic, hate and slay by stealth, so shall evil be lessened in the world.'

'Peace!' said Eric; 'if anything of this passes thy lips thou art no longer a thrall of mine, and I give thee up to the men of thy quarter.'

'And I cleave that wolf's head of thine down to thy hawk's eyes; but, otherwise, I give thee peace, and will hold thee from harm, wood-dweller as thou art,' said Asmund.

The Baresark laughed: 'My hands will hold my head against ten such mannikins as thou art, Priest. There was never but one man who might overcome me in fair fight and there he stands, and his bidding is my law. So waste no words and make not niddering threats against greater folk,' and he slouched back to his horse.

'A mighty man and a rough,' said Asmund, looking after him; 'I like his looks little.'

'Natheless a strong in battle,' quoth Eric; 'had he not been at my back some six hours gone, by now the ravens had torn out these eyes of mine. Therefore, for my sake, bear with him.'

Asmund said it should be so, and then they passed on to the stead.

Here Eric stripped off his harness, washed, and bound up his wounds. Then, followed by Skallagrim, axe in hand, he came into the hall as men made ready to sit at meat. Now the tale of the mighty deeds that he had done, except that of the saving of Gudruda, had gone abroad, and as Brighteyes came all men rose and with one voice shouted till the roof of the great hall rocked :

'*Welcome, Eric Brighteyes, thou glory of the south !* '

Only Björn, Asmund's son, bit his hand, and did not shout, for he hated Eric because of the fame that he had won.

Brighteyes stood still till the clamour died, then said :

'Much noise for little deeds, brethren. It is true that I overthrew the Mosfell Baresarks. See, here is one,' and he turned to Skallagrim ; 'I strangled him in my arms on Mosfell's brink, and that was something of a deed. Then he swore fealty to me, and we are blood-brethren now, and therefore I ask peace for him, comrades—even from those whom he has wronged or whose kin he has slain. I know this, that when thereafter we stood back to back and met the company of Ospakar Blacktooth, who came to slay us—ay, and Asmund also, and bear away Gudruda to be his wife—he warred right gallantly, till seven of their band lay stiff on Horse-Head Heights, overthrown of us, and among them Mord, Blacktooth's son ; and Ospakar himself went thence sore smitten by this Skallagrim. Therefore, for my sake, do no harm to this man who was Baresark, but now is my thrall ; and, moreover, I beg the aid and friendship of all men of this quarter in those suits that will be laid against me at the Althing for these slayings, which I hereby give out as done by my hand, and by the hand of Skallagrim Lambstail, the Baresark.'

At these words all men shouted again ; but Atli the Earl sprang from the high seat where Asmund had placed him, and, coming to Eric, he kissed him, and, drawing a gold chain from his neck, flung it about the neck of Eric, crying :

'Thou art a glorious man, Eric Brighteyes. I thought the world had no more of such a breed. Listen to my bidding: come thou to my earldom in Orkneys and be a son to me, and I will give thee all good gifts, and, when I die, thou shalt sit in my seat after me.'

But Eric thought of Swanhild, who must go from Iceland as wife to Atli, and answered:

'Thou doest me great honour, Earl, but this may not be. Where the fir is planted, there it must grow and fall. Iceland I love, and I will stay here among my own people till I am driven away.'

'That may well happen, then,' said Atli, 'for be sure Ospakar and his kin will not let the matter of these slayings rest, and I think that it will not avail thee much that thou smotest for thine own hand. Then, come thou and be my man.'

'Where the Norns lead there I must follow,' said Eric, and sat down to meat. Skallagrim sat down also at the side-bench; but men shrank from him, and he glowered on them in answer.

Presently Gudruda entered, and she seemed pale and faint.

When he had done eating, Eric drew Gudruda on to his knee, and she sat there, resting her golden head upon his breast. But Swanhild did not come into the hall, though ever Earl Atli sought her dark face and lovely eyes of blue, and he wondered greatly how his wooing had sped. Still, at this time he spoke no more of it to Asmund.

Now Skallagrim drank much ale, and glared about him fiercely; for he had this fault, that at times he was drunken. In front of him sat two thralls of Asmund's; they were brothers, and large-made men, and they watched Asmund's sheep upon the fells in winter. These two also grew drunk and jeered at Skallagrim, asking him what atonement he would make for those ewes of Asmund's that he had stolen last Yule, and how it came to pass that he, a Baresark, had been overthrown by an unarmed man.

Skallagrim bore their gibes for a space as he drank on, but suddenly he rose and rushed at them, and, seizing a man's throat in either hand, thrust them to the ground beneath him and nearly choked them there.

Then Eric ran down the hall, and, putting out his strength, tore the Baresark from them.

'This then is thy peacefulness, thou wolf!' Eric cried. 'Thou art drunk!'

'Ay,' growled Skallagrim, 'ale is many a man's doom.'

'Have a care that it is not thine and mine, then!' said Eric. 'Go, sleep; and know that, if I see thee thus once more, I see thee not again.'

But after this men jeered no more at Skallagrim Lambs-tail, Eric's thrall.

CHAPTER XI

HOW SWANHILD BID FAREWELL TO ERIC

Now all this while Asmund sat deep in thought; but when, at length, men were sunk in sleep, he took a candle of fat and passed to the shut bed where Swanhild slept alone. She lay on her bed, and her curling hair was all about her. She was awake, for the light gleamed in her blue eyes, and on a naked knife that was on the bed beside her, half hidden by her hair.

'What wouldst thou, foster-father?' she asked, rising in the couch. Asmund closed the curtains, then looked at her sternly and spoke in a low voice:

'Thou art fair to be so vile a thing, Swanhild,' he said. 'Who now would have dreamed that heart of thine could talk with goblins and with were-wolves—that those eyes of thine could bear to look on murder and those white hands find strength to do the sin?'

She held up her shapely arms and, looking on them, laughed. 'Would that they had been fashioned in a stronger mould,' she said. 'May they wither in their woman's weakness! else had the deed been done outright. Now my crime is as heavy on me and nothing gained by it. Say what fate for me, foster-father—the Stone of Doom and the pool where faithless women lie? Ah, then might Gudruda laugh indeed, and I will not live to hear that laugh. See,' and she gripped the dagger at her side: 'along this bright edge runs the path to peace and freedom, and, if need be, I will tread it.'

'Be silent,' said Asmund. 'This Gudruda, my daughter, whom thou wouldst have foully done to death, is thine own sister, and it is she who, pitying thee, hath pleaded for thy life.'

' I will naught of her pity who have no pity,' she answered ; ' and this I say to thee who art my father : shame be on thee who hast not dared to own thy child ! '

' Hadst thou not been my child, Swanhild, and had I not loved thee secretly as my child, be sure of this, I had long since driven thee hence ; for my eyes have been open to much that I have not seemed to see. But at length thy wickedness has overcome my love. and I will look upon thy face no more. Listen : none have heard of this shameful deed of thine save those who saw it, and their tongues are sealed. Now I give thee choice : wed Atli and go, or stand in the Doom-ring and take thy fate.'

' Have I not said, father, while death may be sought otherwise, that I will never do this last ? Nor will I do the first. I am not all of the tame breed of you Iceland folk—other and quicker blood runs in my veins ; nor will I be sold in marriage to a dotard as a mare is sold at a market. I have answered.'

' Fool ! think again, for I go not back upon my word. Wed Atli or die—by thy own hand, if thou wilt—there I will not gainsay thee ; or, if thou fearest this, then anon in the Doom-ring.'

Now Swanhild covered her eyes with her hands and shook the long hair about her face, and she seemed wondrous fair to Asmund the Priest who watched. And as she sat thus, it came into her mind that marriage is not the end of a young maid's life—that old husbands have been known to die, and that she might rule this Atli and his earldom and become a rich and honoured woman, setting her sails in such fashion that when the wind turned it would fill them. Otherwise she must die —ay, die shamed and leave Gudruda with her love.

Suddenly she slipped from the bed to the floor of the chamber, and, clasping the knees of Asmund, looked up through the meshes of her hair, while tears streamed from her beautiful eyes :

' I have sinned,' she sobbed—' I have sinned greatly against thee and my sister. Hearken : I was mad with love of Eric, whom from a child I have turned to, and Gudruda is fairer than

I and she took him from me. Most of all was I mad this night
when I wrought the deed of shame, for ill things counselled me
—things that I did not call; and oh, I thank the Gods—if
there are Gods—that Gudruda died not at my hand. See now,
father, I put this evil from me and tear Eric from my heart,'
and she made as though she rent her bosom—' I will wed
Atli, and be a good housewife to him, and I crave but this of
Gudruda: that she forgive me her wrong; for it was not
done of my will, but of my madness, and by the driving of
those whom my mother taught me to know.'

Asmund listened and the springs of his love thawed within
him. ' Now thou dost take good counsel,' he said, ' and of this
be sure, that so long as thou art in that mood none shall
harm thee ; and for Gudruda, she is the most gentle of women,
and it may well be that she will put away thy sin. So weep
no more, and have no more dealings with thy Finnish witchcraft, but sleep; and to-morrow I will bear thy word to Atli, for
his ship is bound and thou must swiftly be made a wife.'

He went out, bearing the light with him ; but Swanhild
rose from the ground and sat on the edge of the bed, staring
into the darkness and shuddering from time to time.

' I shall soon be made his wife,' she murmured, ' who
would be but one man's wife—and methinks I shall soon be
made a widow also. Thou wilt have me, dotard—take me
and thy fate ! Well, well ; better to wed an Earl than to be
shamed and stretched across the Doom-stone. Oh, weak arms
that failed me at my need, no more will I put trust in
you ! When next I wound, it shall be with the tongue ; when
next I strive to slay, it shall be by another's hand. Curses
on thee, thou ill counseller of darkness, who didst betray me
at the last ! Is it for this that I worshipped thee and swore
the oath that my mother taught me ?

The morning came, and at the first light Asmund sought the
Earl. His heart was heavy because of the guile that his
tongue must practise, and his face was dark as a winter dawn.

' What news, Asmund ? ' asked Atli. ' Early tidings are
bad tidings, so runs the saw, and thy looks give weight to it.'

' Not altogether bad, Earl. Swanhild gives herself to thee.'

' Of her own will, Asmund ? '

' Ay, of her own will. But I have warned thee of her temper.'

' Her temper! Little hangs to a maid's temper. Once a wife and it will melt in softness like the snow when summer comes. These are glad tidings, comrade, and methinks I grow young again beneath the breath of them. Why art thou so glum then ? '

' There is something that must yet be told of Swanhild,' said Asmund. ' She is called the Fatherless, but, if thou wilt have the truth, why here it is for thee—she is my daughter, born out of wedlock, and I know not how that will please thee.'

Atli laughed aloud, and his bright eyes shone in his wrinkled face. ' It pleases me well, Asmund, for then the maid is sprung from a sound stock. The name of the Priest of Middalhof is famous far south of Iceland ; and never hath Iceland bred a comelier girl. Is that all ? '

' One more thing, Earl. This I charge thee : watch thy wife, and hold her back from witchcraft and from dealings with evil things and trolls of darkness. She is of Finnish blood and the women of the Finns are much given to such wicked work.'

' I set little store by witchwork, goblins and their kin,' said Atli. ' I doubt me much of their power, and I shall soon wean Swanhild from such ways, if indeed she practise them.'

Then they fell to talking of Swanhild's dower, and that was not small. Afterwards Asmund sought Eric and Gudruda, and told them what had come to pass, and they were glad at the news, though they grieved for Atli the Earl. And when Swanhild met Gudruda, she came to her humbly, and humbly kissed her hand, and with tears craved pardon of her evil doing, saying that she had been mad ; nor did Gudruda withhold it, for of all women she was the gentlest and the most forgiving. But to Eric, Swanhild said nothing.

The wedding-feast must be held on the third day from this, for Atli would sail on that same day, since his people wearied of waiting and his ship might lie bound no longer. Blithe was

Atli the Earl, and Swanhild was all changed, for now she seemed
the gentlest of maids, and, as befitted one about to be made a
wife, moved through the house with soft words and downcast
eyes. But Skallagrim, watching her, bethought him of the
grey wolf that he had seen by Goldfoss, and this seemed not
well to him.

'It would be bad,' he said to Eric, as they rode to Coldback, 'to stand in yon old earl's shoes. This woman's weather
has changed too fast, and after such a calm there'll come a
storm indeed. I am now minded of Thorunna, for she went
just so the day before she gave herself to Ospakar, and me
to shame and bonds.'

'Talk not of the raven till you hear his croak,' said Eric.

'He is on the wing, lord,' answered Skallagrim.

Now Eric came to Coldback in the Marsh, and Saevuna his
mother and Unna, Thorod's daughter, the betrothed of Asmund,
were glad to welcome him ; for the tidings of his mighty deeds
and of the overthrow of Ospakar and the slaying of Mord
were noised far and wide. But at Skallagrim Lambstail they
looked askance. Still, when they heard of those things that he
had wrought on Horse-Head Heights, they welcomed him for
his deeds' sake.

Eric sat two nights at Coldback, and on the second day
Saevuna his mother and Unna rode thence with their servants
to the wedding-feast of Swanhild the Fatherless. But Eric
stopped at Coldback that night, saying that he would be at
Middalhof within two hours of sunrise, for he waited to talk
with a shepherd who should come from the fells.

Saevuna and her company came to Middalhof and was
asked, first by Gudruda, then by Swanhild, why Brighteyes
tarried. She answered that he would be there early on the
morrow. Next morning, before it was light, Eric girded on
Whitefire, took horse and rode from Coldback alone, for he
would not bring Skallagrim, fearing lest he should get
drunk at the feast and shed some man's blood.

It was Swanhild's wedding-day; but she greeted it with
little lightsomeness of heart, and her eyes knew no sleep that
night, though they were heavy with tears.

At the first light she rose, and, gliding from the house, walked through the heavy dew down the path by which Eric must draw near, for she desired to speak with him. Gudruda also rose a while after, though she did not know this, and followed on the same path, to greet her lover at his coming.

Now three furlongs or more from the stead stood a vetch stack, and Swanhild waited on the further side of this stack. Presently she heard a sound of singing come from behind the shoulder of the fell and of the tramp of a horse's hoofs. Then she saw the golden wings of Eric's helm all ablaze with the sunlight as he rode merrily along, and great bitterness laid hold of her because Eric could be of such a joyous mood on the day when she who loved him must be made the wife of another man.

Presently he was before her, and Swanhild stepped from the shadow of the stack and laid her hand upon his horse's bridle.

'Eric,' she said humbly and with bowed head, 'Gudruda sleeps still. Canst thou, then, find time to hearken to my words?'

He frowned and said: 'I think, Swanhild, that it would be better if thou gavest thy words to him who is thy lord.'

She let the bridle-rein drop from her hands. 'I am answered,' she said; 'ride on.'

Now pity stirred in Eric's heart, for Swanhild's mien was most heavy, and he leaped down from his horse. 'Nay,' he said, 'speak on, if thou hast anything to tell me.'

'I have this to tell thee, Eric: that now, before we part for ever, I am come to ask thy pardon for my ill-doing—ay, and to wish all joy to thee and thy fair love,' and she sobbed and choked.

'Speak no more of it, Swanhild,' he said, 'but let thy good deeds cover up the ill, which are not small; so thou shalt be happy.'

She looked at him strangely, and her face was white with pain.

'How then are we so differently fashioned that thou,

I

Eric, canst prate to me of happiness when my heart is racked
with grief ? Oh, Eric, I blame thee not, for thou hast not
wrought this evil on me willingly ; but I say this : that my
heart is dead, as I would that I were dead. See those
flowers : they smell sweet—for me they have no odour. Look
on the light leaping from Coldback to the sea, from the
sea to Westman Isles, and from the Westman crown of rocks
far into the wide heavens above. It is beautiful, is it not ?
Yet I tell thee, Eric, that now to my eyes howling winter
darkness is every whit as fair. Joy is dead within me, music's
but a jangled madness in my ears, food hath no savour on
my tongue, my youth is sped ere my dawn is day. Nothing
is left to me, Eric, save this fair body that thou didst scorn,
and the dreams which I may gather from my hours of scanty
sleep, and such shame as befalls a loveless bride.'

' Speak not so, Swanhild,' he said, and clasped her by the
hand, for, though he loathed her wickedness, being soft-hearted
and but young, it grieved him to hear her words and see the
anguish of her mind. For it is so with men, that they are
easily moved by the pleading of a fair woman who loves them,
even though they love her not.

' Yea, I will speak out all my mind before I seal it up for
ever. See, Eric, this is my state and thou hast set this crown
of sorrow on my brows : and thou comest singing down the fell,
and I go weeping o'er the sea ! I am not all so ill at heart.
It was love of thee that drove me down to sin, as love of thee
might otherwise have lifted me to holiness. But, loving thee
as thou seest, this day I wed a dotard, and go his chattel and
his bride across the sea, and leave thee singing on the fell,
and by thy side her who is my foe. Thou hast done great
deeds, Brighteyes, and still greater shalt thou do ; yet but as
echoes they shall reach my ears. Thou wilt be to me as
one dead, for it is Gudruda's to bind the byrnie on thy
breast when thou goest forth to war, and hers to loose the
winged helm from thy brow when thou returnest, battle-worn
and conquering.'

Now Swanhild ceased, and choked with grief ; then spoke
again :

'So now farewell; doubtless I weary thee, and—Gudruda waits. Nay, look not on my foolish tears: they are the heritage of woman, of naught else is she sure! While I live, Eric, morn by morn the thought of thee shall come to wake me as the sun wakes yon snowy peak, and night by night thy memory shall pass as at eve he passes from the valleys, but to dawn again in dreams. For, Eric, 'tis thee I wed to-day— at heart I am thy bride, thine and thine only; and when shalt thou find a wife who holds thee so dear as that Swanhild whom once thou knewest? So now farewell! Yes, this time thou shalt kiss away my tears; then let them stream for ever. Thus, Eric! and thus! and thus! do I take farewell of thee.'

And now she clung about his neck, gazing on him with great dewy eyes till things grew strange and dim, and he must kiss her if only for her love and tender beauty's sake. And so he kissed, and it chanced that as they clung thus, Gudruda, passing by this path to give her betrothed greeting, came upon them and stood astonished. Then she turned and, putting her hands to her head, fled back swiftly to the hall, and waited there, great anger burning in her heart; for Gudruda had this fault, that she was very jealous.

Now Eric and Swanhild did not see her, and presently they parted, and Swanhild wiped her eyes and glided thence.

As she drew near the stead she found Gudruda watching.

'Where hast thou been, Swanhild?' she said.

'To bid farewell to Brighteyes, Gudruda.'

'Then thou art foolish, for doubtless he thrust thee from him.'

'Nay, Gudruda, he drew me to him. Hearken, I say, thou sister. Vex me not, for I go my ways and thou goest thine. Thou art strong and fair, and hitherto thou hast overcome me. But I am also fair, and, if I find space to strike in, I also have a share of strength. Pray thou that I find not space, Gudruda. Now is Eric thine. Perchance one day he may be mine. It lies in the lap of the Norns.'

'Fair words from Atli's bride,' mocked Gudruda.

'Ay, Atli's bride, but never Atli's love!' said Swanhild, and swept on.

A while after Eric rode up. He was shamefaced and vexed at heart, because he had yielded thus to Swanhild's beauty, and been melted by her tender words and kissed her. Then he saw Gudruda, and at the sight of her all thought of Swanhild passed from him, for he loved Gudruda and her alone. He leapt down from his horse and ran to her. But, drawn to her full height, she stood with dark flashing eyes and fair face set in anger.

Still, he would have greeted her loverwise; but she lifted her hand and waved him back, and fear took hold of him.

'What now, Gudruda?' he asked, faltering.

'What now, Eric?' she answered, faltering not. 'Hast seen Swanhild?'

'Yea, I have seen Swanhild. She came to bid farewell to me. What of it?'

'What of it? Why "*thus! and thus! and thus!*" didst thou bid farewell to Atli's bride. Ay, "thus and thus," with clinging lips and twined arms. Warm and soft was thy farewell kiss to her who would have slain me, Brighteyes!'

'Gudruda, thou speakest truth, though how thou sawest I know not. Think no ill of it, and scourge me not with words, for, sooth to say, I was melted by her grief and the music of her talk.'

'It is shame to thee so to speak of her whom but now thou heldest in thine arms. By the grief and the music of the talk of her who would have murdered me thou wast melted into kisses, Eric!—for I saw it with these eyes. Knowest thou what I am minded to say to thee? It is this: "Go hence and see me no more;" for I have little wish to cleave to such a feather-man, to one so blown about by the first breath of woman's tempting.'

'Yet, methinks, Gudruda, I have withstood some such winds. I tell thee that, hadst thou been in my place, thyself hadst yielded to Swanhild and kissed her in farewell, for she was more than woman in that hour.'

'Nay, Eric, I am no weak man to be led astray thus. Yet she is more than woman—troll is she also, that I know; but less than man art thou, Eric, thus to fall before her who hates me. Time may come when she shall woo thee after a stronger sort, and what wilt thou say to her then, thou who art so ready with thy kisses ? '

' I will withstand her, Gudruda, for I love thee only, and this is well known to thee.'

' Truly I know thou lovest me, Eric ; but tell me of what worth is this love of man that eyes of beauty and tongue of craft may so readily bewray ? I doubt me of thee, Eric ! '

' Nay, doubt me not, Gudruda. I love thee alone, but I grew soft as wax beneath her pleading. My heart consented not, yet I did consent. I have no more to say.'

Now Gudruda looked on him long and steadfastly. ' Thy plight is sorry, Eric,' she said, ' and this once I forgive thee. Look to it that thou givest me no more cause to doubt thee, for then I shall remember how thou didst bid farewell to Swanhild.'

' I will give none,' he answered, and would have embraced her ; but this she would not suffer then, nor for many days after, for she was angry with him. But with Swanhild she was still more angry, though she said nothing of it. That Swanhild had tried to murder her, Gudruda could forgive, for there she had failed ; but not that she had won Eric to kiss her, for in this she had succeeded well.

CHAPTER XII

HOW ERIC WAS OUTLAWED AND SAILED A-VIKING

OW the marriage-feast went on, and Swanhild, draped in white and girt about with gold, sat by Atli's side upon the high seat. He was fain of her and drew her to him, but she looked at him with cold calm eyes in which hate lurked. The feast was done, and all the company rode to the sea strand, where the Earl's ship lay at anchor. They came there, and Swanhild kissed Asmund, and talked a while with Groa, her mother, and bade farewell to all men. But she bade no farewell to Eric and to Gudruda.

'Why sayest thou no word to these two?' asked Atli, her husband.

'For this reason, Earl,' she answered, 'because ere long we three shall meet again; but I shall see Asmund, my father, and Groa, my mother, no more.'

'That is an ill saying, wife,' said Atli. 'Methinks thou dost foretell their doom.'

'Mayhap! And now I will add to my redes, for I foretell *thy* doom also: it is not yet, but it draws on.'

Then Atli bethought him of many wise saws, but spoke no more, for it seemed to him this was a strange bride that he had wed.

They hauled the anchor home, shook out the great sail, and passed away into the evening light. But while land could still be seen, Swanhild stood near the helm, gazing with her blue eyes upon the lessening coast. Then she passed to the hold, and shut herself in alone, and there she stayed, saying that she was sick, till at length, after a fair voyage of twenty days, they made the Orkney Islands.

But all this pleased Atli wondrous ill, yet he dared not cross her mood.

Now, in Iceland the time drew on when men must ride to the Althing, and notice was given to Eric Brighteyes of many suits that were laid against him, in that he had brought Mord, Ospakar's son, to his death, dealing him a brain or a body or a marrow wound, and others of that company. But no suits were laid against Skallagrim, for he was already outlaw. Therefore he must go in hiding, for men were out to slay him, and this he did unwillingly, at Eric's bidding. Asmund took up Eric's case, for he was the most famous of all lawmen in that day, and when thirteen full weeks of summer were done, they two rode to the Thing, and with them a great company of men of their quarter.

Now, men go up to the Lögberg, and there came Ospakar, though he was not yet healed of his wound, and all his company, and laid their suits against Eric by the mouth of Gizur the Lawman, Ospakar's son. The pleadings were long and cunning on either side; but the end of it was that Ospakar brought it about, by the help of his friends—and of these he had

many—that Eric must go into outlawry for three years. But
no weregild was to be paid to Ospakar and his men for those
who had been killed, and no atonement for the great wound
that Skallagrim Lambstail gave him, or for the death of
Mord, his son, inasmuch as Eric fought for his own hand to
save his life.

The party of Ospakar were ill pleased at this finding, and
Eric was not over glad, for it was little to his mind that he
should sail a-warring across the seas, while Gudruda sat at
home in Iceland. Still, there was no help for the matter.

Now Ospakar spoke with his company, and the end of it
was that he called on them to take their weapons and avenge
themselves by their own might. Asmund and Eric, seeing
this, mustered their array of free-men and thralls. There
were one hundred and five of them, all stout men ; but Ospakar
Blacktooth's band numbered a hundred and thirty-three, and
they stood with their backs to the Raven's Rift.

'Now I would that Skallagrim was here to guard my
back,' said Eric, 'for before this fight is done few will be left
standing to tell its tale.'

'It is a sad thing,' said Asmund, 'that so many men must
die because some men are now dead.'

'A very sad thing,' said Eric, and took this counsel. He
stalked alone towards the ranks of Ospakar and called in a
loud voice, saying :

'It would be grievous that so many warriors should fall in
such a matter. Now hearken, you company of Ospakar Blacktooth ! If there be any two among you who will dare to
match their might against my single sword in holmgang,
here I, Eric Brighteyes, stand and wait them. It is better
that one man, or perchance three men, should die, than that
anon so many should roll in the dust. What say ye ? '

Now all those who watched called out that this was a good
offer and a manly one, though it might turn out ill for Eric ;
but Ospakar answered :

'Were I but well of my wound I alone would cut that
golden comb of thine, thou braggart ; as it is, be sure that
two shall be found.'

'Who is the braggart?' answered Eric. 'He who twice has learned the weight of this arm and yet boasts his strength, or I who stand craving that two should come against me? Get thee hence, Ospakar; get thee home and bid Thorunna, thy leman, whom thou didst beguile from that Ounound who now is named Skallagrim Lambstail the Baresark, nurse thee whole of the wound her husband gave thee. Be sure we shall yet stand face to face, and that combs shall be cut then, combs black or golden. Nurse thee! nurse thee! cease thy prating —get thee home, and bid Thorunna nurse thee; but first name thou the two who shall stand against me in holmgang in Oxarà's stream.'

Folk laughed aloud while Eric mocked, but Ospakar gnashed his teeth with rage. Still, he named the two mightiest men in his company, bidding them take up their swords against Brighteyes. This, indeed, they were loth to do; still, because of the shame that they must get if they hung back, and for fear of the wrath of Ospakar, they made ready to obey his bidding.

Then all men passed down to the bank of Oxarà, and, on the other side, people came from their booths and sat upon the slope of All Man's Raft, for it was a new thing that one man should fight two in holmgang.

Now Eric crossed to the island where holmgangs are fought to this day, and after him came the two chosen, flourishing their swords bravely, and taking counsel how one should rush at his face, while the other passed behind his back and spitted him, as woodfolk spit a lamb. Eric drew White-fire and leaned on it, waiting for the word, and all the women held him to be wondrous fair as, clad in his byrnie and his golden helm, he leaned thus on Whitefire. Presently the word was given, and Eric, standing not to defend himself as they deemed he surely would, whirled Whitefire round his helm and rushed headlong on his foes, shield aloft.

The great carles saw the light that played on Whitefire's edge and the other light that burned in Eric's eyes, and terror got hold of them. Now he was almost come, and Whitefire sprang aloft like a tongue of flame. Then they stayed no more, but, running one this way and one that, cast themselves into the flood and swam for the river-edge. Now from either bank rose up a roar of laughter, that grew and grew, till it echoed against the lava rifts and scared the ravens from their nests.

Eric, too, stopped his charge and laughed aloud; then he walked back to where Asmund stood, unarmed, to second him in the holmgang.

'I can get little honour from such champions as these,' he said.

'Nay,' answered Asmund, 'thou hast got the greatest honour, and they, and Ospakar, such shame as may not be wiped out.'

Now when Blacktooth saw what had come to pass, he well-nigh choked and fell from his horse in fury. Still, he could find no stomach for fighting, but, mustering his company, rode straightway from the Thing home again to Swinefell. But he caused those two whom he had put up to do battle with Eric to be set upon with staves and driven from his following, and the end of it was that they might stay no more in Iceland, but took ship and sailed south, and now they are out of the story.

On the next day, Asmund, and with him Eric and all their men, rode back to Middalhof. Gudruda greeted Eric well, and for the first time since Swanhild went away she kissed him. Moreover, she wept bitterly when she learned that he was doomed to go into outlawry, while she must bide at home.

'How shall the days pass by, Eric?' she said, 'when thou art far, and I know not where thou art, nor how it goes with thee, nor if thou livest or art already dead?'

'In sooth I cannot say, sweet,' he answered; 'but of this I am sure that, wheresoever I am, yet more weary shall be my hours.'

'Three years,' she went on—'three long, cold years, and no sight of thee, and perchance no tidings from thee, till mayhap I learn that thou art in that land whence tidings cannot come. Oh, it would be better to die than to part thus.'

'Well I wot that it is better to die than to live, and better never to have been born than to live and die,' answered Eric sadly. ' Here, it would seem, is nothing but hate and strife, weariness and bitter envy to fret away our strength, and at last, if we come so far, sickness, sorrowful age and death, and thereafter we know not what. Little of good do we find to our hands, and much of evil ; nor know I for what ill-doing these burdens are laid upon us. Yet must we needs breathe such an air as is blown about us, Gudruda, clasping at that happiness which is given, though we may not hold it. At the worst, the game will soon be played, and others will stand where we have stood, and strive as we have striven, and fail as we have failed, and so on, till man has worked out his doom, and the Gods cease from their wrath, or Ragnarrök come upon them, and they too are lost in the jaws of grey wolf Fenrir.'

' Men may win one good thing, and that is fame, Eric.'

' Nay, Gudruda, what is it to win fame ? Is it not to raise up foes, as it were, from the very soil, who, mad with secret hate, seek to stab us in the back? Is it not to lose peace, and toil on from height to height only to be hurled down at last ? Happy, then, is the man whom fame flies from, for hers is a deadly gift.'

' Yet there is one thing left that thou hast not numbered, Eric, and it is love—for love is to our life what the sun is to the world, and, though it seems to set in death, yet it may rise again. We are happy, then, in our love, for there are many who live their lives and do not find it.'

So these two, Eric Brighteyes and Gudruda the Fair, talked sadly, for their hearts were heavy, and on them lay the shadow of sorrows that were to come.

' Say, sweet,' said Eric at length, ' wilt thou that I go not into banishment ? Then I must fall into outlawry, and my life will be in the hands of him who may take it ; yet I think that my foes will find it hard to come by while my strength remains, and at the worst I do but turn to meet the fate that dogs me.'

' Nay, that I will not suffer, Brighteyes. Now we will go to my father, and he shall give thee his dragon of war—she is a good vessel—and thou shalt man her with the briskest men of our quarter : for there are many who will be glad to fare abroad

with thee, Eric. Soon she shall be bound and thou shalt sail
at once, Eric: for the sooner thou art gone the sooner the
three years will be sped, and thou shalt come back to me.
But, oh ! that I might go with thee.'

Now Gudruda and Eric went to Asmund and spoke of this
matter.

'I desired,' he answered, 'that thou, Eric, shouldst
bide here in Iceland till after harvest, for it is then that I
would take Unna, Thorod's daughter, to wife, and it was
meet that thou shouldst sit at the wedding-feast and give her
to me.'

'Nay, father, let Eric go,' said Gudruda, 'for well begun is,
surely, half done. He must remain three years in outlawry :
add thou no day to them, for, if he stays here for long, I know
this : that I shall find no heart to let him go, and, if go he
must, then I shall go with him.'

'That may never be,' said Asmund ; 'thou art too young
and fair to sail a-viking down the sea-path. Hearken, Eric : I
give thee the good ship, and now we will go about to find stout
men to man her.'

'That is a good gift,' said Eric ; and afterwards they rode
to the seashore and overhauled the vessel as she lay in her
shed. She was a great dragon of war, long and slender, and
standing high at stem and prow. She was fashioned of oak,
all bolted together with iron, and at her prow was a gilded
dragon most wonderfully carved.

Eric looked on her and his eyes brightened.

'Here rests a wave-horse that shall bear a viking well,' he
said.

'Ay,' answered Asmund, 'of all the things I own this ship
is the very best. She is so swift that none may catch her, and
she can almost go about in her own length. That gale must
be heavy that shall fill her, with thee to steer ; yet I give her to
thee freely, Eric, and thou shalt do great deeds with this my
gift, and, if things go well, she shall come back to this shore at
last, and thou in her.'

'Now I will name this war-gift with a new name,'
said Eric. ' "Gudruda," I name her : for, as Gudruda here

is the fairest of all women, so is this the fairest of all war-
dragons.'

' So be it,' said Asmund.

Then they rode back to Middalhof, and now Eric Brighteyes let it be known that he needed men to sail the seas with
him. Nor did he ask in vain, for, when it was told that Eric
went a-viking, so great was his fame grown, that many a stout
yeoman and many a great-limbed carle reached down sword
and shield and came up to Middalhof to put their hands in
his. For mate, he took a certain man named Hall of Lithdale,
and this because Björn asked it, for Hall was a friend to Björn,
and he had, moreover, great skill in all manner of seamanship,
and had often sailed the Northern Seas—ay, and round England
to the coast of France.

But when Gudruda saw this man, she did not like him, because of his sharp face, uncanny eyes, and smooth tongue, and
she prayed Eric to have nothing to do with him.

' It is too late now to talk of that,' said Eric. ' Hall is a
well-skilled man, and, for the rest, fear not : I will watch him.'

' Then evil will come of it,' said Gudruda.

Skallagrim also liked Hall little, nor did Hall love Skallagrim and his great axe.

At length all were gathered ; they were fifty in number
and it is said that no such band of men ever took ship from
Iceland.

Now the great dragon was bound and her faring goods were
aboard of her, for Eric must sail on the morrow, if the wind
should be fair. All day long he walked to and fro among his
men ; he would trust nothing to others, and there was no sword
or shield in his company but he himself had proved it. All
day long he walked, and at his back went Skallagrim Lambstail, axe on shoulder, for he would never leave Eric if he had
his will, and they were a mighty pair.

At length all was ready and men sat down to the faring-
feast in the hall at Middalhof, and that was a great feast.
Eric's folk were gathered on the side-benches, and by the high
seat at Asmund's side sat Brighteyes, and near to him were
Björn, Asmund's son, Gudruda, Unna, Asmund's betrothed,

and Saevuna, Eric's mother. For this had been settled between Asmund and Eric, that his mother Saevuna, who was now somewhat sunk in age, should flit from Coldback and come with Unna to dwell at Middalhof. But Eric set a trusty grieve to dwell at Coldback and mind the farm.

When the faring-toasts had been drunk, Eric spoke to Asmund and said : 'I fear one thing, lord, and it is that when I am gone Ospakar will trouble thee. I pray you all to beware of Blacktooth, for, though the hound is whipped, he can still bite, and it seems that he has not yet put Gudruda from his mind.'

Now Björn had sat silently, thinking much and drinking more, for he loved Eric less than ever on this day when he saw how all men did him honour and mourned his going, and his father not the least of them.

' Methinks it is thou, Eric,' he said, ' whom Ospakar hates, and thee on whom he would work his vengeance, and that for no light cause.'

' When bad fortune sits in thy neighbour's house, she knocks upon thy door, Björn. Gudruda, thy sister, is my betrothed, and thou art a party to this feud,' said Eric. ' Therefore it becomes thee better to hold her honour and thy own against this Northlander, than to gird at me for that in which I have no blame.'

Björn grew wroth at these words. ' Prate not to me,' he said. ' Thou art an upstart who wouldst teach their duty to thy betters—ay, puffed up with light-won fame, like a feather on the breeze. But I say this : the breeze shall fail, and thou shalt fall upon the goose's back once more. And I say this also, that, had I my will, Gudruda should wed Ospakar : for he is a mighty chief, and not a long-legged carle, outlawed for man-slaying.'

Now Eric sprang from his seat and laid hand upon the hilt of Whitefire, while men murmured in the hall, for they held this an ill speech of Björn's.

' In thee, it seems, I have no friend,' said Eric, ' and hadst thou been any other man than Gudruda's brother, forsooth thou shouldst answer for thy mocking words. This I tell thee, Björn, that, wert thou twice her brother, if thou plottest with Ospakar when I am gone, thou shalt pay dearly for it when I come back again. I know thy heart well : it is cunning and greedy of gain, and filled with envy as a cask with ale ; yet, if thou lovest to feel it beating in thy breast, strive not to work me mischief and to put Gudruda from me.'

Now Björn sprang up also and drew his sword, for he was white with rage ; but Asmund his father cried, ' Peace ! ' in a great voice.

' Peace ! ' he said. ' Be seated, Eric, and take no heed of this foolish talk. And for thee, Björn, art thou the Priest of Middalhof, and Gudruda's father, or am I ? It has pleased me to betroth Brighteyes to Gudruda, and it pleased me not to betroth her to Ospakar, and that is enough for thee. For the rest, Ospakar would have slain Eric, not he Ospakar, therefore Eric's hands are clean. Though thou art my son, I say this, that, if thou workest ill to Eric when he is over sea, thou shalt rightly learn the weight of Whitefire : it is a niddering deed to plot against an absent man.'

Eric sat down, but Björn strode scowling from the hall, and, taking horse, rode south ; nor did he and Eric meet again till three years were come and gone, and then they met but once.

' Maggots shall be bred of that fly, nor shall they lack flesh to feed on,' said Skallagrim in Eric's ears as he watched Björn pass. But Eric bade him be silent, and turned to Gudruda.

' Look not so sad, sweet,' he said, ' for hasty words rise like the foam on mead and pass as soon. It vexes Björn that thy father has given me the good ship : but his anger will pass, or, at the very worst, I fear him not while thou art true to me.'

' Then thou hast litte to fear, Eric,' she answered. ' Look now on thy hair : it grows long as a woman's, and that is ill, for at sea the salt will hang to it. Say, shall I cut it for thee ? '

' Yes, Gudruda.'

So she cut his yellow locks, and one of them lay upon her heart for many a day.

κ

'Now thou shall swear,' she whispered in his ear, 'that no other man or woman shall cut thy hair till thou comest back to me and I clip it again.'

'That I swear, and readily,' he answered. 'I will go long-haired like a girl for thy sake, Gudruda.'

He spoke low, but Koll the Half-witted, Groa's thrall, heard this oath and kept it in his mind.

Very early on the morrow all men rose, and, taking horse, rode once more to the seaside, till they came to that shed where the Gudruda lay.

Then, when the tide was high, Eric's company took hold of the black ship's thwarts, and at his word they dragged her with might and main. She ran down the greased blocks and sped on quivering to the sea, and as her dragon-prow dipped in the water people cheered aloud.

Now Eric must bid farewell to all, and this he did with a brave heart till at the last he came to Saevuna, his mother, and Gudruda, his dear love.

'Farewell, son,' said the old dame ; 'I have little hope that these eyes shall look again upon that bonny face of thine, yet I am well paid for thy birth-pains, for few have borne such a man as thou. Think of me at times, for without me thou hadst never been. Be not led astray by women, nor lead them astray, or ill shall overtake thee. Be not quarrelsome because of thy great might, for there is a stronger than the strongest. Spare a fallen foe, and take not a poor man's goods or a brave man's sword ; but, when thou smitest, smite home. So shalt thou win honour, and, at the last, peace, that is more than honour.'

Eric thanked her for her counsel and kissed her, then turned to Gudruda, who stood, white and still, plucking at her golden girdle.

'What can I say to thee ?' he asked.

'Say nothing, but go,' she answered : 'go before I weep.'

'Weep not, Gudruda, or thou wilt unman me. Say, thou wilt think on me ?'

'Ay, Eric, by day and by night.'

'And thou wilt be true to me?'

'Ay, till death and after, for so long as thou cleavest to me I will cleave to thee. I will first die rather than betray thee. But of thee I am not so sure. Perchance thou mayst find Swanhild in thy journeyings and crave more kisses from her?'

'Anger me not, Gudruda! thou knowest well that I hate Swanhild more than any woman. When I kiss her again, then thou mayst wed Ospakar.'

'Speak not so rashly, Eric,' she said, and as she spoke Skallagrim drew near.

'If thou lingerest here, lord, the tide will serve us little round Westmans,' he said, eyeing Gudruda as it were with jealousy.

'I come,' said Eric. 'Gudruda, fare thee well!'

She kissed him and clung to him, but did not answer, for she could not speak.

CHAPTER XIII

HOW HALL THE MATE CUT THE GRAPNEL CHAIN

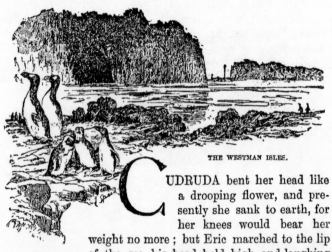

THE WESTMAN ISLES.

CUDRUDA bent her head like a drooping flower, and presently she sank to earth, for her knees would bear her weight no more; but Eric marched to the lip of the sea, his head held high and laughing merrily to hide his pain of heart. Here stood Asmund, who gripped him by both hands, and kissed him on the brow, bidding him good luck.

'I know not whether we shall meet again,' he said; 'but, if my hours be sped before thou returnest, this I charge thee: that thou mindest Gudruda well, for she is the sweetest of all women that I have known, and I hold her the most dear.'

'Fear not for that, lord,' said Eric; 'and I pray thee this, that, if I come back no more, as well may happen, do not force Gudruda into marriage, if she wills it not, and I think she will have little leaning that way. And I say this also : do not count overmuch on Björn thy son, for he has no loyal heart ; and beware of Groa, who was thy housekeeper, for she loves not that Unna should take her place and more. And now I thank thee for many good things, and farewell.'

'Farewell, my son,' said Asmund, 'for in this hour thou seemest as a son to me.'

Eric turned to enter the sea and wade to the vessel, but Skallagrim caught him in his arms as though he were but a child, and, wading into the surf till the water covered his waistbelt, he bore him to the vessel and lifted him up so that Eric reached the bulwarks with his hands.

Then they loosed the cable and got out the oars and soon were dancing over the sea. Presently the breeze caught them, and they set the great sail and sped away like a gull towards the Westman Isles. But Gudruda sat on the shore watching till, at length, the light faded from Eric's golden helm as he stood upon the poop, and the world grew dark to her.

Now Ospakar Blacktooth had news of this sailing and took counsel of Gizur his son, and the end of it was that they made ready two great ships, dragons of war, and, placing sixty fighting men in each of them, sailed round the Iceland coast to the Westmans and waited there to waylay Eric. They had spies on the land, and from them they learned of Brighteyes' coming, and sailed out to meet him in the channel between the greater and the lesser islands, where they knew that he must pass.

Now it drew towards evening when Eric rowed down this channel, for the wind had fallen and he desired to be clear at sea. Presently, as the Gudruda came near to the mouth of the channel, that had high cliffs on either hand, Eric saw two long dragons of war—for their bulwarks were shield-hung— glide from the cover of the island and take their station side by side between him and the open sea.

'Now here are vikings,' said Eric to Skallagrim.

'Now here is Ospakar Blacktooth,' answered Skallagrim, 'for well I know that raven banner of his. This is a good voyage, for we must seek but a little while before we come to fighting.'

Eric bade the men lay on their oars, and spoke :

' Before us is Ospakar Blacktooth with two great dragons, and he is here to cut us off. Now two choices are left to us : one is to bout ship and run before him, and the other to row on and give him battle. What say ye, comrades ? '

Hall of Lithdale, the mate, answered, saying :

' Let us go back, lest we die. The odds are too great, Eric.'

But a man among the crew cried out, ' When thou didst go on holmgang at Thingvalla, Eric, Ospakar's two chosen champions stood before thee, yet at Whitefire's flash they skurried through the water like startled ducks. It was an omen, for so shall his great ships fly when we swoop on them.' Then the others shouted :

' Ay, ay ! Never let it be said that we fled from Ospakar —fie on thy woman's talk, Hall ! '

' Then we are all of one mind, save Hall only,' said Eric. ' Let us put Ospakar to the proof.' And while men shouted ' Yea ! ' he turned to speak with Skallagrim. The Baresark was gone, for, wasting no breath in words, already he was fixing the long shields on the bulwark rail.

The men busked on their harness and made them fit for fight, and, when all was ready, Eric mounted the poop, and with him Skallagrim, and bade the rowers give way. The Gudruda leapt forward and rushed on towards Ospakar's ships. Now they saw that these were bound together with a cable and yet they must go betwixt them.

Eric ran forward to the prow, and with him Skallagrim, and called aloud to a great man who stood upon the ship to starboard, wearing a black helm with raven's wings :

' Who art thou that bars the seas against me ? '

' I am named Ospakar Blacktooth,' answered the great man.

' And what must we lose at thy hands, Ospakar ? '

' But one thing—your lives ! ' answered Blacktooth.

' Thrice have we stood face to face, Ospakar,' said Eric,

'and it seems that hitherto thou hast won no great glory. Now it shall be proved if thy luck has bettered.'

' Art yet healed, lord, of that prick in the shoulder which thou camest by on Horse-Head Heights ? ' roared Skallagrim.

For answer, Oskapar seized a spear and hurled it straight at Eric, and it had been his death had he not caught it in his hand as it flew. Then he cast it back, and that so mightily that it sped right through the shield of Ospakar and was the bane of a man who stood beside him.

' A gift for a gift ! ' laughed Eric. On rushed the Gudruda, but now the cable was strained six fathoms from her bow that held together the ships of Ospakar and it was too strong for breaking. Eric looked and saw. Then he drew Whitefire, and while all men wondered, leaped over the prow of the ship and, clasping the golden dragon's head with his arm, he set his feet upon its claws and waited. On sped the ship and spears flew thick and fast about him, but there Brighteyes hung. Now the Gudruda's bow caught the great rope and strained it taut and, as it rose beneath her weight, Eric smote swift and strong with Whitefire and clove it in two, so that the severed ends fell with a splash into the quiet water.

Eric sprang back to deck while stones and spears hissed about him.

' That was well done, lord,' said Skallagrim ; ' now we shall be snugly berthed.'

' In oars and out grappling-irons,' shouted Eric.

Up rose the rowers, and their war-gear rattled as they rose. They drew in the long oars, and not before it was time, for now the Gudruda forced her way between the two dragons of Ospakar and lay with her bow to their sterns. Then with a shout Eric's men cast the irons and soon the ships were locked fast and the fight began. The spears flew thick, and on either side some got their death before them. Then the men of that vessel, named the Raven, which was to larboard of the Gudruda made ready to board. On they came with a rush, and were driven back, though hardly, for they were many, and those who stood against them few. Again they came, scrambling over the bulwarks, and this time a score of them leapt aboard.

Eric turned from the fight against the dragon of Ospakar and saw it. Then, with Skallagrim, he rushed to meet the boarders as they swarmed along the hold, and naught might they withstand that axe and sword.

Through and through them swept the mighty pair, now Whitefire flashed, and now the great axe fell, and at every stroke a man lay dead or wounded. Six of the boarders turned to fly, but just then the grappling-iron broke, and their ship drifted out with the tide towards the open sea, and presently no man of that twenty was left alive.

Now the men of the ship of Ospakar and of the Gudruda pressed each other hard. Thrice did Ospakar strive to come aboard and thrice he was pushed back. Eric was ever where he was most needed, and with him Skallagrim, for these two threw themselves about from side to side, and were now here and now there, so that it seemed as though there were not one golden helm and one black, but rather four on board the Gudruda.

Eric looked and saw that the other ship was drawing round, though somewhat slowly, to come alongside of them once more.

'Now we must make an end of Ospakar, else our hands will be overfull,' he said, and therewith sprang up upon the bulwarks and after him many men. Once they were driven back, but came on again, and now they thrust all Ospakar's men before them and passed up his ship on both boards. By the mast stood Ospakar and with him Gizur his son, and Eric strove to come at him. But many men were between them, and he could not do this.

Presently, while the fight yet went on hotly and men fell fast, Brighteyes felt the dragon of Ospakar strike, and, looking, saw that they had drifted with the send of the tide on to the rocks of the island. There was a great hole in the hull amidships and the water rushed in fast.

'Back! men; back!' he cried, and all his folk that were unhurt, ran, and leapt on board the Gudruda; but Ospakar and his men sprang into the sea and swam for the shore. Then Skallagrim cut loose the grappling-irons with his axe, and that not too soon, for, scarcely had they pushed clear with great toil when the long warship slipped from the rock and foundered, taking many dead and wounded men with her.

Now Ospakar and some of his people stood safe upon the rocks, and Eric called to him in mockery, bidding him come aboard the Gudruda.

Ospakar made no answer, but stood gnawing his hand, while the water ran from him. Only Gizur his son cursed them aloud.

Eric was greatly minded to follow them, and land and fight them there ; but he might not do this, because of the rocks and of the other dragon, that hung about them, fearing to come on and yet not willing to go back.

' We will have her, at the least, said Eric, and bade the rowers get out their oars.

Now, when the men on board the other ship saw the Gudruda drawing on, they took to their oars at once and rowed swiftly for the sea, and at this a great roar of laughter went down Eric's ship.

' They shall not slip from us so easily,' said Eric ; ' give way, comrades, and after them.'

But the men were much wearied with fighting, and the decks were all cumbered with dead and wounded, so that by the time that the Gudruda had put about, and come to the mouth of the waterway, Ospakar's vessel had shaken out her sails and caught the wind, that now blew strong off shore, and sped away six furlongs or more from Eric's prow.

' Now we shall see how the Gudruda sails,' said Eric, and they spread their canvas and gave chase.

Then Eric bade men clear the decks of the dead, and tend the wounded. He had lost seven men slain outright, and three were wounded, one to death. But on board the ship there lay of Ospakar's force twenty and three dead men.

When all were cast into the sea, men ate and rested.

' We have not done so badly,' said Eric to Skallagrim.

' We shall do better yet,' said Skallagrim to Eric ; ' rather had I seen Ospakar's head lying in the scuppers than those of all his carles ; for he may get more men, but never another head ! '

Now the wind freshened till by midnight it blew strongly. The mate Hall came to Eric and said :

'The Gudruda dips her nose deep in Ran's cup. Say, Eric, shall we shorten sail ? '

'Nay,' answered Eric, 'keep her full and bail. Where yonder Raven flies, my Sea-stag must follow,' and he pointed to the warship that rode the waves before them.

After midnight clouds came up, with rain, and hid the face of the night-sun and the ship they sought. The wind blew ever harder, till at length, when the rain had passed and the clouds lifted, there was much water in the hold and the bailers could hardly stand at their work.

Men murmured, and Hall the mate murmured most of all ; but still Eric held on, for there, not two furlongs ahead of them, rode the dragon of Ospakar. But now, being afraid of the wind and sea, she had lowered her sail somewhat, and made as though she would put about and run for Iceland.

'That she may not do,' called Eric to Skallagrim, 'if once she rolls side on to those seas Ran has her, for she must fill and sink.'

'So they hold, lord,' answered Skallagrim ; 'see, once more she runs ! '

'Ay, but we run faster—she is outsailed. Up, men, up : for presently the fight begins '

'It is bad to join battle in such a sea,' quoth Hall.

'Good or bad,' growled Skallagrim, 'do thou thy lord's bidding,' and he half lifted up his axe.

The mate said no more, for he misdoubted him of Skallagrim Lambstail and his axe.

Then men made ready for the fray as best they might, and stood, sword in hand and drenched with foam, clinging to the bulwarks of the Gudruda as she wallowed through the seas.

Eric went aft to the helm and seized it. Now but a length ahead Ospakar's ship laboured on beneath her small sail, but the Gudruda rushed towards her with all canvas set and at every leap she plunged her golden dragon beneath the surf and shook the water from her foredeck.

'Make ready the grapnel ! ' shouted Eric through the storm.

Skallagrim seized the iron and stood by. Now the Gudruda
rushed alongside the Raven, and Eric steered so skilfully that
there was a fathom space, and no more, between the ships.

Skallagrim cast the iron well and truly, so that it hooked
and held. On sped the Gudruda and the cable tautened—now
her stern kissed the bow of Ospakar's ship, as though she was
towing her, and thus for a space they travelled through the seas.

Eric's folk shouted and strove to cast spears ; but they did
this but ill, because of the rocking of the vessel. As for
Ospakar's men, they clung to the bulwarks and did nothing, for
all the heart was out of them between fear of Eric and terror
of the sea. Eric called to a man to hold the helm, and Skallagrim crept aft to where he stood.

' What counsel shall we take now ? ' said Eric, and as he
spoke a sea broke over them—for the gale was strong.

' Board them and make an end,' answered Skallagrim.

' Rough work ; still, we will try it,' said Eric, ' for we may
not lie thus for long, and I am loath to leave them.'

Then Eric called for men to follow him, and many
answered, creeping as best they might to where he stood.

' Thou art mad, Eric,' said Hall the mate ; ' cut loose and
let us drive, else we shall both founder, and that is a poor tale
to tell.'

Eric took no heed, but, watching his chance, leapt on to the
bows of the Raven, and after him leapt Skallagrim. Even as
he did so, a great sea came and swept past and over them, so
that half the ship was hid for foam. Now, Hall the mate
stood near to the grapnel cable, and, fearing lest they should
sink, out of the cowardice of his heart, he let his axe fall upon
the chain, and severed it so swiftly that no man saw him,
except Skallagrim only. Forward sprang the Gudruda, freed
from her burden, and rushed away before the wind, leaving
Eric and Skallagrim alone upon the Raven's prow.

' Now we are in evil plight,' said Eric, ' the cable has
parted ! '

' Ay,' answered Skallagrim, ' and that losel Hall hath
parted it ! I saw his axe fall.'

CHAPTER XIV

HOW ERIC DREAMED A DREAM

Now, when the men of Ospakar, who were gathered on the poop of the Raven, saw what had come about, they shouted aloud and made ready to slay the pair. But Eric and Skallagrim clambered to the mast and got their backs against it, and swiftly made themselves fast with a rope, so that they might not fall with the rolling of the ship. Then the people of Ospakar came on to cut them down.

But this was no easy task, for they might scarcely stand, and they could not shoot with the bow. Moreover, Eric and Skallagrim, being bound to the mast, had the use of both hands and were minded to die hard. Therefore Ospakar's folks got but one thing by their onslaught, and that was death, for three of their number fell beneath the long sweep of Whitefire, and one bowed before the axe of Skallagrim. Then they drew back and strove to throw spears at these two, but they flew wide because of the rolling of the vessel. One spear struck the mast near the head of Skallagrim. He drew it out, and, waiting till the ship steadied herself in the trough of the sea, hurled it at a knot of Ospakar's thralls, and a man got his death from it. After that they threw no more spears.

Then once more the crew came on with swords and axes, but faint-heartedly, and the end of it was that they lost some more men dead and wounded and fell back again.

Skallagrim mocked at them with bitter words, and one of them, made mad by his scoffing, cast a heavy ballast-stone at him. It fell upon his shoulder and numbed him.

'Now I am unmeet for fight, lord,' said Skallagrim, 'for my right arm is dead and I can scarcely hold my axe.'

'That is ill, then,' said Eric, 'for we have little help, except from each other, and I, too, am well-nigh spent. Well, we have done a great deed and now it is time to rest.'

'My left arm is yet whole, lord, and I can make shift for a while with it. Cut loose the cord before they bait us to death, and let us rush upon these wolves and fall fighting.'

'A good counsel,' said Eric, 'and a quick end; but stay a while : what plan have they now ? '

Now the men of Ospakar, having little heart left in them for such work as this, had taken thought together.

'We have got great hurt, and little honour,' said the mate. 'There are but nineteen of us left alive, and that is scarcely enough to work the ship, and it seems that we shall be fewer before Eric Brighteyes and Skallagrim Lambstail lie quiet by yonder mast. They are mighty men, indeed, and it would be better, methinks, to deal with them by craft, rather than by force.'

The sailors said that this was a good word, for they were weary of the sight of Whitefire as he flamed on high and the sound of the axe of Skallagrim when it crashed through helm and byrnie : and as fear crept in valour fled out.

'This is my rede, then,' said the mate : ' that we go to them and give them peace, and lay them in bonds, swearing that we will put them ashore when we are come back to Iceland. But when we have them fast, as they sleep at night, we will creep on them and hurl them into the sea, and afterwards we will say that we slew them fighting.'

'A shameful deed ! ' said a man.

'Then go thou up against them,' answered the mate. 'If we slay them not, then shall this tale be told against us throughout Iceland : that a ship's company were worsted by two men, and we may not live beneath that dishonour.'

The man held his peace, and the mate, laying down his arms, crept forward alone, towards the mast, just as Eric and Skallagrim were about to cut themselves loose and rush on them.

'What wouldest thou?' shouted Eric. 'Has it gone so well with you with arms that ye are minded to come up against us bearing none?'

'It has gone ill, Eric,' said the mate, 'for ye twain are too mighty for us. We have lost many men, and we shall lose more ere ye are laid low. Therefore we make you this offer: that you lay down your weapons and suffer yourselves to be bound till such time as we touch land, where we will set you ashore, and give you your arms again. Meanwhile, we will deal with you in friendly fashion, giving you of the best we have; nor will we set on foot any suit against you for those of our number whom ye two have slain.'

'Wherefore then should we be bound?' said Eric.

'For this reason only: that we dare not leave you free within our ship. Now choose, and, if ye will, take peace, which we swear by all the Gods we will keep towards you, and, if ye will not, then we will bear you down with beams and sails and stones, and kill you.'

'What thinkest thou, Skallagrim?' said Eric beneath his breath.

'I think that I find little faith in yon carle's face,' answered Skallagrim. 'Still, I am unfit to fight, and thy strength is spent, so it seems that we must lie low if we would rise again. They can scarcely be so base as to do murder having handselled peace to us.'

'I am not so sure of that,' said Eric; 'still, starving beggars must eat bones. Hearken thou: we take the terms, trusting to your honour; and I say this: that ye shall get shame and death if ye depart from them to harm us.'

'Have no fear, lord,' said the mate, 'we are true men.'

'That we shall look to your deeds to learn,' said Eric, laying down his sword and shield.

Skallagrim did likewise, though with no good grace. Then men came with strong cords and bound them fast hand and foot, handling them fearsomely as men handle a live bear in a net. Then they led them forward to the prow.

As they went Eric looked up. Yonder, twenty furlongs and more away, sailed the Gudruda.

'This is good fellowship,' said Skallagrim, 'thus to leave us in the trap.'

'Nay,' answered Eric. 'They cannot put about in such a sea, and doubtless also they think us dead. Nevertheless, if ever it comes about that Hall and I stand face to face again, there will be need for me to think of gentleness.'

'I shall think little thereon,' growled Skallagrim.

Now they were come to the prow, and there was a half deck under which they were set, out of reach of the wind and water. In the deck was a stout iron ring, and the men made them fast with ropes to it, so that they might move but little, and they set their helms and weapons behind them in such fashion that they could not come at them. Then they flung cloaks about them, and brought them food and drink, of which they stood much in need, and treated them well in every way. But for all this Skallagrim trusted them no more.

'We are new-hooked, lord,' he said, 'and they give us line. Presently they will haul in.'

'Evil comes soon enough,' answered Eric, 'no need to run to greet it,' and he fell to thinking of Gudruda, and of the day's deeds, till presently he dropped asleep, for he was very weary.

Now it chanced that as Eric slept he dreamed a dream so strong and strange that it seemed to live within him. He dreamed that he slept there beneath the Raven's deck, and that a rat came and whispered spells into his ear. Then he dreamed that Swanhild glided towards him, walking on the stormy seas. He saw her afar, and she came swiftly, and ever the sea grew smooth before her feet, nor did the wind so much as stir her hair. Presently she stood by him in the ship, and, bending over him, touched him on the shoulder, saying:

'Awake, Eric Brighteyes! Awake! awake!'

It seemed to him that he awoke and said 'What tidings, Swanhild?' and that she answered:

'Ill tidings, Eric—so ill that I am come hither from

L

Straumey [1] to tell of them—ay, come walking on the seas. Had Gudruda done as much, thinkest thou ? '

' Gudruda is no witch,' he said in his dream.

' Nay, but I am a witch, and it is well for thee, Eric. Ay, I am a witch. Now do I seem to sleep at Atli's side, and lo ! here I stand by thine, and I must journey back again many a league before another day be born—ay, many a league, and all for love of thee, Eric ! Hearken, for not long may the spell endure. I have seen this by my magic : that these men who bound thee come even now to take thee, sleeping, and cast thee and thy thrall into the deep, there to drown.'

' If it is fated it will befall,' he said in his dream.

' Nay, it shall not befall. Put forth all thy might and burst thy bonds. Then fetch Whitefire ; cut away the bonds of Skallagrim, and give him his axe and shield. This done, cover yourselves with your cloaks, and wait till ye hear the murderers come. Then rise and rush on them, the two of you, and they shall melt before your might. I have journeyed over the great deep to tell thee this, Eric ! Had Gudruda done as much, thinkest thou ? '

And it seemed to him that the wraith of Swanhild kissed him on the brow, sighed and vanished, bearing the rat in her bosom.

Eric awoke suddenly, just as though he had never slept, and looked around. He knew by the lowness of the sun that it was far into the night, and that he had slept for many hours. They were alone beneath the deck, and far aft, beyond the mast, as the vessel rose upon the waves—for the sea was still rough, though the wind had fallen—Eric saw the mate of the Raven talking earnestly with some men of his crew. Skallagrim snored beside him.

' Awake ! ' Eric said in his ear, ' awake and listen ! '

He yawned and roused himself. ' What now, lord ? ' he said.

' This,' said Eric, and he told him the dream that he had dreamed.

_____
[1] Stroma, the southernmost of the Orkneys.

'That was a fey dream,' said Skallagrim, 'and now we must do as the wraith bade thee.'

'Easy to say, but hard to seek,' quoth Eric; 'this is a great rope that holds us, and a strong.'

'Yes, it is great and strong ; still, we must burst it.'

Now Eric and Skallagrim were made fast in this fashion : their hands were bound behind them, and their legs were lashed above the feet and above the knee. Moreover, a thick cord was fixed about the waist of each, and this cord was passed through the iron ring and knotted there. But it chanced that beneath the hollows of their knees ran an oaken beam, which held the forepart of the dragon together.

'We may try this,' said Eric: 'to set our feet against the beam, and strain with all our strength upon the rope ; though I think that no two men can part it.'

'We shall know that presently,' said Skallagrim, gathering up his legs.

Then they set their feet against the beam and pulled till it groaned ; but, though the rope gave somewhat, it would not break. They rested a while, then strained again till the sweat burst out upon them and the rope cut into their flesh, but still it would not part.

'Now we have found our match,' said Eric.

'That is not altogether proved yet,' answered the Baresark. 'Many a shield is riven at the third stroke.'

So once again they set their feet against the beam, and put out all their strength.

'The ring bends,' gasped Eric. 'Now, when the roll of the ship throws our weight to leeward, in the name of Thor pull ! '

They waited, then put out their might, and lo! though the rope did not break, the iron ring burst asunder and they rolled upon the deck.

'Well pulled, truly,' said Skallagrim as he struggled to his haunches : 'I am marked about the middle with rope-twists for many a day to come, that I will swear. What next, lord ?'

'Whitefire,' answered Eric.

Now, their arms were piled a fathom or more from where they sat, and right in the prow of the ship. Hither, then, they must crawl upon their knees, and this was weary work, for ever as the ship rolled they fell, and could in no wise. save themselves from hurt. Eric was bleeding at the brow, and bloody was the hooked nose of Skallagrim, before they came to where Whitefire was. At length they reached the sword, and pushed aside the bucklers that were over it with their heads. The great war-blade was sheathed, and Eric must needs lie upon his breast and draw the weapon some inches with his teeth.

' This is an ill razor to shave with,' he said, rising, for the keen blade had cut his chin.

' So some have thought and perchance more shall think,' answered Skallagrim. 'Now set the rope on the edge and rub.'

This they did, and presently the thick cord that bound them was in two. Then Eric knelt upon the deck and pressed the bonds that bound his legs upon the blade, and after him Skallagrim. They were free now, except for their hands, and it was no easy thing to cut away the bonds upon their wrists. It was done thus : Skallagrim sat upon the deck, and Eric pushed the sword between his fingers with his feet. Then the Baresark rose, holding the sword, and Eric, turning back to back with him, fretted the cords upon his wrists against the blade. Twice he cut himself, but the third time the cord parted and he was free. He stretched his arms, for they were stiff ; then took Whitefire and cut away the bonds of Skallagrim.

' How goes it with that hurt of thine ? ' he asked.

' Better than I had thought,' answered Skallagrim ; ' the soreness has come out with the bruise.'

''That is good news,' said Eric, ' for methinks, unless Swanhild walked the seas for nothing, thou wilt soon need thine arms.'

' They have never failed me yet,' said Skallagrim and took his axe and shield. ' What counsel now ? '

'This, Skallagrim : that we lie down as we were, and put the cloaks about us as though we were yet in bonds. Then, if these knaves come, we can take them unawares as they think to take us.'

So they went again to where they had been bound, and lay down upon their shields and weapons, drawing cloaks over them. Scarcely had they done this and rested a while, when they saw the mate and all the crew coming along both boards towards them. They bore no weapons in their hands.

' None too soon did Swanhild walk,' said Eric ; ' now we shall learn their purpose. Be thou ready to leap forth when I give the word.'

' Ay, lord,' answered Skallagrim as he worked his stiff arm to and fro. ' In such matters few have thought me backward.'

' What news, friends ? ' cried Eric as the men drew near.

' Bad news for thee, Brighteyes,' answered the mate, ' and that Baresark thrall of thine, for we must loose your bands.'

' That is good news, then,' said Eric, ' for our limbs are numb and dead because of the nipping of the cords. Is land in sight ? '

' Nay, nor will be for thee, Eric.'

' How now, friend ? how now ? Sure, having hand-selled peace to us, ye mean no harm towards two unarmed men ? '

' We swore to do you no harm, nor will we, Eric ; this only will we do : deliver you, bound, to Ran, and leave her to deal with you as deal she may.'

' Bethink you, sirs,' said Eric : ' this is a cruel deed and most unmanly. We yielded to you in faith—will ye break your troth ? '

' War has no troth,' he answered, ' ye are too great to let slip between our fingers. Shall it be said of us that two men overcame us all ? '

' Mayhap ! ' murmured Skallagrim beneath his breath.

' Oh, sirs, I beseech you,' said Eric ; ' I am young, and there is a maid who waits me out in Iceland, and it is hard to die,' and he made as though he wept, while Skallagrim laughed within his sleeve, for it was strange to see Eric feigning fear.

But the men of the Raven mocked aloud.

'This is the great man,' they cried, 'this is that Eric of whose deeds folk sing! Look! he weeps like a child when he sees the water. Drag him forth and away with him into the sea!'

'Little need for that,' cried Eric, and lo! the cloaks about him and Skallagrim flew aside. Out they came with a roar; they came out as a she-bear from her cave, and high above Brighteyes' golden curls Whitefire shone in the pale light, and nigh to it shone the axe of Skallagrim. Whitefire flared aloft, then down he fell and sought the false heart of the mate. The great axe of Skallagrim shone and was lost in the breast of a carle who stood before him.

'Trolls!' shrieked one. 'Here are trolls!' and turned to fly. But again Whitefire was up and that man flew not far— one pace, no more. Then they fled screaming and after them came axe and sword. They fled, they fell, they leaped into the sea, till none were left to fall and leap, for they had no time or heart to find or draw their weapons, and presently Eric Brighteyes and Skallagrim Lambstail stood alone upon the deck—alone with the dead.

'Swanhild is a wise witch,' gasped Eric, 'and, whatever ill she has done, I will remember this to her honour.'

'Little good comes of witchcraft,' answered Skallagrim, wiping his brow: 'to-day it works for our hands, to-morrow it shall work against them.'

'To the helm,' said Eric; 'the ship yaws and comes side on to the seas.'

Skallagrim sprang to the tiller and put his strength on it, and but just in time, for one big sea came aboard them and left much water in the hold.

'We owe this to thy Baresark ways,' said Eric. 'Hadst thou not slain the steersman we had not filled with water.'

'True, lord,' answered Skallagrim; 'but when once my axe is aloft, it seems to fly of itself, till nothing is left before it. What course now?'

'The same on which the Gudruda was laid. Perhaps, if we may endure till we come to the Farey Isles,[1] we shall find her in harbour there.'

'There is not much chance of that,' said Skallagrim ; ' still, the wind is fair and we fly fast before it.'

Then they lashed the tiller and set to bailing. They bailed long, and it was heavy work, but they rid the ship of much water. After that they ate food, for it was now morning, and it came on to blow yet more strongly.

For three days and three nights it blew thus, and the Raven fled along before the gale. All this time, turn and turn about, Eric and Skallagrim stood at the helm and tended the sails. They had little time to eat, and none to sleep. They were so hard pressed also, and must harbour their strength so closely, that the bodies of the dead men yet cumbered the hold. Thus they grew very weary and like to fall from faintness, but still they held the Raven on her course. In the beginning of the fourth night a great sea struck the good ship so that she quivered from stem to stern.

' Methinks I hear water bubbling up,' said Skallagrim in a hoarse voice.

Eric climbed down into the well and lifted the bottom planks, and there beneath them was a leak through which the water spouted in a thin stream. He stopped up the rent as best he might with garments from the dead men, and placed ballast stones upon them, then clambered on to deck again.

' Our hours are short now,' he said, ' the water rushes in apace.'

' Well, it is time to rest,' said Skallagrim ; ' but see, lord ! ' and he pointed ahead. ' What land is that ? '

' It must be the Fareys,' answered Eric ; ' now, if we can but keep afloat for three hours more, we may yet die ashore.'

After this the wind began to fall, but still there was enough to drive the Raven on swiftly.

And ever the water gained in the hold.

Now they were not far from land, for ahead of them the

[1] The Faroes.

bleak hills towered, shining in the faint midnight light, and between the hills was a cleft that seemed to be a fjord. Another hour passed, and they were no more than ten furlongs from the mouth of the fjord, when suddenly the wind fell, and they were in calm water under shelter of the land. They went amidships and looked. The hold was half full of water, and in it floated the bodies of Ospakar's men.

'She has not long to live,' said Skallagrim, 'but we may still be saved if the boat is not broken.'

Now aft, near the tiller, a small boat was bound on the half deck of the Raven. They went to it and looked; it was whole, with oars lashed in it, but half full of water, which they must bail out. This they did as swiftly as they could; then they cut the little boat loose, and, having made it fast with a rope, lifted it over the side-rail and let it fall into the sea, and that was no great way, for the Raven had sunk deep. It fell on an even keel, and Eric let himself down the rope into it and called to Skallagrim to follow.

'Bide a while, lord,' he answered; 'there is that which I would bring with me,' and he went.

For a space Eric waited and then called aloud, 'Swift! thou fool; swift! the ship sinks!'

And as he called, Skallagrim came, and his arms were full of swords and byrnies, and red rings of gold that he had found time to gather from the dead and out of the cabin.

'Throw all aside and come,' said Eric, laying on to the oars, for the Raven wallowed before she sank.

'There is yet time, lord, and the gear is good,' answered Skallagrim, and one by one he threw pieces down into the boat. As the last fell the Raven sank to her bulwarks. Then Skallagrim stepped from the sinking deck into the boat, and cut the cord, not too soon.

Eric gave way with all his strength, and, as he pulled, when he was no more than five fathoms from her, the Raven vanished with a huge swirl.

'Hold still,' he said, 'or we shall follow.'

Round spun the boat in the eddy, she was sucked down

till the water trickled over her gunwale, and for a moment they did not know if they were lost or saved. Eric held his breath and watched, then slowly the boat lifted her nose, and they were safe from the whirlpool of the lost dragon.

'Greed is many a man's bane,' said Eric, 'and it was nearly thine and mine, Skallagrim.'

'I had no heart to leave the good gear,' he answered; 'and thou seest, lord, it is safe and we with it.'

Then they got the boat's head round slowly into the mouth of the fjord, pausing now and again to rest, for their strength was spent. For two hours they rowed down a gulf, as it were, and on either side of them were barren hills. At length the water-way opened out into a great basin, and there, on the further side of the basin, they saw green slopes running down to the water's edge, strewn with white stock-fish set to dry in the wind and sun, and above the slopes a large hall, and about it booths. Moreover, they saw a long dragon of war at anchor near the shore. For a while they rowed on, easing now and again. Then Eric spoke to Skallagrim.

'What thinkest thou of yonder ship, Lambstail?'

'I think this, lord: that she is fashioned wondrous like to the Gudruda.'

'That is in my mind also,' said Eric, 'and our fortune is good if it should be she.'

They rowed on again, and presently a ray from the sun came over the hills—for now it was three hours past midnight —and, the ship having swung a little with the tide, lit upon her prow, and lo! there gleamed the golden dragon of the Gudruda.

'This is a strange thing,' said Eric.

'Ay, lord, a strange and a merry, for now I shall talk with Hall the mate,' and the Baresark smiled grimly.

'Thou shalt do no hurt to Hall,' said Eric. 'I am lord here, and I must judge.'

'Thy will is my will,' said Skallagrim; 'but if my will were thine, he should hang on the mast till sea-birds nested amidst his bones.'

Now they were close to the ship, but they could see no

man. Skallagrim would have called aloud, but Eric bade him hold his peace.

'Either they are dead, and thy calling cannot wake them, or perchance they sleep and will wake of themselves. We will row under the stern, and, having made fast, climb aboard and see with our own eyes.'

This, then, they did as silently as might be, and saw that the Gudruda had not been handled gently by the winds and waves, for her shield-rail was washed away. This they found also, that all men were deep in sleep. Now, amidships a fire still burned, and by it was food. They came there and ate of the food, of which they had great need. Then they took two cloaks that lay on the deck, and, throwing these about them, warmed themselves over the fire: for they were cold and wet, ay, and utterly outworn.

As they sat thus warming themselves, a man of the crew awoke and saw them, and, being amazed, at once called to his fellows, saying that two giants were aboard, warming themselves at the fire. Now men sprang up, and, seizing their weapons, ran towards them, and among them was Hall the mate.

Then suddenly Eric Brighteyes and Skallagrim Lambstail threw aside the cloaks and stood up. They were gaunt and grim to see. Their cheeks were hollow and their eyes stared wide with want of sleep. Thick was their harness with brine, and open wounds gaped upon their faces and their hands. Men saw and fell back in fear, for they held them to be wizards risen from the sea in the shapes of Eric and the Baresark.

Then Eric sang this song:

> Swift and sure across the Swan's Bath
> Sped Sea-stag on Raven's track,
> Heav'd Ran's breast in raging billows,
> Stream'd gale-banners through the sky!
> Yet did Eric the war-eager
> Leap with Baresark-mate aboard,
> Fierce their onset on the foemen!
> Wherefore brake the grapnel-chain?

Hall heard and slunk back, for now he saw that these were

indeed Eric and Skallagrim come up alive from the sea, and
that they knew his baseness.

Eric looked at him and sang again :

> Swift away sped ship Gudruda,
> Left her lord in foeman's ring ;
> Brighteyes back to back with Baresark
> Held his head 'gainst mighty odds.
> Down amidst the ballast tumbling,
> Ospakar's shield-carles were rolled.
> Holy peace at length they handselled,
> Eric must in bonds be laid !
>
> Came the Grey Rat, came the Earl's wife,
> Came the witch-word from afar ;
> Cag'd wolves roused them, and with struggling
> Tore their fetter from its hold.
> Now they watch upon their weapons ;
> Now they weep and pray for life ;
> Now they leap forth like a torrent—
> Swept away is foeman's strength !
>
> Then alone upon the Raven
> Three long days they steer and sail,
> Till the waters, welling upwards,
> Wash dead men about their feet.
> Fails the gale and sinks the dragon,
> Barely may they win the boat :
> Safe they stand on ship Gudruda—
> Say, who cut the grapnel-chain ?

CHAPTER XV

HOW ERIC DWELT IN LONDON TOWN

MEN stood astonished, but Hall the mate slunk back.

'Hold, comrade,' said Eric, 'I have something to say that songs cannot carry. Hearken, my shield-mates: we swore to be true to each other, even to death: is it not so? What then shall be said of that man who cut loose the Gudruda and left us two to die at the foeman's hand?'

'Who was the man?' asked a voice.

LADY ELFRIDA.

'That man was Hall of Lithdale,' said Eric.

'It is false!' said Hall, gathering up his courage; 'the cable parted beneath the straining of the ship, and afterwards we could not put about because of the great sea.'

'Thou art false!' roared Skallagrim. 'With my eyes I saw thee let thine axe fall upon the cable. Liar art thou and dastard! Thou art jealous also of Brighteyes thy lord, and this was in thy mind: to let him die upon the Raven and then to bind his shoes upon thy cowardly feet. Though none else saw, I saw; and I say this: that if I may have my will,

I will string thee, living, to the prow in that same cable till gulls tear out thy fox-heart!'

Now Hall grew very white and his knees trembled beneath him. 'It is true,' he said, 'that I cut the chain, but not from any thought of evil. Had I not cut it the vessel must have sunk and all been lost.'

'Did we not swear, Hall,' said Eric sternly, 'together to fight and together to fall—together to fare and, if need be, together to cease from faring, and dost thou read the oath thus? Say, mates, what reward shall be paid to this man

HALL THE LIAR ROWS ASHORE.

for his good fellowship to us and his tenderness for your lives?'

As with one voice the men answered '*Death!*'

'Thou hearest, Hall?' said Eric. 'Yet I would deal more gently with one to whom I swore fellowship so lately. Get thee gone from our company, and let us see thy cur's face no more. Get thee gone, I say, before I repent of my mercy.'

Then amidst a loud hooting, Hall took his weapons and without a word slunk into the boat of the Raven that lay astern, and rowed ashore; nor did Eric see his face for many months.

'Thou hast done foolishly, lord, to let that weasel go,' said Skallagrim, 'for he will live to nip thy hand.'

'For good or ill, he is gone,' said Eric, 'and now I am worn out and desire to sleep.'

After this Eric and Skallagrim rested three full days, and they were so weary that they were awake for little of this time. But on the third day they rose up, strong and well, except for their hurts and soreness. Then they told the men of that which had come to pass, and all wondered at their might and hardihood. To them indeed Eric seemed as a God, for few such deeds as his had been told of since the God-kind were on earth.

But Brighteyes thought little of his deeds, and much of Gudruda. At times also he thought of Swanhild, and of that witch-dream she sent him : for it was wonderful to him that she should have saved him thus from Ran's net.

Eric was heartily welcomed by the Earl of the Farey Isles, for, when he heard his deeds, he made a feast in his honour, and set him in the high seat. It was a great feast, but Skallagrim became drunk at it and ran down the chamber, axe aloft, roaring for Hall of Lithdale.

This angered Eric much and he would scarcely speak to Skallagrim for many days, though the great Baresark slunk about after him like his shadow, or a whipped hound at its master's heel, and at length he humbled his pride so far as to ask pardon for his fault.

'I grant it for thy deeds' sake,' said Eric shortly; 'but this is upon my mind : that thou wilt err thus again, and it shall be my cause of death—ay, and that of many more.'

'First may my bones be white,' said Skallagrim.

'They shall be white thereafter,' answered Eric.

At Fareys Eric shipped twelve good men and true, to take the seats of those who had been slain by Ospakar's folk. Afterwards, when the wounded were well of their hurts (except one man who died), and the Gudruda was made fit to take the sea again, Brighteyes bade farewell to the Earl of those Isles, who gave him a good cloak and a gold ring at parting, and sailed away.

Now, it were too long to tell of all the deeds that Eric and his

men did. Never, so scalds sing, was there a viking like him
for strength and skill and hardihood, and, in those days,
no such war-dragon as the Gudruda had been known upon the
sea. Wherever Eric joined battle, and that was in many places,
he conquered, for none prevailed against him, till at last foes
would fly before the terror of his name, and earls and kings
would send from far craving the aid of his hands. Withal he
was the best and gentlest of men. It is said of Eric that in
all his days he did no base deed, nor hurt the weak, nor
refused peace to him who prayed it, nor lifted sword against
prisoner or wounded foe. From traders he would take a toll
of their merchandise only and let them go, and whatever
gains he won he would share equally, asking no larger part
than the meanest of his band. All men loved Eric, and even
his foes gave him honour and spoke well of him. Now that
Hall of Lithdale was gone, there was no man among his
mates who would not have passed to death for him, for they
held him dearer than their lives. Women, too, loved him
much; but his heart was set upon Gudruda, and he seldom
turned to look on them.

The first summer of his outlawry Eric warred along the
coast of Ireland, but in the winter he came to Dublin, and for
a while served in the body-guard of the king of that town,
who held him in honour, and would have had him stay
there. But Eric would not bide there, and next spring,
the Gudruda being ready for sea, he sailed for the shores of
England. There he gave battle to two vikings' ships of war,
and took them after a hard fight. It was in this fight that
Skallagrim Lambstail was wounded almost to death. For when,
having taken one ship, Eric boarded the other with but few
men, he was driven back and fell over a beam, and would
have been slain, had not Skallagrim thrown himself across
his body, taking on his own back that blow of a battle-axe
which was aimed at Eric's head. This was a great wound, for
the axe shore through the steel of the byrnie and sank into
the flesh. But when Eric's men saw their lord down, and
Skallagrim, as they deemed, dead athwart him, they made
so fierce a rush that the foemen fell before them like leaves

before a winter gale, and the end of it was that the vikings
prayed peace of Eric. Skallagrim lay sick for many days,
but he was hard to kill, and Eric nursed him back to life.
After this these two loved each other as brother loves twin
brother, and they could scarcely bear to be apart. But other
people did not love Skallagrim, nor he them.

Eric sailed on up the Thames to London, bringing the
viking ships with him, and he delivered their captains bound
to Edmund, Edward's son, the king who was called Edmund
the Magnificent. These captains the King hung, for they
had wrought damage to his ships.

Eric found much favour with the King, and, indeed, his
fame had gone before him. So when he came into the court,
bravely clad, with Skallagrim at his back, who was now almost
recovered of his wound, the King called out to him to draw
near, saying that he desired to look on the bravest viking and
most beauteous man who sailed the seas, and on that fierce
Baresark whom men called 'Eric's Death-shadow.'

So Eric came forward up the long hall that was adorned
with things more splendid than ever his eyes had seen, and
stood before the King. With him walked Skallagrim, driving
the two captive viking chiefs before him with his axe, as a
flesher drives lambs. Now, during these many months
Brighteyes had grown yet more great in girth and glorious to
look on than he was before. Moreover, his hair was now
so long that it flowed like a flood of gold down towards his
girdle, for since Gudruda trimmed it no shears had come near
his head, and his locks grew fast as a woman's. The King
looked at him and was astonished.

'Of a truth,' he said, ' men have not lied about thee, Icelander, nor concerning that great wolf-hound of thine,' and
he pointed at Skallagrim with his sword of state. 'Never
saw I such a man ; ' and he bade all the mightiest men of
his body-guard stand forward that he might measure them
against Eric. But Brighteyes was an inch taller than the
tallest, and measured half a span more round the chest than
the biggest.

'What wouldst thou of me, Icelander ?' asked the King.

'This, lord,' said Eric : ' to serve thee a while, and all my men with me.'

'That is an offer that few would turn from,' answered the King. 'Thou shalt go into my body-guard, and, if I have my will, thou shalt be near me in battle, and thy wolf-dog also.'

Eric said that he asked no better, and thereafter he went up with Edmund the King to make war on the Danes of Mercia, and he and Skallagrim did great deeds before the eyes of the Englishmen.

That winter Eric and his company came back to London, and abode with the King in much state and honour. Now, there was a certain lady of the court named Elfrida. She was both fair and wealthy, the sweetest of women, and of royal blood by her mother's side. So soon as her eyes fell on Eric she loved him, and no one thing did she desire more than to be his wife. But Brighteyes kept aloof from her, for he loved Gudruda alone ; and so the winter wore away, and in the spring he went away warring, nor did he come back till autumn was at hand.

The Lady Elfrida sat at a window when Eric rode through London Town in the King's following, and as he passed she threw him a wreath of flowers. The King saw it and laughed.

'My cold kinswoman seems to melt before those bright eyes of thine, Icelander,' he said, ' as my foes melt before Whitefire's flame. Well, I could wish her a worse mate,' and he looked on him meaningly.

Eric bowed, but made no answer.

That night, as they sat at meat in the palace, the Lady Elfrida, being bidden in jest of Edmund the King to fill the cup of the bravest, passed down the board, and, before all men, poured wine into Eric's cup, and, as she did so, welcomed him back with short sweet words.

Eric grew red as dawn, and thanked her graciously ; but after the feast he spoke with Skallagrim, asking him of the Gudruda, and when she could be ready to take the sea.

'In ten days, lord,' said Skallagrim ; ' but stay we not here with the King this winter ? It is late to sail.'

M

'Nay,' said Eric, 'we bide not here. I wish to winter this year in Fareys, for they are the nighest place to Iceland that I may reach. Next summer my three years of outlawry are over, and I would fare back homewards.'

'Now, I see the shadow of a woman's hand,' said Skalla-grim. 'It is very late to face the northern seas, and we may sail to Iceland from London in the spring.'

'It is my will that we should sail now,' answered Eric.

'Past Orkneys runs the road to Fareys,' said Skallagrim, 'and in Orkneys sits a hawk to whom the Lady Elfrida is but a dove. In faring from ill we may happen on worse.'

'It is my will that we sail,' said Eric stubbornly.

'As thou wilt, and as the King wills,' answered Skalla-grim.

On the morrow Eric went in before the King, and craved a boon.

'There is little that thou canst ask, Brighteyes,' said the King, 'that I will not give thee, for, by my troth, I hold thee dear.'

'I am come to seek no great thing, lord,' answered Eric, 'but this only: leave to bid thee farewell. I wish to wend homeward.'

'Say, Eric,' said the King, 'have I not dealt well with thee?'

'Well, and overwell, lord.'

'Why, then, wouldst thou leave me? I have this in my mind—to bring thee to great honour. See, now, there is a fair lady in this court, and in her veins runs blood that even an Iceland viking might be proud to mate with. She has great lands, and, mayhap, she shall have more. Canst thou not find a home on them, thinkest thou, Brighteyes?'

'In Iceland only I am at home, lord,' said Eric.

Then the King was wroth, and bade him begone when it pleased him, and Eric bowed before him and went out.

Two days afterwards, while Eric was walking in the Palace gardens he met the Lady Elfrida face to face. She held white flowers in her hand, and she was fair to see and pale as the flowers she bore.

He greeted her, and, after a while, she spoke to him in a gentle voice : ' They say that thou goest from England, Brighteyes ? ' she said.

' Yes, lady ; I go,' he answered.

She looked on him once and twice and then burst out weeping. ' Why goest thou hence to that cold land of thine ? ' she sobbed—' that hateful land of snow and ice ! Is not England good enough for thee ? '

' I am at home there, lady, and there my mother waits me.'

' " There thy mother waits thee," Eric ?—say, does a maid called Gudruda the Fair wait thee there also ? '

' There is such a maid in Iceland,' said Eric.

' Yes ; I know it—I know it all,' she answered, drying her tears, and of a sudden growing cold and proud : ' Eric, thou art betrothed to this Gudruda ; and, for thy welfare, somewhat overfaithful to thy troth. For hearken, Eric Brighteyes. I am sure of this : that little luck shall come to thee from the maid Gudruda. It would become me ill to say more ; nevertheless, this is true—that here, in England, good fortune waits thy hand, and there in Iceland such fortune as men mete to their foes. Knowest thou this ? '

Eric looked at her and answered : ' Lady,' he said, ' men are not born of their own will, they live and do little that they will, they die and go, perchance, whither they would not. Yet it may happen to a man that one meets him whose hand he fain would hold, if it be but for an hour's travel over icy ways ; and it is better to hold that hand for this short hour than to wend his life through at a stranger's side.'

' Perhaps there is wisdom in thy folly,' said the Lady Elfrida. ' Still, I tell thee this : that no good luck waits thee there in Iceland.'

' It well may be,' said Eric : ' my days have been stormy, and the gale is still brewing. But it is a poor heart that fears the storm. Better to sink ; for, coward or hero, all must sink at last.'

' Say, Eric,' said the lady, ' if that hand thou dost desire to hold is lost to thee, what then ? '

M 2

'If that hand is cold in death, then henceforth I wend my ways alone.'

'And if it be held by another hand than thine?'

'Then I will journey back to England, lady, and here in this fair garden I may crave speech of thee again.'

They looked one on another. 'Fare thee well, Eric!' said the Lady Elfrida. 'Here in this garden we may talk again; and, if we talk no more—why, fare thee well! Days come and go; the swallow takes flight in winter, and lo! at spring it twitters round the eaves. And if it should not return, then farewell to that swallow. The world is a great house, Eric, and there is room for many swallows. But alas! for her who is left desolate—alas, alas!' And she left him and went her ways.

It is told of this Lady Elfrida that she became very wealthy and was much honoured for her gentleness and wisdom, and that, when she was old, she built a great church and named it Ericskirk. It is also said that, though many sought her in marriage, she wedded none.

CHAPTER XVI

HOW SWANHILD WALKED THE SEAS

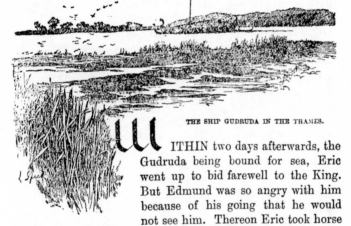

THE SHIP GUDRUDA IN THE THAMES.

ITHIN two days afterwards, the
Gudruda being bound for sea, Eric
went up to bid farewell to the King.
But Edmund was so angry with him
because of his going that he would
not see him. Thereon Eric took horse
and rode down sadly from the Palace to the river-bank where
the Gudruda lay. But when he was about to give the word to
get out the oars, the King himself rode up, and with him men
bearing costly gifts. Eric went ashore to speak with him.

'I am angry with thee, Brighteyes,' said Edmund, 'yet it
is not in my heart to let thee go without words and gifts of
farewell. This only I ask of thee now, that, if things go
not well with thee there, out in Iceland, thou wilt come back
to me.'

'I will—that I promise thee, King,' said Eric, 'for I shall never find a better lord.'

'Nor I a braver servant,' said the King. Then he gave him the gifts and kissed him before all men. To Skallagrim also he gave a good byrnie of Welsh steel coloured black.

Then Eric went aboard again and dropped down the river with the tide.

For five days all went well with them, the sea being calm and the winds light and favourable. But on the fifth night, as they sailed slowly along the coasts of East Anglia over against Yarmouth sands, the moon rose red and ringed and the sea fell dead calm.

'Yonder hangs a storm-lamp, lord,' said Skallagrim, pointing to the angry moon. 'We shall soon be bailing, for the autumn gales draw near.'

'Wait till they come, then speak,' said Eric. 'Thou croakest ever like a raven.'

'And ravens croak before foul weather,' answered Skallagrim, and just as he spoke a sudden gust of wind came up from the south east and laid the Gudruda over. After this it came on to blow, and so fiercely that for whole days and nights their clothes were scarcely dry. They ran northwards before the storm and still northward, sighting no land and seeing no stars. And ever as they scudded on the gale grew fiercer, till at length the men were worn out with bailing and starved with wet and cold. Three of their number also were washed away by the seas, and all were in sorry plight.

It was the fourth night of the gale. Eric stood at the helm, and by him Skallagrim. They were alone, for their comrades were spent and lay beneath decks, waiting for death. The ship was half full of water, but they had no more strength to bail. Eric seemed grim and gaunt in the white light of the moon, and his long hair streamed about him wildly. Grimmer yet was Skallagrim as he clung to the shield-rail and stared across the deep.

'She rolls heavily, lord,' he shouted, 'and the water gains fast.'

'Can the men bail no more?' asked Eric.

'Nay, they are outworn and wait for death.'

'They need not wait long,' said Eric. 'What do they say of me?'

'Nothing.'

Then Eric groaned aloud. 'It was my stubbornness that brought us to this pass,' he said; 'I care little for myself, but it is ill that all should die for one man's folly.'

'Grieve not, lord,' answered Skallagrim, 'that is the world's way, and there are worse things than to drown. Listen! methinks I hear the roar of breakers yonder,' and he pointed to the left.

'Breakers they surely are,' said Eric. 'Now the end is near. But see, is not that land looming up on the right, or is it cloud?'

'It is land,' said Skallagrim, 'and I am sure of this, that we run into a firth. Look, the seas boil like a hot spring. Hold on thy course, lord, perchance we may yet steer between rocks and land. Already the wind falls and the current lessens the seas.'

'Ay,' said Eric, 'already the fog and rain come up,' and he pointed ahead where dense clouds gathered in the shape of a giant, whose head reached to the skies and moved towards them, hiding the moon.

Skallagrim looked, then spoke: 'Now here, it seems, is witchwork. Say, lord, hast thou ever seen mist travel against wind as it travels now?'

'Never before,' said Eric, and as he spoke the light of the moon went out.

Swanhild, Atli's wife, sat in beauty in her bower on Straumey Isle and looked with wide eyes towards the sea. It was midnight. None stirred in Atli's hall, but still Swanhild looked out towards the sea.

Now she turned and spoke into the darkness, for there was no light in the bower save the light of her great eyes.

'Art thou there?' she said. 'I have summoned thee thrice in the words thou knowest. Say, Toad, art there?'

'Ay, Swanhild the Fatherless! Swanhild, Groa's daughter!
Witch-mother's witch-child! I am here. What is thy will
with me?' piped a thin voice like the voice of a dying
babe.

Swanhild shuddered a little and her eyes grew brighter—
bright as the eyes of a cat.

'This first,' she said: 'that thou show thyself. Hideous
as thou art, I had rather see thee, than speak with thee seeing
thee not.'

'Mock not my form, lady,' answered the thin voice, 'for it
is as thou dost fashion it in thy thought. To the good I am
fair as day; to the evil, foul like their heart. *Toad* thou didst
call me: look, now I come as a toad!'

Swanhild looked, and behold! a ring of the darkness grew
white with light, and in it crouching a thing hideous to see. It
was shaped like a great spotted toad, and on it was set a hag's
face, with white locks hanging down on either side. Its eyes
were blood-red and sunken, black were its fangs, and its skin
was dead yellow. It grinned horribly as Swanhild shrank
from it, then spoke again:

'*Grey Wolf* thou didst call me once, Swanhild, when thou
wouldst have thrust Gudruda down Goldfoss gulf, and as a
grey wolf I came, and gave thee counsel that thou tookest
but ill. *Rat* didst thou call me once, when thou wouldst
save Brighteyes from the carles of Ospakar, and as a rat
I came and in thy shape I walked the seas. *Toad* thou
callest me now, and as a toad I creep about thy feet. Name
thy will, Swanhild, and I will name my price. But be swift,
for there are other fair ladies whose wish I must do ere
dawn.'

'Thou art hideous to look on!' said Swanhild, placing her
hand before her eyes.

'Say not so, lady; say not so. Look at this face of mine.
Knowest thou it not? It is thy mother's—dead Groa lent it
me. I took it from where she lies; and my toad's skin I drew
from thy spotted heart, Swanhild, and more hideous than I
am shalt thou be in a day to come, as once I was more fair
than thou art to-day.'

Swanhild opened her lips to shriek, but no sound came.

'Troll,' she whispered, 'mock me not with lies, but hearken to my bidding : where sails Eric now ? '

'Look out into the night, lady, and thou shalt see.'

Swanhild looked, and the ways of the darkness opened before her witch-sight. There at the mouth of Pentland Firth the Gudruda laboured heavily in the great seas, and by the tiller stood Eric, and with him Skallagrim.

'Seest thou thy love ? ' asked the Familiar.

'Yea,' she answered, 'full clearly ; he is worn with wind and sea, but more glorious than aforetime, and his hair is long. Say, what shall befall him if thou aidest not ? '

'This, that he shall safely pass the Firth, for the gale falls, and come safely to Fareys, and from Fareys isles to Gudruda's arms.'

'And what canst thou do, Goblin ? '

'This : I can lure Eric's ship to wreck, and give his comrades, all save Skallagrim, to Ran's net, and bring him to thy arms, Swanhild, witch-mother's witch-child ! '

She hearkened. Her breast heaved and her eyes flashed.

'And thy price, Toad ? '

'*Thou* art the price, lady,' piped the goblin. 'Thou shalt give thyself to me when thy day is done, and merrily will we sisters dwell in Hela's halls, and merrily for ever will we fare about the earth o' nights, doing such tasks as this task of thine, Swanhild, and working wicked woe till the last woe is worked on us. Art thou content ? '

Swanhild thought. Twice her breath went from her lips in great sighs. Then she stood, pale and silent.

'Safely shall he sail the Firth,' piped the thin voice. 'Safely shall he sit in Fareys. Safely shall he lie in white Gudruda's arms—*hee ! hee !* Think of it, lady ! '

Then Swanhild shook like a birch-tree in the gale, and her face grew ashen.

'I am content,' she said.

'*Hee ! hee !* Brave lady ! She is content. Ah, we sisters shall be merry. Hearken : if I aid thee thus I may do no more. Thrice has the night-owl come at thy call—now it must wing away. Yet things will be as I have said; thine own wisdom shall guide the rest. Ere morn Brighteyes shall stand in Atli's hall, ere spring he will be thy love, and ere autumn Gudruda shall sit on the high seat in the hall of Middalhof the bride of Ospakar. Draw nigh, give me thine arm, sister, that blood may seal our bargain.'

Swanhild drew near the toad, and, shuddering, stretched out her arm, and then and there the red blood ran, and there they sealed their sisterhood. And while the nameless deed was wrought, it seemed to Swanhild as though fire shot through her veins, and fire surged before her eyes, and in the fire a shape passed up weeping.

'It is done, Blood-sister,' piped the voice; 'now I must away in thy form to be about thy tasks. Seat thee here before me—so. Now lay thy brow upon my brow—fear not, it was thy mother's—life on death! curling locks on corpse hair! See, so we change—we change. Now thou art the Death-toad and I am Swanhild, Atli's wife, who shall be Eric's love.'

Then Swanhild knew that her beauty had entered into the foulness of the toad, and the foulness of the toad into her beauty, for there before her stood her own shape and here she crouched a toad upon the floor.

'Away to work, away!' said a soft low voice, her own voice speaking from her own body that stood before her, and lo! it was gone.

But Swanhild crouched, in the shape of a hag-headed toad, upon the ground in her bower of Atli's hall, and felt wickedness and evil longings and hate boil and seethe within her heart. She looked out through her sunken horny eyes and she seemed to see strange sights. She saw Atli, her lord, dead upon the grass. She saw a woman asleep, and above her flashed a sword. She saw the hall of Middalhof red with blood. She saw a great gulf in a mountain's heart, and men fell down it. And, last, she saw a war-ship sailing fast out on the sea, afire, to vanish there.

Now the witch-hag who wore Swanhild's loveliness stood upon the cliffs of Straumey and tossed her white arms towards the north.

'Come, fog! come, sleet!' she cried. 'Come, fog! come, sleet! Put out the moon and blind the eyes of Eric!' And as she called, the fog rose up like a giant and stretched his hands from shore to shore.

'Move, fog! beat, rain!' she cried. 'Move and beat against the gale, and blind the eyes of Eric!'

And the fog moved on against the wind, and with it sleet and rain.

'Now I am afeared,' said Eric to Skallagrim, as they stood in darkness upon the ship: 'the gale blows from behind us, and yet the mist drives fast in our faces. What comes now?'

'This is witch-work, lord,' answered Skallagrim, 'and in such things no counsel can avail. Hold the tiller straight and drive on, say I. Methinks the gale lessens more and more.'

So they did for a little while, and all around them sounded the roar of breakers. Darker grew the sky and darker yet, till at the last, though they stood side by side, they could not see each other's shapes.

'This is strange sailing,' said Eric. 'I hear the roar of breakers as it were beneath the prow.'

'Lash the helm, lord, and let us go forward. If there are breakers, perhaps we shall see their foam through the blackness,' said Skallagrim.

Eric did so, and they crept forward on the starboard board right to the prow of the ship, and there Skallagrim peered into the fog and sleet.

'Lord,' he whispered presently, and his voice shook strangely, 'what is that yonder on the waters? Seest thou aught?'

Eric stared and said, 'By Odin! I see a shape of light like to the shape of a woman; it walks upon the waters towards us and the mist melts before it, and the sea grows calm beneath its feet.'

' I see that also ! ' said Skallagrim.

' She comes nigh ! ' gasped Eric. ' See how swift she
comes ! By the dead, it is Swanhild's shape ! Look, Skallagrim ! look how her eyes flame !—look how her hair streams
upon the wind ! '

' It is Swanhild and we are fey ! ' quoth Skallagrim, and
they ran back to the helm, where Skallagrim sank upon the
deck in fear.

' See, Skallagrim, she glides before the Gudruda's beak !
she glides backwards and she points yonder—there to the
right ! Shall I put the helm down and follow her ? '

' Nay, lord, nay ; set no faith in witchcraft or evil will
befall us.'

As he spoke a great gust of wind shook the ship, the
music of the breakers roared in their ears, and the gleaming
shape upon the waters tossed its arms wildly and pointed to
the right.

' The breakers call ahead,' said Eric. ' The Shape points
yonder, where I hear no sound of sea. Once before, thou
mindest, Swanhild walked the waves to warn us and thereby
saved us from the men of Ospakar. Ever she swore she
loved me ; now she is surely come in love to save us and all
our comrades. Say, shall I put about ? Look : once more
she waves her arms and points,' and as he spoke he gripped
the helm.

' I have no rede, lord,' said Skallagrim, ' and I love not
witch-work. We can die but once, and death is all around ;
be it as thou wilt.'

Eric put down the helm with all his might. The good
ship answered, and her timbers groaned loudly, as though in
woe, when the strain of the sea struck her abeam. Then once
more she flew fast across the waters, and fast before her
glided the wraith of Swanhild. Now it pointed here and
now there, and as it pointed so Eric shaped his course.
For a while the noise of breakers lessened, but now again
came a thunder, like the thunder of waves smiting on a cliff,
and about the sides of the Gudruda the waters hissed like
snakes.

Suddenly the Shape threw up its arms and seemed to sink beneath the waves, while a sound like the sound of a great laugh went up from sea to sky.

'Now here is the end,' said Skallagrim, 'and we are lured to doom.'

Ere ever the words had passed his lips the ship struck, and so fiercely that they were rolled upon the deck. Suddenly the sky grew clear, the moon shone out, and before them were cliffs and rocks, and behind them a great wave rushed on. From the hold of the ship there came a cry, for now their comrades were awake and they knew that death was here.

Eric gripped Skallagrim round the middle and looked aft. On rushed the wave, no such wave had he ever seen. Now it struck and the Gudruda burst asunder beneath the blow.

But Eric Brighteyes and Skallagrim Lambstail were lifted on its crest and knew no more.

Swanhild, crouching in hideous guise upon the ground in the bower of Atli's hall, looked on the visions that passed before her. Suddenly a woman's shape, her own shape, was there.

'It is done, Blood-sister,' said a voice, her own voice. 'Merrily I walked the waves, and oh, merry was the cry of Eric's folk when Ran caught them in her net! Be thyself, again, Blood-sister—be fair as thou art foul; then arise, wake Atli thy lord, and go down to the sea's lip by the southern cliffs and see what thou shalt find. We shall meet no more till all this game is played and another game is set,' and the shape of Swanhild crouched upon the floor before the hag-headed toad muttering 'Pass! pass!'

Then Swanhild felt her flesh come back to her, and as it grew upon her so the shape of the Death-headed toad faded away.

'Farewell, Blood-sister!' piped a voice; 'make merry as thou mayest, but merrier shall be our nights when thou hast gone a-sailing with Eric on the sea. Farewell! farewell!

Were-wolf thou didst call me once, and as a wolf I came.
Rat thou didst call me once, and as a rat I came. *Toad* didst
thou call me once, and as a toad I came. Say, at the last,
what wilt thou call me and in what shape shall I come, Blood-
sister ? Till then farewell ! '

And all was gone and all was still.

CHAPTER XVII

HOW ASMUND THE PRIEST WEDDED UNNA, THOROD'S DAUGHTER

Now the story goes back to Iceland.

When Brighteyes was gone, for a while Gudruda the Fair moved sadly about the stead, like one new-widowed. Then came tidings. Men told how Ospakar Blacktooth waylaid Eric on the seas with two long ships, dragons of war, and how Eric had given him battle and sunk one dragon with great loss to Ospakar. They told also how Blacktooth's other dragon, the Raven, sailed away before the wind, and Eric had sailed after it in a rising gale. But of what befell these ships no news came for many a month, and it was rumoured that this had befallen them—that both had sunk in the gale, and Eric was dead.

But Gudruda would not believe this. When Asmund the Priest, her father, asked her why she did not believe it, she answered that, had Eric been dead, her heart would surely have spoken to her of it. To this Asmund said that it might be so.

Hay-harvest being done, Asmund made ready for his wedding with Unna, Thorod's daughter and Eric's cousin.

Now it was agreed that the marriage-feast should be held at Middalhof; for Asmund wished to ask a great company to the wedding, and there was no place at Coldback to hold so many. Also some of the kin of Thorod, Unna's father, were bidden to the feast from the east and north. At length all was prepared and the guests came in great companies, for no such feast had been made in this quarter for many years.

N

On the eve of the marriage Asmund spoke with Groa. The witch-wife had borne herself humbly since she was recovered from her sickness. She passed about the stead like a rat at night, speaking few words and with downcast eyes. She was busy also making all things ready for the feasting.

Now as Asmund went up the hall seeing that everything was in order, Groa drew near to him and touched him gently on the shoulder.

'Are things to thy mind, lord?' she said.

'Yes, Groa,' he answered, 'more to my mind than to thine I fear.'

'Fear not, lord; thy will is my will.'

'Say, Groa, is it thy wish to bide here in Middalhof when Unna is my housewife?'

'It is my wish to serve thee as aforetime,' she answered softly, 'if so be that Unna wills it.'

'That is her desire,' said Asmund and went his ways.

But Groa stood looking after him and her face was fierce and evil.

'While bane has virtue, while runes have power, and while hand has cunning, never, Unna, shalt thou take my place at Asmund's side! Out of the water I came to thee, Asmund; into the water I go again. Unquiet shall I lie there—unquiet must I wend through Hela's halls; but Unna shall rest at Asmund's side—in Asmund's cairn!'

Then again she moved about the hall, making all things ready for the feast. But at midnight, when the light was low and folk slept, Groa rose, and, veiled in a black robe, with a basket in her hand, passed like a shadow through the hall out upon the meads. Thence she glided into the mists that hang about the river's edge, and in silence, always looking behind her, like one who fears a hidden foe, culled flowers of the noisome plants that grow in the marsh. Her basket being filled, she passed round the stead to a hidden dell upon the mountain side. Here a man stood waiting, and near him burned a fire of turf. In his hand he held an iron-pot. It was Koll the Half-witted, Groa's thrall.

'Are all things ready, Koll?' she said.

'Yes,' he answered ; ' but I like not these tasks of thine, mistress. Say now, what wouldst thou with the fire and the pot ?'

'This, then, Koll. I would brew a love-potion for Asmund the Priest as he has bidden me to do.'

'I have done many an ill deed for thee, mistress, but of all of them I love this the least,' said the thrall, doubtfully.

'I have done many a good deed for thee, Koll. It was I who saved thee from the Doom-stone, seeming to prove thee innocent—ay, even when thy back was stretched on it, because thou hadst slain a man in his sleep. Is it not so?'

'Yea, mistress.'

'And yet thou wast guilty, Koll. And I have given thee many good gifts, is it not so ?'

'Yes, it is so.'

'Listen then: serve me this once and I will give thee one last gift— thy freedom, and with it two hundred in silver.'

GROA BREWS A LOVE-POTION.

Koll's eyes glistened. 'What must I do, mistress?'

'To-day at the wedding-feast it will be thy part to pour the cups while Asmund calls the toasts. Last of all, when men are merry, thou wilt mix that cup in which Asmund shall pledge Unna his wife and Unna must pledge Asmund. Now, when thou hast poured, thou shalt pass the cup to me, as I stand at the foot of the high seat, waiting to give the bride greeting on behalf of the serving-women of the household. Thou shalt hand the cup to me as though in error, and that is but a little thing to ask of thee.'

'A little thing indeed,' said Koll, staring at her, and pulling with his hand at his red hair, 'yet I like it not. What if I say no, mistress?'

'Say no or speak of this and I will promise thee one thing only, thou knave, and it is, before winter comes, that the crows shall pick thy bones! Now, brave me, if thou darest,' and straightway Groa began to mutter witch-words.

'Nay,' said Koll, holding up his hand as though to ward away a blow. 'Curse me not: I will do as thou wilt. But when shall I touch the two hundred in silver?'

'I will give thee half before the feast begins, and half when it is ended, and with it freedom to go where thou wilt. And now leave me, and on thy life see that thou fail me not.'

'I have never failed thee yet,' said Koll, and went his ways.

Now Groa set the pot upon the fire, and, placing in it the herbs that she had gathered, poured water on them. Presently they began to boil and as they boiled she stirred them with a peeled stick and muttered spells over them. For long she sat in that dim and lonely place stirring the pot and muttering spells, till at length the brew was done.

She lifted the pot from the fire and smelt at it. Then drawing a phial from her robe she poured out the liquor and held it to the sky. The witch-water was white as milk, but presently it grew clear. She looked at it, then smiled evilly.

'Here is a love-draught for a queen—ah, a love-draught for a queen!' she said, and, still smiling, she placed the phial in her breast.

Then, having scattered the fire with her foot, Groa took the pot and threw it into a deep pool of water, where it could not be found readily, and crept back to the stead before men were awake.

Now the day wore on and all the company were gathered at the marriage-feast to the number of nearly two hundred. Unna sat in the high seat, and men thought her a bonny bride, and by her side sat Asmund the Priest. He was a hale, strong man to look at, though he had seen some three-score winters;

but his mien was sad and his heart heavy. He drank cup after cup to cheer him, but all without avail. For his thought sped back across the years and once more he seemed to see the face of Gudruda the Gentle as she lay dying, and to hear her voice when she foretold evil to him if he had aught to do with Groa the Witch-wife. And now it seemed to him that the evil was at hand, though whence it should come he did not know. He looked up. There Groa moved along the hall, ministering to the guests; but he saw as she moved that her eyes were always fixed, now on him and now on Unna. He remembered that curse also which Groa had called down upon him when he had told her that he was betrothed to Unna, and his heart grew cold with fear. 'Now I will change my counsel,' Asmund said to himself: 'Groa shall not stay here in this stead, for I will look no longer on that dark face of hers. She goes hence to-morrow.'

Not far from Asmund sat Björn, his son. As Gudruda the Fair, his sister, brought him mead he caught her by the sleeve, whispering in her ear. 'Methinks our father is sad. What weighs upon his heart?'

'I know not,' said Gudruda, but as she spoke she looked first on Asmund, then at Groa.

'It is ill that Groa should stop here,' whispered Björn again.

'It is ill,' answered Gudruda, and glided away.

Asmund saw their talk and guessed its purport. Rousing himself he laughed aloud and called to Koll the Half-witted to pour the cups that he might name the toasts.

Koll filled, and, as Asmund called the toasts one by one, Koll handed the cups to him. Asmund drank deep of each, till at length his sorrow passed from him, and, together with all who sat there, he grew merry.

Last of all came the toast of the bride's cup. But before Asmund called it, the women of the household drew near the high seat to welcome Unna, when she should have drunk. Gudruda stood foremost, and Groa was next to her.

Now Koll filled as before, and it was a great cup of gold that he filled.

Asmund rose to call the toast, and with him all who were in the hall. Koll brought up the cup, and handed it, not to Asmund, but to Groa; but there were few who noted this, for all were listening to Asmund's toast and most of the guests were somewhat drunken.

'The cup,' cried Asmund—'give me the cup that I may drink.'

Then Groa started forward, and as she did so she seemed to stumble, so that for a moment her robe covered up the great bride-cup. Then she gathered herself together slowly, and, smiling, passed up the cup.

Asmund lifted it to his lips and drank deep. Then he turned and gave it to Unna his wife, but before she drank he kissed her on the lips.

Now while all men shouted such a welcome that the hall shook, and as Unna, smiling, drank from the cup, the eyes of Asmund fell upon Groa who stood beneath him, and lo! her eyes seemed to flame and her face was hideous like the face of a troll.

Asmund grew white and put his hand to his head, as though to think, then cried aloud:

'Drink not, Unna! the draught is drugged!' and he struck at the vessel with his hand.

He smote it indeed, and so hard that it flew from her hold far down the hall.

But Unna had already drunk deep.

'The draught is drugged!' Asmund cried, and pointed to Groa, while all men stood silent, not knowing what to do.

'The draught is drugged!' he cried a third time, 'and that witch has drugged it!' And he began to tear at his breast.

Then Groa laughed so shrilly that men trembled to hear her.

'Yea, lord,' she screamed, 'the draught is drugged, and Groa the Witch-wife hath drugged it! Ay, tear thy heart out, Asmund, and, Unna, grow thou white as snow—soon, if my medicine has virtue, thou shalt be whiter yet! Hearken all men. Asmund the Priest is Swanhild's father, and for many a year I have been Asmund's mate. What did I tell thee, lord?—that I would see the two of you dead ere Unna should take my place!—ay, and on Gudruda the Fair, thy daughter, and Björn thy son, and Eric Brighteyes, Gudruda's love, and many another man—on them too shall my curse fall! Tear thy heart out, Asmund! Unna, grow thou white as snow! The draught is drugged and Groa, Ran's gift! Groa the witch-wife! Groa, Asmund's love! hath drugged it!'

And ere ever a man might lift a hand to stay her Groa glided past the high seat and was gone.

For a space all stood silent. Asmund ceased clutching at his breast. Rising he spoke heavily:

'Now I learn that sin is a stone to smite him who hurled it. Gudruda the Gentle spoke sooth when she warned me against this woman. *New wed, new dead!* Unna, fare thee well!'

And straightway Asmund fell down and died there by the high seat in his own hall.

Unna gazed at him with an ashen face. Then, plucking at her bosom, she sprang from the daïs and rushed along the hall, screaming. Men made way for her, and at the door she also fell dead.

This then was the end of Asmund Asmundson the Priest, and of Unna, Thorod's daughter, Eric's cousin, his new-made wife.

For a moment there was silence in the hall. But before the echoes of Unna's screams had died away, Björn called aloud:

'The witch! where is the witch?'

Then with a yell of rage, men leaped to their feet, seizing their weapons, and rushed from the stead. Out they ran. There, on the hill-side far above them, a black shape climbed and leapt swiftly. They gave tongue like dogs set upon a wolf and sped up the hill.

They gained the crest of the hill, and now they were at Goldfoss brink. Lo! the witch-wife had crossed the bed of the torrent, for little rain had fallen and the river was low.

She stood on Sheep-saddle, the water running from her robes. On Sheep-saddle she stood and cursed them.

Björn took a bow and set a shaft upon the string. He drew it and the arrow sung through the air and smote her, speeding through her heart. With a cry Groa threw up her arms.

Then down she plunged. She fell on Wolf's Fang, where Eric once had stood and, bounding thence, rushed to the boiling deeps below and was no more seen for ever.

Thus, then, did Asmund the Priest wed Unna, Thorod's daughter, and this was the end of the feasting.

Thereafter Björn, Asmund's son, ruled at Middalhof, and was Priest in his place. He sought for Koll the Half-witted to kill him, but Koll took to the fells, and after many months he found passage in a ship that was bound for Scotland.

Now Björn was a hard man and a greedy. He was no friend to Eric Brighteyes, and always pressed it on Gudruda that she should wed Ospakar Blacktooth. But to this counsel Gudruda would not listen, for day and night she thought upon her love. Next summer there came tidings that Eric was safe in Ireland, and men spoke of his deeds, and of how he and Skallagrim had swept the ship of Ospakar single-handed. Now after these tidings, for a while Gudruda walked singing through the meads, and no flower that grew in them was half so fair as she.

That summer also Ospakar Blacktooth met Björn, Asmund's son, at the Thing, and they talked much together in secret.

CHAPTER XVIII

HOW EARL ATLI FOUND ERIC AND SKALLAGRIM ON THE SOUTHERN ROCKS OF STRAUMEY ISLE

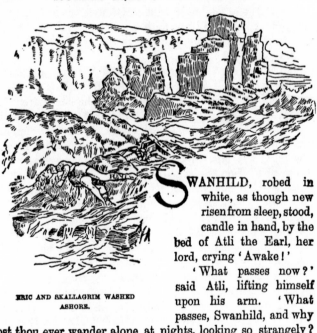

ERIC AND SKALLAGRIM WASHED ASHORE.

SWANHILD, robed in white, as though new risen from sleep, stood, candle in hand, by the bed of Atli the Earl, her lord, crying 'Awake!'

'What passes now?' said Atli, lifting himself upon his arm. 'What passes, Swanhild, and why dost thou ever wander alone at nights, looking so strangely? I love not thy dark witch-ways, Swanhild, and I was wed to thee in an ill hour, wife who art no wife.'

'In an ill hour indeed, Earl Atli,' she answered, 'an ill hour for thee and me, for, as thou hast said, eld and youth are strange yokefellows and pull different paths. Arise now, Earl, for I have dreamed a dream.'

'Tell it to me on the morrow, then,' quoth Atli; 'there is small joyousness in thy dreams, that always point to evil, and I must bear enough evil of late.'

'Nay, lord, my rede may not be put aside so. Listen now : I have dreamed that a great dragon of war has been cast away upon Straumey's south-western rocks. The cries of those who drowned rang in my ears. But I thought that some came living to the shore, and lie there senseless, to perish of the cold. Arise, therefore, take men and go down to the rocks.'

'I will go at daybreak,' said Atli, letting his head fall upon the pillow. 'I have little faith in such visions, and it is too late in the year for long ships of war to try the passage of the Firth.'

'Arise, I say,' answered Swanhild sternly, 'and do my bidding, else I will myself go to search the rocks.'

Then Atli rose grumbling, and shook the heavy sleep from his eyes : for of all living folk he most feared Swanhild his wife. He donned his garments, threw a thick cloak about him, and, going to the hall where men snored around the dying fires, for the night was bitter, he awoke some of them. Now among those men whom he called was Hall of Lithdale, Hall the mate who had cut the grapnel-chain. For this Hall, fearing to return to Iceland, had come hither saying that he had been wounded off Fareys, in the great fight between Eric and Ospakar's men, and left there to grow well of his hurt or die. Then Atli, not knowing that the carle lied, had bid him welcome for Eric's sake, for he still loved Eric above all men.

But Hall loved not labour and nightfarings to search for shipwrecked men of whom the Lady Swanhild had chanced to dream. So he turned himself upon his side and slept again. Still, certain of Atli's folk rose at his bidding, and they went together down to the south-western rocks.

But Swanhild, a cloak thrown over her night-gear, sat herself in the high seat of the hall and fixing her eyes, now upon the dying fires and now upon the blood-marks in her arm, waited in silence. The night was cold and windy, but the moon

shone bright, and by its light Atli and his people made their
way to the south-western rocks, on which the sea beat madly.

'What lies yonder?' said Atli, pointing to some black thing
that lay beneath them upon the rock, cast there by the waves.
A man climbed down the cliff's side that is here as though it
were cut in steps, and then cried aloud :

'A ship's mast, new broken, lord.'

'It seems that Swanhild dreams true,' muttered Atli;
'but I am sure of this : that none have come ashore alive in
such a sea.'

Presently the man who searched the rocks below cried
aloud again :

'Here lie two great men, locked in each other's arms.
They seem to be dead.'

Now all the men climb down the slippery rocks as best they
may, though the spray wets them, and with them goes Atli. The
Earl is a brisk man, though old in years, and he comes first to
where the two lie. He who was undermost lay upon his back, but
his face was hid by the thick golden hair that flowed across it.

'Man's body indeed, but woman's locks,' said Atli as he
put out his hand and drew the hair away, so that the light of
the moon fell on the face beneath.

He looked, then staggered back against the rock.

'By Thor !' he cried, 'here lies the corpse of Eric Brighteyes !' and Atli wrung his hands and wept, for he loved Eric
much.

'Be not so sure that the men are dead, Earl,' said one,
'I thought I saw yon great carle move but now.'

'He is Skallagrim Lambstail, Eric's Death-shadow,' said
Atli again. 'Up with them, lads—see, yonder lies a plank—and
away to the hall. I will give twenty in silver to each of you
if Eric lives,' and he unclasped his cloak and threw it over
both of them.

Then with much labour they loosed the grip of the two
men one from the other, and they set Skallagrim on the plank.
But eight men bore Eric up the cliff between them, and the
task was not light, though the Earl held his head, from which
the golden hair hung like seaweed from a rock.

At length they came to the hall and carried them in. Swan-hild, seeing them come, moved down from the high seat.

'Bring lamps, and pile up the fires,' cried Atli. 'A strange thing has come to pass, Swanhild, and thou dost dream wisely, indeed, for here we have Eric Brighteyes and Skallagrim Lambstail. They were locked like lovers in each other's arms, but I know not if they are dead or living.'

Now Swanhild started and came on swiftly. Had the Familiar tricked her and had she paid the price for nothing? Was Eric taken from Gudruda and given to her indeed—but given dead? She bent over him, gazing keenly on his face. Then she spoke.

'He is not dead but senseless. Bring dry cloths, and make water hot,' and, kneeling down, she loosed Eric's helm and harness and ungirded Whitefire from his side.

For long Swanhild and Atli tended Eric at one fire, and the serving women tended Skallagrim at the other. Presently there came a cry that Skallagrim stirred, and Atli with others ran to see. At this moment also the eyes of Eric were unsealed, and Swanhild saw them looking at her dimly from beneath. Then, moved to it by her passion and her joy that he yet lived, Swan-hild let her face fall till his was hidden in her unbound hair, and kissed him upon the lips. Eric shut his eyes again, sighing heavily, and presently he was asleep. They bore him to a bed and heaped warm wrappings upon him. At daybreak he woke, and Atli, who sat watching by his side, gave him hot mead to drink.

'Do I dream?' said Eric, 'or is it Earl Atli who tends me, and did I but now see the face of Swanhild bending over me?'

'It is no dream, Eric, but the truth. Thou hast been cast away here on my isle of Straumey.'

'And Skallagrim—where is Skallagrim?'

'Skallagrim lives—fear not!'

'And my comrades, how went it with them?'

'But ill, Eric. Ran has them all. Now sleep!'

Eric groaned aloud. 'I had rather died also than live to hear such heavy tidings,' he said. 'Witch-work! witch-work! and that fair witch-face wrought it.' And once again he slept,

nor did he wake till the sun was high. But Atli could make
nothing of his words.

When Swanhild left the side of Eric she met Hall of Lithdale face to face and his looks were troubled.

'Say, lady,' he asked, ' will Brighteyes live? '

'Grieve not, Hall,' she answered, 'Eric will surely live and
he will be glad to find a messmate here to greet him, having
left so many yonder,' and she pointed to the sea.

'I shall not be glad,' said Hall, letting his eyes fall.

'Why not, Hall? Fearest thou Skallagrim? or hast
thou done ill by Eric? '

'Ay, lady, I fear Skallagrim, for he swore to slay me, and
that kind of promise he ever keeps. Also, if the truth must
out, I have not dealt altogether well by Eric, and of all men
I least wish to talk with him.'

'Speak on,' she said.

Then, being forced to it, Hall told her something of the tale
of the cutting of the cable, being careful to put another colour
on it.

'Now it seems that thou art a coward, Hall,' Swanhild said
when he had done, ' and I scarcely looked for that in thee,' for
she had not been deceived by the glozing of his speech. 'It
will be bad for thee to meet Eric and Skallagrim, and this is
my counsel: that thou goest hence before they wake, for they
will sit this winter here in Atli's hall.'

'And whither shall I go, lady? '

Swanhild gazed on him, and as she did so a dark thought
came into her heart: here was a knave who might serve her
ends.

'Hall,' she said, ' thou art an Icelander, and I have known
of thee from a child, and therefore I wish to serve thee in
thy strait, though thou deservest it little. See now, Atli
the Earl has a farm on the mainland not two hours' ride from
the sea. Thither thou shalt go, if thou art wise, and thou
shalt sit there this winter and be hidden from Eric and Skallagrim. Nay, thank me not, but listen: it may chance that I
shall have a service for thee to do before spring is come.'

'Lady, I shall wait upon thy word,' said Hall.

'Good. Now, so soon as it is light, I will find a man to sail with thee across the Firth, for the sea falls, and bear my message to the steward at Atli's farm. Also if thou needest faring-money thou shalt have it. Farewell.'

Thus then did Hall fly before Eric and Skallagrim.

On the morrow Eric and Skallagrim arose, sick and bruised indeed, but not at all harmed, and went down to the shore. There they found many dead men of their company, but never a one in whom the breath of life remained.

Skallagrim looked at Eric and spoke: 'Last night the mist came up against the wind : last night we saw Swanhild's wraith upon the waves, and yonder is the path it showed, and there'—and he pointed to the dead men—'is the witch-seed's flower. Now to-day we sit in Atli's hall and here we must stay this winter at Swanhild's side, and in all this lies a riddle that I cannot read.'

Eric shook his head, making no answer. Then, leaving Skallagrim with the dead, he turned, and striding back alone towards the hall, sat down on a rock in the home meadows, and, covering his face with his hands, he wept for his comrades.

As he wept Swanhild came to him, for she had seen him from afar, and touched him gently on the arm.

'Why weepest thou, Eric ? ' she said.

'I weep for the dead, Swanhild,' he answered.

'Weep not for the dead—they are at peace ; if thou must weep, weep for the living. Nay, weep not at all ; rejoice rather that thou art here to mourn. Hast thou no word of greeting for me who have not heard thy voice these many months ? '

'How shall I greet thee, Swanhild, who would never have seen thy face again if I might have had my will ? Knowest thou that yesternight, as our ship laboured in yonder Firth, we saw a shape walking the waters to lead us to our doom ? How shall I greet thee, Swanhild, who art a witch and evil ? '

'And knowest thou, Eric, that yesternight I woke from sleep, having dreamed that thou didst lie upon the shore, and thus I saved thee alive, as perchance I have saved thee aforetime? If thou didst see a shape walking the waters it was that shape which led thee here. Hadst thou sailed on, not only those thou mournest, but Skallagrim and thou thyself had now been numbered with the lost.'

'Better so than thus,' said Brighteyes. 'Knowest thou also, Swanhild, that when last night my life came back again in Atli's hall, methought that Atli's wife leaned over me and kissed me on the lips? That was an ill dream, Swanhild.'

'Some had found it none so ill, Eric,' she made answer, looking at him strangely. 'Still, it was but a dream. Thou didst dream that Atli's wife breathed back the breath of life into thy pale lips—be sure of it thou didst but dream. Ah, Eric, fear me no more; forget the evil that I have wrought in the blindness and folly of my youth. Now things are otherwise with me. Now I am a wedded wife and faithful hearted to my lord. Now, if I still love thee, it is with a sister's love. Therefore forget my sins, remember only that as children we played upon the Iceland fells. Remember that, as boy and girl, we rode along the marshes, while the sea-mews clamoured round our heads. The world is cold, Eric, and few are the friends we find in it; many are already gone, and soon the friend-less dark draws near. So put me not away, my brother and my friend; but, for a little space, whilst thou art here in Atli's hall, let us walk hand in hand as we walked long years ago in Iceland, gathering the fifa-bloom, and watching the mid-night shadows creep up the icy jökul's crests.'

Thus Swanhild spoke to him most sweetly, in a low voice of music, while the tears gathered in her eyes, talking ever of Iceland that he loved, and of days long dead, till Eric's heart softened in him.

'Almost do I believe thee, Swanhild,' he said, stretching out his hand; 'but I know this: that thou art never twice in the same mood, and that is beyond my measuring. Thou hast done much evil and thou hast striven to do more; also I love not those who seem to walk the seas o' nights. Still, hold thou to this last saying of thine and there shall be peace between us while I bide here.'

She touched his hand humbly and turned to go. But as

she went Eric spoke again : 'Say, Swanhild, hast thou tidings
from Iceland yonder? I have heard no word of Asmund or
of Gudruda for two long years and more.'

She stood still, and a dark shadow that he could not see
flitted across her face.

'I have few tidings, Eric,' she said, turning, 'and those
few, if I may trust them, bad enough. For this is the rumour
that I have heard : that Asmund the Priest, my father, is dead ;
that Groa my mother is dead—how, I know not; and, lastly,
that Gudruda the Fair, thy love, is betrothed to Ospakar Blacktooth and weds him in the spring.'

Now Eric sprang up with an oath and grasped the hilt of
Whitefire. Then he sat down again upon the stone and
covered his face with his hands.

'Grieve not, Eric,' she said gently; 'I put no faith in
this news, for rumour, like the black-backed gull, often
changes colour in its flight across the seas. Also I had it
but at fifth hand. I am sure of this, at least, that Gudruda
will never forsake thee without a cause.'

'It shall go ill with Ospakar if this be true,' said Eric,
smiling grimly, 'for Whitefire is yet left me and with it one
true friend.'

'Run not to meet the evil, Eric. Thou shalt come to Iceland with the summer flowers and find Gudruda faithful and
yet fairer than of yore. Knowest thou that Hall of Lithdale,
who was thy mate, has sat here these two months? He is
gone but this morning, I know not whither, leaving a message
that he returns no more.'

'He did well to go,' said Eric, and he told her how Hall
had cut the cable.

'Ay, well indeed,' answered Swanhild. 'Had Atli known
this he would have scourged Hall hence with rods of seaweed.
And now, Eric, I desire to ask thee one more thing : why
wearest thou thy hair long like a woman's? Indeed, few
women have such hair as thine is now.'

'For this cause, Swanhild : I swore to Gudruda that none
should cut my hair till she cut it once more. It is a great burden to me surely, for never did hair grow so fast and strong as

mine, and once in a fray I was held fast by it and went near
to the losing of my life.   Still, I will keep the oath even if it
grows on to my feet,' and he laughed a little and shook back
his golden locks.

Swanhild smiled also and, turning, went.   But when her
face was hidden from him she smiled no more.

' As I live,' she said in her heart, ' before spring rains fall
again I will cause thee to break this oath, Eric.   Ay, I will
cut a lock of that bright hair of thine and send it for a love-
token to Gudruda.'

But Eric still sat upon the rock thinking.   Swanhild had set
an evil seed of doubt in his heart, and already it put forth roots.
What if the tale were true?   What if Gudruda had given herself to Ospakar ?   Well, if so—she should soon be a widow, that
he swore.

Then he rose, and stalked grimly towards the hall.

CHAPTER XIX

HOW KOLL THE HALF-WITTED BROUGHT TIDINGS FROM ICELAND

THE BROKEN LOVE-TOKEN.

RESENTLY as Eric walked he met Atli the Earl seeking him. Atli greeted him.

'I have seen strange things happen, Eric,' he said, 'but none more strange than this coming of thine and the manner of it. Swanhild is fore-sighted, and that was a doom-dream of hers.'

'I think her fore-sighted also,' said Eric. 'And now, Earl, knowest thou this: that little good can come to thee at the hands of one whom thou hast saved from the sea.'

'I set no faith in such old wives' tales,' answered Atli. 'Here thou art come, and it is my will that thou shouldest sit here. At the least, I will give thee no help to go hence.'

'Then we must bide in Straumey, it seems,' said Eric: 'for of all my goods and gear this alone is left me,' and he looked at Whitefire.

'Thou hast still a gold ring or two upon thy arm,' answered the Earl, laughing. 'But surely, Eric, thou wouldst not begone?'

'I know not, Earl. Listen: it is well that I should be

plain with thee. Once, before thou didst wed Swanhild, she had another mind.'

'I have heard something of that, and I have guessed more, Brighteyes; but methinks Swanhild is little given to gadding now. She is as cold as ice, and no good wife for any man,' and Atli sighed, '"Snow melts not if sun shines not," so runs the saw. Thou art an honest man, Eric, and no whisperer in the ears of others' wives.'

'I am not minded indeed to do thee such harm, Earl, but this thou knowest: that woman's guile and beauty are swords few shields can brook. Now I have spoken—and they are hard words to speak—be it as thou wilt.'

'It is my will that thou shouldest sit here this winter, Eric. Had I my way, indeed, never wouldest thou sit elsewhere. Listen: things have not gone well with me of late. Age hath a grip of me, and foes rise up against one who has no sons. That was an ill marriage, too, which I made with Swanhild yonder: for she loves me not, and I have found no luck since first I saw her face. Moreover, it is in my mind that my days are almost sped. Swanhild has already foretold my death, and, as thou knowest well, she is foresighted. So I pray thee, Eric, bide thou here while thou mayest, for I would have thee at my side.'

'It shall be as thou wilt, Earl,' said Eric.

So Eric Brighteyes and Skallagrim Lambstail sat that winter in the hall of Atli the Earl at Straumey. For many weeks all things went well and Eric forgot his fears. Swanhild was gentle to him and kindly. She loved much to talk with him, even of Gudruda her rival; but no word of love passed her lips. Nevertheless, she did but bide her time, for when she struck she determined to strike home. Atli and Eric were ever side by side, and Eric gave the Earl much good counsel. He promised to do this also, for now, being simple-minded, his doubts had passed and he had no more fear of Swanhild. On the mainland lived a certain chief who had seized large lands of Atli's, and held them for a year or more. Now Eric gave his word that, before he sailed for Iceland in the early summer, he would go up against this man and drive him from the lands, if he could. For Brighteyes might not come to Iceland till hard upon midsummer, when his three years of outlawry were spent.

The winter wore away and the spring came. Then Atli gathered his men and went with Eric in boats to where the chief dwelt who held his lands. There they fell on him and that was a fierce fight. But in the end the man was slain by Skallagrim, and Eric did great deeds, as was his wont. Now in this fray Eric was wounded in the foot by a spear, so that he must be borne back to Straumey, and he lay there in the hall for many days. Swanhild nursed him, and often he sat talking with her in her bower.

When Eric was nearly healed of his hurt, the Earl went with all his people to a certain island of the Orkneys to gather scat [1] that was unpaid, and Skallagrim went with him. But Eric did not go, because of his hurt, fearing lest the wound should open if he walked overmuch. Thus it came to pass that, except for some women, he was left almost alone with Swanhild.

Now, when Atli had been gone three days, it chanced on an afternoon that Swanhild heard how a man from Iceland sought speech with her. She bade them bring him in to where she was alone in her bower, for Eric was not there, having gone down to the sea to fish.

The man came and she knew him at once for Koll the Half-witted, who had been her mother Groa's thrall. On his shoulders was the cloak that Ospakar Blacktooth gave him; it was much torn now, and he had a worn and hungry look.

'Whence comest thou, Koll?' she asked, 'and what are thy tidings?'

'From Scotland last, lady, where I sat this winter; before that, from Iceland. As for my tidings, they are heavy, if thou hast not heard them. Asmund the Priest is dead, and dead is Unna his wife, poisoned by thy mother, Groa, at their marriage-feast. Dead, too, is thy mother, Groa. Björn, Asmund's

[1] Tribute.

son, shot her with an arrow, and she lies in Goldfoss
pool.'

Now Swanhild hid her face for a while in her hands.
Then she lifted it and it was white to see. 'Speakest thou
truth, fox? If thou liest, this I swear—thy tongue shall be
dragged from thee by the roots!'

'I speak the truth, lady,' he answered. But still he spoke
not all the truth, for he said nothing of the part which he had
played in the deaths of Asmund and Unna. Then he told
her of the manner of their end.

Swanhild listened silently—then said:

'What news of Gudruda, Asmund's daughter? Is she
wed?'

'Nay, lady. Folk spoke of her and Ospakar, that was
all.'

'Hearken, Koll,' said Swanhild, 'bearing such heavy tidings,
canst thou not weight the ship a little more? Eric Brighteyes
is here. Canst thou not swear to him that, when thou didst
leave Iceland it was said without question that Gudruda had
betrothed herself to Ospakar, and that the wedding-feast was
set for this last Yule? Thou hast a hungry look, Koll, and
it seems that things have not gone altogether well with thee
of late. Now, if thou canst so charge thy memory, thou shalt
lose little by it. But, if thou canst not, then thou goest hence
from Straumey with never a luck-penny in thy purse, and
never a sup to stay thy stomach.'

Now of all things Koll least desired to be sent from
Straumey; for, though Swanhild did not know it, he was
sought for on the mainland as a thief.

'That I may do, lady,' he said, looking at her cunningly.
'Now I remember that Gudruda the Fair charged me with
a certain message for Eric Brighteyes, if I should chance to
see him as I journeyed.'

Then Swanhild, Atli's wife, and Koll the Half-witted talked
long and earnestly together.

At nightfall Eric came in from his fishing. His heart
was light, for the time drew near when he should sail for

home, and he did not think on evil. For now he feared
Swanhild no longer, and, no fresh tidings having come from
Iceland about Ospakar and Gudruda, he had almost put the
matter from his mind. On he walked to the hall, limping
somewhat from his wound, but singing as he came, and bearing
his fish slung upon a pole.

At the men's door of the hall a woman stood waiting.
She told Eric that the Lady Swanhild wished to speak with
him in her bower. Thither he went and knocked. Getting
no answer he knocked again, then entered.

Swanhild sat on a couch. She was weeping, and her hair
fell about her face.

'What now, Swanhild?' he said.

She looked up heavily. 'Ill news for thee and me, Eric.
Koll, who was my mother's thrall, has come hither from Iceland, and these are his tidings: that Asmund is dead, and
Unna, thy cousin, Thorod of Greenfell's daughter, is dead, and
my mother Groa is dead also.'

'Heavy tidings, truly!' said Eric; 'and what of Gudruda,
is she also dead?'

'Nay, Eric, she is wed—wed to Ospakar.'

Now Eric reeled against the wall, clutching it, and for a
space all things swam round him. 'Where is this Koll?' he
gasped. 'Send me Koll hither.'

Presently he came, and Eric questioned him coldly and
calmly. But Koll could lie full well. It is said that in his
day there was no one in Iceland who could lie so well as Koll
the Half-witted. He told Eric how it was said that Gudruda
was plighted to Ospakar, and how the match had been agreed
on at the Althing in the summer that was gone (and indeed
there had been some such talk), and how that the feast was
to be at Middalhof on last Yule Day.

'Is that all thy tidings?' said Eric. 'If so, I give no
heed to them: for ever, Koll, I have known thee for a liar!'

'Nay, Eric, it is not all,' answered Koll. 'As it chanced,
two days before the ship in which I sailed was bound, I saw
Gudruda the Fair. Then she asked me whither I was going,
and I told her that I would journey to London, where men

said thou wert, and asked her if she desired to send a message. Then she alighted from her horse, Blackmane, and spoke with me apart. 'Koll,' she said, 'it well may happen that thou wilt see Eric Brighteyes in London town. Now, if thou seest him, I charge thee straightly tell him this. Tell him that my father is dead, and my brother Björn, who rules in his place, is a hard man, and has ever urged me on to wed Ospakar, till at last, having no choice, I have consented to it. And say to Eric that I grieve much and sorely, and that, though we twain should never meet more, yet I shall always hold his memory dear.'

'It is not like Gudruda to speak thus,' said Eric : 'she had ever a stout heart and these are craven words. Koll, I hold that thou liest ; and, if indeed I find it so, I'll wring the head from off thee ! '

'Nay, Eric, I lie not. Wherefore should I lie ? Hearken : thou hast not heard all my tale. When the lady Gudruda had made an end of speaking she drew something from her breast and gave it me, saying : " Give this to Eric, in witness of my words." '

' Show me the token,' said Eric.

Now, many years ago, when they were yet boy and girl, it chanced that Eric had given to Gudruda the half of an ancient gold piece that he had found upon the shore. He had given her half, and half he had kept, wearing it next his heart. But he did not know, for she feared to tell him, that Gudruda had lost her half. Nor indeed had she lost it, for Swanhild had taken the love-token and hidden it away. Now she brought it forth for Koll to build his lies upon.

Then Koll drew out the half piece from a leather purse and passed it to him. Eric plunged his hand into his breast and found his half. He placed the two side by side, while Swanhild watched him. Lo ! they fitted well.

Then Eric laughed aloud, a hard and bitter laugh. ' There will be slaying,' he cried, ' before all this tale is told. Take thy fee and begone, thou messenger of ill,' and he cast the broken piece at Koll. ' For once thou hast spoken the truth.'

Koll stooped, found the gold and went, leaving Brighteyes and Swanhild face to face.

He hid his brow in his arms and groaned aloud. Softly Swanhild crept up to him—softly she drew his hands away, holding them between her own.

'Heavy tidings, Eric,' she said, 'heavy tidings for thee and me! She is a murderess who gave me birth and she has slain my own father—my father and thy cousin Unna also. Gudruda is a traitress, a traitress fair and false. I did ill to be born of such a woman; thou didst ill to put thy faith in such a woman. Together let us weep, for our woe is equal.'

'Ay, let us weep together,' Eric answered. 'Nay, why should we weep? Together let us be merry, for we know the worst. All words are said—all hopes are sped! Let us be merry, then, for now we have no more tidings to fear.'

'Ay,' Swanhild answered, looking on him darkly, 'we will be merry and laugh our sorrows down. Ah! thou foolish Eric, under what unlucky star wast thou born that thou knewest not true from false?' and she called the serving-women, bidding them bring food and wine.

Now Eric sat alone with Swanhild in her bower and made pretence to eat. But he could eat little, though he drank deep of the southern wine. Close beside him sat Swanhild, filling his cup. She was wondrous fair that night, and it seemed to Eric that her eyes gleamed like stars. Sweetly she spoke also and wisely. She told strange tales and she sang strange songs, and ever her eyes shone more and more, and ever she crept closer to him. Eric's brain was afire, though his heart was cold and dead. He laughed loud and mightily, he told great tales of deeds that he had done, growing boastful in his folly, and still Swanhild's eyes shone more and more, and still she crept closer, wooing him in many ways.

Now of a sudden Eric thought of his friend, Earl Atli, and his mind grew clear.

'This may not be, Swanhild,' he said. 'Yet I would that I had loved thee from the first, and not the false Gudruda: for, with all thy dark ways, at least thou art better than she.'

'Thou speakest wisely, Eric,' Swanhild answered, though she did not mean that he should go. 'The Norns have appointed us an evil fate, giving me as wife to an old man whom I do not love, and thee for a lover to a woman who has betrayed thee. Ah, Eric Brighteyes, thou foolish Eric! why knewest thou not the false from the true while yet there was time? Now are all words said and all things done—nor can they be undone. Go hence, Eric, ere ill come of it; but before thou goest, drink one cup of parting, and then farewell.'

And she slipped from him and filled the cup, mixing in it a certain love-potion that she had made ready.

'Give it me that I may swear an oath on it,' said Eric.

Swanhild gave him the cup and stood before him, watching him.

'Hearken,' he said: 'I swear this, that before snow falls again in Iceland I will see Ospakar dead at my feet or lie dead at the feet of Ospakar.'

'Well spoken, Eric,' Swanhild answered. 'Now, before thou drinkest, grant me one little boon. It is but a woman's fancy, and thou canst scarce deny me. The years will be long when thou art gone, for from this night it is best that we should meet no more, and I would keep something of thee to call back thy memory and the memories of our youth when thou hast passed away and I grow old.'

'What wouldst have then, Swanhild? I have nothing left to give, except Whitefire alone.'

'I do not ask Whitefire, Eric, though Whitefire shall kiss the gift. I ask nothing but one tress of that golden hair of thine.'

'Once I swore that none should touch my hair again except Gudruda's self.'

'It will grow long, then, Eric, for now Gudruda tends black locks and thinks little on golden. Broken are all oaths.'

Eric groaned. 'All oaths are broken in sooth,' he said. 'Have then thy will;' and, loosing the peace-strings, he drew Whitefire from its sheath and gave her the great war-sword.

Swanhild took it by the hilt, and, lifting a tress of Eric's yellow hair, she shore through it deftly with Whitefire's razor edge, smiling as she shore. With the same war-blade on which Eric and Gudruda pledged their troth, did Swanhild cut the locks that Eric had sworn no hand should clip except Gudruda's.

He took back the sword and sheathed it, and, knotting the long tress, Swanhild hid it in her bosom.

' Now drink the cup, Eric,' she said—' pledge me and go.'

Eric drank to the dregs and cast the cup down, and lo ! all things changed to him, for his blood was afire, and seas seemed to roll within his brain. Only before him stood Swanhild like a shape of light and glory, and he thought that she sang softly over him, always drawing nearer, and that with her came a scent of flowers like the scent of the Iceland meads in May.

' All oaths are broken, Eric,' she murmured, ' all oaths are broken indeed, and now must new oaths be sworn. For cut is thy golden hair, Brighteyes, and not by Gudruda's hand ! '

CHAPTER XX

HOW ERIC WAS NAMED ANEW

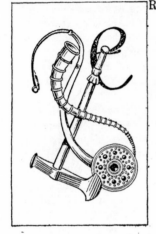

RIC dreamed. He dreamed that Gudruda stood by him looking at him with soft, sad eyes, while with her hand she pointed to his hair, and spake.

'Thou hast done ill, Eric,' she seemed to say. ' Thou hast done ill to doubt me ; and now thou art for ever shamed, for thou hast betrayed Atli, thy friend. Thou hast broken thy oath, and therefore hast thou fallen into this pit ; for when Swanhild shore that lock of thine, my watching Spirit passed, leaving thee to Swanhild and thy fate. Now, I tell thee this : that shame shall lead to shame, and many lives shall pay forfeit for thy sin, Eric.'

Eric awoke, thinking that this was indeed an evil dream which he had dreamed. He woke, and lo! by him was Swanhild, Atli's wife. He looked upon her beauty, and fear and shame crept into his heart, for now he knew that it was no dream, but he was lost indeed. He looked again at Swanhild, and hatred and loathing of her shook him. She had overcome him by her arts ; that cup was drugged which he had drunk, and he was mad with grief. Yes, she had played upon his woe like a harper on a harp, and now he was shamed—now he had betrayed his friend who loved him! Had White-fire been to his hand at that moment, Eric had surely slain himself. But the great sword was not there, for it hung in Swanhild's bower. Eric groaned aloud, and Swanhild turned at the sound. But he sprang away and stood over her, cursing her.

'Thou witch!' he cried, 'what hast thou done? What didst thou mix in that cup yestre'en? Thou hast brought me to this that I have betrayed Atli, my friend—Atli, thy lord, who left thee in my keeping!'

He seemed so terrible in his woe and rage that Swanhild shrank from him, and, throwing her hair about her face, peeped at him through its meshes as once she had peeped at Asmund.

'It is like a man,' she said, gathering up her courage and her wit; ''tis like a man, having won my love, now to turn upon me and upbraid me. Fie upon thee, Eric! thou hast dealt ill with me to bring me to this.'

Now Eric ceased his raving, and spoke more calmly.

'Well thou knowest the truth, Swanhild,' he said.

'Hearken, Eric,' she answered. 'Let this be secret between us. Atli is old, and methinks that not for long shall he bide here in Straumey. Soon he will die; it is upon my mind that he will die quickly, and, being childless, his lands and goods pass to me. Then, Eric, thou shalt sit in Atli's hall, and in all honour shall Atli's wife become thy bride.'

Eric listened coldly. 'I can well believe,' he said, 'that thou hast it in thy thoughts to slay thy lord, for all evil is in thy heart, Swanhild. Now know this: that if in honour or dishonour my lips touch that fair face of thine again, may the limbs rot from my trunk, and may I lie a log for ever in the halls of Hela! If ever my eyes of their own will look again upon thy beauty, may I go blind and beg my meat from homestead to homestead! If ever my tongue whisper word of love into thy ears, may dumbness seize it, and may it wither to the root!'

Swanhild heard and sank upon the ground before him, her head bowed almost to her feet.

'Now, Swanhild, fare thee well,' said Eric. 'Living or dead, may I never see thy face again!'

She gazed up through her falling hair; her face was wild and white, and her eyes glowed in it as live embers glow in the ashes of burnt wood.

'We are not so easily parted, Eric,' she said. 'Not for this came I to witchcraft and to sin. Thou fool! hast thou never heard that, of all the foes a man may have, none is so terrible as the woman he has scorned? Thou shalt learn this lesson, Eric Brighteyes, Thorgrimur's son : for here we have but the beginning of the tale. Its end I will write in runes of blood.'

'Write on,' said Eric. 'Thou canst do no worse than thou hast done,' and he passed thence.

For a while Swanhild crouched upon the ground, brooding in silence. Then she rose, and, throwing up her arms, wept aloud.

'Is it for this that I have sold my soul to the Hell-hag?' she cried. 'Is it for this that I have become a witch, and sunk so low as I sank last night—to be scorned, to be hated, to be betrayed? Now Eric will go to Atli and tell this tale. Nay, there I will be beforehand with him, and with another story—an ancient wile of women truly, but one that never yet has failed them, nor ever will. And then for vengeance! I will see thee dead, Eric, and dead will I see Gudruda at thy side! Afterwards let darkness come—ay, though the Horror rides it! Swift!—I must be swift!'

Eric passed into Swanhild's bower, and finding Whitefire bore it thence. On the table was food. He took it. Then, going to the place where he was wont to sleep, he armed himself, girding his byrnie on his breast and his golden helm upon his head, and taking shield and spear in his hand. Then he passed out. By the men's door he found some women spreading fish in the sun. Eric greeted them, saying that when the Earl came back, for he was to come on that morning, he would find him on the south-western rocks nigh to where the Gudruda sank. This he begged of them to tell Atli, for he desired speech with him.

P

The women wondered that Brighteyes should go forth thus and fully armed, but, holding that he had some deed to do, they said nothing.

Eric came to the rocks, and there he sat all day long looking on the sea, and grieving so bitterly that he thought his heart would burst within him. For of all the days of Eric's life this was the heaviest, except one other only.

But Swanhild, going to her bower, caused Koll the Half-witted to be summoned. To him she spoke long and earnestly, and they made a shameful plot together. Then she bade Koll watch for Atli's coming and, when he saw the Earl leave his boats, to run to him and say that she wished to speak with him.

After this Swanhild sent a man across the firth to the stead where Hall of Lithdale sat, bidding him come to her at once.

When the afternoon grew towards the evening, Koll, watching, saw the boats of Atli draw to the landing-place. Then he went down, and, going to the Earl, bowed before him:

'What wouldst thou, fellow, and who art thou?' asked Atli.

'I am a man from Iceland; perchance, lord, thou sawest me in Asmund's hall at Middalhof. I am sent here by the Lady Swanhild to say that she desires speech with thee, and that at once.' Then, seeing Skallagrim, Koll fled back to the house, for he feared Skallagrim.

Now Atli was uneasy in his mind, and, saying nothing, he hurried up to the hall, and through it into Swanhild's bower.

There she sat on a couch, her eyes red with weeping, and her curling hair unbound.

'What now, Swanhild?' he asked. 'Why lookest thou thus?'

'Why look I thus, my lord?' she answered heavily. 'Because I have to tell thee that which I cannot find words to fit,' and she ceased.

'Speak on,' he said. 'Is aught wrong with Eric?'

Then Swanhild drew near and told him a false tale.

When it was done for a moment or so Atli stood still, and

grew white beneath his ruddy skin, white as his beard. Then
he staggered back against the wainscotting of the bower.

'Woman, thou liest!' he said. 'Never will I believe so
vile a thing of Eric Brighteyes, whom I have loved.'

'Would that I could not believe it!' she answered. 'Would
that I could think it was but an evil dream! But alas! it is
no dream. That which I tell thee, this man has done.
Nay, I will prove it. Suffer that I summon Koll, the Icelander, who was my mother's thrall—Groa who now is dead,
for I have that tidings also. He saw something of this thing,
and he will bear me witness.'

'Call the man,' said Atli sternly.

So Koll was summoned, and told his lies with a bold face.
He was so well taught, and so closely did his story tally with
that of Swanhild, that Atli could find no flaw in it.

'Now I am sure, Swanhild, that thou speakest truth,' said
the Earl when Koll had gone. 'And now also I have somewhat to say to this Eric. For thee, rest thyself; that which
cannot be mended must be borne,' and he went out.

Now, when Skallagrim came to the house he asked for
Eric. The women told him that Brighteyes had gone down to
the sea, fully armed, in the morning, and had not returned.

'Then there must be fighting toward, and that I am loth
to miss,' said Skallagrim, and, axe aloft, he started for the
south-western rocks at a run. Skallagrim came to the rocks.
There he found Eric, sitting in his harness, looking out across
the sea. The evening was wet and windy; the rain beat
upon him as he sat, but Eric took no heed.

'What seekest thou, lord?' asked the Baresark.

'Rest,' said Eric, 'and I find none.'

'Thou seekest rest helm on head and sword in hand?
This is a strange thing, truly!'

'Stranger things have been, Skallagrim. Wouldst thou
hear a tale?' and he told him all.

'What said I?' asked Skallagrim. 'We had fared better
in London town. Flying from the dove thou hast found the
falcon.'

'I have found the falcon, comrade, and she has pecked out my eyes. Now I would speak with Atli, and then I go hence.'

'Hence go the twain of us, lord. The Earl will be here presently and rough words will fly in this rough weather. Is Whitefire sharp, Brighteyes?'

'Whitefire was sharp enough to shear my hair, Skallagrim; but if Atli would strike let him lay on. Whitefire will not be aloft for him.'

'That we shall see,' said Skallagrim. 'At least, if thou art harmed because of this loose quean, my axe will be aloft.'

'Keep thou thine axe in its place,' said Eric, and as he spoke Atli came, and with him many men.

Eric rose and turned to meet the Earl, looking on him with sad eyes. Atli's face was as the face of a trapped wolf, for he was mad with rage at the shame that had been put upon him and the ill tale that Swanhild had told of Eric's dealings with her.

'It seems that the Earl has heard of these tidings,' said Skallagrim.

'Then I shall be spared the telling of them,' answered Eric.

Now they stood face to face; Atli leaned upon his drawn sword, and his wrath was so fierce that for a while he could not speak. At length he found words.

'See ye that man, comrades?' he said, pointing at Eric with the sword. 'He has been my guest these many months. He has sat in my hall and eaten of my bread, and I have loved him as a son. And wot ye how he has repaid me? He has put me to the greatest shame, me and my wife the Lady Swanhild, whom I left in his guard—to such shame, indeed, that I cannot speak it.'

'True words, Earl,' said Eric, while folk murmured and handled their swords.

'True, but not all the truth,' growled Skallagrim. 'Methinks the Earl has heard a garbled tale.'

'True words, thyself thou sayest it,' went on Atli, 'thou hound that I saved from the sea! " Ran's gift, Hela's gift," so

runs the saw, and now from Ran to Hela shalt thou go, thou
mishandler of defenceless women ! '

' Here is somewhat of which I know nothing,' said
Eric.

' And here is something of which thou shalt know,'
answered Atli, and he shook his sword before Eric's eyes.
' Guard thyself ! '

' Nay, Earl ; thou art old, and I have done the wrong—I
will not fight with thee.'

' Art thou a coward also ? ' said the Earl.

' Some have deemed otherwise,' said Eric, ' but it is true
that heavy heart makes weak hand. Nevertheless this is my
rede. With thee are ten men. Stand thou aside and let
them fall on me till I am slain.'

' The odds are too heavy even for thee,' said Skallagrim.
' Back to back, lord, as we have stood aforetime, and let
us play this game together.'

' Not so,' cried Atli, ' this shame is mine, and I have
sworn to Swanhild that I will wipe it out in Eric's blood.
Stand thou before me and draw ! '

Then Eric drew Whitefire and raised his shield. Atli the
Earl rushed at him and smote a great two-handed blow. Eric
caught it on his shield and suffered no harm ; but he would
not smite back.

Atli dropped his point. ' Niddering art thou, and coward
to the last ! ' he cried. ' See, men, Eric Brighteyes fears to
fight. I am not come to this that I will cut down a man who
is too faint-hearted to give blow for blow. This is my word :
take ye your spear-shafts and push this coward to the shore.
Then put him in a boat and drive him hence.'

Now Eric grew red as the red light of sunset, for his manhood might not bear this.

' Take shield,' he said, ' and, Earl, on thine own head be
thy blood, for none shall live to call Eric niddering and
coward.'

Atli laughed in his folly and his rage. He took a shield,
and, once more springing on Brighteyes, struck a great blow.

Eric parried, then whirled Whitefire on high and smote—

once and once only! Down rushed the bright blade like a
star through the night. Sword and shield did Atli lift to
catch the blow. Through shield it sheared, and arm that
held the shield, through byrnie mail and deep into Earl Atli's
side. He fell prone to earth, while men held their breath,
wondering at the greatness of that stroke.

But Eric leaned on Whitefire and looked at the old Earl
upon the rock.

'Now, Atli, thou hast had thy way,' he said, 'and
methinks things are worse than they were before. But I will
say this: would that I lay there and thou stoodest to watch
me die, for as lief would I have slain my father as thee, Earl
Atli. There lies Swanhild's work!'

Atli gazed upwards into Eric's sad eyes and, while he
gazed so, his rage left him, and of a sudden a light brake
upon his mind, as even then the light of the setting sun broke
through the driving mist.

'Eric,' he said, 'draw near and speak with me ere I am
sped. I think that I have been beguiled and that thou didst
not do this thing which Swanhild said and Koll bore witness to.'

'What did Swanhild say, then, Earl Atli?'

The Earl told him.

'It was to be looked for from her,' said Eric, 'though I
never thought of it. Now hearken!' and he told him all.

Atli groaned aloud. 'I know this now, Eric,' he said:
'that thou speakest truth, and once more I have been deceived. Eric, I forgive thee all, for no man may fight against
woman's witchcraft and witch's wine. Swanhild is evil to
the heart. Yet, Eric, I lay this doom upon thee—I do not
lay it of my own will, for I would not harm thee, whom I love,
but because of the words that the Norns put in my mouth,
for now I am fey in this the hour of my death. Thou hast
sinned, and that thou didst sin against thy will shall avail
thee nothing, for of thy sin fate shall fashion a handle to the
spear which pierces thee. Henceforth thou art accursed. For
I tell thee that this wicked woman Swanhild shall drag thee
down to death, and worse than death, and with thee those

thou lovest. By witchcraft she brought thee to Straumey, by lies she laid me here before thee. Now by hate and might and cruel deeds shall she bring thee to lie more low than I do. For, Eric, thou art bound to her, and thou shalt never loose the bond!'

Atli ceased a while, then spoke again more faintly :

'Hearken, comrades,' he cried ; 'my strength is well-nigh spent. Ye shall swear four things to me—that ye will give Eric Brighteyes and Skallagrim Lambstail safe passage from Straumey. That ye will tell Swanhild the Fatherless, Groa's daughter and Atli's wife, that, at last, I know her for what she is—a murderess, a harlot, a witch and a liar ; and that I forgive Eric whom she tricked, but that her I hate and spit upon. That ye will slay Koll the Half-witted, Groa's thrall, who came hither two days gone, since by his lies he hath set an edge upon this sword of falsehood. That ye will raise no blood-feud against Eric for this my slaying, for I goaded him to the deed. Do ye swear ? '

'We swear,' said the men.

'Then, farewell! And to thee farewell, also, Eric Bright-eyes! Now take my hand and hold it while I die. Behold! I give thee a new name, and by that name thou shalt be called in story. I name thee *Eric the Unlucky*. Of all tales that are told, thine shall be the greatest. A mighty stroke that was of thine—a mighty stroke! Farewell!'

Then his head fell back upon the rock and Earl Atli died. And as he died the last rays of light went out of the sky.

CHAPTER XXI

HOW HALL OF LITHDALE TOOK TIDINGS TO ICELAND

NOW on the same night that Atli died at the hand of Eric, Swanhild spake with Hall of Lithdale, whom she had summoned from the mainland. She bade him do this: take passage in a certain ship that should sail for Iceland on the morrow from the island that is called Westra, and there tell all these tidings of the ill-doings of Eric and of the slaying of Atli by his hand. 'Thou shalt say,' she went on, 'that Eric had been my love for long, but that at length the matter came to the ears of Atli, the Earl. Then, holding this the greatest shame, he went on holmgang with Eric and was slain by him. This shalt thou add to thy tale also, that presently Eric and I will wed, and that Eric shall rule as Earl in Orkneys. Now these tidings must soon come to the ears of Gudruda the Fair, and she will send for thee, and question thee straightly concerning them, and thou shalt tell her the tale as thou toldest it at first. Then thou shalt give Gudruda this packet, which I send her as a gift, saying, that I bade her remember a certain oath which Eric took as to the cutting of his hair. And when she sees that which is within the packet is somewhat stained, tell her that it is but the blood of Atli which is upon it, as his blood is upon Eric's hands. Now remember thou this, Hall, that if thou fail in the errand thy life shall pay forfeit, for presently I will also come to Iceland and hear how thou hast sped.'

Then Swanhild gave him faring-money and gifts of wadmal cloth and gold rings, promising that he should have so much again when she came to Iceland.

Hall said that he would do all these things, and went at once ; nor did he fail in his tasks.

Atli being dead, Eric loosed his hand and called to the men to take up his body and bear it to the hall. This they did. Eric stood and watched them till they were lost in the darkness.

' Whither now, lord ? ' said Skallagrim.

' It matters little,' said Eric. ' What is thy counsel ? '

' This is my counsel. That we take ship and sail back to the King in London. There we will tell all this tale. It is a far cry from Straumey to London town, and there we shall sit in peace, for the King will think little of the slaying of an Orkney Earl in a brawl about a woman. Mayhap, too, the Lady Elfrida will not set great store by it. Therefore, I say, let us fare back to London.'

' In but one place am I at home, and that is Iceland,' said Eric. ' Thither I will go, Skallagrim, though it be but to miss friend from stead and bride from bed. At the least I shall find Ospakar there.'

'Listen, lord!' said Skallagrim. 'Was it not my rede that we should bide this winter through in London? Thou wouldest none of it, and what came about? Our ship is sunk, gone are our comrades, thine honour is tarnished, and dead is thy host at thine own hand. Yet I say all is not lost. Let us hence south, and see no more of Swanhild, of Gudruda, of Björn and Ospakar. So shall we break the spell. But if thou goest to Iceland, I am sure that the evil fate which Atli foretold will fall on thee, and the days to come shall be even more unlucky than the days that have been.'

'It may be so,' said Eric. 'I think, indeed, that it will be so. Henceforth I am Eric the Unlucky. Yet I will go back to Iceland and there play out the game. I care little if I live or am slain—I have no more joy in my life. I stand alone, like a fir upon a mountain-top, and every wind from heaven and every storm of hail and snow beats upon my head. But I say to thee, Skallagrim: go thy road, and leave a luckless man to his ill fate. Otherwise it shall be thine also. Good friend hast thou been to me; now let us part and wend south and north. The King will be glad to greet thee yonder in London, Lambstail.'

'But one severing shall we know, lord,' said Skallagrim, 'and that shall be sword's work, nor will it be for long. It is ill to speak such words as these of the parting of lord and thrall. Bethink thee of the oath I swore on Mosfell. Let us go north, since it is thy will: in fifty years it will count for little which way we wended from the Isles.'

So they went together down to the shore, and, finding a boat and men who as yet knew nothing of what had chanced to Atli, they sailed across the firth at the rising of the moon.

Two days afterwards they found a ship at Wick that was bound for Fareys, and sailed in her, Eric buying a passage with the half of a gold ring that the King had given him in London.

Here at Fareys they sat a month or more; but not in the Earl's hall as when Eric came with honour in the Gudruda, but in a farmer's stead. For the tale of Eric's dealings with Atli and Atli's wife had reached Fareys, and the Earl there had been a friend of Atli's. Moreover, Eric was now a poor man, having neither ship nor goods, nor friends. Therefore all looked coldly on him, though they wondered at his beauty and his might. Still, they dared not to speak ill or make a mock of him ; for, two men having done so, were nearly slain of Skallagrim, who seized the twain by the throat, one in either hand, and dashed their heads together. After that men said little.

They sat there a month, till at length a chapman put in at Fareys, bound for Iceland, and they took passage with him, Eric paying the other half of his gold ring for ship-room. The chapman was not willing to give them place at first, for he, too, had heard the tale ; but Skallagrim offered him choice, either to do so or to go on holmgang with him. Then the chapman gave them passage.

Now it is told that when his thralls and house-carles bore the corpse of Atli the Earl to his hall in Straumey, Swanhild met it and wept over it. And when the spokesman among them stood forward and told her those words that Atli had bidden them to say to her, sparing none, she spoke thus :

' My lord was distraught and weak with loss of blood when he spoke thus. The tale I told him was true, and now Eric has added to his sin by shedding the blood of him whom he wronged so sorely.'

And thereafter she spoke so sweetly and with so much gentleness, craft, and wisdom that, though they still doubted them, all men held her words weighty. For Swanhild had this art, that she could make the false sound true in the ears of men and the true sound false.

Still, being mindful of their oath, they hunted for Koll and found him. And when the thrall knew that they would slay him he ran thence screaming. Nor did Swanhild lift a hand to save his life, for she desired that Koll should die, lest he should bear witness against her. Away he ran towards the cliffs, and after him sped Atli's house-carles, till he came to the great cliffs that edge in the sea. Now they were close upon him and their swords were aloft. Then, sooner than know the kiss of steel, the liar leapt from the cliffs and was crushed, dying miserably on the rocks below. This was the end of Koll the Half-witted, Groa's thrall.

Swanhild sat in Straumey for a while, and took all Atli's heritage into her keeping, for he had no male kin ; nor did any say her nay. Also she called in the moneys that he had out at interest, and that was a great sum, for Atli was a careful and a wealthy man. Then Swanhild made ready to go to Iceland. Atli had a great dragon of war, and she manned that ship and filled it with stores and all things needful. This done, she set stewards and grieves over the Orkney lands and farms, and, when the Earl was six weeks dead, she sailed for Iceland, giving out that she went thither to set a blood-suit on foot against Eric for the death of Atli, her lord. There she came in safety just as folk rode to the Thing.

Now Hall of Lithdale reached Iceland and told his tale of the doings of Eric and the death of Atli. Oft and loud he told it, and soon people gossiped of it in field and fair and stead. Björn, Asmund's son, heard this talk and sent for Hall. To him also Hall told the tale.

'Now,' said Björn, ' we will go to my sister Gudruda the Fair, and learn how she takes these tidings.'

So they went in to where Gudruda sat spinning in the hall, singing as she span.

'Greeting, Gudruda,' said Björn ; ' say, hast thou tidings of Eric Brighteyes, thy betrothed ? '

' I have no tidings,' said Gudruda.

' Then here is one who brings them.'

Now for the first time Gudruda the Fair saw Hall of Lithdale. Up she sprang. ' Thou hast tidings of Eric, Hall ? Ah ! thou art welcome, for no tidings have come of him for many a month. Speak on,' and she pressed her hand against her heart and leaned towards him.

' My tidings are bad, lady.'

' Is Eric dead ? Say not my love is dead ! '

' He is worse than dead,' said Hall. ' He is shamed.'

'There thou liest, Hall,' she answered. 'Shame and Eric are things apart.'

'Mayst thou think so when thou hast heard my tale, lady,' said Hall, 'for I am sad at heart to speak it of one who was my mate.'

'Speak on, I say,' answered Gudruda, in such a voice that Hall shrank from her. 'Speak on; but of this I warn thee: that if in one word thou liest, that shall be thy death when Eric comes.'

Now Hall was afraid, thinking of the axe of Skallagrim. Still, he might not go back upon his word. So he began at the beginning, telling the story of how he was wounded in the fight with Ospakar's ships and left at Farey isles, and how he came thence to Scotland and sat in Atli's hall on Orkneys. Then he told how the Gudruda was wrecked on Straumey, and, of all aboard, Eric and Skallagrim alone were saved because of Swanhild's dream.

'Herein I see witch-work,' said Gudruda.

Then Hall told that Eric became Swanhild's love, but of the other tale which Swanhild had whispered to Atli he said nothing. For he knew that Gudruda would not believe this, and, moreover, if it were so, Swanhild had not sent the token which he should give.

'It well may be,' said Gudruda, proudly; 'Swanhild is fair and light of mind. Perchance she led Brighteyes into this snare.' But, though she spoke thus, bitter jealousy and anger burned in her breast and she remembered the sight which she had seen when Eric and Swanhild met on the morn of Atli's wedding.

Then Hall told of the slaying of Atli the Good by Eric, but he said nothing of the Earl's dying words, nor of how he goaded Brighteyes with his bitter words.

'It was an ill deed in sooth,' said Gudruda, 'for Eric to slay an old man whom he had wronged. Still, it may chance that he was driven to it for his own life's sake.'

Then Hall said that he had seen Swanhild after Atli's slaying, and that she had told him that she and Eric should wed shortly, and that Eric would rule in Orkneys by her side.

Gudruda asked if that was all his tale.

'Yes, lady,' answered Hall, 'that is all my tale, for after that I sailed and do not know what happened. But I am charged by the Lady Swanhild to give something to thee. She bade me say this also: that, when thou lookest on the gift, thou shouldst think on a certain oath which Eric took as to the cutting of his hair.' And he drew a linen packet from his breast and gave it to her.

Thrice Gudruda looked at it, fearing to open it. Then, seeing the smile of mockery on Björn's cold face, she took the shears that hung at her side and cut the thread with them. And as she cut, a lock of golden hair rose from the packet, untwisting itself like a living snake. The lock was long, and its end was caked with gore.

'Whose hair is this?' said Gudruda, though she knew the hair well.

'Eric's hair,' said Hall, 'that Swanhild cut from his head with Eric's sword.'

Now Gudruda put her hand to her bosom. She drew out a satchel, and from the satchel a lock of yellow hair. Side by side she placed the locks, looking first at one and then at the other.

'This is Eric's hair in sooth,' she said—'Eric's hair that he swore none but I should cut! Eric's hair that Swanhild shore with Whitefire from Eric's head—Whitefire whereon we plighted troth! Say now, whose blood is this that stains the hair of Eric?'

'It is Atli's blood, whom Eric first dishonoured and then slew with his own hand,' answered Hall.

Now there burned a fire on the hearth, for the day was cold. Gudruda the Fair stood over the fire and with either hand she let the two locks of Eric's hair fall upon the embers. Slowly they twisted up and burned. She watched them burn, then she threw up her hands and with a great cry fled from the hall.

Björn and Hall of Lithdale looked on each other.

'Thou hadst best go hence!' said Björn; 'and of this I warn thee, Hall, though I hold thy tidings good, that, if thou

hast spoken one false word, that will be thy death. For then
it would be better for thee to face all the wolves in Iceland
than to stand before Eric in his rage.'

Again Hall bethought him of the axe of Skallagrim, and
he went out heavily.

That day a messenger came from Gudruda to Björn,
saying that she wished to speak with him. He went to where
she sat alone upon her bed. Her face was white as death,
and her dark eyes glowed.

'Eric has dealt badly with thee, sister, to bring thee to
this sorrow,' said Björn.

'Speak no ill of Eric to me,' Gudruda answered. 'The
evil that he has done will be paid back to him ; there is little
need for thee to heap words upon his head. Hearken, Björn
my brother : is it yet thy will that I should wed Ospakar
Blacktooth ? '

'That is my wish, surely. There is no such match in
Iceland as this Ospakar, and I should win many friends
by it.'

'Do this then, Björn. Send messengers to Swinefell and
say to Ospakar that if he still desires to wed Gudruda the
Fair, Asmund's daughter, let him come to Middalhof when
folk ride from the Thing and he shall not go hence alone.
Nay, I have done. Now, I pray thee speak no more to me
of Eric or of Ospakar. Of the one I have seen and heard
enough, and of the other I shall hear and see enough in the
years that are to come.

CHAPTER XXII

HOW ERIC CAME HOME AGAIN

SWANHILD made a good passage from the Orkneys, and was in Iceland thirty-five days before Eric and Skallagrim set foot there. But she did not land by Westman Isles, for she had no wish to face Gudruda at that time, but by Reyjaness. Now she rode thence with her company to Thingvalla, for here all men were gathered for the Thing. At first people hung aloof from her, notwithstanding her wealth and beauty; but Swanhild knew well how to win the hearts of men. For now she told the same story of Eric that she had told to Atli, and there were none to say her nay. So it came to pass that she was believed, and Eric Brighteyes held to be shamed indeed. Now, too, she set a suit on foot against Eric for the death of Atli at his hand, claiming that sentence of the greater outlawry should be passed against him, and that his lands at Coldback in the Marsh on Ran River should be given, half to her in atonement for the Earl's death, and half to the men of Eric's quarter.

On the day of the opening of the Thing Ospakar Blacktooth came from the north, and with him his son Gizur and a great company of men. Ospakar was blithe, for from the Thing he should ride to Middalhof, there to wed Gudruda the Fair. Then Swanhild clad herself in beautiful attire, and, taking men with her, went to the booth of Ospakar.

Blacktooth sat in his booth and by him sat Gizur his son the Lawman. When he saw a beauteous lady, very richly clad, enter the booth he did not know who it might be. But Gizur knew her well, for he could never put Swanhild from his mind.

'Lo! here comes Swanhild the Fatherless, Atli's widow,' said Gizur, flushing red with joy at the sight of her.

Then Ospakar greeted her heartily, and made place for her by him at the top of the booth.

'Ospakar Blacktooth,' she said, 'I am come to ask this of thee: that thou shalt befriend me in the suit which I have against Eric Brighteyes for the slaying of Earl Atli, my husband.'

'Thou couldst have come to no man who is more willing,' said Ospakar, 'for, if thou hast something against Eric, I have yet more.'

'I would ask this, too, Ospakar: that thy son Gizur should take up my suit and plead it; for I know well that he is the most skilful of all lawmen.'

'I will do that,' said Gizur, his eyes yet fixed upon her face.

'I looked for no less from thee,' said Swanhild, 'and be sure of this, that thou shalt not plead for nothing,' and she glanced at him meaningly. Then she set out her case with a lying tongue, and afterwards went back to her booth, glad at heart. For now she learned that Hall had not failed in his errand, seeing that Gudruda was about to wed Ospakar.

Gizur gave warning of the blood-suit, and the end of it was that, though he had no notice and was not there to answer to the charge, against all right and custom Eric was declared outlaw and his lands were given, half to Swanhild and half to the men of his quarter. For now all held that Swanhild's was a true tale, and Eric the most shameful of men, and therefore they were willing to stretch the law against him. Also, being absent, he had few friends, and those men of small account; whereas Ospakar, who backed Swanhild's suit, was the most powerful of the northern chiefs, as Gizur was the most skilled lawman in Iceland. Moreover, Björn the Priest, Asmund's son, was among the judges, and, though Swanhild's tale seemed strange to him after that which he had heard

Q

from Hall of Lithdale, he loved Eric little. He feared also that if Eric came a free man to Iceland before Gudruda was wed to Ospakar, her love would conquer her anger, for he could see well that she still loved Brighteyes. Therefore he strove with might and main that Eric should be brought in guilty, nor did he fail in this.

So the end of it was that Eric Brighteyes was outlawed, his lands declared forfeit, and his head a wolf's head, to be taken by him who might, should he set root in Iceland.

Thereafter, the Althing being ended, Björn, Gizur, and Ospakar, with all their company, rode away to Middalhof to sit at the marriage-feast. But Swanhild and her folk went by sea in the long war-ship to Westmans. For this was her plan : to seize on Coldback and to sit there for a while, till she saw if Eric came out to Iceland. Also she desired to see the wedding of Ospakar and Gudruda, for she had been bidden to it by Björn, her half-brother.

Now Ospakar came to Middalhof, and found Gudruda waiting his coming.

She stood in the great hall, pale and cold as April snow, and greeted him courteously. But when he would have kissed her, she shrank from him, for now he was more hideous in her sight than he had ever been, and she loathed him in her heart.

That night there was feasting in the hall, and at the feast Gudruda heard that Eric had been made outlaw. Then she spoke :

'This is an ill deed, thus to judge an absent man.'

'Say, Gudruda,' said Björn in her ear, 'hast thou not also judged Eric who is absent ?'

She turned her head and spoke no more of Eric ; but Björn's words fixed themselves in her heart like arrows. The tale was strange to her, for it seemed that Eric had been made outlaw at Swanhild's suit, and yet Eric was Swanhild's love : for Swanhild's self had sent the lock of Brighteyes' hair by Hall, saying that he was her love and soon would wed her. How, then, did Swanhild bring a suit against him who should be her husband ? Moreover, she heard that Swanhild sailed

down to Coldback, and was bidden to the marriage-feast, that
should be on the third day from now. Could it be, then, when
all was said and done, that Eric was less faithless than she
deemed? Gudruda's heart stood still and the blood rushed to
her brow when she thought on it. Also, even if it were so, it
was now too late. And surely it was not so, for had not Eric
been made outlaw? Men were not made outlaw for a little
thing. Nay, she would meet her fate, and ask no more of
Eric and his doings.

On the morrow, as Gudruda sat in her chamber, it was
told her that Saevuna, Thorgrimur's widow and Eric's mother,
had come from Coldback to speak with her. For, after the
death of Asmund and of Unna, Saevuna had moved back to
Coldback in the Marsh.

'Nay, how can this be?' said Gudruda astonished, for she
knew well that Saevuna was now both blind and bed-ridden.

'She has been borne here in a chair,' said the woman
who told her, 'and that is a strange sight to see.'

At first Gudruda was minded to say her nay; but her heart
softened, and she bade them bring Saevuna in. Presently she
came, being set in a chair upon the shoulders of four men.
She was white in hue, for sickness had aged her much, and
she stared about her with sightless eyes. But she was still
tall and straight, and her face was stern to look on. To
Gudruda it seemed like that of Eric when he was angered.

'Am I nigh to Gudruda the Fair, Asmund's daughter?'
asked Saevuna. 'Methinks I hear her breathe.'

'I am here, mother,' said Gudruda. 'What is thy will
with me?'

'Set down, carles, and begone!' quoth Saevuna; 'that
which I have to say I would say alone. When I summon
you, come.

The carles set down the chair upon the floor and went.

'Gudruda,' said the dame, 'I am risen from my deathbed, and I have caused myself to be borne on my last
journey here across the meads, that I may speak with thee and
warn thee. I hear that thou hast put away my son, Eric
Brighteyes, to whom thou art sworn in marriage, and **art**

about to give thyself to Ospakar Blacktooth. I hear also that thou hast done this deed because a certain man, Hall of Lithdale—whom from his youth up I have known for a liar and a knave, and whom thou thyself didst mistrust in years gone by—has come hither to Iceland from Orkneys, bearing a tale of Eric's dealings with thy half-sister Swanhild. This I hear, further : that Swanhild, Atli's widow, hath come out to Iceland and laid a suit against Eric for the slaying of Atli the Earl, her husband, and that Eric has been outlawed and his lands at Coldback are forfeit. Tell me now, Gudruda, Asmund's daughter, if these tales be true ? '

' The tales are true, mother,' said Gudruda.

' Then hearken to me, girl. Eric sprang from my womb, who of all living men is the best and first, as he is the bravest and most strong. I have reared this Eric from a babe and I know his heart well. Now I tell thee this, that, whatever Eric has done or left undone, naught of dishonour is on his hands. Mayhap Swanhild hath deceived him—thou art a woman, and thou knowest well the arts which women have, and the strength that Freya gives them. Well thou knowest, also, of what breed this Swanhild came ; and perchance thou canst remember how she dealt with thee, and with what mind she looked on Eric. Perchance thou canst remember how she plotted against thee and Eric—ay, how she thrust thee from Goldfoss brink. Say, then, wilt thou take her word ? Wilt thou take the word of this witch-daughter of a witch ? Wilt thou not think on Groa, her mother, and of Groa's dealings with thy father, and with Unna my kinswoman ? As the mother is, so shall the daughter be. Wilt thou cast Eric aside, and that unheard ? '

' There is no more room for doubt, mother,' said Gudruda. ' I have proof of this : that Eric has forsaken me.'

' So thou thinkest, child ; but I tell thee that thou art wrong ! Eric loves thee now as he loved thee aforetime, and will love thee always.'

' Would that I could believe it ! ' said Gudruda. ' If I could think that Eric still loved me—ay, even though he had been faithless to me—I would die ere I wed Ospakar ! '

'Thou art foolish, Gudruda, and thou shalt rue thy folly bitterly. I am outworn, and death draws near to me—far from me now are hates and loves, hopes and fears ; but I know this : that woman is mad who, loving a man, weds where she loves not. Shame shall be her portion and bitterness her bread. Unhappy shall she live, and when she comes to die, but as a wilderness—but as the desolate winter snow, shall be the record of her days ! '

Now Gudruda wept aloud. ' What is done is done,' she cried : ' the bridegroom sits within the hall—the bride awaits him in the bower. What is done is done—I may hope no more to be saved from Ospakar.'

' What is done is done, yet it can be brought to nothing ; but soon that shall be done which may never be undone! Gudruda, fare thee well! Never shall I listen to thy voice again. I hold thee shameless, thou unfaithful woman, who in thy foolish jealousy art ready to sell thyself to the arms of one thou hatest! Ho! carles ; come hither. Bear me hence! '

Now the men came in and took up Saevuna's chair. Gudruda watched them carry her forth. Then suddenly she sprang from her seat and ran after her into the hall, weeping bitterly.

Now as Saevuna, Eric's mother, was borne out she was met by Ospakar and Björn.

' Stay,' said Björn. ' What does this carline here?—and why weeps Gudruda, my sister ? '

The men halted. ' Who calls me "carline" ? ' said Saevuna. ' Is the voice I hear the voice of Björn, Asmund's son ? '

' It is my voice, truly,' said Björn, ' and I seek to know this—and this would Ospakar, who stands at thy side, know also—why thou comest here, carline ? and why Gudruda weeps ? '

' Gudruda weeps because she has good cause to weep, Björn. She weeps because she has betrayed her love, Eric Brighteyes, my son, and is about to be sold in marriage—to be sold to thee, Ospakar Blacktooth, like a heifer at a fair.'

Then Björn grew angry and cursed Saevuna, nor did Ospakar spare to add to his ill words. But the old dame sat in her chair, listening silently till all their curses were spent.

'Ye are evil, the twain of you,' she said, 'and ye have told lies of Eric, my son; and ye have taken his bride for lust and greed, playing upon the jealous folly of a maid like harpers on a harp. Now I tell you this, Björn and Ospakar! My blind eyes are opened and I see this hall of Middalhof, and lo! it is but a gore of blood! Blood flows upon the board—blood streams along the floor, and ye—ye twain!—lie dead thereon, and about your shapes are shrouds, and on your feet are Hell-shoon! Eric comes and Whitefire is aloft, and no more shall ye stand before him whom ye have slandered than stands the birch before the lightning stroke! Eric comes! I see his angry eyes—I see his helm flash in the door-place! Red was that marriage-feast at which sat Unna, my kinswoman, and Asmund, thy father—redder shall be the feast where sit Gudruda, thy sister, and Ospakar! The wolf howls at thy door, Björn! the grave-worm opens his mouth! trolls run to and fro upon thy threshold, and the ghosts of men speed Hellwards! Ill were the deeds of Groa—worse shall be the deeds of Groa's daughter! Red is thy hall with blood, Björn! —for Whitefire is aloft and—*I tell thee Eric comes!*'—and with one great cry she fell back—dead.

Now they stood amazed, and trembling in their fear.

'Saevuna hath spoken strange words,' said Björn.

'Shall we be frightened by a dead hag?' quoth Ospakar, drawing his breath again. 'Fellows, bear this carrion forth, or we will fling it to the dogs.'

Then the men tied the body of Saevuna, Thorgrimur's widow, Eric's mother, fast in the chair and bore it thence. But when at length they came to Coldback, they found that Swanhild was there with all her following, and had driven Eric's grieve and his folk to the fells. But one old carline, who had been nurse to Eric, was left there, and she sat wailing in an outhouse, being too weak to move.

Then the men set down the corpse of Saevuna in the outhouse, and, having told all their tale to the carline, they fled also.

That night passed, and passed the morrow; but on the next day at dawn Eric Brighteyes and Skallagrim Lambstail landed near Westman Isles. They had made a bad passage from Fareys, having been beat about by contrary winds; but at length they came safe and well to land.

Now this was the day of the marriage-feast of Gudruda the Fair and Ospakar; but Eric knew nothing of these tidings.

'Where to now, lord?' said Skallagrim.

'To Coldback first, to see my mother, if she yet lives, and to learn tidings of Gudruda. Then as it may chance.'

Near to the beach was a yeoman's house. Thither they went to hire horses; but none were in the house, for all had gone to Gudruda's marriage-feast. In the home meadow ran two good horses, and in the outhouses were saddles and bridles. They caught the horses, saddled them and rode for Coldback. When they had ridden for something over an hour they came to the crest of a height whence they could see Coldback in the Marsh.

Eric drew rein and looked, and his heart swelled within him at the sight of the place where he was born. But as he looked he saw a great train of people ride away from Coldback towards Middalhof—and in the company a woman wearing a purple cloak.

'Now what may this mean?' said Eric.

'Ride on and we shall learn,' answered Skallagrim.

So they rode on, and as they rode Eric's breast grew heavy with fear. Now they passed up the banked way through the home meadows of the house, but they could see no one; and now they were at the door. Down sprang Eric and walked into the hall. But none were there to greet him, though a fire yet burned upon the hearth. Only a gaunt hound wandered about the hall, and, seeing him, sprang towards him, growling. Eric knew him for his old wolf-hound, and called him by his name. The dog listened, then ran up and smelt his hands, and straightway howled with joy and leapt upon him. For a while he leapt thus, while Eric stared around him wondering and sad at heart. Then the dog ran to the door and stood there, whining. Eric followed after him. The hound passed through the entrance, and across the yard till he came to an outhouse. Here the dog stopped and scratched at the door, still whining. Eric thrust it open. Lo! there before him sat Saevuna, his mother, dead in a chair, and at her feet crouched the carline—she who had been Eric's nurse.

Now he grasped the door-posts to steady himself, and his shadow fell upon the white face of his mother and the old carline at her feet.

CHAPTER XXIII

HOW ERIC WAS A GUEST AT THE WEDDING-FEAST OF GUDRUDA THE FAIR

RIC looked, but said nothing.

'Who art thou?' whined the carline, gazing up at him with tear-blinded eyes. But Eric's face was in the shadow, and she only saw the glint of his golden hair and the flash of the golden helm. For Eric could not speak yet a while.

'Art thou one of Swanhild's folk, come to drive me hence with the rest? Good sir, I cannot go to the fells, my limbs are too weak. Slay me, if thou wilt, but drive me not from this,' and she pointed to the corpse.

'Say now, wilt thou not help me to give it burial? It is unmeet that she who in her time had husband, and goods, and son, should lie unburied like a dead cow on the fells. I have still a hundred in silver, if I might but come at it. It is hidden, sir, and I will pay thee if thou wilt help me to bury her. These old hands are too feeble to dig a grave, nor could I bear her there alone if it were dug. Thou wilt not help me?—then may thine own mother's bones lie uncovered, and be picked by gulls and ravens. Oh, that Eric Brighteyes would come home again! Oh, that Eric was here! There is work to do and never a man to do it.'

Now Eric gave a great sob and cried, 'Nurse, nurse! knowest thou me not? *I* am Eric Brighteyes.'

She uttered a loud cry, and, clasping him by the knees, looked up into his face.

'Thanks be to Odin! Thou art Eric—Eric come home again! But alas, thou hast come too late!'

'What has happened, then?' said Eric.

'What has happened? All evil things. Thou art outlawed, Eric, at the suit of Swanhild for the slaying of Atli the Earl. Swanhild sits here in Coldback, for she hath seized thy lands. Saevuna, thy mother, died two days ago in the hall of Middalhof, whither she went to speak with Gudruda.'

'Gudruda! what of Gudruda?' cried Eric.

'This, Brighteyes: to-day she weds Ospakar Black-tooth.'

Eric covered his face with his hand. Presently he lifted it.

'Thou art rich in evil tidings, nurse, though, it would seem, poor in all besides. Tell me at what hour is the wedding-feast?'

'An hour after noon, Eric; but now Swanhild has ridden thither with her company.'

'Then room must be found at Middalhof for one more guest,' said Eric, and laughed aloud. 'Go on!—pour out thy evil news and spare me not!—for nothing has any more power to harm me now! Come hither, Skallagrim, and see and hearken.'

Skallagrim came and looked on the face of dead Saevuna.

'I am outlawed at Swanhild's suit, Lambstail. My life lies in thy hand, if so be thou wouldst take it! Hew off my head, if thou wilt, and bear it to Gudruda the Fair—she will thank thee for the gift. Lay on, Lambstail; lay on with that axe of thine.'

'Child's talk!' said Skallagrim.

'Child's talk, but man's work! Thou hast not heard the tale out. Swanhild hath seized my lands and sits here at Cold-back! And—what thinkest thou, Skallagrim?—but now she has ridden a-guesting to the marriage-feast of Ospakar Blacktooth with Gudruda the Fair! Swanhild at Gudruda's wedding!—the eagle in the wild swan's nest! But there will be another guest,' and again he laughed aloud.

'*Two* other guests,' said Skallagrim.

'More of thy tale, old nurse !—more of thy tale !' quoth Eric. 'No better didst thou ever tell me when, as a lad, I sat by thee, in the ingle o' winter nights—and the company is fitting to the tale !' and he pointed to dead Saevuna.

Then the carline told on. She told how Hall of Lithdale had come out to Iceland, and of the story that he bore to Gudruda, and of the giving of the lock of hair.

'What did I say, lord ?' broke in Skallagrim—'that in Hall thou hadst let a weasel go who would live to nip thee ?'

'Him I will surely live to shorten by a head,' quoth Eric.

'Nay, lord, this one for me—Ospakar for thee, Hall for me !'

'As thou wilt, Baresark. Among so many there is room to pick and choose. Tell on, nurse !'

Then she told how Swanhild came out to Iceland, and, having won Ospakar Blacktooth and Gizur to her side, had laid a suit against Eric at the Thing, and there bore false witness against him, so that Brighteyes was declared outlaw, being absent. She told, too, how Gudruda had betrothed herself to Ospakar, and how Swanhild had moved down to Coldback and seized the lands. Lastly she told of the rising of Saevuna from her deathbed, of her going to Middalhof, of the words she spoke to Björn and Ospakar, and of her death in the hall at Middalhof.

When all was told, Eric stooped and kissed the cold brow of his mother.

'There is little time to bury thee now, my mother,' he said, 'and perchance before six hours are sped there will be one to bury at thy side. Nevertheless, thou shalt sit in a better place than this.'

Then he cut loose the cords that bound the body of Saevuna to the chair, and, lifting it in his arms, bore it to the hall. There he set the corpse in the high seat of the hall.

'We need not start yet a while, Skallagrim,' said Eric, 'if indeed thou wouldst go a-guesting with me to Middalhof. Therefore let us eat and drink, for there are deeds to do this day.'

So they found meat and mead and ate and drank. Then Eric washed himself, combed out his golden locks, and looked well to his harness and to Whitefire's edge. Skallagrim also ground his great axe upon the whetstone in the yard, singing as he ground. When all was ready, the horses were caught, and Eric spoke to the carline :

'Hearken, nurse. If it may be that thou canst find any of our folk—and perchance now when they see that Swanhild has ridden to Middalhof some one of them will come down

to spy—thou shalt say this to them. Thou shalt say that, if Eric Brighteyes yet lives, he will be at the foot of Mosfell to-morrow before midday, and if, for the sake of old days and fellowship, they are minded to befriend a friendless man, let them come thither with food, for by then food will be needed, and I will speak with them. And now farewell,' and Eric kissed her and went, leaving her weeping.

As it chanced, before another hour was sped, Jon, Eric's thrall, who had stayed at home in Iceland, seeing Coldback empty, crept down from the

SKALLAGRIM GROUND HIS AXE.

fells and looked in. The carline saw him, and told him these tidings. Then he went thence to find the other men. Having found them he told them Eric's words, and a great gladness came upon them when they learned that Brighteyes still lived and was in Iceland. Then they gathered food and gear, and rode away to the foot of Mosfell that is now called Ericsfell.

Ospakar sat in the hall at Middalhof, near to the high seat. He was fully armed, and a black helm with a raven's crest

was on his head. For, though he said nothing of it, not a little
did he fear that Saevuna spoke sooth—that her words would
come true, and, before this day was done, he and Eric should
once more stand face to face. At his side sat Gudruda the
Fair, robed in white, a worked headdress on her head, golden
clasps upon her breast and golden rings about her arms.
Never had she seemed more beautiful; but her face was
whiter than her robes. She looked with loathing on Blacktooth at her side, rough like a bear, and hideous as a troll.
But he looked on her with longing, and laughed from side to
side of his great mouth when he thought that at last he had
got her for his own.

'Ah, if Eric would but come, faithless though he be!—if
Eric would but come!' thought Gudruda; but no Eric came
to save her. The guests gathered fast, and presently Swanhild
swept in with all her company, wrapped about in her purple
cloak. She came up to the high seat where Gudruda sat, and
bent the knee before her, looking on her with lovely mocking
face and hate in her blue eyes.

'Greeting, Gudruda, my sister!' she said. 'When last we
met I sat, Atli's bride, where to-day thou sittest the bride of
Ospakar. Then Eric Brighteyes held thy hand, and little
thou didst think of wedding Ospakar. Now Eric is afar—so
strangely do things come about—and Blacktooth, Brighteyes'
foe, holds that fair hand of thine.'

Gudruda looked on her and turned whiter yet in her pain,
but she answered never a word.

'What! no word for me, sister?' said Swanhild. 'And
yet it is through me that thou comest to this glad hour. It is
through me that thou art rid of Eric, and it is I who have
given thee to the arms of mighty Ospakar. No word of
thanks for so great a service!—fie on thee, Gudruda! fie!'

Then Gudruda spoke: 'Strange tales are told of thee
and Eric, Groa's daughter! I have done with Eric, but I
have done with thee also. Thou hast thrust thyself here
against my will, and, if I may, I would see thy face no more.'

'Wouldst thou see Eric's face, Gudruda?—say, wouldst
see Eric's face? I tell thee it is fair!'

But Gudruda answered nothing, and Swanhild fell back, laughing.

Now the feast began, and men waxed merry. But ever Gudruda's heart grew heavier, for in it echoed those words that Saevuna had spoken. Her eyes were dim, and she seemed to see naught but the face of Eric as it had looked when he came back to her that day on the brink of Goldfoss Falls and she had thought him dead. Oh! what if he still loved her and were yet true at heart? Swanhild mocked her!—what if this was a plot of Swanhild's? Had not Swanhild plotted aforetime, and could a wolf cease from ravening or a witch from witch-work? Nay, she had seen Eric's hair— that he had sworn none save she should touch! Perchance he had been drugged, and the hair shorn from him in his sleep? Too late to think! Of what use was thought?—beside her sat Ospakar, in one short hour she would be his. Ah! that she could see him dead—the troll who had trafficked her to shame, the foe she had summoned in her wrath and jealousy! She had done ill—she had fallen into Swanhild's snare, and now Swanhild came to mock her!

The feast went on—cup followed cup. Now they poured the bride-cup! Before her heart beat two hundred times she would be the wife of Ospakar!

Blacktooth took the cup—pledged her in it, and drank deep. Then he turned and strove to kiss her. But Gudruda shrank from him with horror in her eyes, and all men wondered. Still she must drink the bridal cup. She took it. Dimly she saw the upturned faces, faintly she heard the murmur of a hundred voices.

What was that voice she caught above them all—there— without the hall?

Holding the cup in her hand, Gudruda bent forward, staring down the skali. Then she cried aloud, pointing to the door, and the cup fell clattering from her hand and rolled along the ground.

Men turned and looked. They saw this: there on the threshold stood a man, glorious to look at, and from his winged helm of gold the rays of light flashed through the dusky hall. The man was great and beautiful. He had long yellow hair bound in about his girdle, and in his left hand he held a pointed shield, in his right a spear, and at his thigh there hung a mighty sword. Nor was he alone, for by his side, a broad axe on his shoulder and shield in hand, stood another man, clad in black-hued mail—a man well-nigh as broad and big, with hawk's eyes, eagle beak, and black hair streaked with grey.

For a moment there was silence. Then a voice spoke:

'Lo! here be the Gods Baldur and Thor!—come from Valhalla to grace the marriage-feast!'

Then the man with golden hair cried aloud in a voice that made the rafters ring:

'Here are Eric Brighteyes and Skallagrim Lambstail, his thrall, come from over sea to grace the feast, indeed!'

'I could have looked for no worse guests,' said Björn beneath his breath, and rose to bid men thrust them out. But before he could speak, lo! gold-helmed Eric and black-helmed Skallagrim were stalking up the length of that great hall. Side by side they stalked, with faces fierce and cold; nor stayed they till they stood before the high seat. Eric looked up and round, and the light of his eyes was as the light of a sword. Men marvelled at his greatness and his wonderful beauty, and to Gudruda he seemed like a God.

'Here I see faces that are known to me,' said Eric. 'Greeting, comrades!'

'Greeting, Brighteyes!' shouted the Middalhof folk and the company of Swanhild; but the carles of Ospakar laid hand on sword—they too knew Eric. For still all men loved Eric, and the people of his quarter were proud of the deeds he had done oversea.

'Greeting, Björn, Asmund's son!' quoth Eric. 'Greeting, Ospakar Blacktooth! Greeting, Swanhild the Fatherless, Atli's witch-wife—Groa's witch-bairn! Greeting, Hall of Lithdale, Hall the liar—Hall who cut the grapnel-chain! And to thee, sweet Bride, to thee Gudruda the Fair, greeting!'

Now Björn spoke: 'I will take no greeting from a shamed and outlawed man. Get thee gone, Eric Brighteyes, and

R 2

take thy wolf-hound with thee, ere thou bidest here stiff and cold.'

'Squeak not so loud, rat, lest hound's fang worry thee!' growled Skallagrim.

But Eric laughed aloud and cried—

'Words must be said, and perchance men shall be dead, ere ever I leave this hall. Björn!'

CHAPTER XXIV

HOW THE FEAST WENT

EARKEN all men!' said Eric. 'Thrust him out!' quoth Björn.

'Nay, cut him down!' said Ospakar, 'he is an outlawed man.'

'Words first, then deeds,' answered Skallagrim. 'Thou shalt have thy fill of both, Blacktooth, before day is done.'

'Let Eric say his say,' said Gudruda, lifting her head. 'He has been doomed unheard, and it is my will that he shall say his say.'

'What hast thou to do with Eric?' snarled Ospakar.

'The bride-cup is not yet drunk, lord,' she answered.

'To thee, then, I will speak, lady,' quoth Eric. 'How comes it that, being betrothed to me, thou dost sit there the bride of Ospakar?'

'Ask of Swanhild,' said Gudruda in a low voice. 'Ask also of Hall of Lithdale yonder, who brought me Swanhild's gift from Straumey.'

'I must ask much of Hall and he must answer much,' said Eric. 'What tale, then, did he bring thee from Straumey?'

'He said this, Eric,' Gudruda answered : 'that thou wast Swanhild's love : that for Swanhild's sake thou hadst basely killed Atli the Good, and that thou wast about to wed Swan-hild's self and take the Earl's seat in Orkneys.'

'And for what cause was I made outlaw at the Althing?'

'For this cause, Eric,' said Björn, 'that thou hadst dealt evilly with Swanhild, bringing her to shame against her will, and thereafter that thou hadst slain the Earl, her husband.'

'Which, then, of these tales is true? for both cannot be true,' said Brighteyes. 'Speak, Swanhild.'

'Thou knowest well that the last is true, Eric,' said Swanhild boldly.

'How then comes it that thou didst charge Hall with that message to Gudruda? How then comes it that thou didst send her the lock of hair which thou didst cozen me to give thee?'

'I charged Hall with no message, and I sent no lock of hair,' Swanhild answered.

'Stand thou forward, Hall!' said Eric, 'and liar and coward though thou art, dare not to speak other than the truth! Nay, look not at the door: for, if thou stirrest, this spear shall find thee before thou hast gone a pace!'

Now Hall stood forward, trembling with fear, for he saw the eye of Skallagrim watching him close, and while Lambstail watched, his fingers toyed with the handle of his axe.

'It is true, lord, that Swanhild charged me with that message which I gave to the Lady Gudruda. Also she bade me give the lock of hair.'

'And for this service thou didst take money, Hall?'

'Ay, lord, she gave me money for my faring.'

'And all the while thou knewest the tidings false?'

Hall made no reply.

'Answer! thundered Eric—'answer the truth, knave, or by every God that passes the hundred gates I will not spare thee twice!'

It is so, lord,' said Hall.

'Thou liest, fox!' cried Swanhild, white with wrath and casting a fierce look upon Hall. But men took no heed of Swanhild's words, for all eyes were bent on Eric.

' Is it now your pleasure, comrades, that I should tell you the truth ? ' said Brighteyes.

The most part of the company shouted ' Yea ! ' but the men of Ospakar stood silent.

' Speak on, Eric,' quoth Gudruda.

This is the truth, then : Swanhild the Fatherless, Atli's wife, has always sought my love, and she ever hated Gudruda whom I loved. From a child she has striven to work mischief between us. Ay, and she did this, though till now it has been hidden : she strove to murder Gudruda; it was on the day that Skallagrim and I overcame Ospakar and his band on Horse-Head Heights. She thrust Gudruda from the brink of Golden Falls while she sat looking on the waters, and as she hung there I dragged her back. Is it not so, Gudruda ? '

' It is so,' said Gudruda.

Now men murmured and looked at Swanhild. But she shrank back, plucking at her purple cloak.

' It was for this cause,' said Eric, ' that Asmund, Swanhild's father, gave her choice to wed Atli the Earl and pass over sea or to take her trial in the Doom-Ring. She wedded Atli and went away. Afterwards, by witchcraft, she brought my ship to wreck on Straumey's Isle—ay, she walked the waters like a shape of light and lured us on to ruin, so that all were drowned except Skallagrim and myself. Is it not so, Skallagrim ? '

' It is so, lord. I saw her with my eyes.'

Again folk murmured.

' Then we must sit in Atli's hall,' said Eric, ' and there we dwelt last winter. For a while Swanhild did no harm, till I feared her no more. But some three months ago, I was left with her : and a man called Koll, Groa's thrall, of whom ye know, came out from Iceland, bringing news of the death of Asmund the priest, of Unna my cousin, and of Groa the witch. To these ill-tidings Swanhild bribed him to add something. She bribed him to add this : that thou, Gudruda, wast betrothed to Ospakar, and wouldst wed him on last Yule Day. Moreover, he gave me a certain message from thee, Gudruda,

and, in token of its truth, the half of that coin which I broke
with thee long years ago. Say now, lady, didst thou send
the coin ? '

'Nay, never ! ' cried Gudruda ; 'many years ago I lost
the half thou gavest me, though I feared to tell thee.'

'Perchance one stands there who found it,' said Eric,
pointing with his spear at Swanhild. 'At the least I was
deceived by it. Now the tale is short. Swanhild mourned
with me, and in my sorrow I mourned bitterly. Then it
was she asked a boon, that lock of mine, Gudruda, and,
thinking thee faithless, I gave it, holding all oaths broken.
Then too, when I would have left her, she drugged me with a
witch-draught—ay, she drugged me, and I woke to find myself
false to my oath, false to Atli, and false to thee, Gudruda. I
cursed her and I left her, waiting for the Earl, to tell him all.
But Swanhild outwitted me. She told him that other tale of
shame that ye have heard, and brought Koll to him as witness
of the tale. Atli was deceived by her, and not until I had cut
him down in anger at the bitter words he spoke, calling
me coward and niddering, did he know the truth. But
before he died he knew it ; and he died, holding my hand and
bidding those about him find Koll and slay him. Is it not
so, ye who were Atli's men ? '

'It is so, Eric ! ' one cried ; 'we heard it with our own
ears, and we slew Koll. But afterwards Swanhild brought
us to believe that Earl Atli was distraught when he spoke
thus, and that things were indeed as she had said.'

Again men murmured, and a strange light shone in
Gudruda's eyes.

'Now, Gudruda, thou hast heard all my story,' said Eric.
'Say, dost thou believe me ? '

'I believe thee, Eric.'

'Say then, wilt thou still wed yon Ospakar ? '

Gudruda looked on Blacktooth, then she looked at golden
Eric and opened her lips to speak. But before a word could pass
them Ospakar rose in wrath, laying his hand upon his sword.

'Thinkest thou thus to lure away my dove, outlaw ?
First I will see thee food for crows.'

'Well spoken, Blacktooth,' laughed Eric. 'I waited for such words from thee. Thrice have we striven together—once out yonder in the snow, once on Horse-Head Heights, and once by Westman Isles—and still we live to tell the tale. Come down, Ospakar; come down from that soft seat of thine and here and now let us put it to the proof who is the better man. When we met before, the stake was Whitefire set against my eye. Now the stake is our lives and fair Gudruda's hand. Talk no more, Ospakar, but fall to it.'

'Gudruda shall never wed thee, while I live!' said Björn; 'thou art a landless loon, a brawler, and an outlaw. Get thee gone, Eric, with thy wolf-hound!'

'Squeak not so loud, rat—squeak not so loud, lest hound's fang worry thee!' said Skallagrim.

'Whether I wed Gudruda or whether I wed her not is a matter that shall be known in its season,' said Eric. 'For thy words, I say this: that it is risky to hurl names at such as I am, Björn, lest perchance I answer them with spear-thrusts. Thy answer, Ospakar! What need to wait? Thy answer!'

Now Ospakar looked at Brighteyes and grew afraid. He was a mighty man, but he knew the weight of Eric's arm.

'I will not fight with thee, carle,' he said, 'who hast naught to lose.'

'Then thou art coward and niddering!' said Eric. 'Ospakar *Niddering* I name thee here before all men! What! thou couldst plot against me—thou couldst waylay me, ten to one and two ships to one, but face to face with me alone thou dost not dare to stand? Comrades, look on your lord!—look at Ospakar the *Niddering!*'

Now the swarthy brow of Blacktooth grew red with rage, and his breath came in great gasps. 'Ho, men!' he cried, 'drive this knave away. Strip his harness off him and whip him hence with rods.'

'Let but a man stir towards me and this spear flies through thy heart, Niddering,' cried Eric. 'Gudruda, what thinkest thou of thy lord?'

'I know this,' said Gudruda, 'that I will not wed a man who is named "Niddering" in the face of all and lifts no sword.'

Gudruda spoke thus, because she was mad with love and fear and shame, and she desired that Eric should stand face to face with Ospakar Blacktooth, for thus, alone, she might perhaps be rid of Ospakar.

'Such words do not come well from gentle lips,' said Björn.

'Is it to be borne, brother,' answered Gudruda, 'that the man who would call me wife should be named Ospakar the Niddering? When that shame is washed away, and then only, can I think on marriage. I will never be Niddering's bride!'

'Thou hearest, Ospakar Niddering?' said Eric. Then he gave the spear in his hand to Skallagrim, and, gripping Whitefire's hilt, he burst the peace-strings, and tore it from the scabbard.

Now the great sword shone on high like lightning leaping from a cloud, and as it shone men shouted, '*Ospakar! Ospakar Niddering!* Come, win back Whitefire from Eric's hand, or be for ever shamed!'

Blacktooth could endure this no more. He snatched sword and shield, and, like a bear from a cave, like a wolf from his lair, rushed roaring from his seat. On he came, and the ground shook beneath his bulk.

'At last, Niddering!' cried Eric, and sprang to meet him.

'Back! all men, back!' shouted Skallagrim, 'now we shall see blows.'

As he spoke the great swords flashed aloft and clanged upon the iron shields. So heavy were the blows that fire leapt out from them. Ospakar reeled back beneath the shock, and Eric was beaten to his knee. Now he was up, but as he rushed, Ospakar struck again and swept away half of Brighteyen's pointed shield so that it fell upon the floor. Eric smote also, but Ospakar dropped his knee to earth and the sword hissed over him. Blacktooth cut at Eric's legs; but Brighteyes sprang from the ground and took no harm.

Now some cried, '*Eric! Eric!*' and some cried '*Ospakar! Ospakar!*' for no one knew how the fight would go.

Gudruda sat watching in the high seat, and as blows fell her colour came and went.

Swanhild drew near, watching also, and she desired in

her fierce heart to see Eric brought to shame and death, for, should he win, then Gudruda would be rid of Ospakar. Now, by her side stood Gizur, Ospakar's son, and near to her was Björn. These two held their breath, for, if Eric conquered, all their plans were brought to nothing.

Even as he sprang into the air, Eric smote down with all his strength. The blow fell on Ospakar's shield. It shore through the shield and struck on the shoulder beneath. But Blacktooth's byrnie was good, nor did the sword bite on it. Still the stroke was so heavy that Ospakar staggered back four paces beneath it, then fell upon the ground.

Now folk raised a shout of '*Eric! Eric!*' for it seemed that Ospakar was sped. Brighteyes, too, cried aloud, then rushed forward. Now, as he came, Swanhild whispered an eager word into the ear of Björn. By Björn's foot lay that half of Eric's shield that had been shorn away by the sword of Ospakar. Gudruda, watching, saw Björn push it with his shoe so that it slid before the feet of Brighteyes. His right foot caught on it, he stumbled heavily—stumbled again, then fell prone on his face, and, as he fell, stretched out his sword-hand to save himself, so that Whitefire flew from his grasp. The blade struck its hilt against the ground, then circled in the air and fixed itself, point downwards, in the clay of the flooring. The hand of Ospakar rising from the ground smote against the hilt of Whitefire. He saw it, with a shout he cast his own sword away and clasped Whitefire.

Away circled the sword of Ospakar; and of that cast this strange thing is told, false or true. Far in the corner of the hall lurked Thorunna, she who had betrayed Skallagrim when he was named Ounound. She had come with a heavy heart to Middalhof in the company of Ospakar; but when she saw Skallagrim, her husband—whom she had betrayed, and who had turned Baresark because of her wickedness—shame smote her, and she crept away and hid herself behind the hangings of the hall. The sword sped along point first, it rushed like a spear through the air. It fell on the hangings, piercing them, piercing the heart of Thorunna, who cowered behind them, so that with one cry she sank dead to earth, slain by her lover's hand.

Now when men saw that Ospakar once more held White-fire in his hand—Whitefire that Brighteyes had won from him—they called aloud that it was an omen. The sword of Blacktooth had come back to Blacktooth and now Eric would surely be slain by it!

Eric sprang from the ground. He heard the shouts and saw Whitefire blazing in Ospakar's hand.

'Now thou art weaponless, fly! Brighteyes; fly!' cried some.

Gudruda's cheek grew white with fear, and for a moment Eric's heart failed him.

'Fly not!' roared Skallagrim. 'Björn tripped thee. Yet hast thou half a shield!'

Ospakar rushed on, and Whitefire flickered over Eric's helm. Down it came and shore one wing from the helm. Again it shone and fell, but Brighteyes caught the blow on his broken shield.

Then, while men waited to see him slain, Eric gave a great war-shout and sprang forward.

'Thou art mad!' shouted the folk.

'Ye shall see! Ye shall see!' screamed Skallagrim.

Again Ospakar smote, and again Eric caught the blow; and behold! he struck back, thrusting with the point of the shorn shield straight at the face of Ospakar.

'Peck! Eagle; peck!' cried Skallagrim.

Once more Whitefire shone above him. Eric rushed in beneath the sword, and with all his mighty strength thrust the buckler-point at Blacktooth's face. It struck fair and full, and lo! the helm of Ospakar burst asunder. He threw wide his giant arms, then fell as a pine falls upon the mountain edge. He fell back, and he lay still.

But Eric, stooping over him, took Whitefire from his hand.

CHAPTER XXV

HOW THE FEAST ENDED

OR a moment there was silence in the hall, for men had known no such fight as this.

'Why, then, do ye gape, comrades?' laughed Skallagrim, pointing with the spear. 'Dead is Ospakar!— slain by a swordless man! Eric Brighteyes hath slain Ospakar Blacktooth!'

Then there went up such a shout as never was heard in the hall of Middalhof.

Now when Gudruda knew that Ospakar was sped, she looked at Eric as he rested, leaning on his sword, and her heart was filled with awe and love. She sprang from her seat, and, coming to where Brighteyes stood, she greeted him.

'Welcome to Iceland, Eric!' she said. 'Welcome, thou glory of the south!'

Now Swanhild grew wild, for she saw that Eric was about to take Gudruda in his arms and kiss her before all men.

'Say, Björn,' she cried: 'wilt thou suffer that this outlaw, having slain Ospakar, should lead Gudruda hence as wife?'

'He shall never do so while I live,' cried Björn, nearly mad with rage. 'This is my command, sister: that thou dost see Eric no more.'

'Say, Björn,' answered Gudruda, 'did I dream, or did I

indeed see thee thrust the broken buckler before Eric's feet, so that he stumbled on it and fell ? '

'That thou sawest, lady,' said Skallagrim; 'for I saw it also.'

Now Björn turned white in his anger. He did not answer Gudruda, but called aloud to his men to slay Eric and Skallagrim. Gizur called also to the folk of Ospakar, and Swanhild to those who came with her.

Then Gudruda fled back to her seat.

But Eric cried aloud also : ' Ye who love me, cleave to me. Suffer it not that Brighteyes be cut down of northerners and outland men. Hear me, Atli's folk; hear me, carles of Cold-back and of Middalhof ! '

And so greatly did many love Eric that half of the thralls of Björn, and almost all of the company of Swanhild who had been Atli's shield-men and Brighteyes' comrades, drew swords, shouting ' Eric! Eric ! ' But the carles of Ospakar came on to make an end of him.

Björn saw, and, drawing sword, smote at Brighteyes, taking him unawares. But Skallagrim caught the blow upon his axe, and before Björn could smite again Whitefire was aloft and down fell Björn, dead !

This was the end of Björn, Asmund's son.

' Thou hast squeaked thy last, rat ! What did I tell thee ? ' cried Skallagrim. ' Take Bjorn's shield and back to back, lord, for here come foes.'

' There goes one,' answered Eric, pointing to the door.

Now Hall of Lithdale slunk through the doorway—Hall, the liar, who cut the grapnel-chain—for he wished to see the last of Skallagrim. But the Baresark still held Eric's spear in his hand. He whirled it aloft, and it hissed through the air. The aim was good, for, as he crept away, the spear struck Hall between neck and shoulder, pinning him to the doorpost, and there the liar died.

' Now the weasel is nailed to the beam,' said Skallagrim. ' Hall of Lithdale, what did I promise thee ? '

' Guard thy head and my back,' quoth Eric ; ' blows fall ! '

Now men smote at Eric and Skallagrim, nor did they

spare to smite in turn. And as foes fell before him, Eric stepped one pace forward towards the door, and Skallagrim, who, back to back with him, held off those who pressed behind, took one step rearwards. Thus, a foe for every step, they won their way down the long hall. Fierce raged the fray around them, for, mad with hate and drink and the lust of fight, Swanhild's folk—Eric's friends—remembering the words of Atli, fell on Ospakar's; and the people of Björn fell on each other, brother on brother, and father on son— nor might the fray be stayed. The boards were overthrown, dead men lay among the meats and mead, and the blood of freeman, lord and thrall ran adown the floor. Everywhere through the dusky hall glittered the sheen of flashing swords and rose the clang of war. Darts clove the air like tongues of flame, and the clamour of battle beat against the roof.

Blinded of the Norns who brought these things to pass, men sought no mercy and they gave none, but smote and slew till few were left to slay.

And still Gudruda sat in her bride-seat, and, with eyes fixed in horror, watched the waxing of the war. Near to her stood Swanhild, marking all things with fierce-set face, and calling down curses on her folk, who one and all cried '*Eric! Eric!*' and swept the thralls of Ospakar as corn is swept of the sickle.

And there, nigh to the door, pale of face and beautiful to see, golden Eric clove his way, and with him went black Skallagrim. Terrible was the flare of Whitefire as he flickered aloft like the levin in the cloud. Terrible was the flare of Whitefire; but more terrible was the light of Eric's eyes, for they seemed to flame in his head, and wherever that fire fell it lighted men the way to death. Whitefire sung and flickered, and crashed the axe of Skallagrim, and still through the press of war they won their way. Now Gizur stands before them, spear aloft, and Whitefire leaps up to meet him. Lo! he turns and flies. The coward son of Ospakar does not seek the fate of Ospakar!

The door is won. They stand without but little harmed, while women wail aloud.

'To horse!' cried Skallagrim; 'to horse, ere our luck fail us!'

'There is no luck in this,' gasped Eric; 'for I have slain many men, and among them is Björn, the brother of her whom I would make my bride.'

'Better one such fight than many brides,' said Skallagrim, shaking his red axe. 'We have won great glory this day, Brighteyes, and Ospakar is dead — slain by a swordless man!'

Now Eric and Skallagrim ran to their horses, none hindering them, and, mounting, they rode towards Mosfell.

All that evening and all the night they rode, and at morning they came across the black sand to Mosfell slopes that are by the Hecla. Here they rested, and, taking off their armour, washed themselves in the stream: for they were very weary and foul with blood and wounds. When they had finished washing and had buckled on their harness again, Skallagrim, peering across the plain with his hawk's eyes, saw men riding fast towards them.

'Foes are soon afoot, lord,' he said. 'I thought we had stayed their hunger for a while.'

'Would that I might stay mine,' quoth Eric. 'I am weary, and unfit for fight.'

'I have still strength for one or two,' said Skallagrim, 'and then good-night! But these are no foes. They are of the Coldback folk. The carline has kept her word.'

Then Eric was glad, and presently six men, headed by Jon his thrall, the same man who had watched on Mosfell when Eric went up to slay the Baresark, rode to them and greeted them. 'Beggar women,' said Jon, 'whom they met at Ran River, had told them of the death of Ospakar, and of the great slaying at Middalhof, and they would know if the tidings were true.'

'It is true, Jon,' said Eric; 'but first give us food, if ye have it, for we are hungered and spent. When we have eaten we will speak.'

So they led up a pack-horse and from it took stockfish and

smoked meat, of which Eric and Skallagrim eat heartily, till their strength came back to them.

Then Eric spoke. 'Comrades,' he said, 'I am an outlawed man, and, though I have not sought it, much blood is on my head. Atli is dead at my hand; Ospakar is dead at my hand; Björn the Priest, Asmund's son, is dead at my hand, and with them many another man. Nor may the matter stay here, for Gizur, Blacktooth's son, yet lives, and Björn has kin in the south, and Swanhild will buy friends with gold, and all of these will set on me to slay me, so that at the last I die by the sword.'

'No need for that,' said Skallagrim. 'Our vengeance is wrought, and now, as before, the sea is open, and I think that a welcome awaits us in London.'

'Now Gudruda is widowed before she was fully wed,' said Eric, 'therefore I bide an outlawed man here in Iceland. I go hence no more, though it be death to stay, unless indeed Gudruda the Fair goes with me.'

'It will be death, then,' said Skallagrim, 'and the swords are forged that we shall feel. The odds are too heavy, lord.'

'Mayhap,' answered Eric. 'No man may flee his fate, and I shall not altogether grieve when mine finds me. Hearken, comrades: I go up Mosfell height, and there I stay, till those be found who can drag me from my hole. But this is my counsel to you: that ye leave me to my doom, for I am an unlucky man who always chooses the wrong road.'

'That will not I,' said Skallagrim.

'Nor we,' said Eric's folk; 'Swanhild holds Coldback, and we are driven to the fells. To the fells then we will go with thee, Eric Brighteyes, and become cave-dwellers and outlaws for thy sake. Fear not, thou shalt still find many friends.'

'I did not look for such a thing at your hands,' said Eric; 'but stormy waters shew how the boat is built. May no bad luck come to you from your good fellowship. And now let us to our nest.'

Then they caught the horses, and rode with Brighteyes up the steep side of Mosfell, till at length they came to that secret dell which Skallagrim had once shown to Eric. Here they

s

turned the horses loose to feed, and, going forward on foot, reached the dark and narrow pass that Brighteyes had trod when he sought for his Baresark foe. Skallagrim led the way along it, then came Eric and the rest. One by one they stepped on to the giddy point of rock, and, catching at the birch-bush, entered the hole. So they gained the platform and the great cave beyond; and they found that no man had set foot there since the day when Eric had striven with Skallagrim. For there on the rock, rotten with the weather, lay that haft of wood which Brighteyes had hewed from the axe of Skallagrim, and in the cave were many things beside as the Baresark had left them.

So they took up their dwelling in the cave, Eric, Skallagrim, and the six Coldback men, and there they dwelt many months. But Eric sent out men, one at a time, and got together food and a store of sheepskins, and other needful things. For he knew this well: that Gizur and Swanhild would before long come up against them, and, if they could not take them by force, would set themselves to watch the mountain-path and starve them out.

When Eric and Skallagrim rode away from Middalhof the fight still raged fiercely in the hall, and nothing but death might stay it. The minds of men were mad, and they smote one another, and slew each other, till at length of all that marriage company few were left unharmed, except Gizur, Swanhild, and Gudruda. For the serving thralls and women-folk had fled the hall, and with them some peaceful men.

Then Gudruda spoke as one in a dream.

'Saevuna's prophecy was true,' she said, 'red was the marriage-feast of Asmund my father, redder has been the marriage-feast of Ospakar! She saw the hall of Middalhof one gore of blood, and lo! it is so. Look upon thy work, Swanhild,' and she pointed to the piled-up dead—'look upon thy work, witch-sister, and grow fearful: for all this death is on thy head!'

Swanhild laughed aloud. 'I think it a merry sight,' she cried. 'The marriage-feast of Asmund our father was red, and thy marriage-feast, Gudruda, has been redder. Would that thy blood and the blood of Eric ran with the blood of Björn and Ospakar! That tale must yet be told, Gudruda. There shall be binding on of Hell-shoes at Middalhof, but I bind them not. My task is still to come : for I will live to fasten the Hell-shoes on the feet of Eric, and on thy feet, Gudruda! At the least, I have brought about this much, that thou canst scarcely wed Eric the outlaw : for with his own hand he slew Björn our brother, and because of this I count all that death as nothing. Thou canst not mate with Brighteyes, lest the wide wounds of Björn thy brother should take tongues and cry thy shame from sea to sea!'

Gudruda made no answer, but sat as one carved in stone. Then Swanhild spoke again :

'Let us away to the north, Gizur ; there to gather strength to make an end of Eric. Say, wilt thou help us, Gudruda ? The blood-feud for the death of Björn is thine.'

'Ye are enough to bring about the fall of one unfriended man,' Gudruda said. ' Go, and leave me with my sorrow and the dead. Nay! before thou goest, listen, Swanhild, for there is that in my heart which tells me I shall never look again upon thy face. From evil to evil thou hast ever gone, Swanhild, and from evil to evil thou wilt go. It well may chance that thy wickedness will win. It may well chance that thou wilt crown thy crimes with my slaying and the slaying of the man who loves me. But I tell thee this, traitress—murderess, as thou art—that here the tale ends not. Not by death, Swanhild, shalt thou escape the deeds of life ! *There* they shall rise up against thee, and *there* every shame that thou hast worked, every sin that thou hast sinned, and every soul that thou hast brought to Hela's halls, shall come to haunt thee and to drive thee on from age to age ! That witch-craft which thou lovest shall mesh thee. Shadows shall bewilder thee ; from the bowl of empty longing thou shalt drink and drink, and not be satisfied. Yea! lusts shall mock and madden thee. Thou shalt ride the winds, thou shalt sail the seas, but thou shalt find no harbour, and never shalt thou set foot upon a shore of peace.

s 2

'Go on, Swanhild—dye those hands in blood—wade through the river of shame ! Seek thy desire, and finding, lose ! Work thy evil, and winning, fail ! I yet shall triumph—I yet shall trample thee ; and, in a place to come, with Eric at my side, I shall make a mock of Swanhild the murderess ! Swanhild the liar, and the wanton, and the witch ! Now get thee gone ! '

Swanhild heard. She looked up at Gudruda's face and it was alight as with a fire. She strove to answer, but no words came. Then Groa's daughter turned and went, and with her went Gizur.

Now women and thralls came in and drew out the wounded and those who still breathed from among the dead, taking them to the temple. They bore away the body of Ospakar also, but they left the rest.

All night long Gudruda sat in the bride's seat. There she sat in the silver summer midnight, looking on the slain who were strewn about the great hall. All night she sat alone in the bride's seat thinking—ever thinking.

How, then, would it end ? There her brother Björn lay a-cold—Björn the justly slain by Brighteyes ; yet how could she wed the man who slew her brother ? From Ospakar she was divorced by death ; from Eric she was divorced by the blood of Björn her brother ! How might she unravel this tangled skein and float to weal upon this sea of death ? All things went amiss ! The doom was on her ! She had lived to an ill purpose—her love had wrought evil ! What availed it to have been born to be fair among women and to have desired that which might not be ? And she herself had brought these things to pass—she had loosed the rock which crushed her ! Why had she hearkened to that false tale ?

Gudruda sat on high in the bride's seat, asking wisdom of the piled-up dead, while the cold blue shadows of the nightless night gathered over her and them—gathered, and waned, and grew at last to the glare of day.

CHAPTER XXVI

HOW ERIC VENTURED DOWN TO MIDDALHOF AND WHAT HE FOUND

OSPAKAR'S CAIRN.

GIZUR rode north to Swine-fell, and Swanhild went with him. For now that Ospakar was dead at Eric's hand, Gizur ruled in his place at Swinefell, and was the greatest lord in all the north. He loved Swanhild, and desired to make her his wife; but she played with him, talking darkly of what might be. Swanhild was not minded to be the wife of any man, except of Eric; to all others she was cold as the winter earth. Still, she fooled Gizur as she had fooled Atli the Good, and he grew blind with love of her. For still the beauty of Swanhild waxed as the moon waxes in the sky, and her wicked eyes shone as the stars shine when the moon has set.

Now they came to Swinefell, and there Gizur buried Ospakar Blacktooth, his father, with much state. He set him in a chamber of rock and timbers on a mountain-top, whence his ghost might see all the lands that once were his, and built up a great mound of earth above him. To this day people tell that here on Yule night black Ospakar bursts out, and golden Eric rides down the blast to meet him. Then come the clang of swords, and groans, and the sound of riven helms, till presently Brighteyes passes southward on the wind, bearing in his hand the half of a cloven shield.

So Gizur bound the Hell-shoes on his father, and swore that he would neither rest nor stay till Eric Brighteyes was dead and dead was Skallagrim Lambstail.' Then he gathered a great force of men and rode south to Coldback, to the slaying of Eric, and with him went Swanhild.

Gudruda sat alone in the haunted hall of Middalhof and brooded on her love and on her fate. Eric, too, sat in Mosfell cave and brooded on his evil chance. His heart was sick with sorrow, and there was little that he could do except think about the past. He would not go to foray, after the fashion of outlaws, and there was no need of this. For the talk of his mighty deeds spread through the land, so that people spoke of little else. And the men of his quarter were so proud of these deeds of Eric's that, though some of their kin had fallen at his hands in the great fight of Middalhof and some at the hands of Skallagrim, yet they spoke of him as men speak of a God. Moreover they brought him gifts of food and clothing and arms, as many as his people could carry away, and laid them in a booth that is on the plain near the foot of Mosfell, which thenceforth was named Ericsfell. Further, they bade his thralls tell him that, if he wished it, they would find a good ship of war to take him from Iceland—ay, and man it with loyal men and true.

Eric thanked them through Jon his thrall, but answered that he wished to die here in Iceland.

Now, when Eric had sat two months and more in Mosfell cave and autumn was coming, he learned that Gizur and Swanhild had moved down to Coldback, and with them a great company of men who were sworn to slay him. He asked if Gudruda the Fair had also gathered men for his slaying. They told him no; that Gudruda stayed with her thralls and women at Middalhof, mourning for Björn her brother. From these tidings Eric took some heart of hope: at the least Gudruda laid no blood-feud against him. For he waited, thinking, if indeed she yet loved him, that Gudruda would send him some word or token of her love. But no word came, since between them ran the blood of Björn. On the morrow of these tidings Skallagrim spoke to Eric.

'This is my counsel, lord,' he said, 'that we ride out by night and fall on the folk of Gizur at Coldback, and burn the stead over them, putting them to the sword. I am weary of sitting here like an eagle in a cage.'

'Such is no counsel of mine, Skallagrim,' answered Brighteyes. 'I am weary of sitting here, indeed ; but I am yet more weary of bringing men to their death. I will shed no more blood, unless it is to save my own head. When the people of Gizur come to seek me on Mosfell, they shall find me here ; but I will not go to them.'

'Thy heart is out of thee, lord,' said Skallagrim ; 'thou wast not wont to speak thus.'

'Ay, Skallagrim,' said Eric, 'the heart is out of me. Yet I ride from Mosfell to-day.'

'Whither, lord ? '

'To Middalhof, to have speech with Gudruda the Fair.'

'Like enough, then, thou wilt be silent thereafter.'

'It well may be,' said Eric. 'Yet I will ride. I can bear this doubt no longer.'

'Then I shall come with thee,' said Skallagrim.

'As thou wilt,' answered Eric.

So at midday Eric and Skallagrim rode away from Mosfell in a storm of rain. The rain was so heavy that those of Gizur's spies who watched the mountain did not see them. All that day they rode and all the night, till by morning they came to Middalhof. Eric told Skallagrim to stay with the horses and let them feed, while he went on foot to see if by chance he might get speech with Gudruda. This the Baresark did, though he grumbled at the task, fearing lest Eric should be done to death and he not there to die with him.

Now Eric walked to within two bowshots of the house, then sat down in a dell by the river, from the edge of which he could see those who passed in and out. Presently his heart gave a leap, for there came out from the women's door a tall and beautiful lady, with golden hair that flowed about her breast. It was Gudruda, and he saw that she bore a napkin in her hand. Then Eric knew, according to her custom on the warm mornings, that she came alone to bathe in the river, as she had always done from a child. It was her habit to bathe here in this place: for at the bottom of the dell is a spot where reeds and bushes grow thick, and the water lies in a basin of rock and is clear and still. For at this spot a hot spring runs into the river.

Eric went down the dell, hid himself close in the bushes and waited, for he feared to speak with Gudruda in the open field. A while passed, and presently the shadow of the lady crept over the edge of the dell, then she came herself in that beauty which since her day has not been known in Iceland. Her face was sad and sweet, her dark and lovely eyes were sad. On she came, till she stood within a spear's length of where Eric lay, crouched in the bush, and looking at her through the hedge of reeds. Here a flat rock overhung the water, and Gudruda sat herself on this rock, and, shaking off her shoes, dipped her white feet in the water. Then suddenly she threw aside her cloak, baring her arms, and, gazing upon the shadow of her beauty in the mirror of the water, sighed and sighed again, while Eric looked at her with a bursting heart, for as yet he could find no words to say.

Now she spoke aloud. 'Of what use to be so fair?' she said. 'Oh, wherefore was I born so fair to bring death to many and sorrow on myself and him I love?' And she shook her golden hair about her arms of snow, and, holding the napkin to her eyes, wept softly. But it seemed to Eric that between her sobs she called upon his name.

Now Eric could no longer bear the sight of Gudruda weeping. While she wept, hiding her eyes, he rose from behind the screen of reeds and stood beside her in such fashion that his shadow fell upon her. She felt the sunlight pass and looked up. Lo! it was no cloud, but the shape of Eric, and the sun glittered on his golden helm and hair.

'Eric!' Gudruda cried; 'Eric!' Then, remembering how she was attired, snatching her cloak, she threw it about her arms and thrust her wet feet into her shoes. ' Out upon thee ! ' she said ; ' is it not enough, then, that thou shouldst break thy troth for Swanhild's sake, that thou shouldst slay my brother and turn my hall to shambles ? Wouldst now steal upon me thus ! '

' I thought that thou didst weep and call upon my name, Gudruda,' he said humbly.

' By what right art thou here to hearken to my words ? ' she answered. ' Is it, then, strange that I should speak the name of him who slew my brother ? Is it strange that I should weep over that brother whom thou didst slay ? Get thee gone, Erighteyes, before I call my folk to kill thee ! '

' Call on, Gudruda. I set but a small price upon my life. I laid it in the hands of chance when I came from Mosfell to speak with thee, and now I will pay it down if so it pleases thee. Fear not, thy thralls shall have an easy task : for I shall scarcely care to hold my own. Say, shall I call for thee ? '

' Hush ! Speak not so loud ! Folk may hear thee, Eric, and then thou wilt be in danger—I would say that, then shall ill things be told of me, because I am found with him who slew my brother ? '

' I slew Ospakar also, Gudruda. Surely the death of him by whose side thou didst sit as wife is more to thee than the death of Björn ? '

' The bride-cup was not yet drunk, Eric ; therefore J have no blood-feud for Ospakar.'

' Is it, then, thy will that I should go, lady ? '

' Yes, go !—go ! Never let me see thy face again ! '

Brighteyes turned without a word. He took three paces and Gudruda watched him as he went.

' Eric ! ' she called. ' Eric ! thou mayest not go yet : for at this hour the thralls bring down the kine to milk, and they will see thee. Lie thou hid here. I—I will go. For though, indeed, thou dost deserve to die, I am not willing to bring thee to thy end—because of old friendship I am not willing ! '

' If thou goest I will go also,' said Eric. ' Thralls or no thralls, I will go, Gudruda.'

'Thou art cruel to drive me to such a choice, and I have a mind to give thee to thy fate.'

'As thou wilt,' said Eric ; but she made as though she did not hear his words.

'Now,' she said, 'if we must stay here, it is better that we hide where thou didst hide, lest some come upon thee.' And she passed through the screen of rushes and sat down in a grassy place beyond, and spoke again.

'Nay, sit not near me; sit yonder. I would not touch thee, nor look upon thee, who wast Swanhild's love, and didst slay Björn my brother.'

'Say, Gudruda,' said Eric, 'did I not tell thee of the magic arts of Swanhild? Did I not tell thee before all men yonder in the hall, and didst thou not say that thou didst believe my words ? Speak.'

'That is true,' said Gudruda.

'Wherefore, then, dost thou taunt me with being Swanhild's love—with being the love of her whom of all alive I hate the most—and whose wicked guile has brought these sorrows on us ? '

But Gudruda did not answer.

'And for this matter of the death of Björn at my hands, think, Gudruda : was I to blame in it ? Did not Björn thrust the cloven shield before my feet, and thus give me into the hand of Ospakar ? Did he not afterwards smite at me from behind, and would he not have slain me if Skalla-grim had not caught the blow? Was I, then, to blame if I smote back and if the sword flew home ? Wilt thou let the needful deed rise up against our love ? Speak, Gudruda ! '

'Talk no more of love to me, Eric,' she answered ; 'the blood of Björn has blotted out our love : it cries to me for vengeance. How may I speak of love with him who slew my brother ? Listen ! ' she went on, looking on him side-long, as one who wished to look and yet not seem to see : ' here thou must hide an hour, and, since thou wilt not sit in silence, speak no tender words to me, for it is not fitting ; but tell me of those deeds thou didst in the south lands over sea, before thou wentest to woo Swanhild and camest hither to kill my brother. For till then thou wast mine—till then I loved thee—who now love thee not. Therefore I would hear of the deeds of that Eric whom once I loved, before he became as one dead to me.'

'Heavy words, lady,' said Eric—'words to make death easy.'

'Speak not so,' she said ; 'it is unmanly thus to work upon my fears. Tell me those tidings of which I ask.'

So Eric told her all his deeds, though he showed small boastfulness about them. He told her how he had smitten the war-dragons of Ospakar, how he had boarded the Raven and with Skallagrim slain those who sailed in her. He told her also of his deeds in Ireland, and of how he took the viking ships and came to London town.

And as he told, Gudruda listened as one who hangs upon her lover's dying words, and there was but one light in the world for her, the light of Eric's eyes, and there was but one music, the music of his voice. Now she looked upon him sidelong no longer, but with open eyes and parted lips she drank in his words, and always, though she knew it not herself, she crept closer to his side.

Then he told her how he had been greatly honoured by the King of England, and of the battles he had fought in at his side. Lastly, Eric told her how the King would have given him a certain great lady of royal blood in marriage, and how Edmund had been angered because he would not stay in England.

'Tell me of this lady,' said Gudruda, quickly. 'Is she fair, and how is she named ?'

'She is fair, and her name is Elfrida,' said Eric.

'And didst thou have speech with her on this matter ?'

'Somewhat.'

Now Gudruda drew herself away from Eric's side.

'What was the purport of thy speech ?' she said, looking down. 'Speak truly, Eric.'

'It came to little,' he answered. 'I told her that there was one in Iceland to whom I was betrothed, and to Iceland I must go.'

' And what said this Elfrida, then ? '

' She said that I should get little luck at the hands of Gudruda the Fair. Moreover, she asked, if my betrothed chanced to be faithless to me, or put me from her, whether I should come again to England.'

Now Gudruda looked him in the face and spoke. ' Say, Eric, is it in thy mind to sail for England in the spring, if thou canst escape thy foes so long ? '

Now Eric took counsel with himself, and in his love and doubt grew guileful as he had never been before. For he knew well that Gudruda had this weakness—she was a jealous woman.

' Since thou dost put me from thee, that is in my mind, lady, for there good fortune waits me,' he answered.

Gudruda heard. She thought on the great and beauteous Lady Elfrida, far away in England, and of Eric walking at her side, and sorrow took hold of her. She said no word, but fixed her dark eyes on Brighteyes' face, and lo ! they filled with tears.

Eric might not bear this sight, for his heart beat within him as though it would burst the byrnie over it. Suddenly he stretched out his arms and swept her to his breast. Soft and sweet he kissed her, again and yet again, and she did not struggle, though she wept a little.

' It is small blame to me,' she whispered, ' if thou dost hold me on thy breast and kiss me, for thou art more strong than I. Björn must know this if his dead eyes see aught. Yet for thee, Eric, it is the greatest shame of all thy shames.'

' Talk not, my sweet ; talk not,' said Eric, ' but kiss thou me : for thou knowest well that thou lovest me yet as I love thee.'

Now the end of it was that Gudruda yielded and kissed him whom she had not kissed for three long years and more.

' Loose me, Eric,' she said ; ' I would speak with thee,' and he loosed her, though unwillingly.

' Hearken,' she went on, hiding her fair face in her hands: ' it is true that for life and death I love thee now as ever—how much thou mayest never know. Though Björn be dead at thy hands, yet I love thee ; but how I may wed thee and not win the greatest shame I do not know. I am sure of one thing, that we may not bide here in Iceland. Now if, indeed, thou lovest me, listen to my rede. Get thee back to Mosfell, Eric, and sit there in safety through this winter, for they may not come at thee yonder on Mosfell. Then, if thou art willing, in the spring I will make ready a ship, for I have no ship now, and, moreover, it is too late to sail. Then, perchance, leaving all my lands and goods, I will take thy hand, Eric, and we will fare together to England, seeking such fortune as the Norns may give us. What sayest thou ? '

' I say it is a good rede, and would that the spring were come.'

' Ay, Eric, would that the spring were come. Our lot has been hard, and I doubt much if things will go well with us at the last. And now thou must hence, for presently the serving-women will come to seek me. Guard thyself, Eric, as thou lovest me—guard thyself, and beware of Swanhild ! ' Then once more they kissed soft and long, and Eric went.

But Gudruda sat a while behind the screen of reeds, and was very happy for a space. For it was as though the winter were past and summer shone upon her heart again.

CHAPTER XXVII

HOW GUDRUDA WENT UP TO MOSFELL

ERIC walked warily till he came to the dell where he had left Skallagrim and the horses. It was that same dell in which Groa had brewed the poison-draught for Asmund the Priest and Unna, Thorod's daughter.

'What news, lord?' said Skallagrim. 'Thou wast gone so long that I thought of seeking thee. Hast thou seen Gudruda?'

'Ay,' said Eric, 'and this is the upshot of it, that in the spring we sail for England and bid farewell to Iceland and our ill luck.'

'Would, then, that it were spring,' said Skallagrim, speaking Brighteyes' own words. 'Why not sail now and make an end?'

'Gudruda has no ship and it is late to take the sea. Also I think that she would let a time go by because of the blood-feud which she has against me for the death of Björn.'

'I would rather risk these things than stay the winter through in Iceland,' said Skallagrim, 'it is long from now to spring, and yon wolf's den is cold-lying in the dark months, as I know well.'

'There is light beyond the darkness,' said Eric, and they rode away. Everything went well with them till late at night they came to the slopes of Mosfell. They were half asleep on their horses, being weary with much riding, and the horses were weary also. Suddenly Skallagrim, looking up, caught the faint gleam of light from swords hidden behind some stones.

'Awake, lord!' he cried, 'here are foes ahead.'

Gizur's folk behind the stones heard his voice and came out from their ambush. There were six of them, and they formed in line before the pair. They were watching the mountain, for a rumour had reached them that Eric was abroad, and, seeing him, they had hidden hastily behind the stones.

'Now what counsel shall we take?' said Eric, drawing Whitefire.

'We have often stood against more men than six, and sometimes we have left more men than six to mark where we had stood,' answered Skallagrim. 'It is my counsel that we ride at them!'

'So be it,' said Eric, and spurred his tired horse with his heels. Now when the six saw Eric and Skallagrim charge on them boldly, they wavered, and the end of it was that they broke and fled to either side before a blow was struck. For it had come to this pass, so great was the terror of the names of Eric Brighteyes and Skallagrim Lambstail, that no six men dared to stand before them in open fight.

So the path being clear they rode on up the slope. But when they had gone a little way, Skallagrim turned his horse, and mocked those who had lain in ambush, saying:

'Ye fight well, ye carles of Gizur, Ospakar's son! Ye are heroes, surely! Say now, mighty men, will ye stand there if I come down alone against you?'

At these words the men grew mad with wrath, and flung their spears. Skallagrim caught one on his shield and it fell to the earth, but another passed over his head and struck Eric on the left shoulder, near the neck, making a deep wound. Feeling the spear fast in him, Eric grasped it with his right hand, drew it forth and, turning, hurled it so hard, that the man before it got his death from the blow, for his shield did not serve to stay it. Then the rest fled.

Skallagrim bound up Eric's wound as well as he could, and they went on to the cave. But when Eric's folk, watching above, saw the fight they ran down and met him. Now the hurt was bad and Eric bled much; still, within ten days it healed up for the time.

But a little while after Eric's wound was skinned over, the snows set in on Mosfell, and the days grew short and the nights long. Once Gizur's men to the number of fifty came half way up the mountain to take it; but, when they saw how strong the place was, they feared, and went back, and after that returned no more, though they always watched the fell.

It was very dark and lonesome there upon the mountain. For a while Eric kept in good heart, but as the days went by he grew troubled. For since he was wounded this had come upon him, that he feared the dark, and the death of Atli at his hand and Atli's words weighed more and more upon his mind. They had no candles on the fell, yet, rather than stay in the blackness of the cave, Eric would wrap sheepskins about him and sit by the edge of that gulf down which the head of the Baresark had foretold his fall, and look out at the wide plains and fells and ice-rivers, gleaming in the silver shine of the Northern lights or in the white beams of the stars.

It chanced that Eric had bidden the men who stayed with him to build a stone hut upon the flat space of rock before the cave, and to roof it with turves. He had done this that work might keep them in heart, also that they might have a place to store such goods as they had gathered. Now there was one stone lying near that no two men of their number could move, except Skallagrim and one other. One day, while it was light, Eric watched these two rolling the stone along to where it must stand, and it was slow work. Presently they stayed to rest. Then Eric came and putting his hands beneath the stone, lifted, and while men wondered, he rolled the mass alone, to where it should be set as the corner stone of the hut.

'Ye are all children,' he said, and laughed merrily.

'Ay, when we set our strength against thine, lord,' answered Skallagrim; 'but look: the blood runs from thy neck—the spear-wound has broken out afresh.'

'So it is, surely,' said Eric. Then he washed the wound and bound it up, thinking little of the matter.

But that night, according to his custom, Eric sat on the

edge of the gulf and looked at the winter lights as they played over Hecla's snows. He was sad and heavy at heart, for he thought of Gudruda and wondered much if they should live to wed. Remembering Atli's words, he had little faith in his good luck. Now as Eric sat and thought, the bandage on his neck slipped, so that the hurt bled, and the frost got hold of the wound and froze it, and froze his long hair to it also, in such fashion that when he went to the cave where all men slept, he could not loose his hair from the sore, but lay down with it frozen to him. On the morrow the hair was caked so fast about his neck that it could only be freed by shearing it. But this Eric would not suffer. None, he said, should shear his hair, except Gudruda. Thus he had sworn, and when he broke the oath misfortune had come of it. He would break that vow no more, if it cost him his life. For sorrow and his ill luck had taken so great a hold of Eric's mind that in some ways he was scarcely himself.

So it came to pass that he fell more and more sick, till at length he could not rise from his bed in the cave, but lay there all day and night, staring at the little light which pierced the gloom. Still, he would not suffer that anyone should touch his hair. And when one stole upon him sleeping, thinking so to cut it before he woke, and come at the wound, suddenly he sat up and dealt the man such a buffet on the head that he went near to death from it.

Then Skallagrim spoke.

' On this matter,' he said, ' it seems that Brighteyes is mad. He will not suffer that any touch his hair, except Gudruda, and yet, if his hair is not shorn, he must die, for the wound festers under it. Nor may we cut it by strength, for then he will kill himself in struggling. It is come to this then : either Gudruda must be brought hither or Eric will shortly die.'

' That may not be,' they answered. ' How can the lady Gudruda come here across the snows, even if she will come ? '

' Come she can, if she has the heart,' said Skallagrim, ' though I put little trust in women's hearts. Still, I ride down to Middalhof, and thou, Jon, shalt go with me. For the rest

I charge you watch your lord ; for, if I come back and **find** anything amiss, that shall be the death of some, and if I do not come back but perish on the road, yet I will haunt you.'

Now Jon did not like this task ; still, for love of Eric and fear of Skallagrim he set out with the Baresark. They had a hard journey through the snow-drifts and the dark, but on the third day they came to Middalhof, knocked upon the door and entered.

Now it was supper-time, and people, sitting at meat, saw a great black man, covered with snow and rime, stalk up the hall, and after him another smaller man, who groaned with the cold, and they wondered at the sight. Gudruda sat on the high seat and the firelight beat upon her face.

' Who comes here ? ' she said.

' One who would speak with thee, lady,' answered Skallagrim.

' Here is Skallagrim the Baresark,' said a man. ' He is an outlaw, let us kill him ! '

' Ay, it is Skallagrim,' he answered, ' and if there is killing to be done, why here's that which shall do it,' and he drew out his axe and smiled grimly.

Then all held their peace, for they feared the axe of Skallagrim.

' Lady,' he said, ' I do not come for slaying or such child's play, I come to speak a word in thine ear—but first I ask a cup of mead and a morsel of food, for we have spent three days in the snows.'

So they ate and drank. Then Gudruda bade the Baresark draw near and tell her his tale.

' Lady,' said he, ' Eric, my lord, lies dying on Mosfell.'

Gudruda turned white as the snow.

' Dying?—Eric lies dying? ' she said. ' Why, then, art thou here? '

' For this cause, lady : I think that thou canst save him, if he is not already sped.' And he told her all the tale.

Now Gudruda thought a while.

' This is a hard journey,' she said, ' and it does not become a maid to visit outlaws in their caves. Yet I am come to this,

that I will die before I shrink from anything that may save
the life of Eric. When must we ride, Skallagrim ? '

' This night,' said the Baresark. 'This night while men
sleep, for now night and day are almost the same. The snow
is deep and we have no time to lose if we would find Brighteyes living.'

' Then we will ride to-night,' answered Gudruda.

Afterwards, when people slept, Gudruda the Fair summoned her women, and bade them say to all who asked for
her that she lay sick in bed. But she called three trusty thralls,
bidding them bring two pack-horses laden with hay, food,
drugs, candles made of sheep's fat, and other goods, and ride

RIDING OVER THE SNOWS.

with her. Then, all being ready, they rode away secretly up
Stonefell, Gudruda on her horse Blackmane, and the others
on good geldings that had been hay-fed in the yard, and by
daylight they passed up Horse-Head Heights. They slept
two nights in the snow, and on the second night almost
perished there, for much soft snow fell. But afterwards
came frost and a bitter northerly wind and they passed on.
Gudruda was a strong woman and great of heart and will,
and so it came about that on the third day she reached
Mosfell, weary but little harmed, though the fingers of her left
hand were frostbitten. They climbed the mountain, and when
they came to the dell where the horses were kept, certain of
Eric's men met them and their faces were sad.

' How goes it now with Brighteyes ? ' said Skallagrim, for

Gudruda could scarcely speak because of doubt and cold. 'Is he dead, then?'

'Nay,' they answered, 'but like to die, for he is beside himself and raves wildly.'

'Push on,' quoth Gudruda; 'push on, lest it be too late.'

So they climbed the mountain on foot, won the pass and came to that giddy point of rock where he must tread who would reach the platform that is before the cave. Now since she had hung by her hands over Goldfoss gulf, Gudruda had feared to tread upon a height with nothing to hold to. Skallagrim went first, then called to her to follow. Thrice she looked, and turned away, trembling, for the place was awful and the fall bottomless. Then she spoke aloud to herself:

'Eric did not fear to risk his life to save me when I hung over Golden Falls; less, then, should I fear to risk mine to save him,' and she stepped boldly down upon the point. But when she stood there, over the giddy height, shivers ran along her body, and her mind grew dark. She clutched at the rock, gave one low cry and began to fall. Indeed she would have fallen and been lost, had not Skallagrim, lying on his breast in the narrow hole, stretched out his arms, caught her by the cloak and kirtle and dragged her to him. Presently her senses came back.

'I am safe!' she gasped, 'but by a very little. Methinks that here in this place I must live and die, for I can never tread yonder rock again.'

'Thou shalt pass it safe enough, lady, with a rope round thee,' said Skallagrim, and led the way to the cave.

Gudruda entered, forgetting all things in her love of Eric. A great fire of turf burned in the mouth of the cave to temper the bitter wind and frost, and by its light Gudruda saw her love through the smoke-reek. He lay upon a bed of skins at the far end of the cave and his bright grey eyes were wild, his wan face was white, and now of a sudden it grew red with fever, and then was white again. He had thrown the sheep-skins from his mighty chest, the bones of which stood out grimly. His long arms were thrust through the locks of his golden hair, and on one side of his neck the hair clung to him and it was but a black mass.

He raved loudly in his madness. ' Touch me not, carles, touch me not; ye think me spent and weak, but, by Thor ! if ye touch my hair, I will loosen the knees of some. Gudruda alone shall shear my hair : I have sworn and I will keep the oath that I once broke. Give me snow ! snow ! my throat burns ! Heap snow on my head, I bid you. Ye will not? Ye mock me, thinking me weak ! Where, then, is Whitefire ?— I have yet a deed to do ! Who comes yonder ? Is it a woman's shape or is it but a smoke-wraith ? 'Tis Swanhild the Father-less who walks the waters. Begone, Swanhild, thou witch ! thou hast worked evil enough upon me. Nay, it is not Swan-hild, it is Elfrida; lady, here in England I may not stay. In Iceland I am at home. Yea, yea, things go crossly; perchance in this garden we may speak again ! '

Now Gudruda could bear his words no longer, but ran to him and knelt beside him.

' Peace, Eric ! ' she whispered. ' Peace ! It is I, thy love. It is Gudruda, who am come to thee.'

He turned his head and looked upon her strangely.

'No, no,' he said, ' it is not Gudruda the Fair. She will have little to do with outlaws, and this is too rough a place for her to come to. It is dark also and Atli speaks in the darkness. If thou art Gudruda, give me a sign. Why comest thou here and where is Skallagrim ? Ah ! that was a good fight—

> Down amongst the ballast tumbling
> Ospakar's shield-carles were rolled.

But he should never have slain the steersman. The axe goes first and Skallagrim follows after. Ha, ha ! Ay, Swanhild, we'll mingle tears ! Give me the cup. Why, what is this ? Thou art afire, a glory glows about thee, and from thee floats a scent like the scent of the Iceland meads in May.'

' Eric ! Eric ! ' cried Gudruda, ' I am come to shear thy hair, as thou didst swear that I alone should do.'

' Now I know that thou art Gudruda,' said the crazed

man. 'Cut, cut; but let not those knaves touch my head, lest I should slay them.'

Then Gudruda drew out her shears, and without more ado shore off Brighteyes' golden locks. It was no easy task, for they were thick as a horse's mane, and glued to the wound. Yet when she had cut them, she loosened the hair from the flesh with water which she heated upon the fire. The wound was festered and blue, still Eric never winced while she dragged the hair from it. Then she washed the sore clean, and put sweet ointment on it and covered it with napkins.

This done, she gave Eric broth and he drank. Then, laying her hand upon his head, she looked into his eyes and bade him sleep. And presently he slept—which he had scarcely done for many days—slept like a little child.

Eric slept for a day and a night. But at that same hour of the evening, when he had fallen asleep, Gudruda, watching him by the light of a taper that was set upon a rock, saw him smile in his dreams. Presently he opened his eyes and stared at the fire which glowed in the mouth of the cave, and the great shadows that fell upon the rocks.

' Strange!' she heard him murmur, it is very strange! but I dreamed I slept, and that Gudruda the Fair leaned over me as I slept. Where, then, is Skallagrim? Perhaps I am dead and that is Hela's fire,' and he tried to lift himself upon his arm, but fell back from faintness, for he was very weak. Then Gudruda took his hand, and, leaning over him, spoke:

' Hush, Eric!' she said; 'that was no dream, for I am here. Thou hast been sick to death, Eric; but now, if thou wilt rest, things shall go well with thee.'

' *Thou* art here?' said Eric, turning his white face towards her. 'Do I still dream, or how camest thou here to Mosfell, Gudruda?'

' I came through the snows, Eric, to cut thy hair, which clung to the festering wound, for in thy madness thou wouldst not suffer anyone to touch it.'

' Thou camest through the snows—over the snows—to nurse me, Gudruda? Thou must love me much then,' and he was so weak that, as he spoke, the tears rolled down Eric's cheeks.

Then Gudruda kissed him, weeping also, and, laying her face by his, bade him be at peace, for she was there to watch him.

CHAPTER XXVIII

HOW SWANHILD WON TIDINGS OF ERIC

Now Eric's strength came back to him and his heart opened in the light of Gudruda's eyes like a flower in the sunshine. For all day long she sat at his side, holding his hand and talking to him, and they found much to say.

But on the fifth day from the day of his awakening she spoke thus :

'Eric, now I must go back to Middalhof. Thou art safe and it is not well that I should stay here.'

'Not yet, Gudruda,' he said ; 'do not leave me yet.'

'Yes, love, I must leave thee. The moon is bright, the sky has cleared, and the snow is hard with frost and fit for the hoofs of horses. I must go before more storms come. Listen now : in the second week of spring, if all is well, I will send thee a messenger with words of token, then shalt thou come down secretly to Middalhof, and there, Eric, we will be wed. Then, on the next day, we will sail for England in a trading-ship that I shall get ready, to seek our fortune there.'

'It will be a good fortune if thou art by my side,' said Eric, 'so good that I doubt greatly if I may find it, for I am Eric the Unlucky. Swanhild must yet be reckoned with, Gudruda. Yes, thou art right : thou must go hence, Gudruda, and swiftly, though it grieves me much to part with thee.'

Then Eric called Skallagrim and bade him make things ready to ride down to Middalhof with the Lady Gudruda.

This Skallagrim did swiftly, and afterwards Eric and Gudruda kissed and parted, and they were sad at heart to part.

Now on the fifth day after the going of Gudruda, Skallagrim came back to Mosfell somewhat cold and weary. And he told Eric, who could now walk and grew strong again, that he and Jon had ridden with Gudruda the Fair to Horse-Head Heights, seeing no man, and had left her there to go on with her thralls. He had come back also meeting no one, for the weather was too cold for the men of Gizur to watch the fell in the snows.

Now Gudruda came safely to Middalhof, having been eleven days gone, and found that few had visited the house, and that these had been told that she lay sick abed. Her secret had been well kept, and, though Swanhild had no lack of spies, many days went by before she learned that Gudruda had gone up to Mosfell to nurse Eric.

After this Gudruda began to make ready for her flight from Iceland. She called in the moneys that she had out at interest, and with them bought from a certain chapman a good trading-ship which lay in its shed under the shelter of Westman Isles. This ship she began to make ready for sea so soon as the heart of the winter was broken, putting it about that she intended to send her on a trading voyage to Scotland in the spring. And to give colour to this tale she bought many pelts and other goods, such as chapmen deal in.

Thus the days passed on—not so badly for Gudruda, who strove to fill their emptiness in making ready for the full and happy time; but for Eric in his cave they were very heavy, for he could find nothing to do except to sleep and eat, and think of Gudruda, whom he might not see.

For Swanhild also, sitting at Coldback, the days did not go well. She was weary of the courting of Gizur, whom she played with as a cat plays with a rat, but found the sport poor, and her heart was sick with love, hate, and jealousy. For she well knew that Gudruda and Eric still clung to each other and had means of greeting, if not of speech. At that time she wished to kill Eric if she could, though she would rather kill Gudruda if she dared. Still, she could not come at Eric, for her men feared to try the narrow way of Mosfell, and when they met him in the open they fled before him.

Presently it came to her ears that Gudruda made a ship ready to sail to Scotland on a trading voyage, and she was perplexed by this tale, for she knew that Gudruda had no love of trading and never thought of gain. So she set spies to watch the ship. Still, the slow days drew on, and at length the air grew soft with spring, and flowers showed through the snow.

Eric sat in his mountain nest waiting for tidings, and watched the nesting eagles wheel about the cliffs. At length news came. For one morning, as he rose, Skallagrim told him that a man wished to speak with him. He had come to the mountain in the darkness, and had lain in a dell till the breaking of the light, for, now that the snows were melting, the men of Gizur and Swanhild watched the pathways.

Eric bade them bring the man to him. When he saw him he knew that he was a thrall of Gudruda's, and welcomed him heartily.

' What tidings ? ' he asked.

' This, lord,' said the thrall : ' Gudruda the Fair bids me say that she is well and that the snows melt on the roof of Middalhof.'

Now this was the signal word that had been agreed upon between Eric and Gudruda, that she should send him when all was ready.

' Good,' said Eric, ' ride back to Gudruda the Fair and say that Eric Brighteyes is well, but on Hecla the snows melt not.'

By this answer he meant that he would be with her presently, though the thrall could make nothing of it. Then Skallagrim asked tidings of the man, and learned that Swanhild was still at Middalhof, and with her Gizur, and that they gave out that they wished to make an end of waiting and slay Eric.

' First snare your bird, then wring his neck,' laughed Skallagrim.

Then Eric did this : among his men were some who he knew were not willing to sail from Iceland, and Jon, his thrall, was of them, for Jon did not love the angry sea. He bade these bide a while on Mosfell and make fires nightly on the platform of rock which is in front of the cave, that the spies of Gizur and Swanhild might be deceived by them, and think that Eric was still on the fell. Then, when they heard that he had sailed, they were to come down and hide themselves with friends till Gizur and his following rode north. But he told two of the men who wished to sail with him to make ready.

That night before the moon rose Eric said farewell to Jon and the others who stayed on Mosfell, and rode away with Skallagrim and the two who went with him. They passed the plain of black sand in safety, and so on to Horse-Head Heights. Now at length, as the afternoon drew on to evening, from Stonefell's crest they saw the Hall of Middalhof before them, and Eric's heart swelled in his breast. Yet they must wait till darkness fell before they dared enter the place, lest they might be seen and notice of their coming should be carried to Gizur and Swanhild. And this came into the mind of Eric, that of all the hours of his life that hour of waiting was the longest. Scarcely, indeed, could Skallagrim hold him back from going down the mountain side, he was so set on coming to Gudruda whom he should wed that night.

At length the darkness fell, and they went on. Eric rode swiftly down the rough mountain path, while Skallagrim and the two men followed grumbling, for they feared that their horses would fall. At length they came to the place, and riding into the yard, Eric sprang from his horse and strode to the women's door. Now Gudruda stood in the porch, listening; and while he was yet some way off, she heard the clang of Brighteyen's harness, and the colour came and went upon her cheek. Then she turned and fled to the high seat of the hall, and sat down there. Only two women were left in Middalhof with her, and some thralls who tended the kine and horses. But these slept, not in the hall, but in an outhouse. Gudruda had sent the rest of her people down to the ship to help in the lading, for it was given out that the vessel sailed on the morrow. She had done this that there might be no talk of the coming of Eric to Middalhof.

Now Brighteyes came to the porch, and, finding the door wide, walked in. But Skallagrim and the men stayed without a while, and tended the horses. A fire burned upon the centre hearth in the hall, and threw shadows on the paneling. Eric walked on by its light, looking to left and right, but seeing neither man nor woman. Then a great fear took him lest Gudruda should be gone, or perhaps slain by Swanhild, Groa's daughter, and he trembled at the thought. He stood near the fire, and Gudruda, watching from the shadow of the high seat, saw the dull light glow upon his golden helm, and a sigh of joy broke from her lips. Eric heard the sigh and looked, and as he looked a stick of pitchy drift-wood fell into the flame and flared up fiercely. Then he saw. There, in the carved high seat, robed all in bridal white, sat Gudruda the Fair, his love. Her golden hair flowed about her breast, her white arms were stretched towards him, and on her sweet face shone such a look of love as he had never seen.

' *Eric !* ' she whispered softly, and the breath of her voice ran down the empty paneled hall, that from all sides seemed to answer, ' *Eric.* '

Slowly he drew near to her. He saw nothing but the glory of Gudruda's face and the light shining on Gudruda's hair ; he heard nothing save the sighing of her breath ; he knew nothing except that before him sat his fair bride, won after many years.

Now he had climbed the high seat, and now, wrapped in each other's arms, they sat and gazed into each other's eyes, and lo ! the air of the great hall rolled round them a sea of glory, and sweet voices whispered in their ears. Now Freya smiled upon them and led them through her gates of love, and they were glad that they had been born.

Thus then they were wed.

Now the story tells that Swanhild spoke with Gizur, Ospakar's son, in the house at Coldback.

'I tire of this slow play,' she said. 'We have tarried here for many weeks, and Atli's blood yet cries out for vengeance, and cries for vengeance the blood of black Ospakar, thy father, and the blood of many another, dead at great Eric's hand.'

'I tire also,' said Gizur, 'and I am much needed in the north. I say this to thee, Swanhild, that, hadst thou not so strictly laid it on me that Eric must die ere thou weddest me, I had flitted back to Swinefell before now, and there bided my time to bring Brighteyes to his end.'

'I will never wed thee, Gizur, till Eric is dead,' said Swanhild fiercely.

'How shall we come at him then?' he answered. 'We may not go up that mountain path, for two men can hold it against all our strength, and folk do not love to meet Eric and Skallagrim in a narrow way.'

'The place has been badly watched,' said Swanhild. 'I am sure of this, that Eric has been down to Middalhof and seen Gudruda, my half-sister. She is shameless, that still holds commune with him who slew her brother and my husband. Death should be her reward, and I am minded to slay her because of the shame which she has brought upon our blood.'

'That is a deed which thou wilt do alone, then,' said Gizur, 'for I will have no hand in the murder of this fair maid—no nor will any who live in Iceland!'

Swanhild glanced at him strangely. 'Hearken, Gizur!' she said: 'Gudruda makes a ship ready to sail with goods to Scotland and bring a cargo thence before winter comes again. Now I find this strange, for never before did I know Gudruda turn her thoughts to trading. I think that she has it in her mind to sail from Iceland with this outlaw Eric, and seek a home over seas, and that I will not bear.'

'It may be,' said Gizur, 'and I should not be sorry to see the last of Brighteyes, for I think that more men will die at his hand before he stiffens in his barrow.'

'Thou art cowardly-hearted, thou son of Ospakar!' Swanhild said. 'Thou sayest thou lovest me and wouldest win me to

U

wife : I tell thee that there is but one road to my arms, and it leads over the corpse of Eric. Now this is my counsel: that we send the most of our men to watch that ship of Gudruda's, and, when she lifts anchor, to board her and search, for she is already bound for sea. Also among the people here I have a carle who was born near Hecla, and he swears to me that, when he was a lad, searching for an eagle's eyrie, he found a path by which Mosfell might be climbed from the north, and that in the end he came to a large flat place, and, looking over, saw that platform where Eric dwells with his thralls. But he could not see the cave, because of the overhanging brow of the rock. Now we will do this : thou and I, and the carle alone—no more, for I do not wish that our search should be noised abroad—to-morrow at the dawn we will ride away for Mosfell, and, passing under Hecla, come round the mountain and see if this path can still be scaled. For, if so, we will return with men and make an end of Brighteyes.'

This plan pleased Gizur, and he said that it should be so.

So very early on the following morning Swanhild, having sent many men to watch Gudruda's ship, rode away secretly with Gizur and the thrall, and before it was again dawn they were on the northern slopes of Mosfell. It was on this same night that Eric went down from the mountain to wed Gudruda.

For a while the climbing was easy, but at length they came to a great wall of rock, a hundred fathoms high, on which no fox might find a foothold, nor anything that had not wings.

'Here now is an end of our journey,' said Gizur, 'and I only pray this, that Eric may not ride round the mountain before we are down again.' For he did not know that Brighteyes already rode hard for Middalhof.

'Not so,' said the thrall, 'if only I can find the place by which, some thirty summers ago, I won yonder rift, and through it the crest of the fell,' and he pointed to a narrow cleft in the face of the rock high above their heads, that was clothed with grey moss.

Then he moved to the right and searched, peering behind stones and birch-bushes, till presently he held up his hand and whistled. They passed along the slope and found him standing by a little stream of water which welled from beneath a great rock.

'Here is the place,' the man said.

'I see no place,' answered Swanhild.

'Still, it is there, lady,' and he climbed on to the rock, drawing her after him. At the back of it was a hole, almost overgrown with moss. 'Here is the path,' he said again.

'Then it is one that I have no mind to follow,' answered Swanhild. 'Gizur, go thou with the man and see if his tale is true. I will stay here till ye come back.'

Then the thrall let himself down into the hole and Gizur went after him. But Swanhild sat there in the shadow of the rock, her chin resting on her hand, and waited. Presently, as she sat, she saw two men ride round the base of the fell, and strike off to the right towards a turf-booth which stood the half of an hour's ride away. Now Swanhild was the keenest-sighted of all women of her day in Iceland, and when she looked at these two men she knew one of them for Jon, Eric's thrall, and she knew the horse also—it was a white horse with black patches, that Jon had ridden for many years. She watched them go till they came to the booth, and it seemed to her that they left their horses there and entered.

Swanhild waited upon the side of the fell for nearly two hours in all. Then, hearing a noise above her, she looked up, and there, black with dirt and wet with water, was Gizur, and with him was the thrall.

'What luck, Gizur?' she asked.

'This, Swanhild: Eric shall hold Mosfell no more, for we have found a way to bolt the fox.'

'That is good news, then,' said Swanhild. 'Say on.'

'Yonder hole, Swanhild, leads to the cleft above, having been cut through the cliff by fire, or perhaps by water. Now up that cleft a man may climb, though hardly, as by a difficult stair, till he comes to the flat crest of the fell. Then, crossing

U 2

the crest, on the further side, perhaps six fathoms below him, he sees that space of rock where is Eric's cave; but he cannot see the cave itself, because the brow of the cliff hangs over. And so it is that, if any come from the cave on to the space of rock, it will be an easy matter to roll stones upon them from above and crush them.'

Now when Swanhild heard this she laughed aloud.

'Eric shall mock us no more,' she said, 'and his might can avail nothing against rocks rolled on him from above. Let us go back to Coldback and summon men to make an end of Brighteyes.'

So they went on down the mountain till they came to the place where they had hidden their horses. Then Swanhild remembered Jon and the other man whom she had seen riding to the booth, and she told Gizur of them.

'Now,' she said, 'we will snare these birds, and perchance they will twitter tidings when we squeeze them.'

So they turned and rode for the booth, and drawing near, they saw the two horses grazing without. Now they got off their horses, and creeping up to the booth, looked in through the door which was ajar, and saw that one man sat on the ground with his back to the door, eating stock-fish, while Jon made bundles of fish and meal ready to tie on the horses. For it was here that those of his quarter who loved Eric brought food to be carried by his men to the cave on Mosfell.

Now Swanhild touched Gizur on the arm, pointing first to the man who sat eating the fish and then to the spear in Gizur's hand. Gizur thought a while, for he shrank from this deed.

Then Swanhild whispered in his ear, 'Slay the man and seize the other; I would learn tidings from him.'

So Gizur cast the spear, and it passed through the man's breast, and he was dead at once. Then he and the thrall leapt into the booth and threw themselves on Jon, hurling him to the ground, and holding swords over him. Now Jon was a man of small heart, and when he saw his plight and his fellow dead he was afraid, and prayed for mercy.

'If I spare thee, knave,' said Swanhild, 'thou shalt do this : thou shalt lead me up Mosfell to speak with Eric.'

'I can not do that, lady,' groaned Jon ; 'for Eric is not on Mosfell.'

'Where is he, then ? ' asked Swanhild.

Now Jon saw that he had said an unlucky thing, and answered :

'Nay, I know not. Last night he rode from Mosfell with Skallagrim Lambstail.'

'Thou liest, knave,' said Swanhild. 'Speak, or thou shalt be slain.'

'Slay on,' groaned Jon, glancing at the swords above him, and shutting his eyes. For, though he feared much to die, he had no will to make known Eric's plans.

'Look not at the swords ; thou shalt not die so easily. Hearken : speak, and speak truly, or thou shalt seek Hela's lap after this fashion,' and, bending down, she whispered in his ear, then laughed aloud.

Now Jon grew faint with fear ; his lips turned blue, and his teeth chattered at the thought of how he should be made to die. Still, he would say nothing.

Then Swanhild spoke to Gizur and the thrall, and bade them bind him with a rope, tear the garments from him, and bring snow. They did this, and pushed the matter to the drawing of knives. But when he saw the steel Jon cried aloud that he would tell all.

'Now thou takest good counsel,' said Swanhild.

Then in his fear Jon told how Eric had gone down to Middalhof to wed Gudruda, and thence to fly with her to England.

Now Swanhild was mad with wrath, for she had sooner died than that this should come about.

'Let us away,' she said to Gizur. 'But first kill this man.'

'Nay,' said Gizur, 'I will not do that. He has told his tidings ; let him go free.'

'Thou art chicken-hearted,' said Swanhild, who, after the fashion of witches, had no mercy in her. 'At the least, he shall not go hence to warn Eric and Gudruda of our coming. If thou wilt not kill him, then bind him and leave him.'

So Jon was bound, and there in the booth he sat two days before anyone came to loose him.

'Whither away?' said Gizur to Swanhild.

'To Middalhof first,' Swanhild answered.

JON BOUND

CHAPTER XXIX

HOW WENT THE BRIDAL NIGHT

NOW Eric and Gudruda sat silent in the high seat of the hall at Middalhof till they heard Skallagrim enter by the women's door. Then they came down from the high seat, and stood hand in hand by the fire on the hearth. Skallagrim greeted Gudruda, looking at her askance, for Skallagrim stood in fear of women alone.

'What counsel now, lord?' said the Baresark.

'Tell us thy plans, Gudruda,' said Eric, for as yet no word had passed between them of what they should do.

'This is my plan, Eric,' she answered. 'First, that we eat; then that thy men take horse and ride hence through the night to where the ship lies, bearing word that we will be there at dawn when the tide serves, and bidding the mate make everything ready for sailing. But thou and I and Skallagrim will stay here till to-morrow is three hours old, and this because I have tidings that Gizur's folk will search the ship to-night. Now, when they search and do not find us, they will go away. Then, at the dawning, thou and I and Skallagrim will row on board the ship as she lies at anchor, and, slipping the cable, put to sea before they know we are there, and so bid farewell to Swanhild and our woes.'

'Yet it is a risk for us to sleep here alone,' said Eric.

'There is little danger,' said Gudruda. 'Nearly all of Gizur's men watch the ship; and I have learned this from a spy, that, two days ago, Gizur, Swanhild, and one thrall rode from Coldback towards Mosfell, and they have not come back yet. Moreover, the place is strong, and thou and Skallagrim are here to guard it.'

'So be it, then,' answered Eric, for indeed he had little thought left for anything, except Gudruda.

After this the women came in and set meat on the board, and all ate.

Now, when they had eaten, Eric bade Skallagrim fill a cup, and bring it to him as he sat on the high seat with Gudruda. Skallagrim did so; and then, looking deep into each other's eyes, Eric Brighteyes and Gudruda the Fair, Asmund's daughter, drank the bride's cup.

'There are few guests to grace our marriage-feast, husband,' said Gudruda.

'Yet shall our vows hold true, wife,' said Eric.

'Ay, Brighteyes,' she answered, 'in life and in death, now and for ever!' and they kissed.

'It is time for us to be going, methinks,' growled Skallagrim to those about him. 'We are not wanted here.'

Then the men who were to go on to the ship rose, fetched their horses, and rode away. Also they caught the horses of Skallagrim, Eric, and Gudruda, saddled them, and, slipping their bridles, made them fast in a shed in the yard, giving them hay to eat. Afterwards Skallagrim barred the men's door and the women's door, and, going to Gudruda, asked where he should stay the night till it was time to ride for the sea.

'In the store-chamber,' she answered, 'for there is a

shutter of which the latch has gone. See that thou watch it well, Skallagrim; though I think none will come to trouble thee.'

'I know the place. It shall go badly with the head that looks through yonder hole,' said Skallagrim, glancing at his axe.

Now Gudruda forgot this, that in the store-chamber were casks of strong ale.

Then Gudruda told him to wake them when the morrow was two hours old, for Eric had neither eyes nor words except for Gudruda alone, and Skallagrim went.

The women went also to their shut bed at the end of the hall, leaving Brighteyes and Gudruda alone. Eric looked at her.

'Where do I sleep to-night?' he asked.

'Thou sleepest with me, husband,' she answered soft, 'for nothing, except Death, shall come between us any more.'

Now Skallagrim went to the store-room, and sat down with his back against a cask. His heart was heavy in him, for he boded no good of this marriage. Moreover, he was jealous. Skallagrim loved but one thing in the world truly, and that was Eric Brighteyes, his lord. Now he knew that henceforth he must take a second place, and that for one thought which Eric gave to him, he would give ten to Gudruda. Therefore Skallagrim was very sad at heart.

'A pest upon the women!' he said to himself, 'for from them comes all evil. Brighteyes owes his ill luck to Swanhild and this fair wife of his, and that is scarcely done with yet. Well, well, 'tis nature; but would that we were safe at sea! Had I my will, we should not have slept here to-night. But they are newly wed, and—well, 'tis nature! Better the bride loves to lie abed than to ride the cold wolds and seek the common deck.'

Now, as Skallagrim grumbled, fear gathered in his heart, he knew not of what. He began to think on trolls and goblins. It was dark in the store-room, except for a little line of light that crept through the crack of the shutter. At length he could bear the darkness and his thoughts no longer, but, rising, threw the shutter wide and let the bright moonlight pour into the chamber, whence he could see the hillside behind, and watch the shadows of the clouds as they floated across it. Again Skallagrim sat down against his cask, and as he sat it moved, and he heard the wash of ale inside it.

'That is a good sound,' said Skallagrim, and he turned and smelt at the cask; 'aye, and a good smell, too! We tasted little ale yonder on Mosfell, and we shall find less at sea.' Again he looked at the cask. There was a spigot in it, and lo! on the shelf stood horn cups.

'It surely is on draught,' he said; 'and now it will stand till it goes sour. 'Tis a pity; but I will not drink. I fear ale— ale is another man! No, I will not drink,' and all the while his hand went up to the cups upon the shelf. 'Eric is better laid yonder in Gudruda's chamber than I am here alone with evil thoughts and trolls,' he said. 'Why, what fish was that we ate at supper? My throat is cracked with thirst! If there were water now I'd drink it, but I see none. Well, one cup to wish them joy! There is no harm in a cup of ale,' and he drew the spigot from the cask and watched the brown drink flow into the cup. Then he lifted it to his lips and drank, saying '*Skoll! skoll!*' [1] nor did he cease till the horn was drained. 'This is wondrous good ale,' said Skallagrim as he wiped his grizzled beard. 'One more cup, and evil thoughts shall cease to haunt me.'

Again he filled, drank, sat down, and for a while was merry. But presently the black thoughts came back into his mind. He rose, looked through the shutter-hole to the hillside. He could see nothing on it except the shadows of the clouds.

'Trolls walk the winds to-night,' he said. 'I feel them pulling at my beard. One more cup to frighten them.'

He drank another draught of ale and grew merry. Then ale called for ale, and Skallagrim drained cup on cup, singing as

[1] 'Health! health!'

he drained, till at last heavy sleep overcame him, and he sank drunken on the ground there by the barrel, while the brown ale trickled round him.

Now Eric Brighteyes and Gudruda the Fair slept side by side, locked in each other's arms. Presently Gudruda was wide awake.

'Rouse thee, Eric,' she said, 'I have dreamed an evil dream.'

He awoke and kissed her.

'What, then, was thy dream, sweet?' he said. 'This is no hour for bad dreams.'

'No hour for bad dreams, truly, husband; yet dreams do not weigh the hour of their coming. I dreamed this: that I lay dead beside thee and thou knewest it not, while Swanhild looked at thee and mocked.'

'An evil dream, truly,' said Eric; 'but see, thou art not dead. Thou hast thought too much on Swanhild of late.'

Now they slept once more, till presently Eric was wide-awake.

'Rouse thee, Gudruda,' he said, 'I too have dreamed a dream, and it is full of evil.'

'What, then, was thy dream, husband?' she asked.

'I dreamed that Atli the Earl, whom I slew, stood by the bed. His face was white, and white as snow was his beard, and blood from his great wound ran down his byrnie. "Eric Brighteyes," he said, "I am he whom thou didst slay, and I come to tell thee this: that before the moon is young again thou shalt lie stiff, with Hell-shoon on thy feet. Thou art Eric the Unlucky! Take thy joy and say thy say to her who lies at thy side, for wet and cold is the bed that waits thee and soon shall thy white lips be dumb." Then he was gone, and lo! in his place stood Asmund, thy father, and he also spoke to me, saying, "Thou who dost lie in my bed and at my daughter's side, know this: the words of Atli are true; but I add these to them: ye shall die, yet is death but the gate of life and love and rest," and he was gone.'

Now Gudruda shivered with fear, and crept closer to Eric's side.

'We are surely fey, for the Norns speak with the voices of Atli and of Asmund,' she said. 'Oh, Eric! Eric! whither go we when we die? Will Valhalla take thee, being so mighty a man, and must I away to Hela's halls, where thou art not? Oh! that would be death indeed! Say, Eric, whither do we go?'

'What said the voice of Asmund?' answered Brighteyes. 'That death is but the gate of life and love and rest. Hearken, Gudruda, my May! Odin does not reign over all the world, for when I sat out yonder in England, a certain holy man taught me of another God—a God who loves not slaughter, a God who died that men might live for ever in peace with those they love.'

'How is this God named, Eric?'

'They name Him the White Christ, and there are many who cling to Him.'

'Would that I knew this Christ, Eric. I am weary of death and blood and evil deeds, such as are pleasing to our Gods. Oh, Eric, if I am taken from thee, swear this to me : that thou wilt slay no more, save for thy life's sake only.'

'I swear that, sweet,' he made answer. 'For I too am weary of death and blood, and desire peace most of all things. The world is sad, and sad have been our days. Yet it is well to have lived, for through many heavy days we have wandered to this happy night.'

'Yea, Eric, it is well to have lived ; though I think that death draws on. Now this is my counsel : that we rise, and that thou dost put on thy harness and summon Skallagrim, so that, if evil comes, thou mayst meet it armed. Surely I thought I heard a sound—yonder in the hall!'

'There is little use in that,' said Eric, 'for things will befall as they are fated. We may do nothing of our own will, I am sure of this, and it is no good to struggle with the Norns. Yet I will rise.'

So he kissed her, and made ready to leave the bed, when suddenly, as he lingered, a great heaviness seized him.

' Gudruda,' he said, ' I am pressed down with sleep.'

' That I am also, Eric,' she said. ' My eyes shut of themselves and I can scarcely stir my limbs. Ah, Eric, we are fey
indeed, and this is—death that comes ! '

' Perchance ! ' he said, speaking heavily.

' Eric !—wake, Eric ! Thou canst not move? Yet hearken
to me—ah ! this weight of sleep ! Thou lovest me, Eric !—is
it not so ? '

' Yea,' he answered.

' Now and for ever thou lovest me—and wilt cleave to me
always wherever we go ? '

' Surely, sweet. Oh, sweet, farewell ! ' he said, and his voice
sounded like the voice of one who speaks across the water.

' Farewell, Eric Brighteyes !—my love—my love, farewell ! '
she answered very slowly, and together they sank into a sleep
that was heavy as death.

Now Gizur, Ospakar's son, and Swanhild, Atli's widow, rode
fast and hard from Mosfell, giving no rest to their horses,
and with them rode that thrall who had showed the secret
path to Gizur. They stayed a while on Horse-Head Heights
till the moon rose. Now one path led hence to the shore that
is against the Westmans, where Gudruda's ship lay bound.
Then Swanhild turned to the thrall. Her beautiful face was
fierce and she had said few words all this while, but in her
heart raged a fire of hate and jealousy which shone through
her blue eyes.

' Listen,' she said to the thrall. ' Thou shalt ride hence
to the bay where the ship of Gudruda the Fair lies at anchor.
Thou knowest where our folk are in hiding. Thou shalt
speak thus to them. Before it is dawn they must take boats
and board Gudruda's ship and search her. And, if they find
Eric, the outlaw, aboard, they shall slay him, if they may.'

' That will be no easy task,' said the thrall.

' And if they find Gudruda they shall keep her prisoner.
But, if they find neither the one nor the other, they shall do
this : they shall drive the crew ashore, killing as few as may
be, and burn the ship.'

'It is an ill deed thus to burn another's ship,' said Gizur.

'Good or ill, it shall be done,' answered Swanhild fiercely. 'Thou art a lawman, and well canst thou meet the suit; moreover Gudruda has wedded an outlaw and shall suffer for her sin. Now go, and see thou tarry not, or thy back shall pay the price.'

The man rode away swiftly. Then Gizur turned to Swanhild, asking: 'Whither, then, do we go?'

'I have said to Middalhof.'

'That is into the wolf's den, if Eric and Skallagrim are there,' he answered: 'I have little chance against the two of them.'

'Nay, nor against the one, Gizur. Why, if Eric's right hand were hewn from him, and he stood unarmed, he would still slay thee with his left, as, swordless, he slew Ospakar thy father. Yet I shall find a way to come at him, if he is there.'

Then they rode on, and Gizur's heart was heavy for fear of Eric and Skallagrim the Baresark. So fiercely did they ride that, within one hour after midnight, they were at the stead of Middalhof.

'We will leave the horses here in the field,' said Swanhild.

So they leaped to earth and, tying the reins of the horses together, left them to feed on the growing grass. Then they crept into the yard and listened. Presently there came a sound of horses stamping in the far corner of the yard. They went thither, and there they found a horse and two geldings saddled, but with the bits slipped, and on the horse was such a saddle as women use.

'Eric Brighteyes, Skallagrim Lambstail, and Gudruda the Fair,' whispered Swanhild, naming the horses and laughing evilly — 'the birds are within! Now to snare them.'

'Were it not best to meet them by the ship?' asked Gizur.

'Nay, thou fool; if once Eric and Skallagrim are back to

back, and Whitefire is aloft, how many shall be dead before they are down, thinkest thou? We shall not find them sleeping twice.'

'It is shameful to slay sleeping men,' said Gizur.

'They are outlaws,' she answered. 'Hearken, Ospakar's son. Thou sayest thou dost love me and wouldst wed me: know this, that if thou dost fail me now, I will never look upon thy face again, but will name thee Niddering in all men's ears.'

Now Gizur loved Swanhild much, for she had thrown her glamour on him as once she did on Atli, and he thought of her day and night. For there was this strange thing about Swanhild, that, though she was a witch and wicked, being both fair and gentle she could lead all men, except Eric, to love her.

But of men she loved Eric alone.

Then Gizur held his peace; but Swanhild spoke again:

'It will be of no use to try the doors, for they are strong. Yet when I was a child before now I have passed in and out the house at night by the store-room casement. Follow me, Gizur.' Then she crept along in the shadow of the wall, for she knew its every stone, till she came to the store-room, and lo! the shutter stood open, and through it the moonlight poured into the chamber. Swanhild lifted her head above the sill and looked, then started back.

'Hush!' she said, 'Skallagrim lies asleep within.'

'Pray the Gods he wake not!' said Gizur beneath his breath, and turned to go. But Swanhild caught him by the arm; then gently raised her head and looked again, long and steadily. Presently she turned and laughed softly.

'Things go well for us,' she said; 'the sot lies drunk. We have nothing to fear from him. He lies drunk in a pool of ale.'

Then Gizur looked. The moonlight poured into the little room, and by it he saw the great shape of Skallagrim. His head was thrown back, his mouth was wide. He snored loudly in his drunken sleep, and all about him ran the brown ale, for the spigot of the cask lay upon the floor. In his left hand was a horn cup, but in his right he still grasped his axe.

'Now we must enter,' said Swanhild. Gizur hung back, but she sprang upon the sill lightly as a fox, and slid thence into the store-room. Then Gizur must follow, and presently he stood beside her in the room, and at their feet lay drunken Skallagrim. Gizur looked first at his sword, then on the Baresark, and lastly at Swanhild.

'Nay,' she whispered, 'touch him not. Perhaps he would cry out—and we seek higher game. He has that within him which will hold him fast a while. Follow where I shall lead.'

She took his hand and, gliding through the doorway, passed along the passage till she came to the great hall. Swanhild could see well in the dark, and moreover she knew the road. Presently they stood in the empty hall. The fire had burnt down, but two embers yet glowed upon the hearth, like red and angry eyes.

For a while Swanhild stood still listening, but there was nothing to hear. Then she drew near to the shut bed where Gudruda slept, and, with her ear to the curtain, listened once more. Gizur came with her, and as he came his foot struck against a bench and stirred it. Now Swanhild heard murmured words and the sound of kisses. She started back, and fury filled her heart. Gizur also heard the voice of Eric, saying : 'I will rise.' Then he would have fled, but Swanhild caught him by the arm.

'Fear not,' she whispered, 'they shall soon sleep sound.'

He felt her stretch out her arms and presently he saw this wonderful thing : the eyes of Swanhild glowing in the darkness as the embers glowed upon the hearth. Now they glowed brightly, so brightly that he could see the outstretched arms and the hard white face beneath them, and now they grew dim, of a sudden to shine bright again. And all the while she hissed words through her clenched teeth.

Thus she hissed, fierce and low :

Gudruda, Sister mine, hearken and sleep !
By the bond of blood I bid thee sleep !—
By the strength that is in me I bid thee sleep !—
    Sleep ! sleep sound !

Eric Brighteyes, hearken and sleep !
By the bond of sin I charge thee sleep !—
By the blood of Atli I charge thee, sleep !—
    Sleep ! sleep sound !

Then thrice she tossed her hands aloft, saying :

From love to sleep !
From sleep to death !
From death to Hela !
Say, lovers, where shall ye kiss again ?

Then the light went out of her eyes and she laughed low. And ever as she whispered, the spoken words of the two in the shut bed grew fainter and more faint, till at length they died away, and a silence fell upon the place.

'Thou hast no cause to fear the sword of Eric, Gizur,' she said. 'Nothing will wake him now till daylight comes.'

'Thou art awesome !' answered Gizur, for he shook with fear. 'Look not on me with those flaming eyes, I pray thee !'

'Fear not,' she said, 'the fire is out. Now to the work.'

'What must we do, then ?'

'*Thou* must do this. Thou must enter and slay Eric.'

'That I can not—that I will not !' said Gizur.

She turned and looked at him, and lo ! her eyes began to flame again —upon his eyes they seemed to burn.

'Thou wilt do as I bid thee,' she said. 'With Eric's sword thou shalt slay Eric, else I will curse thee where thou art, and bring such evil on thee as thou knowest not of.'

'Look not so, Swanhild,' he said. 'Lead on—I come.'

Now they creep into the shut chamber of Gudruda. It is so dark that they can see nothing, and nothing can they hear except the heavy breathing of the sleepers.

This is to be told, that at this time Swanhild had it in her mind to kill, not Eric but Gudruda, for thus she would smite the heart of Brighteyes. Moreover, she loved Eric, and while he lived she might yet win him ; but Eric dead must be Eric

x 2

lost. But on Gudruda she would be bitterly avenged—Gudruda, who, for all her scheming, had yet been a wife to Eric!

Now they stand by the bed. Swanhild puts out her hand, draws down the clothes, and feels the breast of Gudruda beneath, for Gudruda slept on the outside of the bed.

Then she searches by the head of the bed and finds Whitefire which hung there, and draws the sword.

'Here lies Eric, on the outside,' she says to Gizur, 'and here is Whitefire. Strike and strike home, leaving Whitefire in the wound.'

Gizur takes the sword and lifts it. He is sore at heart that he must do such a coward deed; but the spell of Swanhild is upon him, and he dare not flinch from it. Then a thought takes him and he also puts down his hand to feel. It lights upon Gudruda's golden hair, that hangs about her breast and falls from the bed to the ground.

'Here is woman's hair,' he whispers.

'No,' Swanhild answers, 'it is Eric's hair. The hair of Eric is long, as thou hast seen.'

Now neither of them knew that Gudruda had cut Eric's locks when he lay sick on Mosfell, though Swanhild knows well that it is not Brighteyes whom she bids Gizur slay.

Then Gizur, Ospakar's son, lifts the sword, and the faint starlight struggling into the chamber gathers and gleams upon the blade. Thrice he lifts it, and thrice he draws it back. Then with an oath he strikes—and drives it home with all his strength!

From the bed beneath there comes one long sigh and a sound as of limbs trembling against the bed-gear. Then all is still.

'It is done!' he says faintly.

Swanhild puts down her hand once more. Lo! it is wet and warm. Then she bends herself and looks, and behold! the dead eyes of Gudruda glare up into her eyes. She can see them plainly, but none know what she read there. At the least it was something that she loved not, for she reels back against the paneling, then falls upon the floor.

Presently, while Gizur stands as one in a dream, she rises,

saying : ' I am avenged of the death of Atli. Let us hence !—
ah ! let us hence swiftly ! Give me thy hand, Gizur, for I am
faint ! '

So Gizur gives her his hand and they pass thence. Presently they stand in the store-room, and there lies Skallagrim,
still plunged in his drunken sleep.

' Must I do more murder ? ' asks Gizur hoarsely.

' Nay,' Swanhild says. ' I am sick with blood. Leave
the knave.'

They pass out by the casement into the yard and so on till
they find their horses.

' Lift me, Gizur; I can no more,' says Swanhild.

He lifts her to the saddle.

' Whither away ? ' he asks.

' To Coldback, Gizur, and thence to cold Death.'

Thus did Gudruda, Eric's bride and Asmund's daughter, the
fairest woman who ever lived in Iceland, die on her marriage
night by the hand of Gizur, Ospakar's son, and through the
hate and witchcraft of Swanhild the Fatherless, her half-sister.

CHAPTER XXX

HOW THE DAWN CAME

THE dawn broke over Middalhof. Slowly the light gathered in the empty hall, it crept slowly into the little chamber where Eric slept, and Gudruda slept also with a deeper sleep.

Now the two women came from their chamber at the far end of the hall, and drew near the hearth, shivering, for the air was cold. They knelt by the fire, blowing at the embers till the sticks they cast upon them crackled to a blaze.

THE AXE CRASHED
THROUGH THE
PANELING.

'It seems that Gudruda is not yet gone,' said one to the other. 'I thought she should ride away with Eric before the dawn.'

'Newly wed lie long abed!' laughed the other.

'I am glad to see the blessed light,' said the first woman, 'for last night I dreamed that once again this hall ran red with blood, as at the marriage-feast of Ospakar.'

'Ah,' answered the other, 'it will be well for the south when Eric Brighteyes and Gudruda are gone over sea, for their loves have brought much bloodshed upon the land.'

'Well, indeed!' sighed the first. 'Had Asmund the Priest never found Groa, Ran's gift, singing by the sea, Valhalla had not been so full to-day. Mindest thou the day he brought her here?'

'I remember it well,' she answered, 'though I was but a girl at the time. Still, when I saw those dark eyes of hers— just such eyes as Swanhild's!—I knew her for a witch, as most Finn women are. It is an evil world: my husband is dead by the sword; dead are both my sons, fighting for Eric; dead is Unna, Thorod's daughter; Asmund, my lord, is dead, and dead is Björn; and now Gudruda the Fair, whom I have rocked to sleep, leaves us to go over sea. I may not go with her, for my daughter's sake; yet I almost wish that I too were dead.'

'That will come soon enough,' said the other, who was young and fair.

Now the witch-sleep began to roll from Eric's heart, though his eyes were not yet open. But the talk of the women echoed in his ears, and the words '*dead!*' '*dead!*' '*dead!*' fell heavily on his slumbering sense. At length he opened his eyes, only to shut them again, because of a bright gleam of light that ran up and down something at his side. Heavily he wondered what this might be, that shone so keen and bright—that shone like a naked sword.

'Now he looked again. Yes, it was a sword which stood by him upon the bed, and the golden hilt was like the hilt of Whitefire. He lifted up his hand to touch it, thinking that he dreamed. Lo! his hand and arm were red!

Then he remembered, and the thought of Gudruda flashed through his heart. He sat up, gazing down into the shadow at his side.

Presently the women at the fire heard a sound as of a great man falling to earth.

'What is that noise?' said one.

'Eric leaping from his bed,' answered the other. 'He has slept too long, as we have also.'

As they spoke the curtain of the shut bed was pushed away, and through it staggered Eric in his night-gear, and lo! the left side of it was red. His eyes were wide with horror, his mouth was open, and his face was white as ice.

He stopped, looking at them, made as though to speak, and could not. Then, while they shrank from him in terror, he turned, and, walking like a drunken man, staggered from the hall down that passage which led to the store-chamber. The door stood wide, the shutter was wide, and on the floor, soaked in the dregs of ale, Skallagrim yet lay snoring, his axe in one hand and a cup in the other.

Eric looked and understood.

'Awake, drunkard!' he cried, in so terrible a voice that the room shook. 'Awake, and look upon thy work!'

Skallagrim sat up, yawning.

'Forsooth, my head swims,' he said. 'Give me ale, I am thirsty.'

'Never wilt thou look on ale again, Skallagrim, when thou hast seen that which I have to show!' said Eric, in the same dread voice.

Then Skallagrim rose to his feet and gaped upon him.

'What means this, lord? Is it time to ride? and say! why is thy shirt red with blood?'

'Follow me, drunkard, and look upon thy work!' Eric said again.

Then Skallagrim grew altogether sober, and grasping his axe, followed after Brighteyes, sore afraid of what he might see.

They went down the passage, past the high seat of the hall, till they came to the curtain of the shut bed; and after them followed the women. Eric seized the curtain in his hand, rent it from its fastenings, and cast it on the ground. Now the light flowed in and struck upon the bed. It fell upon the bed, it fell upon Whitefire's hilt and ran along the blade, it gleamed on a woman's snowy breast and golden hair, and shone in her staring eyes—a woman who lay stiff and cold upon the bed, the great sword fixed within her heart!

'Look upon thy work, drunkard!' Eric cried again, while the women who peeped behind sent their long wail of woe echoing down the paneled hall.

'Hearken!' said Eric: 'while thou didst lie wallowing in

thy swine's sleep, foes crept in across thy carcase, and this is their handiwork:—yonder she lies who was my bride!—now is Gudruda the Fair a death-wife who last night was my bride! This is thy work, drunkard! and now what meed for thee?'

Skallagrim looked. Then he spoke in a hoarse slow voice: 'What meed, lord? But one—death!'

Then with one hand he covered his eyes and with the other held out his axe to Eric Brighteyes.

Eric took the axe, and while the women ran thence screaming, he whirled it thrice about his head. Then he smote down towards the skull of Skallagrim, but as he smote it seemed to him that a voice whispered in his ear: '*Thy oath!*'—and he remembered that he had sworn to slay no more, save for his life's sake.

The mighty blow was falling and he might only do this—loose the axe before it clove Skallagrim in twain. He opened his hand and away the great axe flew. It passed over the head of Skallagrim, and sped like light across the wide hall, till it crashed through the paneling on the further side, and buried itself to the haft in the wall beyond.

'It is not for me to kill thee, drunkard! Go, die in thy drink!'

'Then I will kill myself!' cried the Baresark, and, rushing across the hall he tore the great axe from its bed.

'Hold!' said Eric; 'perhaps there is yet a deed for thee to do. Then thou mayst die, if it pleases thee.'

'Ay,' said Skallagrim coming back, 'perchance there is still a deed to do!'

And, flinging down the axe, Skallagrim Lambstail the Baresark fell upon the floor and wept.

But Eric did not weep. Only he drew Whitefire from the heart of Gudruda and looked at it.

'Thou art a strange sword, Whitefire,' he said, 'who slayest both friend and foe! Shame on thee, Whitefire! We swore our oath on thee, Whitefire, and thou hast cut its chain! Now I am minded to shatter thee.' And as Eric looked on the great blade, lo! it hummed strangely in answer.

' " First must thou be the death of some," thou sayest ?
Well, maybe, Whitefire ! But never yet didst thou drink
so sweet a life as hers who now lies dead, nor ever shalt
again.'

Then he sheathed the sword, but neither then nor afterwards did he wipe the blood of Gudruda from its blade.

' Last night a-marrying—to-day a-burying,' said Eric, and
he called to the women to bring spades. Then, having
clothed himself, he went to the centre of the hall, and, brushing
away the sand, broke the hard clay-flooring, dealing great
blows on it with an axe. Now Skallagrim, seeing his purpose,
came to him and took one of the spades, and together they
laboured in silence till they had dug a grave a fathom
deep.

' Here,' said Eric, ' here, in thine own hall where thou
wast born and lived, Gudruda the Fair, thou shalt sleep at the
last. And of Middalhof I say this : that none shall live there
henceforth. It shall be haunted and accursed till the rafters
rot and the walls fall in, making thy barrow, Gudruda.'

Now this indeed came to pass, for none have lived at Middalhof since the days of Gudruda the Fair, Asmund's daughter.
It has been ruined these many years, and now it is but a pile
of stones.

When the grave was dug, Eric washed himself and ate
some food. Then he went in to where Gudruda lay dead, and
bade the women make her ready for burial. This they did.
When she was washed and clad in a clean white robe, Eric
came to her, and with his own hand bound the Hell-shoes on
her feet and closed her eyes.

It was just then that a man rode up who said that the
people of Gizur and of Swanhild had burned Gudruda's ship,
driving the crew ashore.

' It is well,' said Eric. ' We need the ship no more ; now
hath she whom it should bear wings with which to fly.' Then
he went in and sat down on the bed by the body of Gudruda,
while Skallagrim crouched upon the ground without, tearing
at his beard and muttering. For the fierce heart of Skallagrim

was broken because of that evil which his drunkenness had brought about.

All day long Eric sat thus, looking on his dead love's face, till the hour came round when he and Gudruda had drunk the bride-cup. Then he rose and kissed dead Gudruda on the lips, saying :

' I did not look to part with thee thus, sweet! It is sad that thou shouldst have gone and left me here. Natheless, I shall soon follow on thy path.'

Then he called aloud :

' Art sober, drunkard ? '

Skallagrim came and stood before him, saying nothing.

' Take thou the feet of her whom thou didst bring to death, and I will take her head.'

So they lifted up Gudruda and bore her to the grave. Then Eric stood near the grave, and, taking dead Gudruda in his arms, he looked upon her face by the light of the fire and of the candles that were set about.

He looked thrice, then sang aloud :

> Long ago, when swept the snow-blast,
> Close we clung and plighted troth.
> Many a year, through storm and sword-song,
> Sore I strove to win thee, sweet !
> But last night I held thee, Fairest,
> Lock'd, a wife, in lover's arms.
> Now, Gudruda, in thy death-rest,
> Sleep thou soft till Eric come !
>
> Hence I go to wreak thy murder.
> Hissing fire of flaming stead,
> Groan of spear-carles, wail of women,
> Soon shall startle through the night.
> Then on Mosfell, Kirtle-Wearer,
> Eric waits the face of Death.
> Freed from weary life and sorrow,
> Soon we'll kiss in Hela's halls !

Then he laid her in the grave, and, having shrouded a sheet over her, they filled it in together, hiding Gudruda the Fair from the sight of men for ever.

Afterwards Eric armed himself, and this Skallagrim did

also. Then he strode from the hall, and Skallagrim followed
him. In the yard those horses were still tied that should have
carried them to the ship, and on one was the saddle of Gudruda.
She had ridden on this horse for many years, and loved it
much, for it would follow her like a dog. Eric looked at him,
then said aloud :

'Gudruda may need thee where she is, Blackmane,' for
so was the horse named. 'At the least, none shall ride thee
more!' And he snatched the axe from the hand of Skallagrim
and killed the horse at a blow.

Then they rode away, heading for Coldback. The night was
wild and windy, and the sky dark with scudding clouds,
through which the moon peeped out at times. Eric looked
up, then spoke to Skallagrim :

'A good night for burning, drunkard!'

'Ay, lord ; the flames will fly briskly,' answered Skallagrim.

'How many, thinkest thou, walked over thee, drunkard,
when thou didst lie yonder in the ale ?'

'I know not,' groaned Skallagrim ; 'but I found this in
the soft earth without: the print of a man's and a woman's feet ;
and this on the hill side: the track of two horses ridden
hard.'

'Gizur and Swanhild, drunkard,' said Eric. 'Swanhild
cast us into deep sleep by witchcraft, and Gizur dealt the
blow. Better for him that he had never been born than
that he has lived to deal that coward's blow!'

Then they rode on, and when midnight was a little while
gone they came to the stead at Coldback. Now this house was
roofed with turves, and the windows were barred so that none
could pass through them. Also in the yard were faggots of
birch and a stack of hay.

Eric and Skallagrim tied their horses in a dell that is to the
north of the stead and crept up to the house. All was still ;
but a fire burnt in the hall, and, looking through a crack,
Eric could see many men sleeping about it. Then he made
signs to Skallagrim and together, very silently, they fetched
hay and faggots, piling them against the north door of the

house, for the wind blew from the north. Now Eric spoke to Skallagrim, bidding him stand, axe in hand, by the south door, and slay those who came out when the reek began to smart them : but he went himself to fire the pile.

When Brighteyes had made all things ready for the burning, it came into his mind that, perhaps, Gizur and Swanhild were not in the house. But he would not hold his hand for this, for he was mad with grief and rage. So once more he prepared for the deed, when again he heard a voice in his ear—the voice of Gudruda, and it seemed to say :

'*Thine oath, Eric ! remember thine oath !* '

Then he turned and the rage went out of his heart.

' Let them seek me on Mosfell,' he said, ' I will not slay them secretly and by reek, the innocent and the guilty together.' And he strode round the house to where Skallagrim stood at the south door, axe aloft and watching.

' Does the fire burn, lord ? I see no smoke,' whispered Skallagrim.

' Nay, I have made none. I will shed no more blood, except to save my life. I leave vengeance to the Norns.'

Now Skallagrim thought that Brighteyes was mad, but he dared say nothing. So they went to their horses, and when they found them, Eric rode back to the house. Presently they drew near, and Eric told Skallagrim to stay where he was, and riding on to the house, smote heavy blows upon the door, just as Skallagrim once had smitten, before Eric went up to Mosfell.

Now Swanhild lay in her shut bed ; but she could not sleep, because of what she saw in the eyes of Gudruda. Little may she sleep ever again, for when she shuts her eyes once more she sees that which was written in the dead eyes of Gudruda. So, as she lay, she heard the blows upon the door, and sprang frightened from her bed. Now there was tumult in the hall, for every man rose to his feet in fear, searching for his weapons. Again the loud knocks came.

' It is the ghost of Eric ! ' cried one, for Gizur had given out that Eric was dead at his hand in fair fight.

' Open ! ' said Gizur, and they opened, and there, a little

way from the door, sat Brighteyes on a horse, great and shadowy to see, and behind him was Skallagrim the Baresark.

'It is the ghost of Eric !' they cried again.

'I am no ghost,' said Brighteyes. 'I am no ghost, ye men of Swanhild. Tell me : is Gizur, the son of Ospakar, among you?'

'Gizur is here,' said a voice; 'but he swore he slew thee last night.'

'Then he lied,' quoth Eric. 'Gizur did not slay me— he murdered Gudruda the Fair as she lay asleep at my side. See!' and he drew Whitefire from its scabbard and held it in the rays of the moon that now shone out between the cloud rifts. 'Whitefire is red with Gudruda's blood—Gudruda slaughtered in her sleep by Gizur's coward hand!'

Now men murmured, for this seemed to them the most shameful of all deeds. But Gizur, hearing, shrank back aghast.

'Listen again!' said Eric. 'I was minded but now to burn you all as ye slept—ay, the firing is piled against the door. Still, I held my hand, for I have sworn to kill no more, except to save my life. Now I ride hence to Mosfell. Thither let Gizur come, Gizur the murderer, and Swanhild the witch, and with them all who will. There I will give them greeting, and wipe away the blood of Gudruda from Whitefire's blade.'

'Fear not, Eric,' cried Swanhild, 'I will come, and there thou mayst kill me, if thou canst.'

'Against thee, Swanhild,' said Eric, 'I lift no hand. Do thy worst, I leave thee to thy fate and the vengeance of the Norns. I am no woman-slayer. But to Gizur the murderer I say, come.'

Then he turned and went, and Skallagrim went with him.

'Up, men, and cut Eric down!' cried Gizur, seeking to cover his shame.

But no man stirred.

CHAPTER XXXI

HOW ERIC SENT AWAY HIS MEN FROM MOSFELL

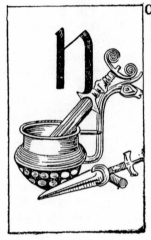OW Eric and Skallagrim came to Mosfell in safety, and during all that ride Brighteyes spoke no word. He rode in silence, and in silence Skallagrim rode after him. The heart of Skallagrim was broken because of the sorrow which his drunkenness had brought about, and the heart of Eric was buried in Gudruda's grave.

On Mosfell Eric found four of his own men, two of whom had been among those that the people of Gizur and Swanhild had driven from Gudruda's ship before they fired her. For no fight had been made on the ship. There also he found Jon, who had been loosed from his bands in the booth by one who heard his cries as he rode past. Now when Jon saw Brighteyes, he told him all, and fell at Eric's feet and wept because he had betrayed him in his fear.

But Eric spoke no angry word to him. Stooping down he raised him, saying, 'Thou wast never overstout of heart, Jon, and thou art scarcely to be blamed because thou didst speak rather than die in torment, though perhaps some had chosen so to die and not to speak. Now I am a luckless man,

Y

and all things happen as they are fated, and the words of Atli come true, as was to be looked for. The Norns, against whom none may stand, did but work their will through thy mouth, Jon; so grieve no more for that which cannot be undone.'

Then he turned away, but Jon wept long and loudly.

That night Eric slept well and dreamed no dreams. But on the morrow he woke at dawn, and clothed himself and ate. Then he called his men together, and with them Skallagrim. They came and stood before him, and Eric, drawing Whitefire, leaned upon it and spoke:

'Hearken, mates,' he said: 'I know this, that my hours are short and death draws on. My years have been few and evil, and I cannot read the purpose of my life. She whom I loved has been slain by the witchcraft of Swanhild and the coward hand of Gizur the murderer, and I go to seek her where she waits. I am very glad to go, for now I have no more joy in life, being but a luckless man; it is an ill world, friends, and all the ways are red with blood. I have killed many men, though but one life haunts me now at the last, and that is the life of Atli the Earl, for he was no match for my might and he is dead because of my sin. With my own blood I will wash away the blood of Atli, and then I seek another place, leaving nothing but a tale to be told in the ingle when fall the winter snows. For to this end we all come at the last, and it matters little if it find us at midday or at nightfall. We live in sorrow, we die in pain and darkness: for this is the curse that the Gods have laid upon men and each must taste it in his season. But I have sworn that no more men shall die for me. I will fight the last great fight alone; for I know this: I shall not easily be overcome, and with my fallen foes I will tread on Bifrost Bridge, after the fashion of my forefathers. Therefore, farewell! When the bones of Eric Brighteyes lie in their barrow, or are picked by ravens on the mountain-side, Gizur will not trouble to hunt out those who clung to him, if indeed Gizur shall live to tell the tale. Nor need ye fear the hate of Swanhild, for she aims her spears at me alone. Go, therefore, and, when I am dead, do not forget me, and do not seek to avenge me, for Death the avenger of all will find these twain also.'

Now Eric's men heard and groaned aloud, saying that they would die with him, for they loved Eric one and all. Only Skallagrim said nothing.

Then Brighteyes spoke again : ' Hear me, comrades. If ye will not go, my blood be on your heads, for I will ride out alone, and meet the men of Gizur in the plain and fall there fighting.'

Then one by one they crept away to seek their horses in the dell. And each man as he went came to Eric and kissed his hand, then passed thence weeping. Jon was the last to go, except Skallagrim only, and he was so moved that he could not speak at all.

It was this Jon who, in after years, when he had grown very old, wandered from stead to stead telling the deeds of Eric Brighteyes, and always finding a welcome because of his tale, till at length, as he journeyed, he was overtaken by a snowstorm and buried in a drift. For Jon, who lacked much, had this gift : he had a skald's tongue. Men have always held that it was to the honour of Jon that he told the tale thus, hiding nothing, seeing that some of it is against himself.

Now when all had gone, Eric looked at Skallagrim, who still stood near him, axe in hand.

' Wherefore goest thou not, drunkard ? ' he said. ' Surely thou wilt find ale and mead in the vales or oversea. Here there is none. Hasten ! I would be alone ! '

Now the great body of Skallagrim shook with grief and shame, and the red blood poured up beneath his dark skin. Then he spoke in a thick voice :

' I did not think to live to hear such words from the lips of Eric Brighteyes. They are well earned, yet it is unmanly of thee, lord, thus to taunt one who loves thee. I would sooner die as Swanhild said yonder thrall should die than live to listen to such words. I have sinned against thee, indeed, and because of my sin my heart is broken. Hast thou, then, never sinned that thou wouldst tear it living from my breast as eagles tear a foundered horse? Think on thine own sins, Eric, and pity mine! Taunt me thus once more or bid me go once more and I will go indeed! I will go thus—on the edge of yonder gulf thou didst overcome me by thy naked might, and there I swore fealty to thee, Eric Brighteyes. Many a year have we wandered side by side, and, standing back to back, we have struck many a blow. I am minded to bide by thee in the last great fight that draws on and to die there with thee. I have loved no other man save thee, and I am too old to seek new lords. Yet, if still thou biddest me, I will go thus. Where I swore my oath to thee, there I will end it. For I will lay me down on the brink of yonder gulf, as once I lay when thy hand was at my throat, and call out that thou art no more my lord and I am no more thy thrall. Then I will roll into the depths beneath, and by this death of shame thou shalt be freed from me, Eric Brighteyes.'

Eric looked at the great man—he looked long and sadly. Then he spoke:

'Skallagrim Lambstail, thou hast a true heart. I too have sinned, and now I put away thy sin, although Gudruda is dead through thee and I must die because of thee. Stay by me if thou wilt and let us fall together.'

Then Skallagrim came to Eric, and, kneeling before him, he took his hands and kissed them.

'Now I am once more a man,' he said, 'and I know this: we two shall die such a great death that it will be well to have lived to die it!' and he arose and shouted:

> A! hai! A! hai! I see foes pass in pride!
> A! hai! A! hai! Valkyries ride the wind!
> Hear the song of the sword!
> Whitefire is aloft—aloft!
> Bare is the axe of the Baresark!
> Croak, ye nesting ravens;
> Flap your wings, ye eagles,
> For bright is Mosfell's cave with blood!
> Lap! lap! thou Grey Wolf,
> Laugh aloud, Odin!

Laugh till shake the golden doors ;
Heroes' feet are set on Bifrost,
Open, ye hundred gates !
  A ! hai ! A ! hai ! red runs the fray !
  A ! hai ! A ! hai ! Valkyries ride the wind !

Then Skallagrim turned and went to clean his harness and the golden helm of Eric.

Now at Coldback Gizur spoke with Swanhild.

'Thou hast brought the greatest shame upon me,' he said, 'for thou hast caused me to slay a sleeping woman. Knowest thou that my own men will scarcely speak with me ? I have come to this evil pass, through love of thee, that I have slain a sleeping woman ! '

'It was not my fault that thou didst kill Gudruda,' answered Swanhild ; 'surely I thought it was Eric whom thy sword pierced ! I have not sought thy love, Gizur, and I say this to thee : go, if thou wilt, and leave me alone ! '

Now Gizur looked at her, and was minded to go ; but, as Swanhild knew well, she held him too fast in the net of her witcheries.

'I would go, if I might go ! ' answered Gizur ; 'but I am bound to thee for good or evil, since it is fated that I shall wed thee.'

'Thou wilt never wed me while Eric lives,' said Swanhild.

Now she spoke thus truthfully, and by chance, as it were, not as driving Gizur on to slay Eric—for, now that Gudruda was dead, she was in two minds as to this matter, since, if she might, she still desired to take Eric to herself—but meaning that while Eric lived she would wed no other man. But Gizur took it otherwise.

'Eric shall certainly die if I can bring it about,' he answered, and went to speak with his men.

Now all were gathered in the yard at Coldback, and that was a great company. But their looks were heavy because of the shame that Gizur, Ospakar's son, had brought upon them by the murder of Gudruda in her sleep.

'Hearken, comrades ! ' said Gizur : 'great shame is come

upon me because of a deed that I have done unwittingly,
for I aimed at the eagle Eric and I have slain the swan
Gudruda.'

Then a certain old viking in the company, named Ketel,
whom Gizur had hired for the slaying of Eric, spoke :

'Man or woman, it is a niddering deed to kill folk in their
sleep, Gizur ! It is murder, and no less, and small luck can
be hoped for from the stroke.'

Now Gizur felt that his people looked on him askance and
heavily, and knew that it would be hard to show them that
he was driven to this deed against his will, and by the
witchcraft of Swanhild.   So, as was his nature, he turned to
guile for shelter, like a fox to his hole, and spoke to them
with the tongue of a lawman ; for Gizur had great skill in
speech.

'That tale is not all true which Eric Brighteyes told
you,' he said.   'He was mad with grief, and moreover it
seems that he slept, and only woke to find Gudruda dead.
It came about thus : I stood with the lady Swanhild, and
was about to call aloud on Eric to arm himself and come
forth and meet me face to face——'

'Then, lord, methinks thou hadst never met another foe,'
quoth the viking Ketel who had spoken first.

'When of a sudden,' went on Gizur, taking no note of
Ketel's words, 'one clothed in white sprang from the bed and
rushed on me.   Then I, thinking that it was Eric, lifted
sword, not to smite, but to ward him away ; but the linen-
wearer met the sword and fell down dead.   Then I fled,
fearing lest men should wake and trap us, and that is all
the tale.   It was no fault of mine if Gudruda died upon the
sword.'

Thus he spoke, but still men looked doubtfully upon him,
for his eye was the eye of a liar—and Eric, as they knew, did
not lie.

'It is hard to find the truth between lawman's brain and
tongue,' said the old viking Ketel.   'Eric is no lawman, but
a true man, and he sang another song.   I would kill Eric
indeed, for between him and me there is a blood-feud, since

my brother died at his hand when, with Whitefire for a crook,
Brighteyes drove armed men like sheep down the hall of Middalhof—ay and swordless, slew Ospakar. Yet I say that Eric
is a true man, and, whether or no thou art true, Gizur the Lawman, that thou knowest best—thou and Swanhild the Fatherless, Groa's daughter. If thou didst slay Gudruda as thou
tellest, say, how came Gudruda's blood on Whitefire's blade?
How did it chance, Gizur, that thou heldest Whitefire in thy
hand and not thine own sword? Now I tell thee this: either
thou shalt go up against Eric and clear thyself by blows, or I
leave thee; and methinks there are others among this company
who will do the same, for we have no wish to be partners with
murderers and their wickedness.'

' Ay, a good word!' said many who stood by. ' Let Gizur
go up with us to Mosfell, and there stand face to face with
Eric and clear himself by blows.'

' I ask no more,' said Gizur; ' we will ride to-night.'

' But much more shalt thou get, liar,' quoth Ketel to
himself, ' for that hour when thou lookest once again on
Whitefire shall be thy last!'

So Gizur and Swanhild made ready to go up against Eric.
That day they rode away with a great company, a hundred
and one in all, and this was their plan. They sent six men with
that thrall who had shown them the secret path, bidding
him guide them to the mountain-top. Then, when they were
come thither, and heard the shouts of those who sought to gain
the platform from the south, they were to watch till Eric and
his folk came out from the cave, and shoot them with arrows
from above or crush them with stones. But if perchance Eric
left the platform and came to meet his foes in the narrow pass,
then they were to let themselves down with ropes from the
height above, and, creeping after him round the rock, must
smite him in the back. Moreover, in secret, Gizur promised
a great reward of ten hundreds in silver to him who should
kill Eric, for he did not long to stand face to face with
him alone. Swanhild also in secret made promise of reward

to those who should bring Eric to her, bound, but living; and she bade them to bear him down with shields and tie him with ropes.

So they rode away, the seven who should climb the mountain from behind going first, and on the morrow morning they crossed the sand and came to Mosfell.

CHAPTER XXXII

HOW ERIC AND SKALLAGRIM GREW FEY

THE GHOST OF THE
BARESARK.

OW the night came down upon Mosfell, and of all nights this was the strangest. The air was quiet and heavy, yet no rain fell. It was so silent, moreover, that, did a stone slip upon the mountain side or a horse neigh far off on the plains, the sound of it crept up the fell and was echoed from the crags.

Eric and Skallagrim sat together on the open space of rock that is before the cave, and great heaviness and fear came into their hearts, so that they had no desire to sleep.

'Methinks the night is ghost-ridden,' said Eric, 'and I am fey, for I grow cold, and it seems to me that one strokes my hair.'

'It is ghost-ridden, lord,' answered Skallagrim. 'Trolls are abroad, and the God-kind gather to see Eric die.'

For a while they sat in silence, then suddenly the mountain heaved up gently beneath them. Thrice it seemed to heave like a woman's breast, and left them frightened.

'Now the dwarf-folk come from their caves,' quoth

Skallagrim, ' and great deeds may be looked for, since they are not drawn to the upper earth by a little thing.'

Then once more they sat silent ; and thick darkness came down upon the mountain, hiding the stars.

' Look,' said Eric of a sudden, and he pointed to Hecla.

Skallagrim looked, and lo! the snowy dome of Hecla was aglow with a rosy flame like the light of dawn.

' Winter lights,' said Lambstail, shuddering.

' Death lights !' answered Eric. ' Look again ! '

They looked, and behold! in the rosy glow there sat three giant forms of fire, and their shapes were the shapes of women. Before them was a loom of blackness that stretched from earth to sky, and they wove at it with threads of flame. They were splendid and terrible to see. Their hair streamed behind them like meteor flames, their eyes shone like lightning, and their breasts gleamed like the polished bucklers of the gods. They wove fiercely at the loom of blackness, and as they wove they sang. The voice of the one was as the wind whistling through the pines ; the voice of the other was as the sound of rain hissing on deep waters ; and the voice of the third was as the moan of the sea. They wove fearfully and they sang loudly, but what they sang might not be known. Now the web grew and the woof grew, and a picture came upon the loom—a great picture written in fire.

Behold! it was the semblance of a storm-awakened sea, and a giant ship fled before the gale—a dragon of war, and in the ship were piled the corses of men, and on these lay another corse, as one lies upon a bed. They looked, and the face of the corse grew bright. It was the face of Eric, and his head rested upon the dead heart of Skallagrim.

Clinging to each other, Eric and Skallagrim saw the sight of fear that was written on the loom of the Norns. They saw it for a breath. Now, with a laugh like the wail of wolves, the shapes of fire sprang up and rent the web asunder. Then the first passed upward to the sky, the second southward towards Middalhof, but the third swept over Mosfell, so that the brightness of her flaming form shone on the rock where they sat by the cave, and the lightning of her eyes was mirrored in the byrnie of Skallagrim and on Eric's golden helm. She swept past, pointing downwards as she went, and lo! she was gone, and once more darkness and silence lay upon the earth.

Now this sight was seen by Jon the thrall also, and he told it in his story of the deeds of Eric. For Jon lay hid in a secret place on Mosfell, waiting for tidings of what came to pass.

For a while Eric and Skallagrim clung to each other. Then Skallagrim spoke.

'We have seen the Valkyries,' he said.

'Nay,' answered Eric, 'we have seen the Norns—who are come to warn us of our doom! We shall die to-morrow.'

'At the least,' said Skallagrim, 'we shall not die alone: we had a goodly bed on yonder goblin ship, and all of our own slaying methinks. It is not so ill to die thus, lord!'

'Not so ill!' said Eric; 'and yet I am weary of blood and war, of glory and of my strength. Now I desire rest alone. Light fire—I can bear this darkness no longer; the marrow freezes in my bones.'

'Fire can be seen by foes,' said Skallagrim.

'It matters little now,' said Eric, 'we are feyfolk.'

So Skallagrim lighted the fire, piling much brushwood and dry turf over it, till presently it burnt up brightly, throwing light on all the space of rock, and heavy shadows against the cliff behind. They sat thus a while in the light of the flames, looking towards the deep gulf, till suddenly there came a sound as of one who climbed the gulf.

'Who comes now, treading where no man may pass?' cried Eric, seizing Whitefire as he sprang to his feet. Presently he sank down again with white face and staring eyes, and pointed at the edge of the cliff. And as he pointed, the neck of a man rose in the shadow above the brink, and the hands of a man grasped the rock. But there was no head on the neck. The shape of the headless man drew itself slowly over the brink, it walked slowly into the light towards the fire, then sat itself down in the glare of the flames, which shrank away

from it as from a draught of wind. Pale with terror, Eric and
Skallagrim looked on the headless thing and knew it. It was
the wraith of the Baresark that Brighteyes had slain—the
first of all the men he slew.

'It is my mate, Eric, whom thou didst kill years ago and
whose severed head spoke with thee!' gasped Skallagrim.

'It is he, sure enough!' said Eric; 'but where may his
head be?'

'Perchance the head will come,' answered Skallagrim. 'He
is an evil sight to see, surely. Say, lord, shall I fall upon
him, though I love not the task?'

'Nay, Skallagrim, let him bide; he does but come to warn
us of our fate. Moreover, trolls can only be laid in one way—
by the hewing off of the head and the laying of it at the
thigh. But this one has no head to hew.'

Now as he spoke the headless man turned his neck as though
to look. Once more there came the sound of feet and lo! men
marched in from the darkness on either side. Eric and Skallagrim looked up and knew them. They were those of Ospakar's
folk whom they had fought with on Horse-Head Heights:
all their wounds were on them and in front of them marched
Mord, Ospakar's son. The ghosts gazed upon Eric and
Skallagrim with cold dead eyes, then they too sat down by the
fire. Now once more there came the sound of feet, and from
every side men poured in who had died at the hands of Eric
and of Skallagrim. First came those who fell on that ship
of Ospakar's which Eric sank by Westmans; then the crew of
the Raven who had perished upon the sea-path. Even as
the man died, so did each ghost come. Some had been drowned
and behold their harness dripped water! Some had died of
spear-thrusts and the spears were yet fixed in their breasts!
Some had fallen beneath the flash of Whitefire and the weight
of the axe of Skallagrim, and there they sat, looking on their
wide wounds!

Then came more and more. There were those whom Eric
and Skallagrim had slain upon the seas, those who had fallen
before them in the English wars, and all that company who had
been drowned in the waters of the Pentland Firth when the

witchcraft of Swanhild had brought the Gudruda to her wreck.

'Now here we have a goodly crew,' said Eric at length. 'Is it done, thinkest thou, or will Mosfell send forth more dead?'

As he spoke the wraith of a grey-headed man drew near. He had but one arm, for the other was hewn from him, and the byrnie on his left side was red with blood.

'Welcome, Earl Atli!' cried Eric. 'Sit thou over against me, who to-morrow shall be with thee.'

The ghost of the Earl seated itself and looked on Eric with sad eyes, but it spake never a word.

Then came another company, and at their head stalked black Ospakar.

'These be they who died at Middalhof,' cried Eric. 'Welcome, Ospakar! that marriage-feast of thine went ill!'

'Now methinks we are overdone with trolls,' said Skallagrim; 'but see! here come more.'

As he spoke, Hall of Lithdale came, and with him Koll the Half-witted, and others. And so it went on till all the men whom Eric and Skallagrim had slain, or who had died because of them, or at their side, were gathered in deep ranks before them.

'Now it is surely done,' said Eric.

'There is yet a space,' said Skallagrim, pointing to the other side of the fire, 'and Hell holds many dead.'

Even as the words left his lips there came a noise of the galloping of horse's hoofs, and one clad in white rode up. It was a woman, for her golden hair flowed down about her white arms. Then she slid from the horse and stood in the light of the fire, and behold! her white robe was red with blood, a great sword was set in her heart, and the face and eyes were the face and eyes of Gudruda the Fair, and the horse she rode was Blackmane, that Eric had killed.

Now when Brighteyes saw her he gave a great cry.

'Greeting, sweet!' he said. 'I am no longer afraid, since thou comest to bear me company. Thou art dear to my sight—ay even in yon death-sheet. Greeting, sweet, my May! I laid thee stiff and cold in the earth at Middalhof, but, like a loving wife, thou hast burst thy bonds, and art come to save me from the grip of trolls. Thou art welcome, Gudruda, Asmund's daughter! Come, wife, sit thou at my side.'

The ghost of Gudruda spake no word. She walked through the fire towards him, and the flames went out beneath her feet, to burn up again when she had passed. Then she sat down over against Eric and looked on him with wide and tender eyes. Thrice he stretched out his arms to clasp her, but thrice their strength left them and they fell back to his side. It was as though they struck a wall of ice and were numbed by the bitter cold.

'Look, here are more,' groaned Skallagrim.

Then Eric looked, and lo! the empty space to the left of the fire was filled with shadowy shapes like shapes of mist. Amongst them was Gizur, Ospakar's son, and many a man of his company. There, too, was Swanhild, Groa's daughter, and a toad nestled in her breast. She looked with wide eyes upon the eyes of dead Gudruda's ghost, that seemed not to see her, and a stare of fear was set on her lovely face. Nor was this all; for there, before that shadowy throng, stood two great shapes clad in their harness, and one was the shape of Eric and one the shape of Skallagrim.

Thus, being yet alive, did these two look upon their own wraiths!

Then Eric and Skallagrim cried out aloud and their brains swam and their senses left them, so that they swooned.

When they opened their eyes and life came back to them the fire was dead, and it was day. Nor was there any sign of that company which had been gathered on the rock before them.

'Skallagrim,' quoth Eric, 'it seems that I have dreamed a strange dream—a most strange dream of Norns and trolls!'

'Tell me thy dream, lord,' said Skallagrim.

So Eric told all the vision, and the Baresark listened in silence.

'It was no dream, lord,' said Skallagrim, 'for I myself have seen the same things. Now this is in my mind, that yonder sun is the last that we shall see, for we have beheld the death-shadows. All those who were gathered here last night wait to welcome us on Bifrost Bridge. And the mist-shapes who sat there, amongst whom our wraiths were numbered, are the shapes of those who shall die in the great fight to-day. For days are fled and we are sped ! '

' I would not have it otherwise,' said Eric. ' We have been greatly honoured of the Gods, and by the ghost-kind that are around us and above us. Now let us make ready to die as becomes men who have never turned back to blow, for the end of the story should fit the beginning, and of us there is a tale to tell.'

' A good word, lord,' answered Skallagrim : ' I have struck few strokes to be ashamed of, and I do not fear to tread Bifrost Bridge in thy company. Now we will wash ourselves and eat, so that our strength may be whole in us.'

So they washed themselves with water, and ate heartily, and for the first time for many months Eric was merry. For now that the end was at hand his heart grew light within him. And when they had put the desire of food from them, and buckled on their harness, they looked out from their mountain height, and saw a cloud of dust rise in the desert plain of black sand beneath, and through it the sheen of spears.

' Here come those of whom, if there is truth in visions, some few shall never go back again,' said Eric. ' Now, what counsel hast thou, Skallagrim ? Where shall we meet them ? Here on the space of rock, or yonder in the deep way of the cliff ? '

' My counsel is that we meet them here,' said Skallagrim, ' and cut them down one by one as they try to turn the rock. They can scarcely come at us to slay us here so long as our arms have strength to smite.'

' Yet they will come, though I know not how,' answered Eric, ' for I am sure of this, that our death lies before us. Here, then, we will meet them.'

Now the cloud of dust drew nearer, and they saw that this was a great company which came up against them.

z

At the foot of the fell the men stayed and rested a while, and it was not till afternoon that they began to climb the mountain.

'Night will be at hand before this game is played,' said Skallagrim. 'See, they climb slowly, saving their strength, and yonder among them is Swanhild in a purple cloak.'

'Ay, night will be at hand, Skallagrim—a last long night! A hundred to two—the odds are heavy; yet some shall wish them heavier. Now let us bind on our helms.'

Meanwhile Gizur and his folk crept up the paths from below. Now that thrall who knew the secret way had gone on with six chosen men, and already they climbed the watercourse and drew near to the flat crest of the fell. But Eric and Skallagrim knew nothing of this. So they sat down by the turning place that is over the gulf and waited, singing of the taking of the Raven and of the slaying in the stead at Middalhof, and telling tales of deeds that they had done. And the thrall and his six men climbed on till at length they gained the crest of the fell, and, looking over, saw Eric and Skallagrim beneath them.

'The birds are in the snare, and hark! they sing,' said the thrall; 'now bring rocks and be silent.'

But Gizur and his people, having learned that Eric and Skallagrim were alone upon the mountain, pushed on.

'We have not much to fear from two men,' said Gizur.

'That we shall learn presently,' answered Swanhild. 'I tell thee this, that I saw strange sights last night, though I did not sleep. I may sleep little now that Gudruda is dead, for that which I saw in her eyes haunts me.'

Then they went on, and the face of Gizur grew white with fear.

CHAPTER XXXIII

HOW ERIC AND SKALLAGRIM FOUGHT THEIR LAST GREAT FIGHT

OW the thrall and those with him on the crest of the fell heard the murmur of the company of Gizur and Swanhild as they won the mountain side, though they could not see them because of the rocks.

'Now it is time to begin and knock these birds from their perch,' said the thrall, 'for that is an awkward corner for our folk to turn with Whitefire and the axe of Skallagrim waiting on the further side.'

So he balanced a great stone, as heavy as three men could lift, on the brow of the rock, and aimed it. Then he pushed and let it go. It smote the platform beneath with a crash, two paces behind the spot where Eric and Skallagrim sat. Then it flew into the air, and, just as Brighteyes turned at the sound, it struck the wings of his helm, and, bursting the straps, tore the golden helm-piece from his head and carried it away into the gulf beneath.

Skallagrim looked up and saw what had come about.

'They have gained the crest of the fell,' he cried. 'Now

z 2

we must fly into the cave or down the narrow way and hold it.'

' Down the narrow way, then,' said Eric, and while rocks, spears and arrows rushed between and around them, they stepped on to the stone and won the path beyond. It was clear, for Gizur's folk had not yet come, and they ran nearly to the mouth of it, where there was a bend in the way, and stood there side by side.

' Thou wast at death's door then, lord ! ' said Skallagrim.

' Head-piece is not head,' answered Eric ; ' but I wonder how they won the crest of the fell. I have never heard tell of any path by which it might be gained.'

' There they are at the least,' said Skallagrim. ' Now this is my will, that thou shouldst take my helm. I am Baresark and put little trust in harness, but rather in my axe and strength alone.'

' I will not do that,' said Eric. ' Listen : I hear them come.'

Presently the tumult of voices and the tramp of feet grew clearer, and after a while Gizur, Swanhild, and the men of their following turned the corner of the narrow way, and lo ! there before them—ay within three paces of them—stood Eric and Skallagrim shoulder to shoulder, and the light poured down upon them from above.

They were terrible to see, and the sun shone brightly on Eric's golden hair and Whitefire's flashing blade, and the shadows lay dark upon the black helm of Skallagrim and in the fierce black eyes beneath.

Back surged Gizur and those with him. Skallagrim would have sprung upon them, but Eric caught him by the arm, saying : ' A truce to thy Baresark ways. Rush not and move not ! Let us stand here till they overwhelm us.'

Now those behind Gizur cried out to know what ailed them that they pushed back.

' Only this,' said Gizur, ' that Eric Brighteyes and Skallagrim Lambstail stand like two grey wolves and hold the narrow way.'

' Now we shall have fighting worth the telling of,' quoth

Ketel the viking. ' On, Gizur, Ospakar's son, and cut them down ! '

' Hold ! ' said Swanhild ; ' I will speak with Eric first,' and, together with Gizur and Ketel, she passed round the corner of the path and came face to face with those who stood at bay there.

' Now yield, Eric,' she cried. ' Foes are behind and before thee. Thou art trapped, and hast little chance of life. Yield thee, I say, with thy black wolf-hound, so perchance thou mayest find mercy even at the hands of her whose husband thou didst wrong and slay.'

' It is not my way to yield, lady,' answered Eric, ' and still less perchance is it the way of Skallagrim. Least of all will we yield to thee who, after working many ills, didst throw me in a witch-sleep, and to him who slew the wife sleeping at my side. Hearken, Swanhild : here we stand, awaiting death, nor will we take mercy from thy hand. For know this, we shall not die alone. Last night as we sat on Mosfell we saw the Norns weave our web of fate upon their loom of darkness. They sat on Hecla's dome and wove their pictures in living flame, then rent the web and flew upward and southward and westward, crying our doom to sky and earth and sea. Last night as we sat by the fire on Mosfell all the company of the dead were gathered round us—ay ! and all the company of those who shall die to-day. Thou wast there, Gizur the murderer, Ospakar's son ! thou wast there, Swanhild the witch, Groa's daughter ! thou wast there, Ketel Viking ! with many another man ; and there were we two also. Valkyries have kissed us and death draws near. Therefore, talk no more, but come and make an end. Greeting, Gizur, thou woman-murderer ! Draw nigh ! draw nigh ! Out sword ! up shield ! and on, thou son of Ospakar ! '

Swanhild spoke no more, and Gizur had no word.

' On, Gizur ! Eric calls thee,' quoth Ketel Viking ; but Gizur slunk back, not forward.

Then Ketel grew mad with rage and shame. He called to the men, and they drew near, as many as might, and looked doubtfully at the pair who stood before them like rocks upon

a plain. Eric laughed aloud and Skallagrim gnawed the
edge of his shield. Eric laughed aloud and the sound of his
laughter rang up the rocks.

'We are but two,' he cried, 'and ye are many! Is there
never a pair among you who will stand face to face with a
Baresark and a helmless man ?' and he tossed Whitefire high
into the air and caught it by the hilt.

Then Ketel and another man of his following sprang forward with an oath, and their axes thundered loud on the
shields of Eric and of Skallagrim. But Whitefire flickered up
and the axe of Skallagrim crashed, and at once their knees
were loosened, so that they sank down dead.

'More men! more men!' cried Eric. 'These were brave,
but their might was little. More men for the Grey Wolf's
maw!'

Then Swanhild lashed the folk with bitter words, and two
of them sprang on. They sprang on like hounds upon a deer
at bay, and they rolled back as gored hounds roll from the
deer's horns.

'More men! more men!' cried Eric. 'Here lie but four
and a hundred press behind. Now he shall win great honour
who lays Brighteyes low and brings down the helm of
Skallagrim.'

Again two came on, but they found no luck, for presently
they also were down upon the bodies of those who went
before. Now none could be found to come up against the
pair, for they fought like Baldur and Thor, and none could
touch them, and no harness might withstand the weight of
their blows that shore through shield and helm and byrnie,
deep to the bone beneath. Then Eric and Skallagrim leaned
upon their weapons and mocked their foes, while these cursed
and tore their beards with rage and shame.

Now it is to be told that when the thrall and those with
him saw that Eric and Skallagrim had escaped their rocks and
spears, they took counsel, and the end of it was that they slid
down a rope to the platform which is under the crest of the
fell. Thence, though they could see nothing, they could hear

the clang of blows and the shouts of those who fought and fell—ay! and the mocking of Eric and of Skallagrim.

'Now it goes thus,' said the thrall, who was a cunning man : 'Eric and Skallagrim hold the narrow way and none can stand against them. This, then, is my rede : that we turn the rock and take them in the back.'

His fellows thought this a good saying, and one by one they stood upon the little stone and won the narrow way. They crept along this till they were near to Eric and Skallagrim. Now Swanhild, looking up, saw them and started. Skallagrim noted it and glanced over his shoulder, and that not too soon, for, as he looked, the thrall lifted sword to smite the head of Eric.

With a shout of ' Back to back ! ' the Baresark swung round and ere ever the sword might fall his axe was buried deep in the thrall's breast.

'Now we must cut our path through them,' said Skallagrim, ' and, if it may be, win the space that is before the cave. Keep them off in front, lord, and I will mind these mannikins.'

Now Gizur's folk, seeing what had come about, took heart and fell upon Eric with a rush, and those who were with the dead thrall rushed at Skallagrim, and there began such a fight as has not been known in Iceland. But the way was so narrow that scarce more than one man could come to each of them at a time. And so fierce and true were the blows of Eric and Skallagrim that of those who came on few went back. Down they fell, and where they fell they died, and for every man who died Eric and Skallagrim won a pace toward the point of rock. Whitefire flamed so swift and swept so wide that it seemed to Swanhild, watching, as though three swords were aloft at once, and the axe of Skallagrim thundered down like the axe of a woodman against a tree, and those groaned on whom it fell as groans a falling tree. Now the shields of these twain were hewn through and through, and cast away, and their blood ran from many wounds. Still, their life was whole in them and they plied axe and sword with both hands. And ever men fell, and ever, fighting hard, they drew nearer to the point of rock.

Now it was won, and now all the company that came with the thrall from over the mountain brow were dead or sorely wounded at the hands of black Skallagrim. Lo! one springs on Eric, and Gizur creeps behind him. Whitefire leaps to meet the man and does not leap in vain; but Gizur smites a coward blow at Eric's uncovered head, and wounds him sorely, so that he falls to his knee.

'Now I am smitten to the death, Skallagrim,' cries Eric. 'Win the rock and leave me.' Yet he rises from his knee.

Then Skallagrim turns, red with blood and terrible to see.

' 'Tis but a scratch. Climb thou the rock—I follow,' he says, and, screaming like a horse, with weapon aloft he leaps alone upon the foe. They break before the Baresark rush; they break, they fall—they are cloven by Baresark axe and trodden of Baresark feet! They roll back, leaving the way clear—save for the dead. Then Skallagrim follows Bright-eyes to the rock.

Now Eric wipes the gore from his eyes and sees. Then, slowly and with a reeling brain, he steps down upon the giddy point. He goes near to falling, yet does not fall, for now he lies upon the open space, and creeps on hands and knees to the rock-wall that is by the cave, and sits resting his back against it, Whitefire on his knee.

Before he is there, Skallagrim staggers to his side with a rush.

'Now we have time to breathe, lord,' he gasps. 'See, here is water,' and he takes a pitcher that stands by, and gives Eric to drink from the pool, then drinks himself and pours the rest of the water on Eric's wound. Then new life comes to them, and they both stand upon their feet and win back their breath.

'We have not done so badly!' says Skallagrim, 'and we are still a match for one or two. See, they come! Say, where shall we meet them, lord?'

'Here,' quoth Eric; 'I cannot stand well upon my legs without the help of the rock. Now I am all unmeet for fight.'

'Yet shall this last stand of thine be sung of!' says Skallagrim.

Now finding none to stay them, the men of Gizur climb one by one upon the stone and win the space that is beyond. Swanhild goes first of all, because she knows well that Eric will not harm her, and after her come Gizur and the others. But many do not come, for they will lift sword no more.

Now Swanhild draws near and looks at Eric and mocks him in the fierceness of her heart and the rage of her wolf-love.

'Now,' she says, 'now are Brighteyes Dim eyes! What! weepest thou, Eric?'

'Ay, Swanhild,' he answered, 'I weep tears of blood for those whom thou hast brought to doom.'

She draws nearer and speaks low to him: 'Hearken, Eric. Yield thee! Thou hast done enough for honour, and thou art not smitten to the death of yonder cowardly hound. Yield and I will nurse thee back to health and bear thee hence, and together we will forget our hate and woes.'

'Not twice may a man lie in a witch's bed,' said Eric, 'and my troth is plighted to other than thee, Swanhild.'

'She is dead,' says Swanhild.

'Yes, she is dead, Swanhild; and I go to seek her amongst the dead—I go to seek her and to find her!'

But the face of Swanhild grew fierce as the winter sea.

'Thou hast put me away for the last time, Eric! Now thou shalt die, as I have promised thee and as I promised Gudruda the Fair!'

'So shall I the more quickly find Gudruda and lose sight of thy evil face, Swanhild the harlot! Swanhild the murderess! Swanhild the witch! For I know this: thou shalt not escape! —thy doom draws on also!—and haunted and accursed shalt thou be for ever! Fare thee well, Swanhild; we shall meet no more, and the hour comes when thou shalt grieve that thou wast ever born!'

Now Swanhild turned and called to the folk : 'Come, cut down these outlaw rogues and make an end. Come, cut them down, for night draws on.'

Then once more the men of Gizur closed in upon them. Eric smote thrice and thrice the blow went home, then he could smite no more, for his strength was spent with toil and wounds, and he sank upon the ground. For a while Skallagrim stood over him like a she-bear o'er her young and held the mob at bay. Then Gizur, watching, cast a spear at Eric. It entered his side through a cleft in his byrnie and pierced him deep.

'I am sped, Skallagrim Lambstail,' cried Eric in a loud voice, and all men drew back to see giant Brighteyes die. Now his head fell against the rock and his eyes closed.

Then Skallagrim, stooping, drew out the spear and kissed Eric on the forehead.

'Farewell, Eric Brighteyes!' he said. 'Iceland shall never see such another man, and few have died so great a death. Tarry a while, lord ; tarry a while—I come—I come ! '

Then crying ' Eric ! Eric ! ' the Baresark fit took him, and once more and for the last time Skallagrim rushed screaming upon the foe, and once more they rolled to earth before him. To and fro he rushed, dealing great blows, and ever as he went they stabbed and cut and thrust at his side and back, for they dared not stand before him, till he bled from a hundred wounds. Now, having slain three more men, and wounded two others, Skallagrim might no more. He stood a moment swaying to and fro, then he let his axe drop, threw his arms high above him, and with one loud cry of ' Eric ! ' fell as a rock falls—dead upon the dead.

But Eric was not yet gone. He opened his eyes and saw the death of Skallagrim and smiled.

'Well ended, Lambstail ! ' he said in a faint voice.

'Lo ! ' cried Gizur, ' yon outlawed hound still lives ! Now I will do a needful task and make an end of him, and so shall Ospakar's sword come back to Ospakar's son.'

'Thou art wondrous brave now that the bear lies dying ! ' mocked Swanhild.

Now it seemed that Eric heard the words, for suddenly his might came back to him, and he staggered to his knees and thence to his feet. Then, as folk fall from him, with all his strength he whirls Whitefire round his head till it shines like a wheel of fire. ' Thy service is done and thou art clean of Gudruda's blood—go back to those who forged thee! ' Brighteyes cries, and casts Whitefire from him towards the gulf.

Away speeds the great blade, flashing like lightning through the rays of the setting sun, and behold! as men watch it is gone—gone in mid-air!

Since that day no such sword as Whitefire has been known in Iceland.

' Now kill thou me, Gizur,' says the dying Eric.

Gizur comes on with little eagerness, and Eric cries aloud :

' Swordless I slew thy father!—swordless, shieldless, and wounded to the death I will yet slay *thee*, Gizur the Murderer ! ' and with a loud cry he staggered toward him.

Gizur smites him with his sword, but Eric does not stay, and while men wait and wonder Brighteyes sweeps him into his great arms—ay, sweeps him up, lifts him from the ground and reels on.

Eric reels on to the brink of the gulf. Gizur sees his purpose, struggles and shrieks aloud. But the strength of the dying Eric is more than the strength of Gizur. Now Brighteyes stands on the dizzy edge and the light of the passing sun flames about his head. And now, bearing Gizur with him, he hurls himself out into the gulf, and lo! the sun sinks !

Men stand wondering, but Swanhild cries aloud :

' Nobly done, Eric ! nobly done ! So I would have seen thee die who of all men wast the first ! '

This then was the end of Eric Brighteyes the Unlucky, who of all warriors that have lived in Iceland was the mightiest, the goodliest, and the best beloved of women and of those who clung to him.

Now, on the morrow, Swanhild caused the body of Eric to be searched for in the cleft, and there they found it, floating in water and with the dead Gizur yet clasped in its bear-grip. Then she cleansed it and clothed it again in its rent armour, and bound on the Hell-shoes, and it was carried on horses to the sea-side, and with it were borne the bodies of Skallagrim Lambstail the Baresark, Eric's thrall, and of all those men whom they had slain in the last great fight on Mosfell, that is now named Ericsfell.

Then Swanhild drew her long dragon of war, in which she had come from Orkneys, from its shed over against Westman Isles, and, in the centre of that ship, she piled the bodies of the slain in the shape of a bed, and lashed them fast. And on this bed she laid the corpse of Eric Brighteyes, and the breast of black Skallagrim the Baresark was his pillow, and the breast of Gizur, Ospakar's son, was his foot-rest.

Then she caused the sails to be hoisted, and went alone aboard the long ship, the rails of which were hung with the shields of the dead men.

And when at evening the breeze freshened to a gale that blew from the land, she cut the cable with her own hand, and the dragon leapt forward like a thing alive, and rushed out in the red light of the sunset towards the open sea.

Now ever the gale freshened and folk, standing on Westman Heights, saw the long ship plunge past, dipping her prow beneath the waves and sending the water in a rain of spray over the living Swanhild, over the dead Eric and those he lay upon.

And by the head of Eric Brighteyes, her hair streaming on the wind, stood Swanhild the Witch, clad in her purple cloak, and with rings of gold about her throat and arms. She stood by Eric's head, swaying with the rush of the dragon, and singing so sweet and wild a song that men grew weak who heard it.

Now, as the people watched, two white swans came down from the clouds and sped on wide wings side by side over the vessel's mast.

The ship rushed on through the glow of the sunset into

the gathering night. On sped the ship, but still Swanhild sung, and still the swans flew over her.

The gale grew fierce, and fiercer yet. The darkness gathered deep upon the raging sea.

Now that war-dragon was seen no more, and the death-song of Swanhild as she passed to doom was never heard again.

For swans and ship, and Swanhild, and dead Eric and his dead foes, were lost in the wind and the night.

But far out on the sea a great flame of fire leapt up towards the sky.

Now this is the tale of Eric Brighteyes, Thorgrimur's son; of Gudruda the Fair, Asmund's daughter; of Swanhild the Fatherless, Atli's wife, and of Ounound, named Skallagrim Lambstail, the Baresark, Eric's thrall, all of whom lived and died before Thangbrand, Wilibald's son, preached the White Christ in Iceland.

THE END